THE GIRL WHO CHEATED THE WIND

M.E.MOIRIN

Want to know more about the world of Syanka?

Visit mmoirin.com for lore, short stories, bonus content, and more!

THE TALE OF THE WELL

There is a tale of a well buried deep in the forest where the town of Morava once stood. Of it, only a clearing remains, and at its centre lies the well. Finding it happens only by chance, never when one is looking. Ancient trees and overgrown bushes hide the way; moss veils the remnants of houses, and creepers stretch green tendrils over once-busy roads. If you stumble upon the clearing, it is only because the forest allowed it. The air is cool and damp, branches concealing the sky in an eerie silence. At the centre, the well waits. You draw closer, curious.

Aside from the toppled statue of a beautiful woman, it appears ordinary: stone-lined walls, an old bucket at its side, moss clinging to cracks. But on a waxing crescent night, a faint whisper rises from its depths. It's a female voice, melodic and tinged with sorrow. Branches part above you, moonlight spilling over the path. As you inch closer, the whisper falters, as if startled, then resumes with urgency. You lean over the well to catch what it has to say. A story, it turns out. Mesmerised, you listen until numbness creeps into your legs.

As if in a dream, you take ink and parchment from your satchel and settle on the forest floor, moss moulding into a cushion. Even the moon has paused its journey, eager to hear her story. Under its silver light, whispered words spill onto the page as you scribble furiously.

By the time you finish, it seems days should have passed, yet dawn is only shyly peeking above the trees. With the last words scrawled, you inspect your hands and, for the first time, notice black ink seeping through your skin like bruises. When you glance around, the voice's story is drawing to an end, fading back into the well's depths.

The silence that follows is short-lived. With dawn, the forest comes to life. A robin stirs in the branches, a bee hums past your ear. Just like that, the spell is broken, and another kind of magic settles in, one of forest green and birdsong. You glance at the pages, her voice still echoing in your ears. A part of you longs for its melody to be unbroken, for the story to be never-ending. If only you could keep listening, the voice's cadence lingering in your mind like the ink stains blooming across your palms. But you must return and tell Jasna's story. After all, you promised the splinter of her soul that still dwells in the well.

CHAPTER 1

OF TENDRILS AND DARKNESS

Nana used to say lingering out after sunset invited shadows in. She was wrong. Mine had always been there, watching. Last night, I saw it stir. By dawn, the Grand Vizier would arrive, and my refusal to marry him would cost me my own shadow.

The morning of his arrival, last night's stolen kiss weighed on my mind. My thoughts kept drifting back to it as I walked along the tree-lined path that led to the well. Above, the ancient trees loomed, their twisted branches like hands reaching to snatch anyone who dared to disrupt their eternal silence.

The clash of metal, the ringing voices, and the vibrant colours flashing between the trees should have tipped me off to the intruders. Like a wave, the restless stir so uncharacteristic of Morava washed over me as I stood on its edge. I would like to think I would have noticed them on any other day. But

1

as my mind kept wandering back to the night before, I missed all the warning signs. By the time I emerged from the last line of trees, the throng of motion swallowed me whole.

Horses and carts overflowing with goods surrounded the well, a motley entourage of people at its centre. State officials, I thought, though usually that would be solely men. This troop, however, also included a handful of women. Merchants, soldiers, even janissaries and other Sultan's emissaries often passed through Morava, but never women.

I paused to admire their ornate clothing, sun-kissed skin, and the elegance with which the women wove their way through the crowd. I wondered what such an opulent group was doing so far from the empire's centre. The blood tax, collected by the Sultan last year, was not due for four more years. So great was my surprise at this unlikely sight that the voice that whispered in my ear caught me off guard, giving me a start.

"What a sight for sore eyes you are, young woman. The Grand Vizier will be most pleased to see you."

I had no time to conceal my shock upon noticing a scrawny old man with jaundiced skin and creases so deep they made Nana's wrinkles seem shallow by comparison. It unsettled me that he had somehow crept to my side unnoticed. The two of us faced each other, assessing the person opposite. His black, worn garments posed a sharp contrast to the colourful clothing surrounding us. For a moment, it felt as though the two of us stood in a void, darkness spilling from his body like ink. I gasped, and the sound broke the illusion. Sunlight reigned once more.

Whether the man had conjured the darkness with unspooling tendrils or I had imagined the scene, I did not know, and it mattered little. I had to get away. Yet when I tried to move my feet, they remained firmly planted on the ground as if commanded by a force other than my body. Ready to dismiss the man mere seconds ago, I now stood frozen, as if the tendrils had taken a hold of me.

"The Grand Vizier would like to see you," repeated the man. "What is your name?"

I hesitated. The man spoke with casual authority, as if he himself was the Vizier, yet his garments were a testament to humble origins. Perhaps one of the Vizier's guards entertained themselves by playing out a prank and my best bet was to humour him.

"Well? Are you mute?"

"Jasna. My name is Jasna. But why would the Grand Vizier want to see me?"

"You will find out soon enough. For now, a lesson in manners will you some good. Lesson one, Jasna: don't keep men like me waiting."

"And who might you be?"

The relief I felt when the man did not seem offended by my upfront question was short-lived. He merely laughed, dismissing my inquiry, though his dark eyes remained shards of black ice. He grabbed my arm so suddenly that the movement attracted nervous glances from the people around. The copper water jug I carried slid down from my fingers and landed on the ground with a muffled thud.

"Let go of me," I said as I tried to yank my arm free, but his grip only tightened. The onlookers who had briefly glanced in our direction averted their eyes, pointedly ignoring us.

"You will come with me, girl." His low voice carried a note of impatience.

"I'd rather not," I said with more conviction than I felt. "I have had enough of this nonsense and will be taking my leave now."

But the scrawny man laughed once again and, without

letting go of my arm, steered me in the well's direction. Though his age and seemingly fragile state left the impression his hand would be easy to shrug off, his tight grip on me said otherwise.

Some regarded me with curiosity, others with indifference. Most paid no attention, yet all tensed when the man passed them by. Their rigid shoulders spoke not of reverence, but of fear that I saw lurking in their postures and tense eyes.

"You aren't the Sultan... are you?" I asked.

For a moment, I thought he hadn't heard me. His eyes remained fixed on what lay ahead. But then he smiled, an oily smile that sat wrong on his thin lips and revealed a set of teeth that were a varying shade of yellow.

"One day the Sultan would wish to be me, girl," was all he said.

I kept silent, thinking. Not only would that statement be considered treasonous, but it would ring ridiculous under different circumstances. Who would be so powerful as to make such a bold claim? Were the man's words a testament to his insanity? The fear in the onlookers' eyes told me otherwise. As for why the Vizier wanted to see me, I had an inkling. It was the same reason nearly every man's eyes followed me with undisguised lust wherever I went. I had the bad luck to be born with a face men called beautiful.

Another cluster of people parted to reveal the well and an ornate chair that looked out of place beside it. Though I had never seen the Grand Vizier for myself, there was no mistaking who the man occupying the chair was. Despite being seated while everyone else was standing, the man loomed larger and more regal than his subjects. Younger than expected, especially considering the stories of countless lands he had subjugated in the Sultan's name, the empire's Grand Vizier suited the role very well. His thick black beard was covered in scented pomade that gave it a sleek shine. It obscured most of his face, yet it brought out the Vizier's dark blue eyes, a colour so rarely seen in our lands that I found myself unable to tear my eyes from his. His kaftan, though much simpler than the clothing of the court surrounding him, hugged his figure, accentuating it in all the right places, its black and red cut underlining his broad shoulders and chest. Yet, only fear coiled in my gut as I stood before the second most powerful man in the empire. I bowed and prayed my tardy display of reverence went unnoticed.

When I lifted my gaze, I found the Vizier's eyes locked on me. He studied me silently and with an intensity that brought redness to my neck and cheeks. My unease only grew stronger when coupled with the realisation that I had allowed myself to feel embarrassed. Redness crept across my face like an itching rash. I had to force myself to remain still despite the intense desire to bolt. All the while, the Vizier's gaze felt as if a predator appraised their dinner. Other men had devoured me with their eyes before, so the Vizier's interest was not new to me, yet it remained equally unwelcome. I sent a silent plea to the gods to end this spectacle. If they were listening, no help arrived. The crowd of onlookers drew closer, eager to hear the exchange.

"What a beauty," said a man with a luscious moustache. Our eyes met, and his assessing look reminded me of a merchant casually discussing the price of a horse at the market.

"Look at that skin, so pristine," a woman chimed in with undisguised jealousy. A glance in her direction told me she had nothing to be envious of. Her own complexion betrayed little time in the sun. My blue cardigan, knitted by Nana, looked like a child's garment compared to the intricate patterns woven into her silk kaftan that likely cost more than my lifetime's outgoings. But the Grand Vizier seemed to have eyes only for me when he asked,

"What is your name, girl?" Referring to me as a girl when it was clear we were of similar age irked me, but I tried not to betray the annoyance. I must have disguised my emotions poorly, for the Vizier's mouth twitched at the corners in a disarming smirk. A few of the noble ladies around sighed longingly.

"Jasna, Grand Vizier," I said. "It's an honour."

The lie rang hollow, but the Grand Vizier ignored it.

"Well done, Yerleg," he said, addressing the man who had dragged me here. "You have outdone yourself."

The man bowed deeply, though it was obvious the sign of reverence was difficult on his bones.

"I live to serve, great one."

My breath caught in my throat at the name as I finally recognised who the scrawny man was. I had thought the story to be only that: a story. Yet Nana knew things no other Moravian did. From chatting with the caravanserai's visitors to the market merchants, she had a way of collecting stories from bits and pieces that she strung together like beads and wove into a story.

Only a few heartbeats had passed in the time these thoughts raced through my mind. Enough for the Vizier's eyes to travel unabashedly across my body.

"Jasna," he said, as if tasting my name on his lips. "It means bright in your tongue. A name befitting such beauty."

"You... flatter me, honourable one," I said, though the words rang hollow once more. My heart pounded against my ribcage, so loud that I had no doubt everyone else could hear it as well.

"Indeed, I do. But enough with the pleasantries. I have found what I was searching for, and in a feat worthy of the greatest of mages, Yerleg has delivered it. You shall accompany me back to Tsargrad and be my wife under the law and God's eyes. In return, you shall want for nothing. Beauty like that is wasted living a peasant's life. You will have the softest silks, the best chambers in my palace, jewels, servants, and gardens at your disposal. And you will be the crown jewel of your court of adoring noblewomen, who have been eagerly awaiting my appointed wife."

As he said that, the Vizier looked at me expectantly, as if my acceptance was a tedious formality to him. I only stared at him, startled at the turn of events his abrupt words had brought with them.

"The highest honour indeed," said a man standing uncomfortably close to me.

"So lucky," echoed a woman's melodic voice, marred with jealousy. I had the urge to inform her she could have the Grand Vizier for herself if she so wished.

"Say you agree, girl, don't keep the Vizier waiting," Yerleg hissed in my ear.

"I am honoured, ćelebi," I said, taken aback, as I bowed. Fear clouded my mind, leaving it blank, and before I knew it, my lips parted to say, "But I am afraid I cannot come with you to Tsargrad to be your wife."

I had expected another round of gasps, but the silence that followed seemed to give my words a hollow echo that magnified their defiance. When I found the courage to look at the Grand Vizier, I found a storm brewing behind his blue eyes. Yet, I thought I glimpsed something unexpected, something much like triumph.

"Don't be a fool, girl," Yerleg whispered. As he said that, the sky darkened with unnatural speed, sending a wave of chill down my spine. Previously white clouds turned heavy with rain, obscuring the sun. Thunder rolled in the distance, the promise of a storm heavy in the air. A single raindrop landed on my forehead and ran down my face. All around me, feet shuffled with discomfort. I did not have to chance a look at the people surrounding us to feel their agitation. Despite the fear lodged in the pit of my stomach, it occurred to me the Grand Vizier's mage had a penchant for the dramatic that felt a little too pronounced, if not forced. Once the sky above us had entirely darkened, the Grand Vizier's eyes pierced through me as he drawled, "And why is that?"

I thought I detected something else behind his cloudy blue eyes: a speck of curiosity.

"I cannot accept your kind offer, for I am already betrothed, honourable one," I said in one breath. "Besides, what do I, a simple peasant, know of jewels and silks meant for real ladies?"

"A valid point, grandest of Viziers," Yerleg said, eager to salvage the situation. "It is better to find a bride of noble origins and have this girl join your future wife's court as occasional entertainment. This was my intent when I brought her to you."

The dark mage pointedly glanced at me as if I was at fault for the Vizier's decision to take me as his bride, his glare a silent vow of retribution. All the while, Yerleg addressed the Grand Vizier as if the question of my fate was outside my hands, giving me time to think my way out of the situation. The first and most painless choice would be for me to accept, though I could not tell whether being married to the Grand Vizier or occasionally sating his appetite would be worse. Both possibilities would tear me away from Nana and force me to venture into an unwelcoming court. Chancing a glance around revealed only a sea of hostile faces that confirmed my suspicions. Even the gathering clouds had paused as if awaiting the outcome.

When I stole a glance at the Grand Vizier, I found his eyes already searching for mine. For a moment, with our gazes locked, all the chatter and whispers around us dissolved into a distant murmur, and only he and I remained in a pool of silence. In his stormy blue eyes, I glimpsed my reflection and the way he saw me: forest-green eyes, pristine skin, an oval face with high cheekbones. Though our lives had been vastly different – he, a leader who lacked nothing; I, a servant in his empire, raised on my grandmother's fairy tales – something familiar sparked between us, a sense that neither had ever belonged to where life had thrown us.

In that brief contact, I knew the Vizier, a man used to getting everything he wished for, would not relent.

He broke the eye contact and regarded the crowd. Then, returning his attention to me, a smile spread across his face, broad and knowing, sending another shiver down my spine. He rose from the chair, and complete stillness descended upon the onlookers, myself included. The Grand Vizier took a step towards me, and I had to harness all my willpower not to cower in front of the empire's second-in-command. We were almost at eye level; for once, I was grateful for my height. It made me stand nearly as tall as he was. His next words were a whisper, yet their certainty rang true above the stilled crowd.

"You will come to me of your own free will. By the end of the summer, you will be at the gates of Tsargrad begging me to take you in."

And with that, the spell was broken. The dark clouds that had formed at such unusual speed dissolved just as quickly. That brought me little solace. Something caught in my throat as I searched my mind for a response to the Grand Vizier's last words. A sense of helplessness washed over me. The words were spoken, and whatever they meant, if they had come from the Vizier's lips, they would come true. That, or his dark mage, who now tugged at my sleeve to steer me away from the scene, would make sure of it.

"One last thing," the Grand Vizier said. Everyone stilled. "Let it be known that I appreciate the display of courage and determination to stay true to what one values most. In honour of that, I will have your image built as a statue above this well. As a reminder to treasure that which matters most."

The crowd burst into applause, and I breathed a sigh of relief. Perhaps that was it; I had escaped whatever fate Yerleg and the Grand Vizier had in store for me. The light feeling did not last long. As the crowd parted to make way for me, I noticed Yerleg's smirk, and my blood ran cold with fear. My sight blurred, and for a moment, the darkness surrounding him made itself visible to my eyes once more. The darkness lashed out a warning tendril, and I recoiled, but to no avail. It caressed my cheek almost gently before vanishing into the daylight. The place where the tendril had met my skin burned as if struck by an invisible whip.

CHAPTER 2

NANA'S WARNING

*O*nce back on the twisted path, I bolted for my life, all the while pressing a hand to my burning cheek where the tendril had touched it. So desperate was I to get away from there that I barely noticed the clouds giving way to sunshine once more.

Nana's throaty voice cut through the panic, Yerleg's story rising unbidden in my mind.

"Grand Viziers come and go at the Sultan's will, but everyone knows the position is short and bloody. At the end of their service, only death awaits. Whenever a Grand Vizier displeases the Sultan, it is because he foolishly dared to conspire against the empire. The Sultan, after all, has the most powerful mage to protect him, but that comes at a cost, for dark mages tamper with forces that lie beyond imagining."

"Why would anyone want to rise against the Sultan, if he is so powerful?" I remembered asking.

"Each believed they could outsmart the Sultan and his dark mage. Fools... Generations of mages remained at the palace, serving Sultan after Sultan, making sure he remained at the seat of power. Until one day, the current Grand Vizier, Temir, who had amassed wealth rivalling that of the Sultan himself, enlisted the help of a dark mage. Temir not only found a more corrupt and powerful mage, but also the means to pay him handsomely for his services. The mage's name was Yerleg. Time will tell if, with the help of Yerleg, Temir will be another head on a spike adorning the Sultan's palace walls."

When I reached home, I latched the door and leaned against it, my heart pounding. Once safe inside, my first thought was of Nana. My frantic mind instantly painted images of the black tendrils holding her so tight she was unable to call for help as life slipped away from her frail body. Then the familiar rhythm of a shovel sounded in the backyard and dispelled my fears.

My relief did not last long before anxiety took over. I hurried to the solitary cupboard in the room we shared and rummaged through the bottom shelf to find Nana's decades-old mirror. Even with its chips and cracks, the mirror showed nothing wrong with my cheek. Contrary to what the burning sensation suggested, it wasn't red or inflamed. I sighed with relief as the pain subsided, fading away as if imagined.

Nana came inside, her arms muddy up to her elbows. Her sharp eyes swept the room and rested on me, giving me little time to compose myself. "All the water from last week's rain is gone, spent on the crops. We could use some from the jug you brought."

A glance at the basin next to which the jugs usually rested revealed the vacant space. Nana raised an eyebrow.

"You look pale. What's wrong?"

But I couldn't reply; my throat felt hoarse and thick with fear as if a lump had settled there.

"Was that boy distracting you again? If so, you had better go back before dark. Even with the days getting longer, night is bound to fall early."

"Why do you always think it's Iliya's fault?" I asked instead.

"Because it usually is." Her sweet voice did not fool me. When I didn't fire my usual retort back, her face grew sombre. Slowly, she walked to the basin and dipped her hands in yesterday's water. It barely covered her palms, but she made do as she scrubbed the soil from her hands. The water browned even more. Nana sat on her chair next to the hearth. "Now tell me. What happened?"

My hand flew to the spot where the tendril had licked. One moment, I was biting back tears and in the next one, the lump in my throat dissolved and the whole story came pouring out in a rush. At some point, I found myself on the rug at Nana's feet, arms hugging my knees as her hand patted my shoulder soothingly. I wiped the last of the tears and mustered the courage to ask, "Do you believe me, Nana? About the mage and the Vizier?"

"Of course I do." Her knotty fingers squeezed my shoulders reassuringly. "What makes the stories I tell so compelling is that the boundary between what is real and what isn't is so thin that the listener's mind cannot tell the difference. Yet, I have seen too much to know that there is some truth to every tale. And Yerleg is not only real enough, but he is also no mere mage, for he is rotten to the core. People like him assume, albeit foolishly, that they have a firm grip on darkness better left alone. Inevitably, whatever foul force they have attempted to bind takes hold of them. And by the time they realise that darkness has been in charge all along, it's too late. So yes, I know what you are saying is true."

"What does it mean for me, Nana?" I asked, still in disbelief that everything I knew of the world seemed to have unravelled in a mere morning.

She rose from the chair and indicated that I take her place. I obliged, slumping heavily with the newfound burden weighing me down. Nana inched closer to the window where her dried herbs hung on long strings from the wall, her back to me. She untied one of the valerian herbs and crushed some of its small white flowers into dust in a wooden bowl.

"Since we have no water, this will have to do," she said, and offered the bowl to me. "Should do you good, even without brewing it into tea. Go on now, eat it."

I ate the crunchy herb, though the valerian dust irritated my throat and worsened the dryness that had settled in after finishing my story. In the meantime, Nana dragged one of the wooden chairs, sat on it, and said with a heavy sigh, "What this means for you, you ask. I could tell you that you're safe – but I'd be lying. I could tell you that the Vizier said you'd go to him of your own free will so that he gets to keep his dignity, but that would mean I would be lying."

She paused, and her eyes rested on my face. The heaviness in her voice eased a little, and she reached a trembling hand that gently touched my cheek.

"There is no point in concealing what I know. I shall tell you the truth, or as much as I know, though I wish it were more. An ordinary man's self-conceit knows no boundaries, and a Grand Vizier's pride is a hundredfold worse. The statue at the well is no coincidence. That's the work of dark forces. To what end, I do not know. Nothing good comes to my old mind, frail as it might be, when I think of the Grand Vizier's pet, or Yerleg, as he calls himself. As for why they are building that statue, I have the feeling we will find out soon enough."

My heart had grown cold by the time Nana fell silent. I

stood there, numbly staring at the hearth. I felt it then, a strong premonition that I would not be emerging from this unscathed, if I would emerge alive at all.

"What am I to do?" I asked, but before Nana's answer came, a knock on the door gave us both a start.

"I heard about the Grand Vizier," said Iliya as he let himself in. Our grave faces made him pause. "What is it?"

Before our betrothal, Iliya and I had been friends for years, and had spent our childhoods playing silly games and dreaming of distant lands together. Because of that, he had more freedom around me than most other promised couples did. One such freedom was walking me home unsupervised, and another was visiting me at home whenever he wished.

"Well, at least someone is happy about the Grand Vizier's proposal," Nana said, not keeping the hostility out of her voice. Iliya frowned.

"What proposal? I thought he wanted a statue of you because he couldn't stop staring at you."

"Is that what they say?"

Iliya, rarely fazed by anything, grew agitated and began fidgeting with his fingers, uncertain how to get hold of the situation. I felt compelled to clarify what my grandmother meant before tension had bloated into disdain. After all, few could withstand Nana's fiery gaze.

"What you said is true, at least somewhat. I chanced upon the Grand Vizier at the well, and he said he would build a statue to honour my looks, which he found… compelling. He also wanted me to marry him."

"He… what?" Iliya asked, his face paling.

"You may not know this, child, as you are so young, but it is not uncommon for the Grand Vizier, and even the Sultan, to take a bride from one of the provinces," Nana said agreeably, though her eyes remained serious.

"But he could have anyone he wishes to," I said. "Why me?"

"Why you?" Iliya said, shaking his head. "Everyone in Morava stares when you walk past. Of course he noticed. Doesn't mean you have to marry him."

He said this bitterly, as if I had somehow cast a spell over him and Morava, though I knew he meant well. The boy who had befriended me when everyone else said my birth was an ill omen would never think badly of me. As for the town, that was another matter entirely. Even my beauty would not salvage their opinion of me.

"Perhaps I am cursed, after all," I blurted, unthinkingly.

"Nonsense!" Iliya reassured me. "Your mother died at childbirth, as many women do, and it was your father's choice to take up the road and search for your brother."

"Yet all my life, they say I was born under an ill omen. My looks and you are the only reason they find it acceptable for me to be around. That, and Nana."

I glanced out the window to steady myself, willing the sting in my eyes not to spill into tears. The sun stood high in the sky, closer to noon than morning. Though I was certain I had no place in Morava, the thought of always being scorned rang hollow in my chest.

"Cursed?" Nana snorted. "The curse lies with the small-minded. A hala's storm at your birth didn't doom you – it marked you as someone who'd stand out."

Iliya, who would usually groan and object when unnatural forces were mentioned, remained silent.

"Those who think they know best are the ones who bear a curse," she continued. "A curse for being shortsighted, above all. For benefitting from the suffering of others and for being the first to point fingers when there is wrongdoing afoot, but never when it's their own. Not you, me, your mother, father or brother, but the ones driven by envy and greed. Those are the ones we should pity."

Such strength emanated from Nana when she said those words, that Iliya and I found ourselves nodding along. A knot that had formed in my stomach when Yerleg's darkness had first tainted the day eased at her words. In my heart, I knew them to be true and Iliya's soft eyes told me he shared that knowledge. My gaze travelled down to his lips, remembering how they had felt on mine the night before. Though it had happened only yesterday, the kiss and the confusion that followed felt like a memory from long ago. I lifted my eyes to meet his and quickly averted them. He had been thinking about the kiss, too, though his lips curled with confidence I no longer shared.

"Maybe he just rewards courage. Or maybe he collects wives like paintings," Iliya said, his eyes still focused on my lips. "Rumour has it he has a passion for the arts."

"What does a provincial boy like you know of the arts?" Nana snapped. Her offhand remark caused redness to creep up Iliya's neck. I cast a warning glance towards her, but there was no need as Iliya held his ground.

"I only meant… people say he spares no means to obtain what he desires. Sculptors, architects. Things of beauty. Maybe this is just some… twisted obsession."

Another warning glance at Nana seemed enough to stop her from pressing on. Instead, she said with another heavy sigh, "I hope you are right. For all our sakes."

Iliya reached for my hand and cupped my palm in his. But the warmth I expected wasn't there – only the sting of Yerleg's touch, still burning beneath my skin.

CHAPTER 3

ILIYA'S STOLEN KISS THE NIGHT BEFORE

I didn't know it then, but the night Iliya and I shared our first kiss would also mark our last. Night after night, we followed the same ritual, where he walked me home just as the sun set beyond the horizon, the last crimson light a sole conspirator to our tryst. Trees lined the path home, birches and oaks heavy with late spring's green crown. Iliya's hand lightly brushed against mine as we chatted about everything and nothing, the way only youth did. Contentment settled over us, the breeze teasing with the promise of an endless summer.

At the end of the road, just where Morava ended, stood Nana's house. Beyond it stretched the woods leading to the well and the caravanserai. We lingered there, reluctant for the day to end, yet also eager to savour its last moments. Our eyes met, and he lifted a hand to brush a stray strand of hair from my brow.

18

"I should go," I said. "Night is near." My throat felt dry from a strange blend of thrill and unease his closeness stirred. If Iliya sensed anything, he did not show it. His hand hesitated on mine a moment longer, and I gently brushed it away.

Iliya leaned closer and, before I knew what he was doing, his lips met mine. He tasted sweet, like the honeyed wine we had sneaked from his father's izba, but the kiss did not last long, and the sweet taste soon turned sour. A brush of lips, and before I knew it, I had stepped away, my tongue running against my lips as if to scrub away the foreign taste. But something else felt off, too, as if we weren't alone. Out of nowhere, a foul feeling swept all else aside as something black formed – as if from thin air – a patch of darkness clouding the sky in the woods behind Iliya. I gasped and blinked against the dusk. Whatever had been there was gone.

"What's the matter?" Iliya asked, oblivious to what I had seen. His eyes sparkled in the aftermath of the stolen kiss.

"You shouldn't have done that," I said, though my voice lacked conviction.

A prickle ran down my neck, the trees too still, the forest too quiet. The sense of being watched still clung to me.

"What's wrong with a kiss? We're to be married," Iliya said. "And share more than that."

"I know." But my eyes kept searching the trees, every shadow a shape, every branch a limb. Iliya turned around and followed my gaze with a raised eyebrow as we both frowned at the empty air.

At last, I forced a smile, feeling foolish for imagining things. Nana's tales had a way of getting into my head. "Sorry. I'm just being silly."

He laughed, unsure, and handed me a fistful of crushed snowdrops.

"For you," he said, as he presented me with the flowers, their white cups already withering. "The last for the season."

"You should go. It's getting dark," I said, suddenly feeling weary and wanting nothing more than to curl up next to Nana in front of the hearth. I knew I was being unreasonable, but I could not shake the feeling of foreboding, so I hurried past Iliya and to Nana's house.

"Jasna, wait!" His outstretched arm beckoned me to take it, but I had already crossed the small flower garden Nana tended to in springtime, the dead snowdrops burning against my palm. Perhaps it was the fading light playing tricks on me, or maybe it was all the tension, but just before closing the door to the house, I thought I spotted, out of the corner of my eye, a dark shape watching me from the line of trees. I closed the door with trembling hands and drew the sign of a cross in the air. Signs and omens always carried meaning if we assigned them one, and even though Nana had raised me without religion, our house held fast to the rule: never ignore the old superstitions.

Once inside, my lips still tingling from the kiss, I found Nana in her chair in front of the hearth. Though springtime brought a gust of balmy winds, the house still had a chill to it. A mouth-watering smell from the pot that bubbled over the fire reached me, chasing the last of my worries away. Without further ado, I walked to the cupboard to fetch a bowl and spooned a generous amount of root vegetable stew into it. Nana, who I had thought asleep, almost gave me a start when her throaty voice broke the silence.

"You look flustered! What's the matter?"

When I spun around, I found her peering from her chair, her greenish eyes boring into me as if she herself had witnessed the scene outside unfold. Her eyes, always a different shade of green, had spots of colour dancing inside, a mesmerising mix that bewitched anyone who met her gaze. I too averted my gaze before falling prey to their beguiling magic.

"Nothing exciting happened, Nana. Iliya and I had a pleasant time, and then he walked me back. We never lingered for too long," I lied, but my shaky voice betrayed the truth. Nana's eyes followed me as I sat on the small table where a freshly baked loaf of bread awaited me. Still avoiding her gaze, I tore into it, unable to resist the smell.

"Did Maruna behave herself?"

I couldn't suppress the flinch at the name and the unpleasant wave of memories it brought.

"She was… well, she was Maruna."

"And that boy…"

"Iliya," I said, aware she was leading me into a trap I was foolishly about to fall into. Belatedly remembering the crumpled snowdrops, I fished them out of the tunic pocket I had tucked them in and showed them to Nana. "He gave me these."

It took but a glance for Nana to grasp the flowers' significance. As soon as she did, a look of pity blossomed in her eyes.

"He can't be expected to remember everything," I mumbled in an attempt to defend Iliya's honour. Just because he gave me the same flowers as the ones my father had left for me before setting off after my brother, making his priorities clear in the process, did not mean Iliya had to take the blame. Although he did know of their significance to me.

Nana cleared her throat. "Of course, dear. Was he at least behaving?"

Having no desire to tell Nana of my first kiss and the confusing feelings it brought, I avoided answering for as long as possible, even when my silence grew into an answer. I finished my dinner and took the bowl to the small, half-full basin. By the time I had scraped the bowl clean in the already darkening water, the shadows outside had lengthened and crept into the room.

"You know, you don't have to marry him. Or anyone, for that matter," came Nana's voice from behind.

"Few will agree with you," I said as I walked to the fireplace and sat on the rug next to her chair. We had spent the whole of last winter weaving that rug while Nana's stories from lands afar had kept us entertained.

"Oh, people with their stuck-up ways be damned," said Nana with a sudden vehemence. "If I had a grosh for every opinion and belief hurled my way, I would be a rich woman indeed. Do you see us living in a palace?"

"Well, you certainly had a much more interesting life than me, so perhaps you should be living in one."

"Had? I'm not dead yet, girl."

"And you won't be for many more years," I said, tempted to draw another sign of protection in the air, then settled for tracing one on the rug with my forefinger instead. "How about we hear tonight's story?"

"Another one? I ran out of stories a long time ago. And I have told you the ones I know ten times over."

"Do it one more time, Nana," I begged.

"Very well. Come closer. An old woman's voice is bound to falter every now and again, so listen closely."

"Once upon a time, a mother lived with her three sons. Though poor, they had each other and a single treasure; an apple tree that grew in the garden outside their house. Except that it was no ordinary tree. Once each year, it yielded a single apple made of gold. But the family never got to enjoy the tree's fruit, for each year, just when the apple ripened, a hala swept from the skies and stole the treasure. The mother and her sons watched helplessly for years, until one day the youngest son took matters into his own hands and confronted the hala."

"Wait, that's not right," I said, interrupting. "It's the eldest son who confronts her first."

"Was it?" Nana said with a smile. "I'm getting too old to remember. Besides, does it matter?"

"I suppose not."

"Now, where was I? One of the brothers, let's say the oldest, resolved to guard the tree on the night it came to full bloom and took a silver knife to slay the hala. Alas, he fell asleep. The next morning the golden apple was gone, snatched just before dawn. The following year, the second son tried his luck, but he too fell asleep, and the hala stole the apple. A year later, the youngest son's turn came. His older brothers, embarrassed by their failure to protect the tree, mocked him and tried to coax him into staying, lest he kill the creature and embarrass them, but the boy stood his ground. When night fell, he climbed the tree with the knife in hand, his eyes never leaving the branch with the golden apple. As the apple came into full bloom, the boy's eyes stung with sleep. With heavy eyelids, he used the knife to make a small cut on his arm, the pain just strong enough to keep him from slipping into slumber. At this moment, the hala landed next to the tree, thinking the boy was asleep. Through half-closed eyelids, the youngest brother saw a breathtakingly beautiful woman with white wings. The hala craned her neck towards the apple and just as she was about to pluck it and fly away, the boy slashed at her neck and nearly killed her. But even though wounded, the hala still escaped, leaving the apple behind. The victorious young son picked the fruit and brought it to his mother, proving his brothers wrong. But his work was not done. He knew the hala would be back the following year, so he and his brothers took off to find the wounded creature and end it."

Silence followed. Nana's voice, always deep and throaty, had grown more sluggish as the story went on. I let her sleep, aware that it would be a few nights before the tale was complete. Feet dragging with the weight of the day, I rose and reached for the blanket resting on her chair. After unfolding it, I covered her shoulders, letting it cascade down to her feet. In about an hour, when the fire's remnants had died, she would wake and follow me into the small bedroom we shared.

Some nights, when sleep evaded me, she would continue the story, her voice filling the otherwise silent room with magic. Then, in the space between waking and dreaming where words came true, her tale would spill over, filling my dreams with distant lands and magical creatures. And though some would mock me the next day at the town square for still listening to children's tales, I had a story each night to go back to, where the wings of zmei, hala, or the wind itself would carry me to the magical place born from Nana's stories.

That night, it seemed I would never fall asleep, yet not even the thought of Iliya's kiss could keep me away from the land of dreams. Later, when Nana joined me in her bed across from mine, I never even stirred, blissfully ignorant of what awaited me the following days.

CHAPTER 4

THE STATUE

 ord of my encounter with the Grand Vizier spread through Morava before the next day's end. By evening, whispers trailed after me. I caught snippets as I passed through the town square – my name, the Grand Vizier's name, and something about a statue. Tiho's mother gave me a lingering look before leaving her son at our small gathering. Across the square, a group of young women giggled behind their hands, but thought better of it when I muttered some gibberish under my breath. Thinking it was a curse, one of them mouthed the word witch before leaving.

Iliya, eager as ever, had taken it upon himself to recount the story to anyone willing to listen. His enthusiasm drowned out my protests, Nana's warning from yesterday all but forgotten. A pleasant breeze ruffled his hair, and his flushed cheeks drew my gaze, distracting me from the exaggerations in his tale.

"The Grand Vizier has the most talented sculptors at his disposal," he said with a solemn certainty. "People from across the empire travel all the way to Tsargrad to work for him. Just ask Boyan – he hears all sorts of stories at court. And now, Morava will have its first true work of art – a statue of Jasna, standing over the well!"

Tiho furrowed a brow. "What's 'work of art' mean?"

Before Iliya could answer, a sharp voice cut through the evening air.

"Do you all really believe this?"

As she said that, Maruna stepped forward, arms crossed, a smirk playing on her lips. "If the Vizier had wanted Jasna as his bride, he would have taken her. Why wouldn't he? He is the empire's most powerful man."

Iliya bristled. "Second most powerful."

Maruna's smirk deepened. "And yet, still powerful enough to take whatever he pleases. But sure, let's believe Jasna's version. Though I think she forced those poor builders into doing her bidding with her magic tricks."

A sharp, burning anger rose in my chest. I clenched my fists, willing myself to stay composed. I was better than this. My next words proved otherwise.

"Willyoudousallafavourandshutup?"

The words came out in a single sputtering breath. Maruna's smile widened.

"There we have it," she said. "The infamous Jasna temper. The true Jasna at last."

The others – all but Iliya – snickered.

Iliya's voice came out strained, as though it physically pained him to hold back his anger. "There is something very wrong with you. No wonder you find it hard to attract a husband. I was fortunate enough to escape that… honour."

Maruna's smirk vanished, replaced by something uglier.

I reached for Iliya's sleeve, gently pulling him away. "Enough," I whispered. "She wants attention. Let's not give her any."

"She deserves to know how repulsive her behaviour is."

"Believe me, she knows. Why do you think she always makes sure everyone is as miserable as she is?"

Iliya hesitated, still seething, but after a moment, he let out a slow breath and nodded.

As we walked away, the sun casting long shadows at our backs, Iliya muttered, "Why do people even like her?"

"She's pretty."

He scoffed. "Debatable."

"You know she is. Besides, she can be decent company when she's not full of spite."

"So… never?" He flashed me a wink, the tension between us finally easing.

"And she isn't born under a bad omen. That seems to be the mark of acceptance."

Iliya halted, and my hand slid away from his. I regretted the bitter words.

"You are not cursed or born under a bad omen," he reassured me in a gentle voice.

"I know."

"And since when are you defending Maruna? The most horrible human being in Morava?"

"She is, isn't she?"

We shared a look and burst into laughter. With that, the unpleasant feeling that Maruna's presence brought dissolved, albeit not for long.

* * *

THE BUILDING of the statue commenced the following day. Once more, I found the well occupied when a group of three workers from Tsargrad spread their tools around the clearing. Their hushed, brusque tones sounded like a growl to those unused to their language. Moravians, myself included, understood bits and pieces. Years of mixing imperial language and local dialect had led to the development of a common tongue spoken throughout the empire. Yet, the men acted as if they were from a different realm altogether.

Moravians believed night belonged to evil – to hala, demons and all things non-human that roamed the earth. It was a time when the veil between worlds thinned, allowing creatures to slip through. The builders did not seem to share that belief. At dawn each morning, they took measures of the well and then proceeded to work until their eyes had strained under the dying light. Not afraid of local superstition of evil born of darkness, they slept in the clearing under the stars. Their presence left me questioning my habit of going to the well first thing in the morning. Each time, a man would take in my face. He'd note my looks, posture, and movement. His dark, sharp eyes missed nothing. It unsettled me to be studied like that, yet I felt helpless given that they modelled the statue after me. The men never approached me or spoke a word, but their scrutiny was enough to unnerve me.

It took only a few days for the rumours to spread, turning the tides once more against me. Martisor, the welcome of spring and the banishing of evil spirits, came and went and the statue's shape slowly took form under the late spring's sun. One morning, I took my time making my way to the well, reluctant to face the builders' probing stares. It felt as if their gaze stole a part of me each time their appraising looks committed my appearance to memory, and I resented giving them the opportunity to do so.

When at last I emerged at the well's clearing, the men were nowhere to be seen. My relief turned out to be short-lived, for it was then that I spotted the three women – Zoaea and two of her friends whose names I couldn't remember. The wary glances they exchanged upon my arrival were not lost on me. I hastened, eager to fill my jug with water and leave. The scene brought memories of the whispers that had trailed me for the better part of my life.

"Oh, her mother, Raya, bless her, she couldn't survive the birth of her second child," the murmurs would go ever since. "And then to have her only son taken as blood-tax, only for their father to follow. What an unfortunate turn of events. Her poor family. Jasna being born under a bad omen wrecked it."

They would click their tongues and stare at me unabashedly, as if I was responsible for causing my family's bad luck. In their eyes, misfortune happened for a reason, and that reason usually meant that the recipient was marked by evil.

The three women shared that look I knew too well. Zoaea lowered her face to the ground as I stepped closer to wait for my turn at the well. They parted to make way for me, and I sensed that I was about to learn what the new wave of nasty looks was all about. The women did not disappoint.

"Statues can hold great power," the one with the fairest hair said in a low voice. She had untied the bucket from the rope at the well's mouth and was filling two smaller jugs as she spoke. I ignored her until my turn came and then tied my own jug to the rope, tipping it down the well. A wave of coolness rose from its depths as her next words echoed inside its walls. "And who knows what evil a statue moulded after this girl would contain? Some say– "

I gave the woman no chance to finish as I spun around, letting go of the jug. It crashed into the water with a dull thump, the worn rope pulled taut. I didn't hide the bitterness from my voice when I rounded on her.

"What exactly do they say? Go on, whisper it loud enough to make sure I've heard. Or even better, let me spare you the effort. That the cursed girl's statue will doom every last one of you – is that what you're whispering? Did I guess correctly, or is there anything else you wish to add?"

Zoaea and the two women froze, their eyes wide with fear. I noted with satisfaction that my outburst, so uncharacteristic for a woman, had left them speechless for a heartbeat. My anger, hot and unbridled, seeped out of me like a burning coal fizzing out under icy water. By then, the three women had distanced themselves, muttering excuses as they retreated from the clearing. Zoaea cast an apologetic look towards me, and our eyes met, fear lurking behind her chestnut eyes.

"Count your blessings," I whispered to myself as I pulled the full jug to the surface. "At least those men aren't around to ogle you for their statue."

* * *

EVENINGS WITH NANA carried the smell of buttery roast potatoes and carrots, mingled with sun-kissed garden tomatoes. There was also white cheese, and, on special occasions, poultry.

"Did you know," Nana said in her throaty voice, "that when I was little, it was unheard of having potatoes and tomatoes until travellers from the free lands brought seeds to trade?"

I shook my head and waited for her to elaborate while she set out the dinner plates, but only silence followed. Instead, Nana walked to the table and beckoned me to join her for dinner. Mouthwatering as the food smelled, a sense of worry lodged itself in the pit of my stomach. We ate in silence, and though the buttery vegetables melted in my mouth, I found them hard to swallow. After dinner, I rinsed the plates while Nana settled in her chair in front of the fireplace, though no fire burned tonight. The balmy air made the house too warm to warrant keeping a fire going as summer approached. Nana waited for me to take my usual spot at her feet before saying with a heavy voice, "By now, you have heard the rumours in town."

"That the statue is a bad omen?"

"Ah. Words are like the weeds in our garden. Even the nastiest of them have a way of spreading if even your old Nana, who barely steps out of the house, has heard them."

"And what am I supposed to do? Stop the whole town from talking? Tear the statue down myself?"

I hadn't meant to lash out like that, but the words came out sounding bitter, reflecting the state of unspoken fear that held me in its clutches.

"For now, do nothing but remain vigilant. When they begin work in earnest, keep an eye out on what materials they use and how they use them. It could be charms, odd carvings in the stone, or even chanting, for who knows what black magic entails? I have taught you how to spot an evil eye. Even better, make that worthless boy of yours keep watch for you. If the builders have no hidden intentions, then they will be happy to explain to a boy keen to learn what they are doing. Just be careful."

I nodded. Nana's words unsettled me, yet they also gave me an odd sense of hope. I vowed to keep healing herbs and protective stones from her storage with me at all times. Iliya would be more than eager to help as well. The feeling of foreboding eased a little at the thought. In the meantime, we readied ourselves for Nana's story. As if having read my mind, she yawned, adjusted in the seat, and continued last night's tale.

"The youngest son knew he had merely wounded the hala and that she still lived. Once she got her strength back, she would return to take what she thought was rightfully hers. The boy and his brothers set off to follow the hala's bloody trail and end her for good. The trail, however, soon ended at a well's entry. 'Someone needs to go down,' the youngest brother said. The first one, after peeking inside and finding the darkness so deep that one could cut through it with a knife, refused. So did the second one. Finally, the youngest one conceded, tied a rope around his waist, and went down to the bottom of the well. Once there, a bright light greeted him. When his vision cleared from the darkness, a house stood before him. Inside, three sisters played with a golden apple each, except for the youngest one, who had only an ordinary red apple. Next to the three sisters lay the hala, wounded and bleeding. 'Open the door, girls,' begged the young man. The youngest and the fairest of the sisters–"

"Why does it always have to be the youngest and fairest?" I muttered. Nana acknowledged my remark with a shrug before continuing.

"She took pity on him and opened the door. Once inside, the youngest brother swiftly ended the hala and implored the young sister, whom he had fallen in love with, to go back with him to the surface. 'You will go up first,' said the boy as he tied the rope around her waist. 'If my brothers quarrel over you when they see you and don't pull me up, know that I will find you no matter what.' 'Take this ring,' the youngest sister said, and gave the boy an emerald ring. 'If your brothers don't pull you back up, I will tell them I would marry whoever gives me clothes made by neither man nor woman. You will need to descend further into the well, where a zmei and a lamia will be waiting. The zmei is good, and the lamia is his evil sister. If you fall on the zmei's back, he will take you to the surface. The lamia will descend further down.'

Once on the surface, it was as the youngest brother had foretold. Upon seeing the young woman, the two brothers began fighting over her, forgetting their younger brother in the well. The boy then jumped down, and as luck would have it, fell on the back of the lamia, who brought him down to another realm. After wandering around this new land for a day, he found a village and a house in which an old woman was kneading dough for bread.

"Did the realm have a name?" I asked, eager for details I might have missed from her previous retellings. Nana closed her eyes, thinking.

"They say the lamia's wings cast a shadow that leads to Syanka. Only fools follow," Nana muttered, her voice heavy with sleep. I did not press further.

Soon after, silence followed, broken only by Nana's rhythmic breathing. I waited until the last embers of the fire had died before heading to bed. Lost in thought, I contemplated the day's events, my mind running back to the Vizier, his dark mage, and the glimpse of the shadows surrounding Yerleg. I wondered what it all meant long after the last faint glow of the fire had faded, but still came short of answers. Before a dreamless sleep finally took hold of me, I thought of Iliya's honeyed lips and their foreign feeling on mine.

CHAPTER 5

A Day At The Market

The market stalls stretched in front of us like a sea of vibrant colours and inviting smells. Every now and again, it came all the way from Tsargrad, popping up in larger villages and towns. It offered a choice of foods, drinks, and crafted goods, at least for those with the means to pay. Spring's first market visit was the most well-attended of the four. Naturally, all of Morava crowded the narrow paths between the stalls and carts. Even Nana had ventured out, though as of late her enthusiasm for any social events had waned, and she rarely left her preferred spot in front of the fireplace. Still, not someone to miss the opportunity to let merchants know her opinion on their prices, she wove her way between stalls.

Her first stop was the cheesemonger, who looked as if he would rather be anywhere but his stall as Nana ogled his produce. She picked a slice of cheese and sniffed it, her nose wrinkling at the pungent smell. The merchant regarded her warily, but she paid no heed when she proceeded to shove the cheese into her mouth. Nana chewed it thoughtfully, her lips smacking with approval. Her next words conveyed nothing of the pleasure she had clearly felt.

"Half a grosh for that! The nerve! You can't pay me to eat what on a good day smells like our pig's pantry. Back in my day, a grosh could buy you the whole stall! Ah, those were the times," she added with half-closed eyes and smacked her lips once more.

The merchant shook his head, prompting the bell at the tail of his fez hat to jingle. Despite her words, Nana produced a small knife from her pocket and cut a slice from another cheese. The merchant glared at her as she delicately put the slice in her mouth and slowly chewed it.

"It's even worse! My words stand true. I will not be buying any."

Her gaze travelled longingly to the remaining cheeses, but the merchant's red face and warning glare prevented her from sampling the rest of the goods his stall offered. I suppressed a smile at Nana's supposed lack of manners.

As we went on, I marvelled at the craft cheeses, dried meats, breads, and honey the market stalls overflowed with. Even the constant buzz of wasps around the sweets couldn't dull the colourful display. Nana huffed and puffed at the prices and on more than one occasion proceeded to help herself to samples. Despite our protests, she treated both Iliya and me to some berry pudding and toasted almonds to share. Iliya was about to take a bite of his pudding when he noticed Nana's empty hands.

"What about you, Nana? Any food for you?"

She smirked as she swallowed a bite-sized piece of baklava she had snatched in passing.

"Oh, markets always have too much commotion. It's bad for appetites."

Nana's good mood warmed us through. I scooped the pudding with more vigour than I had possessed a moment ago, and Iliya followed. The weight I had been carrying since my encounter at the well eased a little. The relief did not last long.

We passed by a couple of jewel makers that caught my attention. I stared longingly at the rows of gems adorning everything from earrings to ankle bracelets. Our own local producers were scattered here and there, but they made a drab contrast to the Ottoman opulence. Our region was renowned for its white cow cheese and bread, so the smell of freshly baked dough signalled to where local stalls hosted their goods. We stocked up on some fresh produce, herbs, and salted dried meat, for which Nana bargained as if negotiating for her life. By the time she marched off, the merchant's face was slick with sweat. I glanced back to watch the realisation that he had sold his goods to her at a loss dawn on him. Nana's smirk told me all I needed to know. I was about to remind her the merchant had a family of his own to feed, when she patted my shoulder reassuringly.

"It's not like he's going to starve. If his rich kaftan embroidery is anything to judge by, his stall was doing more than fine. Now, why don't you take our new produce home while I ask around?"

"Ask around? Whatever for?" I asked, narrowing my eyes suspiciously.

"You know, people always have a thing or two to share. Give them the right reason, and they'll tell you plenty."

"You are going to enquire about the statue, aren't you?"

She was already rummaging through her robe's pockets for charms. A couple of years ago, she had sewn extra pockets meant to carry as many herbs and charms as possible, all hidden safely inside her garments. After a good deal of rooting around and inspecting, she produced a pendant with a tiny amber crystal at its centre. The amber winked at the sun as she clasped the chain around her neck. "Ah, old magic never lies. Words of truth will cling to it like honey now."

"Nana!" My scolding was only half-hearted. In truth, any information would be welcome, so I added, "You'd better find something good!"

"Worry not, child, I will."

* * *

AFTER MY ENCOUNTER with Zoaea and her friends, my desire to venture anywhere near the well had all but evaporated. In the days that followed the market trip, Iliya brought us our daily jugs of water and informed us of any new tidings. The men had initially paid no attention to him and had worked silently on the statue, but as his stream of questions grew, they had told him off.

"They told me to find work in the fields and earn my bread instead of aiming above my station," he said miserably as he recounted the day's events. I had expected Nana to agree with the men, but she waited patiently for Iliya to go on, a larger testament to her worry than any words could have conveyed. "I tried to get some answers, but they shielded their work, coming between the statue and me each time I wanted to take a closer look. The little I saw showed a beautiful – if still crude – rendering of you."

Iliya waited for me to swoon over his flattery, but I felt too exhausted to continue speculating in vain. In truth, I had been under an unusually long spell of fatigue, with no apparent cause, and I kept it to myself. Iliya and Nana had enough on their plates without having to worry about my health. Iliya's dark brows furrowed quizzically at my lack of interest.

"Are you well, Jasna? You look a little pale."

Both Nana and he fixed me with worried eyes. I averted my gaze.

"Everything is fine. I just feel a bit tired. Some rest would do me good."

"Whatever you're looking for, I will be there to provide," he reassured me with the confidence only a young man could possess. For a moment, I imagined him in the role of the youngest brother from Nana's tale. The thought brought a smile to my lips, and Iliya returned it with one of his own. On other occasions, I would blush, thinking of the stolen kiss. That day, my limbs felt heavy, my mind muddled with fear and sudden exhaustion. My withdrawal, coupled with the tiredness that grew in my body with each passing day, should have been a warning sign. By the time I felt something to be irrevocably wrong, it was too late. The statue's unveiling at the well marked the first day of my illness.

* * *

A CLOUDLESS DAY greeted me when I stepped outside our house on a fine, crisp morning. The edges of my vision had a hazy quality to them, but I paid little attention. I breathed the air in, as the dawn chorus of birds broke the silence, first from one tree, then another, until birdsong echoed all around. In the distance, fields of yellow sunflowers and golden wheat, ripe for harvest, stretched as far as the eye could see. My first thought was how quickly this year's yield had ripened. As soon as the thought occurred, something else at the back of my mind began nagging at me. I headed for the beaten path towards the well, but the feeling persisted.

Another look at the crops told me it must be the end of summer.

"This can't be right," I said to myself. "Summer has barely started."

At that, the sky darkened, much like it had during my encounter with Yerleg. Out of nowhere, clouds appeared on the horizon, moving with unnatural speed, as if stirred by a faraway wind. The feeling of wrongness intensified as a ball of fire shot down from the sky and towards the fields. A high-pitched noise pierced the air, and as my ears rang, I watched the fireball crash in the middle of the field, a sense of helplessness numbing the fear that had held me in its grip just a heartbeat ago. The fire spread so fast, setting the fields ablaze in a matter of moments. Suddenly, I found it hard to breathe. Unable to comprehend what was happening, I trembled with fear, my heart ready to jump out of my ribcage.

"Would you stop that? It's rather annoying."

The voice had come from behind me, but when I turned around, no one was there. The noise, I realised, was me shouting. I closed my mouth, my throat raw with screaming, and watched helplessly as Morava's fields got scorched.

"It's your fault. All of it." The voice purred with contentment. In the meantime, clouds heavy with rain finally reached the town. They were too late. Blazing fire burned across the fields. Rain pelted, as if the clouds finally received permission to grieve the death of our harvest. I couldn't let myself wonder how we were to survive the winter with no food, so instead I focused on finding the voice's source, but to no avail. Fumes from the fire reached us and scratched my throat when I breathed them in.

"What do you mean, it's my fault?" I asked the empty air, anger now warring with fear. Only laughter greeted my words. The rising smoke curled upward, unspooling into a faint outline. I saw her then. A creature from myth, an impossible thing that roamed the night. Nana's tales warned of her power, and the way she unleashed her anger on anyone foolish enough to displease her. A force of nature. A winged woman whose beauty had no rival. The woman's red hair complemented the fire that ravaged the fields. She took a step towards me, her eyes black with hunger. I opened my mouth and closed it, lost for words as I stood frozen, waiting for the hala to devour me.

"You reek of dark magic," she said and reached a hand that closed around my shoulder. I tried to shake her off, but her grip only tightened. She leaned down and inhaled my scent, but before she could do anything else, someone shook my shoulders.

"It's nearly noon, Jasna, what are you thinking, girl? Wake up! Jasna, why aren't you answering? Wake up!"

I opened my eyes, and the prodding stopped. Nana's face swam before me, her expression flicking from worry to relief as I came into consciousness. My head pounded with pain, making it impossible to focus. When I closed my eyes, fields scorched with fire sprang to my vision. My body ached as I tried to sit up, limbs groaning in protest. One leg swung heavy from the bed, followed by the other. My eyesight clouded, and I blanched.

Nana's hand shot to my forehead. "You're burning!"

With that, she pushed me back to bed. The gathering dusk outside told me I had been asleep for much longer than I had thought, my chores all but forgotten.

"What's the time? Iliya said he must attend to other errands, so I was going to make the trip to the well. Is it too late? And I need to pay the haberdasher a visit to get buttons so you can mend your summer robe."

"My summer robe is of no importance right now," Nana

cut my rambling, and started fussing around. "And we have enough water from yesterday – Iliya made sure to bring two full jugs. Stale as the water will get, it will do for a couple of days. You need one of my herbal teas, perhaps nettle, to ease your burning."

I found I had no strength to protest. In truth, some respite, despite having just awoken, felt welcome. I worried that the eggs would remain uncollected, and the vegetables unwatered until Nana hushed me and told me to focus on getting better.

"Besides, do you take me for so old and frail as to have no strength to tend to my garden and chickens?" she asked amiably, quieting my feeble protests. Then she busied herself preparing a broth while I slipped in and out of consciousness.

That evening, Nana finished last night's story not from our usual spot by the hearth, but from a chair she had pulled to my bedside. Normally, I would implore her to finish her tale, and she would insist she was too old for her mind to remember an entire story before relenting. Tonight, she needed no prompting.

"Where was I? By a twist of fate, the lamia caught the youngest brother on her back and took him down to the earth below, where he found himself in a village. Once there, he saw a house with an open door, and went in. In the kitchen, an old woman was kneading dough – but instead of water, she used spit."

"That's so repulsive! Last time, you said she used her tears!" I tried to protest, but Nana cut me off.

"It matters little what it was. What matters is that it got our young hero curious, so he asked her, 'Old and wise woman, why are you kneading dough with your tears?' To which the old woman replied, 'A hala has cut off our water. She's made the well her lair, denying us access. Unless we bring her someone to devour and sate her hunger, she lets no one near.

We've given her so many people that there are no maidens left. Even the tsar had to send his own daughter.'"

"Upon hearing that, the hero set off to the well to finish the wounded hala and save the village. There he found the creature, and since he knew she was wounded, he was not afraid to confront her. The young hero ended her and saved the kingdom from a gruesome fate. With tears of gratitude in his eyes, the tsar told the youngest son that he could have anything his heart desired. The young hero wished for a way to return to the surface. 'Alas, that I cannot grant,' replied the tsar. 'But if you find someone to take you there, I will give you all you need for the journey.'"

"So the youngest brother began his search. In his wanderings through Syanka, he came across a tall tree where an eagle mother nested with her eaglets. She was absent, and a great snake slithered up the trunk, making for the nest."

"Without thinking, the hero drew his knife and cut off the snake's head, saving the eaglets from certain death. When the eagle mother returned and saw what he had done, she promised to carry him to the surface – but only if he first paid tribute to the tsar of the forest, where she made her nest. The youngest brother agreed and returned to the human tsar to implore him for gifts worthy of a ruler. The tsar gave him a raskovnik – a plant that can summon powerful beings in times of need. The hero offered it to the forest's tsar, the leshy himself, who used it to bring his wife back from the Nav, the land of the dead."

"The grateful leshy blessed the eagle with power to fly over realms, and so she flew our hero back to the surface. There he found his brothers still fighting over the youngest sister. Upon seeing the youngest brother, the girl said she would marry the man who gave her clothes made neither by a man nor by a woman. The young man remembered the ring she had given him and used it to wish for just that. The two were happily married and spent their lives together. The end."

Nana's voice trailed off, and I barely noticed when sleep came upon me. The day's concerns seeped into my bones, pulling me under the spell of oblivion that sleep brought without warning. For a moment, my eyelids fluttered open, revealing the familiar room, bathed in moonlight.

"Sleep now, child," said Nana with a soft voice. I needed no further prompting. Yet, the night brought little solace and only unsettling dreams. I dreamed of a well and a zmei that whisked me away from home, only for Yerleg to freeze me into a statue. The Grand Vizier's last words haunted me even in the land of dreams.

CHAPTER 6

THE SHADOW ILLNESS

The day my illness took hold, I drifted between fitful sleep and weary wakefulness. Fever weighed down my body. When awake, I sipped tea, swallowed spoonfuls of soup, but everything tasted muted. Nana's stories wove through the haze, half-heard, half-forgotten.

When the sun melted into the horizon, I worried Iliya would not come. And as if summoned by the thought, a knock echoed through the quiet house.

I must have slipped under again, because when I next opened my eyes, he was already there, sitting where Nana had been, his voice low as they spoke. His hazel eyes found mine, and he stopped mid-sentence.

"How bad is it?" I asked. His silence told me enough. I recognised that voice he used with Nana. It was the same one he used to calm a skittish horse.

"We don't know yet," Iliya replied hesitantly. The sincerity in his words told me what he said was true. "I wish you saw the statue. A thing to behold. Everyone from Morava was there to see its unveiling this morning. At first, they admired it… but then the whispers started. The likeness is too perfect, they said. Unnatural even. A statue shouldn't look alive."

Iliya hesitated, casting a troubled look at Nana. Her face remained inscrutable under the fading daylight.

"What does that mean?" I asked, unable to conceal my irritation when no one spoke. It was always something with Morava's townsfolk. A curse, bad omens, evil stars, now this. The angst gave me enough energy to prop myself up on my elbows and rest my back against the bedpost. My head throbbed with the effort. I had expected Iliya to elaborate, but instead it was Nana who answered.

"It means that Yerleg did not deliver idle threats."

"But why would he bring this illness down on me if the Vizier wants me in his palace?" I asked, and Iliya nodded. Nana pursed her lips, thinking.

"I know not what the end goal is. The statue clearly has some sort of dark magic tied to it and it's affecting you. Your illness isn't one of natural causes. This much I know. You must continue what you have been doing and find out more."

Iliya nodded and busied himself with a loose thread from my bedsheet. He curled it around his index finger nervously and then uncurled it in a repetitive motion that made my heart sink. Unless something troubled him enough to make him so restless, he never fidgeted like that. Indeed, upon a closer look at his face, I noticed dark circles under his eyes. His amber skin looked pale, and his shaggy hair, usually sleek and casually falling on one side, now looked dull and in need of a comb.

My hand found his, cupping it with all the reassurance I could muster. After hesitating briefly, he turned his palm to face mine and gave my hand a gentle squeeze. His warmth reminded me of the stolen kiss that felt as if it had happened ages ago, of whispered promises and endless nights. At that moment, I knew with certainty that these were our last moments together, though I couldn't say why. I searched Iliya's eyes to see confirmation of what I knew to be true, but his gaze returned an unwavering belief that things would get better.

Nana, who was brewing more tea to give us some privacy, cleared her throat. Our hands drew apart as if scolded, and we looked at her, flustered.

"Listen," she said. "That's all you need to do. Listen and ask questions when you find it appropriate. We need to learn what that illness is and how the statue is causing it. There is no such thing as coincidence, and Jasna falling ill the day of the statue being placed above the well proves it. Now, it's getting late, and you don't want to be caught in the dark, my dear boy. Not with evil lurking so near."

Iliya nodded, but did not move. His eyes met Nana's, and it seemed to me that an understanding passed between them – a promise that they would not let me succumb to whatever the Grand Vizier's mage had in store for me.

At last, Iliya averted his eyes and said,

"I will go now, but not before I make this clear. I've listened enough and it's yielded nothing. I have asked questions, but maybe it was not the right places I sought answers from. From tomorrow, I will double my efforts until we find out what ails Jasna and get rid of it once and for all."

He gently brushed his fingers against my forehead.

"Rest for now. Things will get back to how they used to be. I promise."

* * *

THE FEVER STARTED LIKE A WHISPER. A chill spread throughout my body, sending shivers along my spine like a slithering snake. Despite the cold coursing through my limbs, sweat drenched my forehead. Then came the fire.

A slow, almost lazy burning sensation replaced the chill, like a flame that ate everything in its wake. I could feel my fingers grasping the drenched sheets, but could not will my eyes to open. I was not alone. Someone was there, in my feverish dreams, quiet and observing. A serpentine presence, there and gone in the blink of an eye. Somewhere far away, Nana chanted. Her throaty voice wove words through the air like magic, but just as they were about to take purchase and shield me from the illness, something dark swept in, a tendril's lash that licked them and dissolved them into dust.

I tried to catch her words of healing and let them take hold, but came short, again and again. Delirium swallowed my thoughts and dragged me under once more. Darkness surged at the edges of my vision. A dream, I thought, just a dream, yet this one felt different, more real. The edges of dreaming and waking dulled until I couldn't tell them apart.

I was running, a scent of fresh grass and blossoming trees at my heels. Leaves and twigs crunched under my feet. Maruna ran ahead, her thick braid bouncing up and down. She turned around and flashed a foxlike smile.

"Hurry up, Jasna," she said, panting. But the goods concealed under my tunic weighed me down, making it harder and harder to keep up.

The world lurched, and I tripped. The pot of coins Maruna had dared me to steal spilled with a dull thud on the forest floor.

"Jasna, you moron," Maruna chided between gasps, just as the scene bled into another.

* * *

"Easy, girl," Nana murmured from afar, and something cool pressed against my brow. "The fever still has you in its clutches."

"You were talking in your sleep, saying things..." Iliya's voice sounded troubled. My mind slipped into oblivion once more.

"Come now, Jasna. It's just a few coins. He won't even notice. They say he barely knows where he is half the time," Maruna was saying. She nudged me towards the sleeping man, and whispered in my ear. "You want to be one of us, don't you?"

"Of course I do," I said, my voice laden with fear, wondering how we'd gone from listening to Nana's stories to Maruna pressuring me to steal. This time her nudge turned into a shove and I stepped towards the homeless man. Before I had time to think twice about it, I reached for the pot of coins and my hand closed around it. But just as I was about to take off, the man's eyes opened and met mine. Unable to shed the guilt, I stood there paralysed and gaped at Gorovoi, Nana's old neighbour. His dark green eyes were pools of calm sadness. No judgement lurked there. Worst of all, he watched me as if he had seen all of this before. Tears filled my eyes. I made a run for it, too scared to see the disappointment written on his face.

The vision blurred and shifted. I had expected my past to hound me again, reminding me of my mistakes. Instead, I soared above the clouds, scales rippling, wings cutting through the wind. The world stretched below, the river's silver veins weaving their way through the land. Fire blazed in my throat. Power throbbed beneath my skin while my scaly body ploughed through the air with barely any resistance. I opened my mouth to ask the empty air what was going on, but the roar that left my throat instead shook me to my core.

Then darkness consumed me once more.

"Who are you?" I asked as we flew past Morava's well and soared above the Gora forest. For the longest time, no reply followed. Instead, images of a great serpentine creature with green and yellow scales ran across my vision. I needn't have seen one to recognise it from Nana's tales.

"A zmei," I spoke inside the shared mind as we flew above the Ezero lake with the sunset behind our back. The creature neither confirmed nor denied it, but I was sure that in my dream, I shared the body of a zmei. I was about to ask him for his name when he spoke with an ancient voice.

"They call me…"

But before he could name himself, the dream ended. I cursed under my breath as I opened my eyes and found Iliya towering over my bed. The moment I came into consciousness, a vicious headache rang inside my head and Iliya, who had been in the middle of talking to Nana, leaned forward.

"Jasna," he said as his palm felt for my forehead. "You've been rambling. It's the fever, it's making you say things."

I groaned instead of replying. Iliya moved, giving up the spot he had occupied to Nana. She pressed a cold cloth soaked in water to my forehead.

"You were saying something?" I croaked and a coughing fit overcame me. My limbs felt swollen and the rest of my body was in no better shape. The burning sensation intensified across my face and chest. It felt as if hives of wasps crawled across my skin.

"We think we know what ails you, my child," Nana said as she gently brushed my cheek with her index finger. I knew it must be bad when she made no haste to share it.

"Is it related to what you found out at the market the other day?" I asked. With my illness and the strange dreams that haunted me day and night, I had completely forgotten about it. She nodded. "Is it curable?"

From the look of defeat in their eyes, I assumed it wasn't. She picked up the needles and yarn lying at her feet and slowly spun the yarn.

"We are not sure yet," Iliya said quickly, eager to reassure me. "Nothing is set in stone."

"A travelling merchant at the market had an interesting story to share. It regarded an unusual subject. At first, I did not pay much attention, but now I see it. Shadow entombment practices are what he called them. I heard of it a long time ago. Once, a traveller at the caravanserai told me what it was that made a builder a master of his craft. I have mentioned some of it to you in my stories."

"The story about the bridge," I confirmed. The story wasn't one that Nana shared often, so I only remembered bits and pieces. Nana nodded and busied herself with her knitting. When she spoke next, her words seemed to weigh her down.

"There is much more to the story, as it usually goes. A builder once entombed a maiden's shadow in the structure of a bridge to make sure that the bridge would withstand the test of time. Some said a shadow might be trapped so the art would last as long as stone. It can be anything, really…"

"Such as a statue," I observed. "With his dark magic, Yerleg trapped my shadow in the statue."

"Still, there are more unknowns to this. The question of why Yerleg would do this to you and to what end remains."

You will come to me of your own free will.

Unbidden, the Grand Vizier's words echoed in my mind. Was this a ploy to bend my will into submission so that I went to Tsargrad as he had foretold? If so, an illness would hardly help me in finding my way to the empire's capital. There was little doubt it was getting worse. Unless the Grand Vizier meant to send my corpse to Tsargrad, I would not be making the trip soon. A thought nagged at me.

"Isn't it obvious?" I asked, if only rhetorically. "Once they have my shadow entombed in the structure, it's easy to control me. How would someone with a splinter of a soul resist?"

"Once your shadow is severed," Nana corrected me, "your soul is split and you'll waste until death claims you. No one gets to live for long after the magic takes place. That's what the merchant said. There will be no controlling you if you are dead, so there must be another explanation."

"I saw the dark mage, Yerleg, do something to the weather," I said, remembering. "It was almost as if he had a sort of darkness about him that seemed out of this world. And he had it bent to his will."

"Perhaps entombing your shadow somehow feeds the darkness," Iliya speculated with a shiver. "Or grows his power."

He continued thinking aloud in that vein while I lay back down, feeling drained. His words rang true. Yerleg had entombed my shadow to further his goals. As to what they were, I had no idea. As days merged into one, my strength waned further and further. I ceased eating and spent more time in the land of dreams than in the waking world – though sleep provided little solace, for it was restless and plagued me with unsettling dreams. I searched for the zmei in vain, but though I felt him trying to link his mind to mine, something stood in his way. Whether it was Yerleg, my weakened state, or something else entirely, I could not tell.

* * *

A DISTANT MUFFLED sound kept saying something so close to my ear it prevented me from sinking back into unconsciousness. The voice sounded familiar, though I felt as if I were underwater and sank deeper and deeper, peace awaiting at the bottom. Still, the voice tugged at me until some words filtered down and I paused to listen.

"I'm going to get your shadow back," the voice was saying. It belonged to Iliya. A stranger really – one somehow related to Jasna, the same Jasna who cared what Morava's people thought of her and tried to make them see reason. With considerable effort, my eyes fluttered open and blinked against the bright sunlight. Forcing them to remain open was not a pleasant feeling.

"Jasna," Iliya said, his shoulders dropping with relief. "You're awake."

When I gave no reply, he went on, "I have a plan, you see. I'll get your shadow back from the Grand Vizier. Since he was the one who had it built, he must know how to get it back from the statue. It's possible that he doesn't even suspect what Yerleg did and might willingly make things right… unless it was him who did this. But don't worry. I'll do anything to get it back. He won't be able to refuse my plea. Just live until then, Jasna. Please, hold on for a little longer."

His hands gripped mine and held them tight, as if willing me to hold on to life. But even after his words, the allure of darkness tugged at the sleeve of my sweat-soaked nightdress, and my eyes refused to remain open. I sank back into oblivion.

CHAPTER 7

NANA'S SPELL

Once more, I soared above the sky, unshackled from all the worries weighing me down on solid ground.

"Extraordinary, isn't it? To be so high above, and see how insignificant human life truly is," said the zmei whose body I shared.

"Who are you?" I demanded, intent on getting answers this time. I had expected him to be evasive, so his next words came as a surprise.

"I go by the name Zhar," he said, then paused, waiting for me to recognise the name. I racked my brains, but fell short of answers. That soured his mood.

"Once I was known among humans," the zmei said, his voice heavy with regret. "Now I am doomed to be imprisoned by foul forces for eternity."

"But who imprisoned you? And how can they do that for eternity?"

"A zmei's life stretches beyond what your human mind can comprehend," he said haughtily. "Your lifetime is but a day to me. As far as who did it, I do not know."

"How come you can speak to me?"

Zhar snorted, a sound that might have been laughter.

"I don't need tricks to reach you. Your scent is strong enough for every creature to smell you. That's why we don't have long. You need to find me and free me before someone else finds you."

I stiffened. "My scent?"

"Not your physical scent," the zmei said, correcting me. "Your shadow's. Part of your essence, or what you humans call a soul, is severed from you, marking you to any creature. And there are those of us in Syanka who very much crave the taste of dark magic."

A chill that had nothing to do with the fever ravaging my body ran down my spine. "Am I in danger?"

His silence was enough of an answer.

"What happens if they find me?"

"Once they find the source and devour the traces of dark magic, they will want more. I'm afraid that from the moment that spell was cast, it marked you. It's like a beacon for creatures that feed off darkness."

I had little to add to that. The sense of inevitable doom grew a little bigger inside my chest.

"Why do you think I can free you? I might not live long enough to try. I am, after all, sick and with my shadow missing."

"Live or not, you are the one I have been able to reach," he said with something akin to sorrow. "But there might be hope yet. Like I said, the magic used on you has made you irresistible to creatures that feed on darkness. They will want to consume your essence, starting from the object that has it trapped." My mind raced ahead of the conversation even as I tried to quiet my frantic heart. Zhar had alerted me to danger, and seemed to possess knowledge that I needed if I wanted to live. I couldn't let him out of my sight now, so I pressed for answers while holding on to the dream for dear life.

"Do you know how to reverse the spell? My shadow was trapped in a statue."

"A statue, yes," the zmei said as if it was obvious, but ignored my first question. "A spell like that needs a vessel to contain the essence. The mage that cast this spell has a soul darker than the Nav's darkest corner. And the dead are growing restless while he's giddy with power."

"The dead?" I frowned. "What do they have to do with anything?"

But before Zhar could reply, a tug at the back of my mind made me falter. Though I tried to hold on to the dream, I found myself slipping away until I was pulled out entirely. It took my eyes a moment to shake off the afterimage of the sky and clouds below me and for the room to come into focus.

A faint light seeped through the window. Night had settled over Morava with a quiet blanket of stars. Flickering yellow lights swam before my vision, making me think I was still in one of my bizarre dreams. The lights pulsed, as if signalling something unseen. Fireflies, I realised with relief. They danced outside the window, a muted sheen of luminescence that lit up the night. It dispelled any lingering suspicions that I still slept.

As my eyes adjusted to the darkness, I spotted Nana sitting at a chair in the corner where she could keep constant vigil on me. I needed to tell her something, but my muddled mind kept going in circles. My breath wheezed in and out unevenly as I struggled to speak. No words came out at first, but that was enough to signal to Nana I was no longer asleep. Her eyes flew open at the change in my breath and found my face. Under the scant moonlight, they seemed ancient and burdened with worry. She got up and tottered to my bed with considerable effort. She then placed a withered hand on my forehead and cocked her ear on one side as she listened to me breathe. Whatever she heard must have been bad, for she shook her head and went on to rummage through the pockets of her robe.

"Where did I put it?" she muttered to herself. A rustling of paper told me she had found what she was looking for. "While you were unconscious, I went out and met the master of the forest. An incantation of sorts is all I got… he claims it could bring back your shadow. Hopefully, this time it's not just empty words."

Nana paused, and her silence hung heavy between us. When she spoke, she sounded tired.

"He promised that, if I used it, at least part of the soul should return, but a part of it will remain trapped forever. What should I do? It shouldn't be up to your old Nana to decide if you should be living with half a soul. But no matter, the spell is here and I told the leshy I would have his head if he lied to me. Master of the forest or not, he better be right. Let's see."

She squinted against the faint light filtering through the open curtain. The strain on her face suggested it was still too dark to read the words. I must have drifted off again, for the next thing I knew was that she was still by my bedside, dawn breaking with a crimson light across the floor. She held the piece of paper close to her eyes and read the words out loud.

"Let what was once broken be whole once more,
Strike this foul magic with your mighty claymore,
I beseech you, O mighty king of the green,
Bestow this child of the forest with your grace,

So she may once more her lost essence interlace."

She read the text thrice before stuffing the paper back in her robe with a dismissive hand.

"Bah! He always makes up silly words like these. Listening to a leshy! What possessed me? I have more sense than that!"

* * *

WHEN I WAS but a little girl, Nana's deep, throaty voice used to intimidate me. It was, after all, the voice of a headstrong person, of a woman who had no second thoughts about voicing her opinion. When that voice finally broke through the fever's barrier, I felt like I got pulled away from deep, cold waters and I was drowning no more.

When next I came into consciousness, Nana was feeling for my forehead once more. She listened to my breathing for a long while.

"Your fever is breaking," she sighed with relief. "Keep fighting it, Jasna. There is hope you will pull through this yet. Keep fighting the illness."

Indeed, I could feel the pain subside. There were no words for the horror of wasting away, trapped in a body too weak to fight back. For the first time in weeks, I felt I could breathe unhindered.

Not long after, I propped myself up to sit while Nana brought a tray with bread, milk, goat's cheese, and jam. I ate with a newfound vigour, everything so flavourful as if tasted for the first time. A swarm of unanswered questions kept springing to my mind, dampening my enthusiasm for food.

"Has there been any word of Iliya since he left for Tsargrad?" I asked the first and most pressing one. My voice came out broken and hoarse, almost as hardened as Nana's. She shook her head.

"It takes two weeks to reach Tsargrad with a horse. Ten days, if he rides with little to no breaks."

"How long ago did he leave?"

"Ten days now, as of today."

Ten days? My tired mind told me I must have battled the illness for over a year. Iliya had been here for the first two weeks of it, which meant it had been close to a month since I'd first fallen ill. I sagged back on my pillow. My treacherous elbows wobbled as I tried to prop myself up after, a reminder that my recovery had just begun.

"Go gently, Jasna. Though it might not seem so now, you are doing very well. Only yesterday you were closer to the dead than the living," Nana said reassuringly. "You will get up eventually. It's a start. Give your body some time to remember its purpose."

She hesitated briefly before her curiosity took over.

"When you were feverish, you kept asking for someone. I think you thought you were a zmei. Or perhaps you searched for one. It was hard to tell as your ramblings made little sense."

"I'm sorry, Nana. For putting you through all this," I said carefully, unsure whether I wanted to share my feverish dreams yet.

"Nonsense, girl. You didn't choose to cross the dark mage's path. Or the Grand Vizier's for that matter."

She waved her hand, as if to say it was water under the bridge. Even so, the deepening creases on her face showed just how much my illness had worn her down.

Her bringing up the zmei unsettled me. Nana's words had steered a memory of soaring above the sky in the body of a winged serpentine creature. I had shared the body of a zmei and he had asked me to help him. More than that, Zhar had revealed to me I was no longer safe. My shadow's severing put a target on my back, which also meant I put Nana in danger. Another thing I remembered was his plea – though it sounded more like a demand from the zmei – to free him from his imprisonment. He had mentioned other familiar words such as Syanka, which I perceived to be a different realm altogether. It was the same realm from Nana's tales, the one I had dreamed of visiting ever since I was but a child.

And the name, Zhar, it meant something, but like all fragile threads I had grasped at in my sleep, it kept eluding me. I was about to ask Nana when she spoke. Her words weighed on her, but she said them nonetheless.

"You kept repeating it was your fault that your brother was taken as blood-tax. That you were cursed," she sighed as she relayed my ramblings. I wished she would not go there, to that vulnerable place my mind had occupied in the past month. "I thought we had put the past behind, that it would cease haunting us once and for all. But a part of you, however small, still believes you were the cause, when you well know it's just people talking. It has to stop, Jasna. It isn't good for you to live in the past."

Despite knowing she spoke the truth, I did exactly what she urged me not to do. My memories went back to all the times Maruna's vitriol had reduced me to tears. Yet, the doubt that she was right festered within me. I could not shake the feeling of guilt, the one that told me I had somehow caused the misfortune that had befallen us. After all, it was because of me that Iliya had left to seek a cure and beseech the Grand Vizier to grant me my shadow back.

"Jasna? You are doing it again. Come back to me." Nana's voice boomed in my ear, jolting me away from my self-pitying. "Iliya made up his mind when you were ill. It was his decision to set off for Tsargrad to seek a cure, one he made of his own free will."

Though she had not intended them to, the words rang in an oddly familiar way. *You will come to me of your own free will.*

"Jasna? Did I upset you? You are so pale still, you need to rest."

"You could never upset me, Nana," I whispered. "It's just that… I feel like a force larger than me, one beyond my comprehension, is pushing me towards something unknown, yet inevitable. Nana… what if I must accept the Grand Vizier's proposal?"

Nana's eyes narrowed, taking on that distant air that said she was thinking of times long gone. She sighed, her eyes fixed on the line of trees outside.

"When I was young, it was unorthodox not to take a husband, but not unheard of." She paused, lost in thought. "Ah, those were the times. I managed just fine raising your mother without the help of a man, much to the chagrin of some. Then your mother had you, and that was a blessing to us all. Do not make the mistake of assuming otherwise. And don't feel obliged to do what we did. Walk your own path and be confident about it. If your old Nana has taught you something, let it be this; don't let a handful of people like Maruna dictate the course of your life. Not even a Vizier, grand or not, holds that power."

She paused, and I had the sudden pang of fear that she was saying farewell with her next words.

"As for Iliya, you are not helpless. Travelling alone as a woman is much more dangerous, but I have a trick or two up my sleeve to help you on your journey."

"Nana, what are you saying? That I should go after Iliya? To the Grand Vizier's palace?"

"I'm saying that if Iliya does not return, you are free to go after him. Or not. Ultimately, it's your choice and what I or anyone else tells you should not matter for as long as you follow your heart. Never forget that."

She turned around and fixed me with her murky eyes. The fading light that spilled behind her cast a shadow across her face, making it impossible to read. For a moment, I saw Nana as she must have been before the years had shrunk her shape and shrivelled her skin. A determined woman who had lived her life to the fullest. Some of that beauty still lurked behind the wrinkles, each having a story to tell. Looking at her, I had the feeling I might turn out fine too.

"Will you tell me a story, Nana?" I asked. Her gaze lingered on my face for a while longer before she smiled.

"I thought you would never ask," she said as she shuffled her feet back to her chair and beckoned for me to take my spot next to her. That night, dark mages, spells, and zmei belonged to her stories only, in faraway lands that we imagined from the warmth of our hearth.

CHAPTER 8

WITH THUNDERSTORM SHE STRIKES

Recovery turned out to be slow and frustrating. More than once, my sluggish body needed to be reassured it still belonged to me – that it could move, get up, walk, and that it was alive. It reminded me of when Nana taught me to ride a horse. I had been ten when she led Naiya from the shed and declared that, despite what others might say, I needed the skill. It was a privilege most girls never had, something men took for granted.

Though only a few years had passed, that moment had been the last time she had harnessed what strength remained of her youth and used it to instil a sense of independence in me. Now, as I recovered, I felt the same frustration I had then – thinking I had mastered a skill, only to be proven wrong.

Days went by. Bit by bit, my strength seeped back, hesitantly at first, then with growing vigour, like a stream breaking free from the obstruction of a fallen tree. Summer greeted us with longer days, and soon, I walked without the help of Nana's cane. Yet, a week since my fever broke rolled into another, and there was no sign of Iliya.

Nana and I avoided speaking of him. He might not be coming back. We could only speculate whether he had reached the capital and secured a meeting with the Vizier, but we suspected his plea had done little to restore my health. Nana's spell had played a role – my fever had subsided shortly after she had read the note. Another topic we skirted around was the king of the forest, the leshy who'd given her the spell.

"Bah, leshy and their flowery poems. Who knows what works and what doesn't work with them?" She would say and wave a hand dismissively as if dealing with him had been nothing short of a nuisance.

"So leshy exist?" I had pressed. "Do they look like us? Or are they more like the trees in your tales?" I wanted to ask about other things too, like how she knew the leshy, but Nana always sensed the direction of my curiosity and steered the conversation away.

"Count on your Nana to always be there for you, leshy or not," she would say vaguely, and that would be it.

Yet I felt the world around me shifting, as though something unseen had been set in motion. It was in the way Nana moved more slowly, her cane now a permanent fixture, and in the wind that carried whispers through the trees, setting my skin prickling. During my sickness and subsequent recovery, Nana had taken the burden upon herself of carrying out all tasks around the house, including fetching water. She spent the entire morning trudging up to the well and back, each step heavier than the one before. As guilty as I felt, I could do little to help her. My strength allowed me only to walk to the thin line of trees, where the twisted path began. Soon, I hoped, I could resume my chores before Nana had foundered under the jug's weight.

Then, one morning, Nana caught me off guard when she said, "You would want to see the statue."

A fine morning greeted me when I followed her outside and assumed my seat on the chair she had set out for me.

I frowned. "I doubt that."

"It's changed," she said, setting down her jug. "A crack appeared the day you recovered. A crack wide enough to make people fear that something crawled out of it."

I shivered. Nana's words unsettled me more than I cared to admit. I didn't need to see it to know what had clawed its way out to reunite with me. I wanted to dismiss Nana's words, to believe the crack meant nothing. But that shifting feeling in the air, the way the trees whispered to each other as if conspiring to something foul, was hard to ignore.

"What do the people say?" I couldn't help but ask.

She paused and studied me. I could see something troubled her, but she only said, "I sense a change in you. Your illness has brought out something different, but I cannot tell what. You know, it's only a handful of people that think ill of you. Most of Morava cares little about badmouthing you. Yes, Zoaea and her friends, the baker and Maruna's family, they all say you have doomed this town with your bad luck. Now they have found a new tune for their old song. They think a demon has crawled out of the statue, set free by you. Let them. Use it to your advantage."

I winced. Though there was some truth in that unnatural forces were at work, blaming me as their source still hurt as much as it had when I had been but a child. Whether it was Maruna reminding me I would have no friends if not for her, or Zoaea's friends crossing themselves at the sight of me, their hostility was too long borne to be erased.

I watched Nana disappear into the woods, and must have dozed off because the next thing I felt was a distant shift in the air. It came with a prickle at the back of my neck. Then, as I blinked my eyes open, a sudden chill pierced my body and my vision darkened. I rubbed my eyes to dispel the confusion. The air was charged with anticipation, like the quiet before a storm. The setting felt somehow too familiar. I watched the sky darken at an unnatural speed. Much like my encounter with Yerleg and my fever dreams, clouds gathered beyond the horizon and sailed towards Morava.

The chill intensified, and goosebumps crept along my arms. A high-pitched scream, seemingly from the sky itself, pierced the air, breaking the silence. I searched frantically for the source, but could see no one else. Unlike my dream, I knew the scream hadn't been mine. I could feel something approach, though I couldn't tell what, and I knew it was both foul and famished. I could only guess at what it needed to sate its hunger. I stood paralysed for longer than I should have, dread gripping me in unrelenting clutches.

At last, I scrambled to get up, throwing the blanket that had covered me a moment ago on the ground. Then, just like that, the feeling was gone, dissipated into thin air, and the goosebumps receded, smoothing the surface of my flesh once again. But the clouds remained, and soon the first raindrops spattered across the ground.

A figure emerged at the path's end. With a sigh of relief, I saw it was Nana, panting under the weight of the jug she still hauled. I hurried across the small garden to help her, my joints protesting from the unexpected strain. Nana refused to cede the jug and ushered me back to the house.

"Hurry, Jasna, or the rain will catch us. We can't have you catching a chill just as you are doing so well."

"It's not rain," I said with certainty when cold droplets splattered across my face. "Nana, that's not rain. It's snowing."

"Nonsense, girl, it's summer."

But she had to admit I was right when white snowflakes swirled around us.

"How is it even possible for it to snow in summer?"

"Worse things have happened than having a bit of unexpected snow," Nana said as we hurried inside the house as fast as we could. By the time our slow pace brought us in, the air outside swelled with dancing snowflakes. Nana could no longer hide the concern in her throaty voice.

"I need to check on the chickens," she cried out as a gust of wind lashed at our backs. I groaned. Nana would never leave her precious chickens outside in such weather. I had to help her.

"I'm coming with you," I said as I pushed the front door open. Nana discarded the jug on the floor and headed towards the back with me trailing her at her heels.

The backyard contained two barracks; the larger one used to house our horse but was now home to the chickens and a pig. When I was little, I had spent countless hours playing make-believe stories stitched together from Nana's tales. As the empty yard gaped at us that day, it made a pitiful sight. The chickens had sought shelter in the shed, an alarmed squeak from that direction notifying us of their location. Nana sighed with relief and we headed back.

The chill that ran in the air outside seemed to follow us in. It lingered for so long that after hours of shivering under the winter blanket, Nana had no choice but to light up the fire with the few remaining logs to feed its flame. Soon enough, a pot simmered merrily over the fire, unperturbed by the sudden cold.

The night stretched long, the storm refusing to settle. I absentmindedly watched snowflakes dance outside the window as snow blanketed the ground and the window ledge, coating it in a fine layer that transformed into a thick white carpet overnight. We kept feeding wood to the hearth while the pile dwindled, until the last log sank into its ever-hungry mouth, leaving us shivering not long after. A small part of me wondered if the storm was my doing, and if my feverish dream had somehow come true.

Then, after a day had passed, an even more unnatural warm wind appeared out of nowhere and blew the snow away, leaving the muddied ground soaked in an ugly shade of brown. But that was not the end.

The first rumble of thunder greeted us on the second morning. Then, something started pounding on the window, like an angry beast trying to force its way in. The sky opened a hungry mouth, ready to devour the earth below, and shortly after, ice-cold hail began punching the ground. That was when the second inhuman scream shook the earth. I let out a shriek, and Nana dropped the breakfast tray she was carrying, tea and warm bread spilling on the floor.

"Nana, please tell me I didn't imagine it," I demanded, my voice laced with fear. Nana's eyes mirrored my dread when they met mine. Before she could say anything, another scream, this time sounding closer, split the sky in two. Nana's face hardened. Something in it told me she recognised the scream's source. With a decisive move, she grabbed my elbow and steered me towards the back of the house.

"It's found us. You need to hide, Jasna, now. Hurry into the closet, just as you used to when you were little. Go on now, before she finds you. I will handle the rest."

The fear in her eyes left no room for argument. I turned and crammed myself into the cupboard's narrow space. When the door closed, darkness enveloped me, and I was alone with my heart pounding against my chest.

The silence that followed lasted only a breath. Then, as if blown by a beating gust of wind, the house shook. A noise, much like the flap of giant wings, was followed by a thump on the ground, where I thought was the front door. It sounded like an enormous bird had landed outside. Then a distinctly feminine voice seeped through the walls.

"Where is the source?"

I heard the front door open and close with a creak, and Nana's muffled voice said something I couldn't catch.

"Do you take me for a fool, old woman? I know what you're hiding. I can feel the working of dark magic between those walls. It calls to me. So close..."

She said the last bit longingly, almost gently. Another muted reply followed before the woman hissed, "Yes, the forest, I feel a trace of it there. Just as well. A captured shadow, you say? How delicious. I will enjoy devouring it very much. And, old woman, beware – if you've lied, I will make you beg for death before I'm done with you."

A beat of wings, a gust of strong wind that shook the house, then silence. Suddenly, I found it hard to breathe, the narrow cupboard too small to confine me.

"You can come out now, Jasna," Nana's coarse voice sounded close by as she opened the cupboard doors and peered in. I crawled out, barely able to contain all the questions. But before I could demand answers, she put a finger to her lips, urging me to keep quiet and listen.

"A hala is bound to feel the workings of dark magic. I had hoped she wouldn't sense you or the well where the spell was cast, but it was callous of me to assume so. Of course there would be traces. More so since you got some of your essence back, the magic imprints must be everywhere."

I stared at Nana in disbelief. Throughout my life, there had been no indication that magical creatures existed. But then I dreamed of one, and suddenly they were all real? It did not seem right. Perhaps I was still bedridden, stuck in one of my delirious dreams. Still, I had to know.

"A hala? As in the one from fairy tales? No one believes in that. Do you?" I asked, my voice rising to a high pitch. "Besides, doesn't evil roam only at night?"

"It's more complicated than that," Nana said with a sigh. "This idea that good belongs to the day and bad roams at night fails the moment you assume people are all good. You, of all people, should know that."

My thoughts went back to Maruna and Zoaea. Their cruelty to me did not make them purely evil. Or did it? Did following her hunting instincts make the hala evil? Perhaps not everything wicked belonged to the night. Nana was growing restless.

"Listen closely, child, we have little time to debate good and evil. Know this. Not all creatures are corrupted, just like not all humans are good simply because they tread in daylight. What matters is that this creature wishes you ill. If you anger a hala, you are bound to pay a price. It's in their nature to bring about storms and destroy villages. By now, she must have realised the well's magic traces are only the appetiser, and will be once again hunting for its source."

A crack of thunder split the sky. Outside, hail resumed, heavier than before, pummelling the earth. Chunks, large as fists, hit the ground, striking everything in their wake, from the house to the fields and beyond. Then, just as suddenly as it had begun, the hail ceased. For a moment, even the air stood breathless, long enough for the hair on the back of my neck to stand. Then, a streak of lightning split the sky open, striking the fields below. Within moments, flames licked hungrily at the crops, turning ice to steam. Soon the horizon was ablaze, the fire spreading fast.

My fever dream was coming true. A terrified cry coming from the town's direction confirmed it.

"The fields are on fire!"

It seemed we had more immediate problems than the hala. Nana grabbed my shoulders, her eyes feverish.

"Jasna, listen to me. You have to leave. While I can hold off one hala, I can't protect you from what the people will do when they turn their fear on you."

CHAPTER 9

Burn Her If You Catch Her

More screams rose above the fire. Apart from the tumult coming from Morava, the sky had gone silent. No more hail fell. In the near horizon where the fields began, thick curls of smoke coiled up from the ground. A crimson wave rose, at first slowly, then faster and faster, the fire's maw devouring everything in its wake like an insatiable beast. Even though the fields were far, smoke already permeated the house. My eyes stung from the fumes, and I had to press the sleeve of my blouse to my mouth and nose to stop gagging.

Nana hurried to the windows and began drawing all curtains closed. Something in her rigid posture and tense shoulders told me trouble still brewed. I scrambled to help her close the curtains, plunging us into gloom. A shadow fell on the last curtain. Both Nana and I froze. She leaned closer and whispered in my ear.

"We're too late. They're here. Promise me that when I tell you to run to the backyard, you will."

Her hand held the curtain so that a sliver of what went outside was still visible. In the distance, a handful of people had gathered in a loose circle, their shouts of fury carrying over the fire. While most of Morava carried buckets of water to the fields, a few held torches, which they lit from the flames that threatened to spill over to the woods.

Something in their postures said they thirsted for blood, and for an instant we forgot about the shadow at the door until a knock startled us. Nana stilled, her eyes travelling to the back door. Silently, she put a finger on her lips and pointed towards the back, her message clear. I motioned for the back door as quietly as I could. Another knock, this time more impatient, made me pause.

"It's me, for old time's sake," said a familiar voice. Nana's shoulders relaxed, if only a little, and relief softened my own limbs. Yet she didn't motion for the door.

"What do you want?" she asked instead.

"Oh, come on, you know they are coming after the girl. We don't have long before they show with their pitchforks and their pyres."

I couldn't do much else besides gape at the door. Pitchforks and pyres – like Nana's stories. I sought Nana's eyes for reassurance, but she only pursed her lips and opened the door, even if barely.

My other grandmother, Ona, pushed past her and let herself in. For a moment, she paused at the doorframe, and the two of them sized each other up with undisguised disdain. While the years had peppered Nana's black hair with greys, grandmother Ona's silvery hair gave her an air of wisdom that, in truth, she lacked. Where Nana stood upright, grandmother Ona walked with a hunch, bringing the two of them to eye level. Grandmother Ona averted her eyes and said, "I'm afraid there's no time for our petty squabbles today. You must have heard them by now. They are coming for her."

"Who is coming for me?"

The two of them ignored my question. They never visited each other, and only rarely acknowledged the other's existence. I hadn't seen Ona since last autumn, a testament to our estrangement.

"I thought it would take them longer to start pointing fingers," Nana said as if it was Ona's fault.

"Well, you were wrong. They have rallied most of the folk to extinguish the fires, but a small crowd figured out they needed a culprit."

"Jasna did nothing wrong." Nana said, her lips tightening.

"I know that, but they don't. As it is, they care little for the truth as long as someone gets punished. And who better than a girl cursed at birth, with a broken statue to attest to it? I assume you saw the hala?"

"I'm not cursed," I managed in a small voice that got lost in their exchange. My cheeks burned with rising anger, but there was fear there too.

"Who else better suited," this time Ona turned towards me, at last acknowledging my presence, "to take that blame than a witch?"

"But I had nothing to do with any of it! And I'm no witch, though, as of now, I wish I was!"

"We know that, girl, but they don't, and neither do they care. After all, it was your shadow that lured the hala from the other realm."

Her words rang true. It mattered little whose fault it was, as long as someone got punished for it. Once, a long time ago, Nana had told me a story from the free lands, of witches being burnt at the stake. I had found it hard to believe that anyone would sentence a woman to such a gruesome death just because she had a mole in the wrong place or had displeased a nasty neighbour. The more I had seen of Moravians, the more I sympathised with those women.

And now, it was evident that they had marked me as a witch, and there was little I could do to change that. I had no place here, and if I wanted to live, I had to get out of Morava. My two grandmothers were already two steps ahead.

"Do you have it?" Ona snapped.

Nana's jaw tightened. "Yes, but we're pressed for time."

The distant shouts had solidified into a fast-approaching mass of discontent. We could hear them clearly now, their incoherent but distinctly angry shouts getting louder and drawing closer. Nana walked up to the cupboard where I had hidden just moments ago and crouched, the effort clearly taxing her. She then proceeded to rummage through scattered baskets, ignoring her cracking joints.

"What an obvious place to hide only the most important portal key," grandmother Ona pursed her lips, voice laden with disapproval.

"Well, it's been kept safe, which is all that matters."

Ona knew better than to dispute that. At last, with a lot more bone cracking and heaving, Nana got up, something sharp glinting in her hand. She met my gaze.

"The time has come for you to leave, so listen carefully. First, go to the backyard–"

"Whatever for?" I interrupted despite her bidding me to keep quiet. "And why isn't the hala coming back for me?"

"I assume she would have come after you if she could. Too many people saw her, and I don't think any of the folk in Syanka would be very pleased with that, given the lengths they go to conceal their existence. Also, not using the guise of night must be costing her considerably."

As she said this, Nana hurried around the house, hurling random supplies into a bag – food, clothes, the blue cardigan she'd knitted for me last year. The noise was near enough to rattle the windows.

"Nana, what's all of this? How do you know of Syanka? And where are you sending me? I can't go all by myself! And what about you and Ona?"

"Oh, we'll be fine, girl, just make sure you look out for yourself," grandmother Ona said as she ushered me out through the back door. Nana slung the bag over my shoulder. The shouts sounded close enough to be coming from the other side of the house. Faces appeared at the front garden just as we exited at the back.

"I would love nothing more than the chance to explain, but I'm afraid there is no time," Nana said. Then she rummaged through her robe, and her hand came out with a metal object that reflected the daylight remnants with a strange glint. She lifted it to her mouth and whispered something I couldn't quite catch, and as I watched in shock, the object began expanding. I gasped. Even before assuming its full form, the outline of an axe became clear. A wooden hilt engraved with unfamiliar symbols served as a body to its double-sided head, which appeared to be made of a material that resembled black glass. Nana gripped the hilt tightly and, without giving it a second thought, swung the axe in the air.

It was too late though. A bang to the front door announced the mob's arrival. A sense of helplessness came over me. My mind painted a picture of what it would be like to be burned alive, and I resolved I would do anything to never find out. Just as panic set in, I caught a glimmer in the air where the axe had struck. In a few seconds, a cut made of soft light appeared, intensifying as it grew into a slit, then a door roughly my size. On the other side, the commotion at the front door intensified, signalling the mob's attempt to break in.

"They could have at least given us the benefit of the doubt," Ona muttered just as Nana prodded me towards the shimmering door.

"We're out of time, Jasna," Nana said tenderly. "But before you go, remember, never let a single person, let alone a handful of people, decide your fate."

While she spoke, a path solidified beyond the gleaming doorframe, silver as the door itself. Behind it, the vague outline of woods came into view, a mirror of our own twisted path, except for the greyish tint of light that coated everything.

"The silver road from your tales." Nana's stories often spoke of a place where all the creatures that roamed the night lived. Confusion, apprehension, and indecisiveness threatened to engulf me. "Will I be safer there? If your stories are all true and creatures roam the silver road... what if the hala finds me?"

The door exploded inward, ripped from its hinges. Shouts sounded just steps away, prompting me to take a step towards the portal despite fear clouding my vision. I had little choice. If I wanted to live, I had to step through.

"One last thing, girl," Ona grabbed my elbow while fishing out a ball of red yarn from her other pocket.

"Only now you remember to give it to her?" Nana's voice, laced with angst, grew even more urgent. Ona ignored her and tossed the ball through the door.

"Follow its lead. And be safe."

"The thread will lead you to the Vizier's palace," added Nana as she nudged me towards the red yarn ball that was already unspooling along the silver road. "Find Iliya. Stay safe. You may not be a witch yet, but remember this – the first spell you ever cast is the defiance you showed the Grand Vizier. You are now bound to the thread. Follow it. And Jasna…"

But before she could finish, the crowd spilled through the open back door. Together, my grandmothers pushed me inside the shimmering portal as the gap that had opened narrowed, the magic that fuelled it open now closing it with haste that mirrored my urgency. Though my heart pounded with fear and my vision blurred, I noticed the axe Nana had been holding in one hand shrink to the size of a child's toy as she tucked it back into her skirts.

One glance at the mob – faces I knew, now twisted with hate – was all I had. I spotted Byan, the town's baker, with his perpetually boyish face, twisted in an angry grimace that marred his features. Zoaea and her two friends were also there, next to Maruna, who clutched a club too big for her hands. Though her presence did little to surprise me, a stab of pain still pierced my chest. Had my life not been at stake, I would have found the scene somewhat foolish, which was what ultimately gave me the courage to jump.

"Give us the witch!" yelled Byan, and a few others joined the chorus. My breath caught in my throat. These were people I knew. And now they wanted me dead. Maruna and her mother saw the portal first, their faces growing pale at the sight. Something ugly twisted my former friend's features and I saw fear there, but also a strange sort of longing. It reminded me of quiet afternoons when she'd listened to my retelling of Nana's stories. Then her voice echoed across the backyard, shattering the illusion.

"Proof!" Maruna yelled, seizing the moment. "Proof she's consorting with the devil! You saw her spells scorching the field and now this! An ungodly door, leading straight to hell! Seize her!"

Not waiting for assent, she reached for me, but I turned

towards the portal and stepped through without as much as a second thought. As soon as I did, something grabbed me, its icy fingers closing around my wrist, there and gone in a flash. Once inside the portal, a sense of weightlessness took over all else. Despite the bright light sifting through the doorway, darkness engulfed me.

I moved through a pool of blackness, sailing blindly towards the other side of the portal. At last, my knees hit the ground.

It took a few moments for my eyes to adjust to a brightness that left my temples throbbing after the portal's darkness. The brilliant day that greeted me was not at all like the gloomy sky coated in smoke that I had just escaped. Under the sun's warmth, all the fear that had gripped me only a moment ago seemed to dissolve.

I was alone, save for the forest path rolling ahead of me. After my shadow had been entombed and a hala hunted me, the thought of a silver road to Tsargrad was easier to swallow than I expected. I couldn't help but marvel at the path's resemblance to the one back home. Except that colour here seemed all wrong. The forest ahead wavered, colours bleeding together into bright hues of green. The sky overhead carried the most pristine shade of blue. Most curious of all was that, further ahead, colours dimmed and flickered, as if uncertain about stretching too far into the distance. Remembering the ball of red yarn Ona had thrown, I searched for the thread.

CHAPTER 10

THE RED THREAD AND THE HAN

The red thread wound along the forest, rolling out of sight and into the unknown, beckoning me to follow. I went down the familiar path, beginning at the place where Nana's house should have been, into the twisted branches that closed around the way to the well. Everything in my immediate vicinity burst into colour the moment I took a step towards it. The path ahead and the world behind me blurred, as if waiting for my footsteps to will them into being.

Yet, something I couldn't put my finger on was lacking. It was eerily quiet. As soon as I thought of the bizarre lack of birds, a robin chirped above. Another followed from the branch ahead. In no time, birdsong, along with bee humming, drowned out my suspicions. Despite the summer warmth caressing my arms, the hairs there stood on end.

Upon exiting the twisted path, I drew closer to the well. In the aftermath of the hala's attack on Morava's crops, I feared she would hunt me here if I didn't find shelter soon. After all, Syanka was her domain, and, according to Zhar, I reeked of black magic. But as I neared the well, something else drew my attention. Above its opening stood a mockery of a statue, a grotesque rendering of my image. A black formless outline towered above an empty opening of a well that had long dried up. Curiosity took over and I drew closer to examine it. The form resembled a human, except that it consisted of the same darkness that Yerleg had summoned. It appeared sad and beaten down.

I saw it then. For the first time, I noticed its absence. The sun stood high in the sky, yet I cast no shadow. No matter how I turned and twisted in trying to evoke it, none appeared. Still, I waved my hand, hoping it would wave back at me. No shadow appeared. Then a twitch caught my eye – the hunched, shadowy figure mirrored my gestures. I stared, though my instinct screamed for me to look away. I took a step backwards. The figure shifted back but stayed rooted above the well.

I peered down the well, which, much like in Nana's story, seemed bottomless. My head nearly touched the shadow, and I had to will myself not to flinch. In the face of my beaten image, anger rushed through me, filling my ears with a sharp ringing. The urge to claw at my face surged – to peel off layer after layer of skin until I found the real me. I was done being reduced to a shadow, a beaten thing that had never had the chance to assume its true form, whatever that might be.

But, for now, I had to leave my shadow tethered to the well. My only hope of finding answers lay ahead. So I tucked the ember of anger in a deep pocket of my mind, scorching as it felt, and followed the red thread.

The path that led to the well's clearing meandered for a little while before I emerged at the woods' edge and at the humpback bridge that opened the way to the caravanserai. Even here, on the silver path, the bridge looked like it had seen better days. Its back arched like an old man ready to draw his last breath, and the basin underneath it had long since dried up. It now served, at least in Morava, as grounds for the circus that passed through town every now and again. Here only wildflowers filled the empty basin.

Once across the bridge, a chilly wave washed over me and my breath steamed. My foot struck something hard and slick, skidding out from under me—

"Ice?" I said to the empty field. Just a moment ago, I was basking in the afternoon sun, and now, as I stepped into the midst of winter, shivers shook my body. Under thin ice, the red yarn stood out like a trail of blood. A distant laughter filled the air. At the same time, a muffled noise of what sounded like a tavern song reached my ears. Its direction, the caravanserai, or what Moravians called the han. As soon as the image sprang to my mind, an icy wind blew across, clearing the horizon, and there it stood; the han, just as I remembered it from back home.

Pillars surrounded the expansive yard, casting a shade that made the wintery day even frostier. Terraces hugged the path to the entrance, extending from the fourth floor to ground level. As I walked, feet crunching over frost, the singing, accompanied by the sound of a poorly handled lute, intensified. A tavern song in a caravanserai so out of place on the side of the silver road made me feel as if my senses had taken leave, though the smell of warm food that wafted from the closed doors felt real enough. Venturing into the han seemed foolish – what would I find there? With Nana's bag, I had food to last me for a few days, but what of the cold and the hala that could already be on my trail? I saw little choice but to go in.

My heart pounded as I closed the door behind, leaving the chill outside.

The nearest tables fell silent as I entered. In my world, the han had been in decay for the past twenty years, with fewer and fewer travellers stopping by to visit Morava in its ever-shrinking importance. In Syanka, the place was bustling with activity. As the chatter resumed, I stood at the entrance, unable to tear my eyes from the han's unlikely patrons. Creatures from Nana's tales breathed, walked around, sat on tables and had drinks and food set out in front of them as if it was the most natural thing. It was I who stood out as a human. A brief glance to my left revealed a woman sprouting white wings spotted with black dots. Her description matched that of hala from Nana's tales. I tensed, but she only regarded me coolly before averting her gaze back to her companion, a woman clad in a long black robe, hood drawn to obscure her face. The air around her appeared to have a life of its own. It expanded and contracted, pulsing with darkness.

Further down, a very sick-looking creature sat at a table placed as far away as possible from the rest of the customers. Warts covered its greenish face. Its nose leaked a pungent, yellowish liquid. Even from where I stood, the foul stench reached my nostrils.

Suppressing the bile rising at the back of my throat, I ventured deeper into the han. A fine sheen of condensation that coated the windows obscured the view outside, the falling dusk making it hard to discern any landscape shapes. I seated myself at a small table close to the roaring fireplace, where warmth soon returned to my body.

"My, my, aren't you a pretty thing?" The voice came seemingly from nowhere, giving me a start.

"Oh, you're a human. Down here," the voice said, and as it did so, a tiny figure no taller than my knees materialised at the side of my chair. Wrinkles and dark circles obscured his eyes, and his shiny forehead glistened with sweat. My first impression from his voice was that he was male, though it was hard to judge. The reassuring smile that played on his thin lips did little to put my mind at ease. I wished to ask him what type of creature he was, but held back at the prospect of him finding the inquiry offensive.

"And what can I get you? The special tonight is mutton and mushroom stew," he said lazily.

"Don't people usually see you?" I asked, stalling while I scanned the crowd to determine what they were having. Ale, raki, among other drinks I couldn't recognise. A tall glass of clear blue liquid with a smoking top caught my eye. The man that nursed it appeared to be human, a promising sign that the drink would not kill me. The creature's lips thinned, but he answered.

"No, humans in your world can't see me unless I decide to reveal myself."

His words struck me as strange. Nana's tales usually held enough detail to identify a creature, but I struggled with this one. Instead, I nodded at the blue liquid glass. "I'll have a room for the night, mushroom stew, and what he's having."

"And have you any coins?"

I hadn't thought that far. Redness crept up my cheeks as I remembered the bag Nana had hastily put together for me. It was still slung around my shoulder. The creature regarded it curiously when I took it off, its bulkiness a reassuring weight on my knees. Its strings were tightly sealed. I hastily undid them and started rummaging through the contents.

"Ouch," something sharp pricked my finger, interrupting my search. A drop of crimson blood blossomed at the tip of my finger. I peered inside the bag, this time feeling my way more carefully, and noticed an unfamiliar dagger wrapped inside a change of clothes. I had neither seen Nana hide the dagger, nor had I suspected I would need one to defend myself. Something metal close to it clunked promisingly, drawing my attention away from its sharp edge and the blossoming red spot on the tip of my finger. I shook the bag, and a pouch hit the wooden table with a dull thump.

"How much?" I said as I fished for coins. My palm closed around a grosh coin and I cheerfully slammed it on the table. The creature shook its head and my heart sank.

"This is not a currency we deal in. But I tell you what. Anger, that you have plenty of. Give us some?"

"Us?" I asked just as another creature like him approached, his skin only a little less wrinkled, revealing an eager set of eyes.

"Give us some of your anger and you can have a warm meal, drinks and room for the night."

The creature's eyes grew darker until they became black beads with no whites remaining. I let out a shriek and as the two creatures edged closer, their beady eyes focused on my bleeding finger.

"What are you?"

"Glad you asked," said the creature as he reached for my arm. "Just a banished domovoy trying to make ends meet. Your rage is a feast for us and would do as payment just fine. After all, you humans were the ones to get rid of us, your hearth's protectors. It's only fair to get something out of it, eh?"

As the grubby hand reached for mine, a slap landed on his outstretched palm. Surprised, the domovoy lifted his eyes up to the rather large woman that had delivered the slap.

"You better keep your hands where I can see them or our little deal where you get to keep your head in exchange for me putting up with you and your measly cooking is off," the woman snapped. "Now bring that supper you promised the young woman and bugger off."

By the time she finished, the second domovoy was long gone and, with one last longing look in my direction, the first one followed. The woman turned her attention to me, though her eyes lingered on the pouch and grosh that still lay on the table.

"You shouldn't let domovoy so close, young woman. Even if your hearth at home is blessed with one of the good ones, a banished domovoy makes for a foul companion, he does." She paused and cast a quizzical look at me. Her eyes widened and her next words burst out of her chest. "But what am I saying? Look at you, my dear, dressed for summer! Your ma should know better than to send you out like that! And what a beauty you are! Unless you possess some great magic, it's not safe for you to travel alone like that! Whereabouts do you come from, dear?"

I hesitated. She seemed well-intended and perhaps even trustworthy, but I had proven a poor judge of character before.

"Are you perchance the innkeeper?" I asked instead. Not missing a heartbeat, she only raised an eyebrow, but answered regardless.

"The innkeeper's daughter. Though with papa being sick, aye, I've been running the place these days."

"Sorry about your father," I said. She shrugged, as if it were nothing.

"Oh, don't be. What did he think would happen when he angered a bunch of mermaids with his suggestions?"

The way she said it suggested it was less of a question and more of a statement.

"You mean actual mermaids?" I blurted out before thinking.

The woman flashed a gummy smile as she nodded. That had sealed it. I had shown my ignorance, and now she knew I wasn't from around. I decided against trying to deceive her – to an extent.

"Yes, fine," I admitted, "I'm not from these parts. There is much I don't know about here. But I'd like to see and learn, and it doesn't mean I'm helpless." I hoped the lie sounded at least a little convincing.

The woman laughed, a sound of merriment. "With that face of yours, I wouldn't say you're helpless, no. I bet you have a trick or two up your sleeve. Everyone from your world who comes here does."

I nodded, though I wasn't sure what she meant. A pleasant smell wafted through as the domovoy appeared again, carrying a tray half his size. He set down a steaming dish and a glass of the blue liquid I had requested. This time, he retreated without offering a comment and avoided meeting my eyes. The woman uncovered the dish, and the smell of buttered wild mushrooms made my mouth water, reminding me I hadn't had anything to eat since breakfast. With decorum out the window, I dug into the mushrooms. The woman pretended not to notice me wolfing down the supper as she continued.

"Narisa is my name. I take care of things around here."

"Jasna," I mumbled with a full mouth, wondering if I should have lied.

"Well, Jasna, welcome. You'll find that many people like it here – it's a place where misfits feel at home. Did you use a ley line to come here?"

I made a noncommittal noise, not wanting to divulge any other information or show my ignorance more than I had already. As I finished the meal, an ordeal that did not take long, a wave of drowsiness washed over my body. The drink, tasting like raki mixed in with something sweet, did not help either. Narisa had her back to me and was speaking to another patron. The domovoy returned, carrying a smaller tray of baked spiced apples. This time, I took my time savouring the dish.

"Your room is ready, dear," said Narisa, breaking her previous conversation. "As for the payment…"

Her voice trailed off as she eyed my purse. I hastily slid the grosh across the table. The purse's reassuring weight made me feel like the richest person in sight. I had never seen more than a single grosh at a time, and having a bag with a nice, heavy feel to it made me wonder where Nana had got all this money from. Narisa cleared her throat, her eyes still lingering on the heavy pouch. The friendliness leeched out from her face, replaced by a greedy look.

"And for the room?"

"The room? It's just for a night."

Back in Morava, one grosh could buy you an entire week of board and meals, so I expected some change back.

"That barely covers your supper, dear. And, in the spirit of honesty, like I said, old papa isn't faring that well, and I need to keep the place afloat," said Narisa. As she spoke, her eyes grew hungrier. She reached for the bag, but before she could grab it, I extended an arm and snatched it away. Her han seemed well-attended for me to fall for such cheap money grabs. I might be new there, but I wouldn't let anyone take advantage of that. I resolved to hide the pouch better next time and not let anyone be tempted by its weight.

"Keep the grosh, but don't think me a fool. And don't even think of getting anywhere near that pouch again. Unless you have a death wish, that is. Like I said, I have a few tricks up my sleeve. I'll let you keep the change if you tell me how far the next caravanserai or similar establishment is."

A shadow fell upon her puffy face as she narrowed her eyes at me. I had the distinct feeling she would like nothing more than to teach me a lesson. Had she only defended me from the domovoy so she could jump at the opportunity to take advantage herself? My heart sank at the thought that she had played nice so that she could get away with a few coins.

Her next words came out as a whisper.

"Now, now, you don't want to make enemies of the first place you find yourself at on the silver path, do you, dear?"

"I think she's paid her board's worth, Narisa," said a soft voice. The winged woman I had seen earlier loomed over the table, making Narisa look like a child in comparison. Her wings brushed against the neighbouring tables, and an instant hush fell over them. "Making a coin at the expense of someone unfamiliar with our customs isn't very nice of you, is it?"

Narisa swallowed and shook her head, though the menace behind her eyes remained. That did little to faze the hala.

"I would make sure the lady has her bed chamber ready. What do you think?"

I almost laughed – or would have, had my knees and arms not been trembling from the tension. Me, in my muddy, thin, and drab dress, being called a lady by a mighty creature. I almost felt sorry for Narisa. The woman I suspected was a hala carried herself regally, making it impossible to say no to. She had an air about her that said 'do my bidding, or else.' I didn't want to make enemies of Narisa, but having the winged woman as an adversary was an option I didn't even wish to consider.

After one long, menacing look, the innkeeper's daughter scurried away, but not before pocketing my grosh. One glare from the hala and the men playing dice on the closest table ceased eavesdropping and returned to their game. The woman's attention fell back on me as she studied me for a moment. Her dark skin stood in contrast to her white wings, and I couldn't help but marvel at the magnificent shape she cut.

"I know what you are running from," she said, startling me out of my reverie. "You have the smell of dark magic about you. My sister is hunting you, isn't she?" The hala nodded as if answering her own question. "Don't worry, I'm not a threat to you, nor will I tell her about you. But your smell is even worse here, and it's only a matter of time before she catches its trail."

Not for the first time, I wondered what dark magic smelled like. Did every creature surrounding me sense it on me? My eyes swept over the motley crowd.

"Worry not," she repeated, and, as if having read my mind, added, "Most aren't sensitive enough to connect the magic to you. Some might feel a tug, but won't know its direction. You can rest assured that nearly everyone present possesses dull senses compared to that of a hala."

"Nearly everyone? But not all?" I asked, not at all reassured.

"You have my word – if anyone does, no harm will come to you while I'm around."

"Why would you protect me? You know nothing about me. You don't know my name, nor I yours for that matter."

She only smiled, and a shade of sadness touched her eyes.

"Because you aren't just a pretty face, no matter what Narisa thinks. And I can see you are a decent person. A little lost, but good. Reminds me of me when I was young, many, many years ago."

"You can't be that old," I said casually, thinking of how breathtaking she looked. She smiled again, this time mischievously.

"Tamara. My name. Never hesitate to seek me if you find

yourself at a crossroads. Should you need a place to rest, the next inn is a day's walk to the west. I hope our paths cross again, Jasna. And, remember, not all is as it seems here in Syanka."

My eyes, heavy with sleep, closed despite my best effort to stay awake. When I opened them again, Tamara was gone. As I made my way through the empty hallway to my room, it occurred to me that I never told her my name.

Narisa led me to one of the more secluded parts of the han, away from the chatter. Despite clearly wanting to give me a piece of her mind, she only grunted as she closed the door behind her. A small fire crackled across from the bed when I closed the door behind me. With the tiredness that had washed over me earlier, I thought I would fall asleep the moment my head hit the pillow. Instead, the anger, carefully stowed away, bubbled back to the surface, threatening to consume me. Being used as a scapegoat for the fires back at Morava and having to rely on the kindness of others for protection against people like Narisa was a thought that suddenly plagued me. A resolution crystallised as I drifted to sleep. I decided I would be the one to forge my path from then on, whatever that might be. With that thought, sleep finally found me.

CHAPTER 11

Unexpected Guests

When sleep arrived, my mind remained restless and half awake before at last it merged with the realm of dreams, and I spread my wings once more. Another presence, a familiar one, emerged from the depths of my stupor.

"I was hoping you would make it to our world," the zmei said.

I wasted no time in pleasantries when I prompted him. "Where are you? Is this the realm you were speaking of?"

"We are in Syanka. Every creature that roams the realms comes from here. Showing you around would be my pleasure, but I cannot greet you unless you come to me. Here it's easier for me to find you and talk to you, even if it happens only in your dreams."

When I took in my surroundings, I saw what he meant. Back home, the shape I had first morphed into had been vague enough to feel like a dream. In this realm, everything possessed substance. This time, though, I flew no more. We were enclosed by stone, with torches lining the walls. More than that, Zhar and I weren't sharing a body and I could finally see him as he was. He was scaly and lizard-like, a massive form that brought nightmares to his enemies and granted favours to those who offered flattery. A true zmei, as if shaped by Nana's stories.

After a day of hala, magic yarn threads, doors, roads and axes, the zmei's existence should not have come as a surprise – yet it did. While other creatures had resembled people and had come in shapes I was familiar with, he was an entirely different being. Under the dream light, his scales shimmered with a copper hue, giving him an air that suggested he was as old as time. His next words proved that his wisdom did not stretch as far.

"I was… deceived," he admitted reluctantly. "I got trapped in your world when a powerful dark mage ensnared me at my weakest not so long ago. He struck a bargain with me, not that I had much choice in the matter. Refusing him would mean death. In exchange for my strength, he would grant me my freedom. I had to let him draw from my powers to summon shadows from the underworld–"

"The underworld?"

"The world of the dead. Mortals are not meant to know of its existence," he snapped. "Now, where was I? I truly don't appreciate being interrupted."

He exhaled, and a frustrated puff of smoke darkened the air. His displeasure radiated from his scaly body like an angry wave. I resolved to avoid angering him further and carefully framed my next question.

"The dark mage who trapped you in our world. Was his name by any chance Yerleg?"

Zhar exhaled another angry puff of smoke. He was too quick to anger, and that left me unsettled.

"Do not speak his name!" He roared. My body shook with fear despite knowing it was just a dream.

"I apologise. It won't happen again if it displeases you, great one."

The zmei huffed, but my gamble of appeasing him with flattery had paid off. He seemed mollified. In truth, I sensed that Zhar was somewhat embarrassed. That a human, however powerful, had tricked him, wounded his pride.

"Yerleg, yes. He had dark and cruel eyes. And quite the annoying voice," the zmei said.

"And he just let you go?"

Zhar let out a low, humourless rumble. "Not exactly."

"Then how did it happen?"

His eyes narrowed, and there was a glint of old pride. "You are quite the curious one. But fine, I will tell you. Nighttime opens the crossroads between worlds. When roaming the realms, I grew complacent. I thought myself untouchable – no one had dared challenge me in centuries. Yerleg ambushed me, with knowledge no mortal should possess. As for how he accomplished his deceit, it matters not. Once he had me trapped, he used me as a channel to the underworld. I had no choice but to divulge my secrets."

"Such as how to sever a shadow."

"Such as that," he agreed morosely.

"And he just kept his promise after?"

"He had no say in the matter, for he is, much like everyone else, bound by the laws of Syanka. Breaking a promise to an ancient creature such as myself would amount to a death sentence for the breaker. You must understand," Zhar said slowly, as if his next words were him unloading a burden he had been carrying for a while. "I never meant to harm you."

"I know." The answer came out easily enough. I knew that if my freedom were at stake, I would likely not hesitate to do my captor's bidding. I wanted to judge him, to be angry for him being complicit in harming me. But what would I have done in his place? Would I have resisted longer? Or would I have yielded just as quickly, hoping to be set free? I had, after all, run from an angry mob at the first whiff of danger. In the end, I needed him and uncertainty stung more than resenting the zmei.

"When that cursed mage harnessed my power to entomb your shadow, his spell created a link between us. I began dreaming of you and, soon enough, I could talk to you in your dreams. Having you in Syanka only makes that link stronger. And I owe it to you to make things right, whatever your quest is. Do you know your whereabouts?"

"I'm at a han, but that's about as much as I know."

I frowned, trying to remember its name. There had been no sign outside. The zmei sensed my agitation and nudged me.

"Anything that stood out to you?"

Once more, I came short of an answer. The caravanserai housed creatures from a realm other than my own, one that belonged to legends and folktales. Yet, that was not what bothered me about it. In a flash, I knew what it was.

"It looks like the caravanserai in my world. The one right outside Morava."

If zmei could frown, I would bet the purse of coins Nana had entrusted me with that this was what his expression resembled at that moment.

"Things in Syanka, they don't always appear as they are. Exercise caution. I know Syanka like the scales on my tail, yet I have no knowledge of this place. You must tell me more about how and why you arrived."

So I told him about the hala at Nana's house and the mob that came after me, the axe that had slashed the door open, and the red yarn thread showing me the way to Tsargrad and Iliya. I glossed over the part about meeting my shadow, careful not to remind Zhar of his part in severing it from me. If the zmei felt I was omitting things, he never showed it. Finally, I ended with the thread bringing me to the caravanserai, the innkeeper's hostility, and my unexpected encounter with the hala. The zmei listened patiently throughout. When silence reigned, he sighed heavily, his glittering scales casting specks of light that danced around us.

"What you have gone through is impressive for someone so young. However, I must warn you to exercise caution. I sense deception. Things do not just appear conveniently when you need them. Unless… but that's so rare, it's near impossible. Sooner or later, deception will reveal itself for what it is, just as unexpectedly. Beware of your surroundings, Jasna. Not all is as it seems."

"You might have mentioned that," I said with a sinking heart.

As if on cue, the frame of my dream shook. My vision blurred. Another tremor followed, and I felt my mind slip away. A feeling of weightlessness I had not known was there left my body, reminding me of all the small aches from the tumultuous previous day. The time to be cautious of wounding the zmei's pride had come to an end, so I pressed, "You can't give me half-truths. I need to know more. Where are you and why do we communicate like that if you are freed from your obligation to Yerleg?"

It had been the wrong thing to ask. The zmei huffed indignantly. His petulance reminded me of Nana's tales, where the hero had to tread cautiously lest he provoke the zmei.

"I will meet you here next time you are in the dream realm and explain," he said, just as my vision shook again.

* * *

I BOLTED UPRIGHT in the inn's bedroom. Pale dawn coloured the sky outside. Rubbing my eyes, I squinted against the thin light filtering through the drawn curtains. The tremors that had yanked me out of my dream had ceased. My first impression was that the room seemed smaller somehow, like it had shrunk overnight. And if my eyes did not deceive me, it was duller than I remembered. When my gaze passed over the fireplace, only a grey wall stared back at me. Had that one drink from last night gotten into my head?

Then I remembered the zmei's warning. In Syanka, not all was as it appeared. I wondered if the tremors had been part of my dream or if someone didn't want me talking to the zmei. Coming short of answers, I focused on my immediate concerns.

Sleep leaving my eyes, I finally took in my surroundings. A feeling of tiredness washed over me despite having had a full night's sleep. I suspected that conversing with Zhar in my dreams came at a price, the exhaustion a compelling sign of the cost. Even through the grogginess, I couldn't deny that the place differed from last night's abode. Apart from being smaller, the room was also drab, and what had felt like the softest bed last night proved to be a thin, hard mattress this morning. I had fallen asleep with most of my clothes on, apart from my shoes, which lay kicked on the bed's side.

After washing my face in the small basin that waited at the wobbly table, I dressed in the spare change of clothes Nana had packed for me and ventured out of my room, expecting the caravanserai's high ceilings. Instead, bare wooden walls closed in around me, the ceiling so low I could almost touch it. The long corridor was gone, replaced by a room like the one in Nana's house – a fireplace with a bubbling cauldron, cupboards lining the walls. An old woman with long silver hair sat before the hearth. She reminded me of Nana, which gave me the courage to speak up.

"Excuse me, but what is this place?" I asked hesitantly.

She shifted in her seat, lifting a gnarled hand to beckon me closer. I approached, in equal measure cautious and eager to see whether she was human or a creature of Syanka. She appeared to be human.

The old woman's blue eyes regarded me for a moment before she said, "Such beauty. Your parents must be so proud of you."

"My parents are dead."

She licked her lips, though there was no remorse in her icy blue eyes.

"Ah, figures. Most of you human folk who come over to Syanka always have something eating at you. A missing part of yourselves – something you would do anything to replace."

"Speaking in riddles seems to be the way to hold a conversation around here," I said dryly. I was tired of creatures – Zhar included – edging close to some truth, only to have them spin their words into a cryptic message.

The old woman cackled. "Your dreams are very loud," she said. I tensed immediately.

"How do you know about my dreams?"

I eyed her suspiciously. Was it possible that it was she who had pulled me out mid-conversation? But the woman followed the thread of her own thoughts.

"The other girl's dreams were fuelled by spite – jealousy and ill-wishing. Yours weren't about hurting people. Though you do keep unusual company."

"The other girl's dreams?" I asked, even more confused. "Who is the other girl?"

Just then, the door next to my bedroom opened, revealing the newcomer. My throat went dry. Maruna stood there, a mocking smile playing on her lips. It didn't fool me, though. Her eyes, darting nervously from wall to wall, were wide with fear.

"It was you!" I gasped. "You followed me through the portal yesterday. That's why it went dark and confusing, because the door was for me, not for you."

"Always quick with the accusations, Jasna," Maruna drawled, but her hands shook. "It must be so tiring always thinking that you're so exceptional."

"At least I'm not pathetic enough to latch onto someone else's journey," I spat back.

"Your journey? You're a witch and needed to be stopped! I only followed you so that I see it done!"

I was about to hurl another accusation at her, when a thought clicked into place. She claimed she didn't want to be here, yet she had followed me through the portal. No one afraid of the unnatural would do that.

"You chose to follow me because you wanted to," I said incredulously. Something in Maruna's face shifted, and for a moment, I saw the confirmation there. Then I remembered. When we were friends, she used to avidly listen to my retellings of Nana's stories. We even imagined flying on zmei's wings and defeating lamia together, before she had a change of heart and started bullying me. Maruna frowned, and rearranged her features into indifference. I was not fooled. "Why did you follow me, Maruna?"

"That's enough, girls," the woman interrupted, standing up. Despite her age, she still loomed over us. "You aren't here to bicker."

"What are we here for?" I asked, low on patience. "And where are we?"

The woman raised an eyebrow. "Why, you are in the caravanserai, girl."

With that, she walked to the door at the far end of the room and opened it. The high corridors of the caravanserai greeted us. And beyond, the courtyard and terraces.

"How did my room change so much?" A terrifying thought that someone had moved me when I was asleep laced my voice with fear. "And you better not conceal the truth with cryptic words like folk here do."

"Naturally, you have to make everything about yourself, Jasna," Maruna interjected, unwilling to be left behind as she followed us outside. At that moment, I hated her more than ever – she just had to ruin everything.

"Gods, but you are arrogant," I said, not holding back. "What happened to you yelling that the portal is the devil's work? Only yesterday you were so eager to accuse me of witchcraft and today I find you in the midst of a land filled with magic. Surely, even you must see the hypocrisy."

She was about to retort, but the old woman lifted her hand and Maruna's protest died on her lips. Maruna and I held each other's gazes as if a contest of willpower would determine who was more righteous. The old woman sighed, muttering something about children. In the end, both she and I averted our gazes.

"The caravanserai shifts and changes to fit all its guests," the woman explained. "Last night, the rooms were full. So when your friend begged to be accommodated, the innkeeper's daughter told the caravanserai to adapt."

"It grew a room?" I asked at the same time as Maruna muttered "I'm not her friend."

"Now, for your payment," the woman turned towards Maruna. "You are doing chores to pay for your housing."

Maruna frowned, clearly not liking the idea. I could not help but gloat a little at the prospect of having her do chores while I had my room paid for with Nana's grosh. The woman turned towards me.

"As for you, your lodgings include breakfast, served in the same place as the tavern. After that, staying will cost extra."

"I have no intention of staying longer than necessary," I said flatly. My thoughts wandered to the red thread and Iliya. I must be on my way, and Maruna's presence only heightened my eagerness. There was one more thing I needed to know. "What's your name?"

"Aellialle, some call me," the woman said – and for a moment, her shadow grew tall, two vast wings unfurling to cover the entire wall. Maruna gasped and backed away, regarding her with a newfound fear and, for once, respect. I stared at the wings with fascination. Just like that, the shadow shrank to reflect Aellialle's current form.

"One more thing, girl," the hala said. "My sister, Tamara, said you might need some protection from our sisters. If you are willing to linger after this one's chores are done, I might have something for you."

My eyes slid back to Maruna, whose face had grown even more ashen. A wide grin spread across my face.

"Why not?" I winked at the hala and headed to the breakfast hall.

CHAPTER 12

THE RIVER'S GIFT

Once finished with breakfast, I headed to the place where the hala had instructed me to wait. To my surprise, a warm gust of wind greeted me outside. Spring had arrived with no memory of yesterday's icy winter. As soon as I left the caravanserai's courtyard, tall sword weeds closed in. The wind brought a murmur of a river's current flowing nearby. Syanka's landscape had reshaped itself overnight.

The red thread ran reassuringly ahead of me, so I paused by the river to wait for the hala and Maruna. The sun rolled across the horizon, reminding me I had little time to spare. I had to find Zhar and Iliya before it was too late.

When the two arrived, Maruna's face was red with tiredness and indignation. I was about to tease her for it, but the hala raised an eyebrow at me, as if to scold me for being so childish, so I said nothing. It mattered little. Soon I would be on my way, hopefully never to see Maruna again.

The old woman's glance slid from me to Maruna, assessing the resentment that hung between us like a stale curtain. Perhaps it was my unwavering stance or Maruna's unveiled hatred that made any attempt at having a conversation futile, but the woman quickly gave up with a shrug.

"Very well, dear girls. You are new in Syanka, and despite what your stories tell you about us, most hala aren't the monsters you make us. There is something here for each of you to aid you on your journey."

That caught Maruna's interest, though she still kept her distance from both me and the hala. Aellialle beckoned us to step closer to the river.

"Take a look, girls, and tell me what you see," she said with a honeyed voice.

At first, I thought it to be an ordinary river, its silvery glint reflecting the sun above. Then the water changed colour, darkening until it ran black as night. We had barely approached the bank when the water thickened with blackness. Maruna froze. I stepped back, suddenly wary. Then, without prior warning, the hala sprang behind Maruna and shoved her towards the river. Maruna stumbled but held her ground, her face registering both surprise and anger.

"Quickly, Maruna, jump!" The hala yelled.

"In the river? Are you insane? It's black!" Maruna shrieked, but Aellialle paid her no heed as she shoved the girl forward once more. Even though Maruna was expecting it this time and had steeled herself, ready to resist, the hala's push must have been inhumanely strong. With a cry full of indignation and fear, my former friend landed hard in the river.

"Catch the first thing you touch, dear!" Aellialle shouted as Maruna flailed in the black water. Whether because she heard the old woman's last words or because of the water's pull, she disappeared beneath the surface. Only the rush of the river remained, echoing louder than before.

I backed away from Aellialle before she could do the same to me. The woman cocked an eyebrow quizzically, but after taking one look at my alarmed face, she burst out laughing.

"Patience, girl, your turn will come, too. Not in these waters, though."

The statement did little to put my mind at ease. I itched to run, but curiosity anchored me by the river, keeping a wary distance from Aellialle.

A moment passed, and then another. I wondered whether I would see Maruna again, a part of me embarrassed at the thought that I wouldn't mind not having to. My insides twisted with guilt. As dread settled in my stomach that she wouldn't be resurfacing, her head broke the black surface. She was wet and gasping and covered in the black tar-like water, but she lived. I had not expected to feel as relieved as I did. Though I had little love for her, I did not wish to see her dead.

"What… did… you… do… to… me… you… old… hag," she spat and coughed black water. Despite Maruna's animosity, the hala retained her composure when she answered.

"Worry not, it won't stain for long. One or two washes when the river runs clear should do the trick. It will be like it never happened. What is it that the river gave you?"

"I tried to grab the largest one," said Maruna as she shook the black droplets from the object in her hands. Dark rivulets ran down her hair and stained the grass upon touching it.

"Of course you did," the old woman said. "Go on, open it."

The river's gift turned out to be a chest with a green snake twisted around the seal. Maruna shook it, and a faint rattle followed. I thought I heard a hiss.

"Is there something alive in there? What's inside better be

good. And valuable," Maruna gasped between breaths as her fingers worked around to break the seal.

"What's inside reflects your true nature," Aellialle said. "You and you alone can break the seal."

One more twist and the seal unlocked into two parts, split by the green snake. Maruna lifted the top eagerly, but before she could peek inside, a tangle of snakes coiling around each other fell out. Maruna yelped, dropped the chest, and stepped away, making sure she had put enough distance between herself and the snakes before letting out a high-pitched scream.

"Ah, the emerald chest," Aellialle beamed at her. "Maybe it will teach you something about respecting other living beings. My own darling snakes would love to hear about it when I get back to them."

"Not the chest of gold you were hoping for, eh, Maruna?" I jeered. I had little sympathy that her greediness had not paid off.

"That can't be all. There must be something they're protecting," Maruna insisted as she eyed the empty chest. Her eyes brimmed with tears, and for a heartbeat, I almost felt sorry for her. Then she rounded on Aellialle. "You vile woman! Keep your disgusting beasts – may they eat you in your sleep!"

She stomped towards the woods, away from the hala and me. Much to her vexation, the snakes followed.

"You won't last long on your own," warned the hala while Maruna was still within earshot. "Better wait here until you have a plan or a way to get back home. We will find a way to get rid of the snakes if that's your wish."

"You've done enough!"

"Maruna, it's not safe to venture out on your own. The sun will be down soon." Despite my better judgement, I tried to reason with her, but Maruna's walk had already turned into a trot with the snakes slithering after her. We watched her disappear into the thicket of bushes that signalled the forest's beginning.

"It's not as easy to get rid of the river's gift," Aellialle shook her head. "Not only does it reflect your true nature, it also teaches you humility. The snakes are bound to her and will follow her from now on. Let's see how she deals with that."

"I'd rather not know," I muttered. The black river ran dry; red bled in its place. Dark crimson coloured the waters at first, followed by paler reddish and pink until all colours drained and the river ran clean.

"It's time for your gift," the old woman said, and I blanched.

"Now that you mention it, I have decided I need no gift. I'm sure I'll manage without one."

The hala's smile did little to help calm my racing heart. I had half a mind to follow Maruna when a glint from the river caught my eye. Without thinking, I turned towards its running waters, only to see them turn into liquid gold.

Belatedly, I realised my mistake. I had inched closer to the river, too fascinated to think twice. It ran bright, its surface as dizzying as the sun above. The brightness became so intense that I had to avert my eyes.

"It's beautiful…," I began saying when the push came and I stumbled straight into the golden waters.

"I'm sorry, girl, but we don't have time to wait for you to come around and jump on your own. It runs gold too rarely to risk that."

My vision blurred when the surprisingly deep water embraced me. For a moment, I sank. Then, with a thrust of my arms, I resisted the cold water that had so willingly engulfed me and emerged, gasping for air. Something dull hit my leg as the current carried me down. Another object, this time sharp as Nana's dagger, bumped against my arm.

"Grab whatever you can, Jasna! Don't worry about anything else but your prize!"

I closed my eyes, sucked in a breath and dived back in as pieces of different sizes swam past. I caught a thin object that felt like a feather, but the current swept it away. Twice I lunged for shapes drifting past, but both times they easily slipped from my hands. Each dive left me dizzier, gasping for breath. Finally, thinking my life was worth more than some whimsical item that might or might not decide to kill me, I gave up and swam towards the surface.

The current had carried me further down the river than expected. Aellialle stood but a tiny figure in the distance. I peddled my way awkwardly against the current and to the shore. Dusk had coloured the sky purple by the time my feet touched the riverbed, my struggle to stay afloat claiming all my strength. Gold paled into yellow, and I felt a pang of worry that I would be disappointing Aellialle. Still, better than getting a chest of snakes, I surmised, though I kept the relief to myself.

Something brushed against my hand just as the river was shallow enough to reach my waist. Instinctively, my fingers closed around it, and I lifted it to eye level to inspect it. A flask, I thought at first. Upon closer inspection, the object turned out to be a glass bottle with a round body and a narrow corkscrew top. Inside, purple liquid sloshed about.

"Well, don't just stand there," came Aellialle's voice, giving me a start. Apart from the inhumane strength with which she had shoved me and Maruna into the river, she appeared to possess an unnatural speed, as she had closed the distance in a matter of moments. I stumbled ashore and thrust the bottle at her.

"Curious," was all she said as she inspected the flask.

"What is it?" I asked. Even though my prize was no chest full of gold, I consoled myself that it was no chest of snakes either. While she turned the bottle in her hand, the river's colour ran silky cream until it too bled out and the water was once again clear.

"This is sniffler draught, I'm almost certain. No, nearly positive."

"Nearly positive? What is it supposed to do?"

Just then, her eyes found the red thread that ran along the river and disappeared into the forest. At least that answered my question on whether the thread was visible to my eyes only.

"It's meant to change the course of a magic object like this one so that it alters its direction to lead to someone – or something."

My heart sank. I already had the thread that led to the Vizier's palace and Iliya. I didn't need it to change its course for anything else.

"What am I supposed to do with it?" I asked, not hiding my disappointment.

"How should I know? It's yours now. Keep it safe – you'll thank me one day."

So I took the potion Aellialle was only almost certain wouldn't kill me, wrapped it in some clothes, and stashed it in Nana's bag.

CHAPTER 13

NEVER TRUST A ZMEI

*A*ellialle sent me off only after kindly packing some apples, bread, and cheese for me, as well as a flask of water. After promising to visit if my path ever wound back to the caravanserai, I left, eager to follow the thread to Tsargrad and Iliya.

To my relief, spring still coloured the leaves green, and a pleasant breeze accompanied me on my way. The thread ran ahead, steady and reassuring. I followed. In the afternoon, I stopped at a meadow to have some of Nana's leftover bread and dried meat. Earlier, I had dismissed Aellialle's suggestion to find a companion, preferably one skilled in fighting.

"I don't need anyone. It shouldn't take long to get to where I'm headed," I had replied foolishly, to which she had shaken her head.

"Still, the road ahead is long and dangerous. Besides, you need someone to talk to. To keep you company. The silver path, much like any path, is a dangerous place for a young woman, especially so for someone with a face like yours."

She had been right, I thought as I stared morosely at the hills ahead. Not for the first time, I thought of Iliya. Surely his road had not been filled with monsters and demons – a hala hungry for magic, a zmei needing to be set free, and worst of all, Maruna. Or had it? Had he faced unknown challenges all so that he could return my shadow back to me?

I had not intended to rest long. Yet I must have dozed off, for a familiar place emerged. This time, the colours in my dream resurfaced as even more finely saturated than they had been the night before. I saw my surroundings with a clarity that none of my previous dreams with Zhar had possessed.

It was Zhar's confinement, the same cave we had conversed in last time. Torchlight illuminated the walls, lending the dreary setting an even more oppressive quality. Light bounced off Zhar's glinting scales, casting dancing figures on the walls.

"Jasna, finally. I was worried you had reconsidered," the zmei said, sounding impatient. It had been less than a day since we had last spoken, but I was coming to see that patience was not among the zmei's qualities. "Why is your skin shimmering with gold?"

"It's a long story," I said with a frown. The river's gift had left a mark, and the hasty scrubbing I had attempted before leaving had not entirely removed the gold. "Where are we? What is this place?"

"This is my prison, I'm afraid. As I said last time we spoke, after the Vizier's mage released me, I was left weakened. Someone captured me when crossing over to Syanka. Again. I need you to find me. To set me free."

That was when I remembered one of Nana's stories. A warning to never trust a zmei. No matter how persuasive they were, they always pursued their own ends. The moment the cautionary tales flooded my mind, I grew certain Zhar was withholding something from me. If he had fulfilled his bargain with Yerleg and things had gone smoothly, he would not have sought me out. Still, he had been used, betrayed, and then trapped again – first by Yerleg, now by someone else, someone powerful enough to curse a zmei.

As if having read my mind, the zmei's eyes narrowed and he exhaled slowly, puffs of smoke escaping his nostrils.

"First," I said with a conviction I did not feel, "I would like to know more. You helped the dark mage who imprisoned you. He used your magic to sever my essence – and the moment he released you, you were captured again. Is that right?"

The zmei grunted in reply, and by his tense posture, I could tell there was nothing more he would have liked than to incinerate me then and there for having so openly voiced his weaknesses. I clenched my fists, unsure whether the dream would allow me to run if the need arose. He needed me, but would that be enough to temper his mood?

Reluctantly, he admitted, "I have been bested once more. Yes, after the dark mage released me from his binding, I found myself in a weakened state. It took my remaining strength to fly back to Syanka, which is the last thing I recall before darkness consumed me, and I awoke to find myself chained."

"And you have no notion of where 'here' is?"

"Now that we are in Syanka, your dreams reflect my reality. As you see, we appear to be in a cave," the zmei said with a haughty voice, "I suspect the cave lies near the sea. I hear the waves crashing during storms. And I taste salt in the air, even in this stuffy chamber. The lanterns that you see are the only light in this constant darkness. More than that, I do not know."

I held my breath. The zmei didn't like being questioned, so I stayed still, trying to read his mood.

"You are the only one who can free me. Only you know I'm here," he admitted, another truth that took a dig at his pride. He frowned. "However, there is something else I saw when I was last in the land of dreams. The caravanserai you described and the well next to it."

He paused, considering his next words. A feeling of foreboding swept over me, sending shivers down my spine.

"There was a shadow at the well that seemed tethered to it, at least at first. Except that when night fell, it slipped from the well and stole into the darkness."

It was almost a relief, I thought with a sigh. My shadow – or the part of it that I had met – remained free, no longer bound, roaming the realms at will.

"You must keep this a secret," Zhar said, though he didn't have to warn me. "If others know a part of you is severed, they will be less inclined to house a creature with no shadow. They know better than to come close to the dark magic that was used in the shadow's severance. Once that happens, the person is marked forever. But fear not. When you free me, we will find your shadow and force that dark mage to bind it back to you."

"I need a favour in return," I said, though the tremble in my treacherous voice betrayed my hesitation. If Nana's tales had taught me anything, it was that creatures like Zhar respected bargains as a form of power. And if stories came to life in Syanka, then I would shape this one with words of my own choosing. I would be more than the girl in someone else's tale. For now, a bargain like the one Zhar had struck with Yerleg would protect me. It was the only way to stop him from using me and then discarding me once I had freed him.

"Are you trying to bargain with me?" asked the zmei, enunciating the last word. I nodded and suppressed the flinch that his probing gaze brought. Then a glint of amusement deepened the yellow in his eyes. He seemed almost proud. I exhaled with relief when he said, "Very well. I owe you that much after the unfortunate shadow magic I performed for that vile mage. In that light, I see no other way but to give you my word that once freed, I will aid you in getting your beloved back from the Grand Vizier's palace or wherever he is being kept. My word is as binding as any signed contract, so fear not that I will break it. Is this the bargain you were seeking to strike?"

But there was something else in the zmei's words that had unsettled me.

"Beloved is a strong word," I said before my mind caught up with my mouth. My eyes grew wide at the unwitting confession, but I couldn't take back the words that were out. Perhaps it was the flickering light, but I thought the zmei's thin lips stretched in something like a smile. I tried to soften the harsh words. "Still, no matter my feelings, I owe it to him. Saving Iliya from whatever the Vizier has done to him is the least I could do after all he has done for me."

"Then I will help you."

I weighed the risks. Trusting Zhar could end in betrayal. But going to the Vizier alone was a doomed mission. If I wanted Iliya back, I needed power beside me. And Zhar, proud as he was, offered that power. What a foolish thing to think, that I could storm the Vizier's palace by myself and demand both my shadow and Iliya back! For the first time since setting foot on the silver road, my plan's foolhardiness glared back at me with a mocking smile.

A sinking feeling that the Grand Vizier had planned all of this settled in my stomach. If severing my shadow did not work, he had all the means to salvage his wounded pride. I had scorned him in front of his retinue. His subordinates had seen him, the second most powerful man in the empire, get rejected by a mere servant of the empire he claimed to rule. If I went willingly to his court, he could salvage that. So I needed allies. And who better than a zmei to intimidate the empire's second most powerful man?

"What happens when we encounter the Vizier's dark mage? After all, he bound you once to his will. What is to say he won't do it again?"

It had been the wrong thing to say. The zmei bristled, finding the very suggestion offensive. I had to take a few breaths and remind myself it was only a dream.

"Do you think me so foolish, girl? To be not once, not twice, but thrice beholden to a lesser? Tell me this then. What is your plan once you get there, if you didn't have me?" Zhar insisted. "The Vizier takes what he desires, and you are what he wants. You will need someone to intimidate him. Someone who holds bargaining power. I could be that for you unless your impertinence gets in the way."

Though he did not need to demonstrate his might for my benefit, it was too much for the zmei to resist the display of power. He narrowed his eyes and flared his nostrils. My knees buckled under me as Zhar roared, his warm breath a wave strong enough to extinguish the torchlight. Suddenly, I wished I would wake before the dream morphed into a nightmare. Petulant like a child despite being ancient, yet holding no reservations about using his power for intimidation; that was the real Zhar, the zmei I was about to ally myself with.

"If you are going to pressure the Vizier into returning Iliya to me, so be it," I conceded, the words coming out as if from someone else's mouth. "But don't pretend it's out of the goodness of your heart. You want to go there as much as I do. Both you and I stand to gain from paying a visit to the Grand

Vizier. I don't doubt you want to see the dark mage get his due as much as I want the same for the Grand Vizier. And if you want my help, zmei, you'll speak to me as an equal."

"You are learning fast how to address an ancient one," he said, and to my relief, the tension eased. "Alas, the dark mage is no fool. The terms of his binding stated that he is not to come to harm, before or after the binding's conclusion." He paused in consideration. Then a slow smile blossomed on his serpentine face and he nodded to himself. "Though perhaps he is not as clever as he thinks if he truly believes he could outsmart me. Ha! Me!"

"I take it you have a way of getting back at him?"

"Leave that to me. For now, we shall speak of my release. What is important is that you know this – only an enchanter or enchantress could have trapped me here. I feel a curse that may be as ancient as I am."

Just then, it occurred to me.

"I have a potion that might help. I obtained it yesterday with the help of a hala."

"Hala demons offer no help," he interrupted with a snort. "They take and they give only if there's something in return."

"Much like you," I said. To my surprise, the zmei chortled.

"For now, I think our best bet would be for me to use the potion and find you. Then you and I will get Iliya and my shadow back, and you can deal with the Vizier's dark mage as you please. Do we have an agreement?"

"We have an agreement," the zmei said. For a moment, I thought I glimpsed a spark of hesitation, there and gone in the blink of an eye. "Now, find your way to me."

I WOKE UP WITH A START. The sun had rolled halfway across the horizon, a reminder of the little time left to find shelter before nightfall. The surrounding silence, broken only by the occasional birdsong and insect buzzing, weighed on me even more so than before. I had to admit that even the zmei had been a preferable companion to the thoughts of self-doubt that flooded my mind. Yet, he had withheld something from me, I was certain of it. After rubbing the last remnants of sleep from my eyelids, I rummaged through my bag's contents for the potion.

It felt too convenient, somehow, needing the potion's effect just a day after obtaining it. Luck had never been a friend of mine. Yet, perhaps for once the scales had tipped in my favour to make up for all the times good fortune had been absent when needed. When I located the potion, I lifted it to an eye level to see the liquid sloshing pleasantly inside, as if in anticipation of the stopper coming off. Deciding there was little sense in putting it off, I uncorked the top and downed its contents.

A heartbeat passed, and then another. Nothing happened. Then, the surrounding colours, the blue in the sky, the green and brown earth, all exploded in hues even fuller than earlier. As if out of nowhere, a tiny goldfinch appeared, shimmering in the air. Like a drawing in the sand brought to life, it darted towards the horizon and paused, beckoning me to follow.

Without further ado, I slung Nana's bag and followed the bird to the mountain ahead, hoping there would be a path I could follow. The red thread snaked forward for a while, then swerved right and disappeared from sight. For a heartbeat, I thought the hope of seeing Iliya again had vanished with it. Then something worse happened.

The goldfinch darted to the right, vanishing into the woods. But before I could follow, the bird shot back, something that looked like a worm in its mouth. With a sinking heart, I saw it was no worm. The red string wound back behind the bird as if it had no end.

Powerless, I watched the bird fly before me. Once it dropped the thread, the red string sank into the ground like ink into paper. This was what Zhar was holding back when he was being coy, I was certain.

"What have you done?" I asked the bird, a growing sense of horror clawing at my throat. Unlike other Syanka creatures, it did not reply; it was just a bird. Instead, it pulsed before my eyes, once, twice, thrice, until its light faded into the day as if it had never been, the thread's new course the only evidence of it.

"It will show me the way… to Zhar," I said, slowly, the realisation taking all hope of reaching Iliya in time. "I was thinking of him when I drank the potion. It must have taken that as my wish. That's why Zhar was evasive. He knew I would lose my chance of finding Iliya."

Tears burned my eyes, but no one was there to confirm or deny my words. The red thread's new direction blurred, but was there, fixed. I had no choice but to follow.

CHAPTER 14

THE TSAR OF THE FOREST

As I walked, I kept thinking. In the silence, Nana's story of Zhar, the zmei who was too vain, came to my mind, at long last answering the question about Zhar's past. To break the stillness, I began narrating it in a soft voice, even though there was no one to hear the tale. Even whispered under my breath, it felt good to break the silence while following the red thread's new direction. I had little trouble imagining the snow-covered trees, the warm hearth back home, and Nana's hoarse voice. Stones crunched beneath my feet as the whole mountain stilled to hear Nana's tale.

"A long time ago, when gods and demons still roamed the earth, there lived a zmei called Zhar. He was a glutton at heart, and no king or queen wished him to visit their feasts, for every time he did, no amount of food would sate his hunger. Still, having zmei as a guest was considered the highest honour. Riches befell those close to a zmei, and besides, no one could say no to a mighty creature such as Zhar. The zmei of great renown visited kingdom after kingdom until one day, the hero Yosha challenged him to a duel. Zhar huffed and puffed with indignation, but couldn't say no to a challenge issued in front of the entire court. Yosha, a clever and striking hero, knew vanity to be every zmei's biggest weakness. On the day of the duel, the king, the queen, and the entire kingdom gathered to witness the feat. No one believed that even a mighty hero like Yosha would defeat an ancient zmei, for his power was unrivalled. And so it happened that the two battled for hours without either of them emerging as a victor, their powers evenly matched. But the crowd knew not that on the day of the duel the fates conspired to let their favourite hero win. Help arrived in the form of rain, sent by the three fates. So powerful was their spell that all of a sudden Zhar's wings thinned until they turned into paper. He could no longer take flight and fell to the ground, finally defeated, his wings crumbling to dust. The great Yosha emerged as the victor. His demand: that the zmei never visit the king's feast again. Zhar had no choice but to oblige. And thus Yosha became the only human to defeat the greatest zmei to roam the realms."

By the time I finished the story, the narrow path snaked through the hills. Cliffs loomed above, their shadows spreading a biting chill. I didn't need to know much about myths to see the story was likely exaggerated, if not completely made up. Even as a child, I had found it hard to believe that zmei wings would so easily turn into paper. There must be some truth to it, though. If Zhar was real, perhaps so were some traits attributed to him. Gluttony and vanity, for one, with the latter quite easy to believe.

"What an entertaining story," a voice sounded from a rocky formation above my head. Too late, I realised I had become caught up in telling Zhar's story and had dropped my guard.

With my heart in my throat, I backed away from the rock's shadow until the darkening sky came back into sight. Even with the help of the dying light, I failed to locate the voice's source. I slid Nana's bag off my shoulder and rummaged through its contents for the dagger, cursing myself for not having it ready.

Though the voice did not sound threatening, I resolved not to trust it until its owner showed himself. My eyes searched for him in vain until I grew certain I had imagined it, and was about to move on. Then the tree moved, and it took all my willpower to keep the rising scream from escaping my lips. When the branches shook like arms and the trunk stepped forward, I saw it was no tree that had spoken, but a person. His proportions were all wrong, though. He was too tall and lean to be human, and his eyes were forest-green, too pristine to belong to a person. Oddly, they reminded me of the colours of my own eyes, the same shade of green that had prompted Moravians to label me a witch. Thick branches made up his legs and arms, with sinews twisting into knots to form knees and elbows. His eyes flickered like fireflies in the growing dusk. From behind one branch, a small rodent-like animal emerged. It looked exactly like a deer if one had become trapped inside a mouse's body, right down to the finest detail. Tiny antlers sprouted atop his head and his hooves appeared well-trodden.

"What are you?" I asked the creature, but it was the tree that answered while the rodent fixed me with its beady eyes.

"Don't you remember me? I suppose it's been a long time since we last saw each other. Only then, it had been on the streets of Morava and you had my coins."

I recognised him then. He looked different in Syanka, his true form more like that of a tree than a man. His voice reminded me of wind whispering between leaves. If anything, his green eyes ought to have given him away. They twinkled much the same as they had all those years ago when I had dropped and scattered his coins. The corners of his mouth curved with amusement in response to the shock that must have shown on my face. The tiny creature grunted, a chirp-like sound for its size.

"Gorovoi?" I asked, uncertain. The tree nodded, dispelling any lingering doubt. "How is this possible?"

"How is it possible for the sun to rise over the horizon each day? For the moon to chase it away, only for it to roll back up the next morning? How is it that every high tide follows a low one?"

"I… get your point?" The tiny deer creature snorted, and I had to suppress the desire to reach out and pet it. Gorovoi's kind eyes shone as his branchlike arm swept wide, as if to encompass the forest below and the hillside trees.

"There are forests both here, in Syanka, and in your realm. I preside over all. The difference is that in your realm, I appear as one of you, while here I can assume my true form."

"All this time you've lived so close to us, and I never knew. I thought you were just a little… odd," I admitted while my mind raced to determine what kind of creature he was. I did not have to wonder for long. His next words provided the answer.

"It is the nature of leshy to help those abandoned or deemed unworthy by others."

"A leshy is a creature as close to a god as any demon," I whispered Nana's words to myself, but Gorovoi must have heard, for a smile tugged at the corners of his lips, prompting me to speak up. "He reigns in the forest and can assume any form he wants. That means he can turn into anything – animal or human – or any other creature, really. His true form is that of a man with forest-green eyes and branches sprouting from his body. Leshy can help travellers if they are so inclined, and even teach them magic. At least in Nana's more fanciful tales."

I hesitated. While Nana's stories had an abundance of leshy, there was a particular tale that had captured my imagination above all others.

"Yes?" Gorovoi said encouragingly.

"Nana used to tell me a different kind of story. I thought she did it to keep me from going out at night, though she had no love for that one tale. Naturally, it was one of my favourite ones to ask for. In it, a leshy steals cursed children."

"And why would I steal cursed children?"

Unexpectedly, the antlered creature leapt forward in an arc that brought it down to where I stood, an impressive feat for a creature of its size. As it did, it began transforming mid-air, growing bigger, its shape expanding until it came into full size. My hand instinctively felt for the dagger once more. I regretted it instantly, but Gorovoi's eyes had already traced my move. I withdrew my hand and stood still.

"None of that," the leshy warned.

"I mean you no harm, I promise. Here, you see my hands – I hold no weapon," I said, and lifted my empty hands in the air to placate him. "And to answer your question, leshy would occasionally take pity on the cursed children, since it was their parents who had, wittingly or not, placed the curse on them. For being different, disobedient, or not turning out at all like the children they had wished for. And you removed the curse and gave them a second chance. Sometimes you replaced those children with one of your own. Much to the parents' great chagrin when they found it was a changeling."

"And why did you find this story so captivating?"

I paused, wondering why I had liked that particular story better than the rest. The answer came easily. My experience with Moravians had allowed me to sympathise with the outcasts.

"Because of what leshy did, giving cursed children a second chance. I fancied myself one of those children. When my imagination ran ahead of me, I believed a leshy was out there, waiting to snatch me away from people like Maruna, who called me all sorts of names, like cursed or stupid, or a witch. But then I remembered I had Nana, and that was more than enough."

His green eyes reminded me of the dancing fireflies outside my window. Perhaps I had not imagined Nana's words when I had been delirious. The realisation prompted me to exclaim, "It was you! You gave Nana the spell that returned my some of my soul to me!"

His eyes sparkled with joy. "Very good, Jasna, very good. Alas, even my spells cannot fix what was severed. You have regained a part of your essence, but another one will remain forever separated from the rest."

I remembered the wretched statue of myself I had seen when I first came to Syanka. Though I kept being told a part of me was missing, I felt no different. Perhaps being whole was never the point, but the search for that elusive self – the shadow that completed us – made the journey worthwhile. Zhar said my shadow had slipped from the well, and the thought made me shudder, so I pushed it aside. For the time being, I had other, more pressing questions.

"Why did you do it? After what I did to you that day at the square? Why did you give Nana that spell? I need to know why you helped me – and no more riddles."

Gorovoi frowned, and his eyes searched mine, as if looking for something that wasn't there. His next words would have made me wince if not delivered in his kind voice.

"Were you not paying attention to my story? I cured you

because it's what I do. I help those cast out. Contrary to what some tales suggest, I do not marry the children I raise or leave my own in their stead. That might tempt lesser leshy than myself, but not me. Under my domain, leshy and forest creatures alike are always welcome to seek protection. Although this one time I did leave Zina, a young leshy, in a human child's stead, and she stirred up all sorts of trouble for them. Imagine the parents' reaction when they found out the child was not theirs at all, but an entirely different creature. Ah, Zina, my wayward child, always up to no good."

His laughter rippled merrily between us, infusing the air with joy. I smiled back in earnest.

"Whatever your reasons for helping me get my shadow back, thank you," I said. Gorovoi inclined his head in acknowledgment. It occurred to me that not all of Nana's tales were to be believed. There, most creatures were mischievous at best, revealing their true nature only when about to take advantage of someone unfortunate enough to cross their path. Mostly, they were bested by human cleverness. But if Gorovoi was nothing like the leshy in fairy tales, perhaps Zhar wasn't either.

"Gorovoi, I need to ask someone, and you appear to possess a great deal of knowledge. Am I truly a witch?"

His wooden lips stretched into a smile when he said, "So what if you are?"

"I suppose… I would like that. I never thought of it as a good thing. But, in truth, it may be. It could give me some armour in the days to come, and aid me in finding Iliya and saving him from the Grand Vizier's punishment."

Gorovoi shot an inquisitive look at me, but was too polite to ask. So I told him, all the while hoping that trusting strangers with my story would not come back to haunt me. I told him about the hala and the mob, the red thread, and how

Iliya had set off to Tsargrad to plead with the Vizier to have my shadow returned to me. Gorovoi listened patiently.

"And now I have lost not only a brother and a father to the palace, but also my betrothed," I finished bitterly.

He considered my words for an instant, then said, "I will travel with you through the hills. It's a dangerous place where my power stretches only in some parts, but it would be enough to signal other creatures to stay away."

Without further ado, he slid off the cliff, his tree-like body moving with surprising fluidity. The fully grown deer followed us as we set off. Grateful for his company, I followed him across the hill, the moon guiding us beneath a blanket of stars long after darkness had settled. Scaling the hill while listening to the leshy's tales kept me going for a time until even that couldn't prevent the chill from settling in. The sparse trees had grown thicker and thickets of bushes littered the landscape.

We found a small clearing surrounded by trees that provided protection from the biting wind. There was enough ground to light a fire with no bushes getting in the way. The leshy helped me by providing flint from the depths of his tattered robes, and I used Nana's dagger to scrape it until a spark flew. Not long after, I huddled near the flames while Gorovoi kept his distance, the branches that made up his body instinctively coiling away from the dangers of fire. If any creatures roamed about, none disturbed us that night. We shared the remainder of Nana's food and the fire's warmth. He told me stories of the forest, of children that had found their freedom there after being driven from their homes. He also warned me that not all leshy were as kind; some of his brethren preferred taking children as servants or even as brides. All along, I listened, mesmerised by his soft rhythmic voice.

"How about we hear another one of your stories in return?" Gorovoi asked some time after drowsiness had settled in. Even as I dozed off, I muttered the beginning of one of Nana's stories.

"One day, the young son of the sun told his father that he would take up his work for the day. The sun's son, the youngest of his children, rolled across the horizon and marvelled at the earth below. So mesmerised was the young sun with the lives of the people below that he belatedly remembered to end the day and roll behind the horizon. Even though he hurried to hide behind the hill, he was too late. A ravenous hala who had long awaited such an opportunity descended upon the sun. Just as she was about to devour him, a young man working in the mountain's woods stepped out and killed the hala with his axe. Grateful, the sun's son brought the young hero to his palace above the clouds so that his father would reward the young man for saving his only son."

The fire crackled, reminding me of Nana's hearth. Its warmth seeped through my tired bones, until, just like Nana, I grew too drowsy to finish the story.

"Sleep, child," Gorovoi said, though his eyes remained open, fixed on the darkness beyond the fire. "Sleep, for the road ahead is winding and shadow-filled."

CHAPTER 15

NOT ALL LAMIA ARE EVIL...

I squinted against the purple streaks of dawn running across the sky. Thin wisps of smoke curled upwards from the fire's remnants. I had slept soundly and without Zhar interrupting my dreams, which I suspected was another gift from Gorovoi. The leshy waited patiently, gazing down below to his domain, the forest.

"Don't you need any sleep?" I asked as I stretched, my body, for once, not aching after the dreamless night.

"What was the sun's gift to the man who rescued his son from the hala?" asked Gorovoy instead. I stared at him, sleep still muddling my thoughts. He sighed and muttered something about humans being slow, but elaborated. "From last night's story."

"Oh, that's right. He gave the hero a stallion swift as the wind, able to tread the clouds and gallop across the sea."

"A wind's blessing, to be gifted wings beneath your

hooves," said Gorovoi wistfully as I nibbled on some stale bread. The leshy shook his head when I offered him some. "And tell me, child, what did the young man do with such a gift?"

"What they all do in such stories. Use it to impress a princess and marry her before she's had time to reconsider."

"Romantic," he offered, his voice the sound of rustling forest leaves. We didn't take long to pack. We were back on the mountain path before the sun had risen, the crisp air still infused with last night's chill.

After a couple of hours of walking in silence, Gorovoi said, "In this realm, your kind holds the power to shape wonders if you know how to dream them."

"What do you mean?" I asked as we slowly emerged from the other side of the hill. The downhill journey was far easier than the climb, and the sun followed us across the sky.

"Think of the horse from your story. What do you imagine it looking like?"

"Well, the story's stallion was white. I always imagined it black, though, after Naiya, the horse we had at Nana's house when I was growing up."

"Very good. Imagine her grazing in front of us."

I looked at him, uncertain of what he was getting at. His kind eyes met mine reassuringly. Despite my doubts, I didn't want to disappoint him after all he'd done to help, so I did as he asked. I thought about the horse, but my mind drifted back to my very first impression of Syanka. In this realm, colours intensified as we drew closer, as though they were solidifying into existence. My guess was that we had some power in shaping the landscape that was not yet formed. So if Gorovoy wanted me to imagine my childhood's horse, it meant he had something in mind.

I didn't need to close my eyes to conjure the image. My

mind held the details cupped in a fist, willing them to come to life. A few more steps and the ground beneath us evened. At the bottom of the mountain, a black horse grazed the almost unnaturally green grass.

"Naiya?" My voice trembled. "Is that you?"

Though I had been imagining it for the past few moments, seeing her again felt quite unreal.

"It's not often that wishes are granted," cautioned Gorovoi. "Syanka is a fickle mistress, so don't rely on conjuring to work all the time, especially not when you expect it. Still, now you have a companion for your next leg of the journey. Doran would have loved to accompany you, but alas, I need him elsewhere."

The deer, who seemed to favour riding on Gorovoi's shoulder rather than staying full size, snorted in agreement. I approached the horse cautiously, hoping to see a glimmer of recognition in her eyes. She grazed calmly, though when I placed a hand on the side of her back, the mare twitched in acknowledgment. Naiya had possessed a similar calmness about her. I needed no convincing to know it was my childhood horse that stood in front of me, waiting to be saddled for a ride.

I halted as Gorovoi's last words filtered through the joy of seeing my old friend again.

"Hold on. You are not coming?"

"I said I'd see you through the mountain. As for the rest, that's your path to walk. Besides, I have a realm to watch over. I have one last parting gift to you. I give you my word: no harm shall come to you whilst in my domain, nor from any creature in my forests."

I nodded, though a heavy feeling settled over my heart. With his spell, Gorovoi had helped me recover from my illness. Now he had offered me both company and protection

– more than anyone in Morava, save Nana, ever had. Solemnly, I offered him my hand the way I had seen the town's officials and rich merchants do, and with a smile that lit his calm eyes, Gorovoi shook it back.

"You deserve to be helped. Now, and back when you were a child. Never forget that, no matter what others might let you believe."

Though I said nothing, his words moved me more than I cared to admit. We lingered some more until the inevitability of saying goodbye weighed on us and the deer grew restless. Doran assumed his true form once more so that Gorovoi could ride on his back. With one last wave, he set off and soon the two disappeared into the woods.

Once more I found myself on the silver road, chasing after the zmei. I was not completely alone, though. I had Naiya, I reminded myself as I climbed on the horse's back. Riding without a saddle or spurs meant I ceded control to my mare, but we soon found balance. She allowed me to steer her without complaints, though using my hands and feet proved to be an awkward and challenging feat. The forest, Gorovoi's domain, stretched ahead of us.

Soon the rhythmic horse canter was the only sound, and my thoughts wandered back to Nana, Iliya, and Morava. Perhaps what other Moravians had said was true, a small, treacherous voice whispered inside my head. Perhaps my family bore a curse. No family lost so many members and got someone recruited in the Vizier's army to fight against his own people, not without a spell of misfortune. Or a curse. I still recalled the night my father had set off for Tsargrad to bring my brother back. He had chosen to go after the son he'd lost, and in that, he had forsaken the daughter who was still there. As a child, I believed that meant he loved me less, if at all. As an adult, I knew better, but that did little to remove the sting.

Lost in thought, I pondered how many creatures had helped me, the hala and Gorovoi, all so that I could find Iliya and my shadow. Yet again, I wondered whether my soul would truly be whole again. I felt no different, except for the searing anger simmering beneath the surface of my mind. My earlier resolve to never be helpless again stood firm.

A rustling sound like leaves dancing in the wind put an end to my bleak thoughts. Naiya came to a halt, and I slid off her back, curious to see what secret Syanka held this time. Just off the road and behind a copse, I found a dozen creatures dancing in a circle, almost as if in a trance. The creatures barely reached my knees in height. Large leaves made up their heads, with tiny mouths and big green eyes protruding from their oval faces. Twigs sprouted where their feet and arms should have been. Their bodies appeared quite nimble for something made out of wood. Their dance involved them tapping their twiglet feet on the moss-ridden forest bed. One of them, a creature with a green leaf for a head, spotted me and paused. Soon, the rest followed until we stared at each other, all rustling gone quiet.

"Are you lost?" asked the leafling that had seen me first, its small voice like a whisper of leaves. Before I could answer, its eyes fell on the red thread.

"Is this..." a brown-leaf-faced creature began, pointing at the string.

"A magic thread that shows you the way?" another one with a face of a rusty leaf finished.

I nodded.

"Who are you searching for?"

"Someone held against his will. A zmei," I said honestly.

"Ohhh," the brown leaf-headed one said. "We don't like him."

"We fear him," added the green leafed one.

"You should never cross a zmei."

"He breathes fire."

"We hate fire."

"Burns our bark, it does."

They spoke over one another, finishing each other's sentences. Their squeaky voices and small stature were an instant charmer.

"Has he actually tried to burn your forest?" I asked when I finally got the chance. The creature that had spoken last hesitated.

"Our forest? No. He used to burn us. For pleasure. So we speak not his name, lest he hear us."

I wondered if they meant Zhar or if other zmei roamed Syanka. The playfulness with which they had spoken over each other dissolved into seriousness as the green one took it upon herself to inform me.

"The zmei is never up to any good. Not every zmei breathes fire, but he does and he uses it to get what he wants. He has made many enemies among the more mighty creatures and even men avoid sharing their burrow with him."

The tiny creature shuddered like a leaf blown by the wind.

"Why are you telling me this?" I asked, confused.

"Because Gorovoi protects you," chirped the rusty-leafed one as if it was the most obvious answer.

"Does everyone in his domain know I have his protection?" I asked, and they all nodded enthusiastically. The thought I was not entirely defenceless in this realm brought a comforting sense of warmth.

"We are part of the trees," explained one with a shrivelled brown face and a decayed body trunk, from which I deduced he was older than his fellows. "We know everything that goes on in the forest."

"And Gorovoi dislikes Zhar?"

"The forest tsar dislikes any creature that would harm a living soul or a tree from his domain."

It sounded like the leshy I had come to know in the brief time we had spent together. Still, I refrained from passing judgment, for I knew little about either Zhar or Gorovoi. The former seemed genuinely distressed that he had done me harm, albeit at someone else's bidding. That did not mean he had no violent tendencies of his own. I decided against lying to the creatures.

"Still, I need to find him. I mean you no harm, but he needs my help and I his. But if it's all the same to you... would you mind telling me what you are?"

Nana's stories had no references to the leafy creatures, and I had to ask, my curiosity having the best of me.

"We are," the older one began, but had no chance to finish. Instead, its mouth hung open mid-sentence, and a frown formed on its face, deepening as it listened intently for something only it and its friends could hear. Nearby, Naiya whinnied with growing agitation. Soon, her neigh remained the only noise in the stillness, loud enough to betray our location.

"What is it?" I asked as the hush that fell amidst the leaflings solidified. In the blink of an eye, the creatures froze before my eyes and turned into lifeless tree logs, scattered about like remnants of a great tree. As soon as they stilled, I heard it, a whooshing noise from above, like a massive body cutting through air thick with resistance. A shadow fell on the clearing and a flap of wings brought a current of air that sent the logs flying across the clearing and forced me to retreat into the first line of woods.

The creature that landed in the quiet clearing barely fit

within its confines. A zmei, I thought at first, although its three heads distinguished it as another kind of creature. Its yellow scales gave off a faint gleam that cast dancing lights around the clearing, visible even in daylight. I knew the creature from Nana's tales. It was the zmei's evil sister, the lamia. As soon as the distinction formed in my frightened mind, I retreated towards Naiya, who, though fidgeting and immensely unsettled, miraculously hadn't bolted yet.

But before I could do much else, all three of the lamia's heads turned towards me and three pairs of eyes stared my way, leaving me rooted to the spot.

"You and your tiny friends playing dead have something I want," she said without a preamble, her voice dripping poison. No magic potions or doors would save me now, and I found I had no tricks up my sleeve. Not even Nana's dagger, tucked in her bag, now pressing uncomfortably against my back, could save me. Had I had the courage to do it, using it on myself would be a preferable death to being devoured by a lamia. The path ahead became clear; I could not fight her, so outsmarting her was my only hope.

My mind frantically sought any clues that might help. Didn't lamia live at the bottom of lakes or rivers, or even seas? Or was it the deepest parts of the woods? I tried to get hold of the half-finished thoughts that raced through my mind, but came up empty-handed. I only recalled that lamia, the enemy of the noble zmei, often fought with him.

None of this helped me.

"Answer me, girl. Where is he?"

"Where is who, o great one?" I asked with a trembling voice.

"Flattery. How quaint. You think I haven't heard this thousandfold over?" she bellowed, and the surrounding trees shuddered from the impact of her voice. "You think you are the first one to try this trick on me? You think others haven't tried to save themselves by flattering me? As if that would work on me! Me! A foolish zmei might fall for such trickery, but not a lamia – never!"

"I can see that," I said with a barely audible trembling voice. "O... wise lamia."

"I said enough with the flattery, girl. I was hunting for prey when the prey revealed itself to me. I couldn't believe my ears when I heard you speak of him so freely. After all the time I spent searching and, of all creatures, these petty saplings playing dead have the answers. Answer me, girl. Where is he? Where is Zhar?"

"I... don't know," I said meekly, waiting for the next outburst from the lamia, but she only growled, leaving me no choice but to fumble for words. "I don't know where he is, but I'm searching for him myself. Please don't kill these creatures because of me. They have no more knowledge of his where-abouts than I do. I beg of you, spare them."

The thought of condemning the tiny creatures to death only because I had chanced upon them felt unbearable.

"Kill the saplings? Why would I do that?" asked the lamia, sounding genuinely confused.

"Because that's what you do," I said before I had the chance to think my words through.

Though serpentine expressions were foreign to me, I could swear the lamia winced.

"I called them prey because I hunted for someone who would lead me to Zhar," she said. I gaped at her in disbelief. The identical expression on her three heads softened. "You must have heard the stories about lamia. They are often misleading since they've had millennia to grow and fester, embellish, and vilify me. But ask yourself this – why is it that when Zhar does something, it's seen as a feat no matter its consequences? What he does is noble. When I do the same thing, it's because I calculated it to benefit me at the expense of someone else."

The lamia paused, giving me time to consider her words. Her tale, handed down from generation to generation, torn apart and mended time and time again until it resembled nothing like its true source, was one of deceit. What if that wasn't how the original story went? I let my body relax a little and studied the lamia's eyes. They returned the stare, all six of them. An unmistakable intelligence lent them depth beyond what I had seen in anyone, human or otherwise. Something else lurked there too. It was sadness. The lamia shifted her eyes. Her mouth hung for a moment, as if uncertain of what to say next. At last, she sighed.

"I mean you and your friends no harm. I have matters yet unsettled with the zmei, and I need to know where to find him. Aid me in my search, and I promise you we will part ways amiably."

"And you don't mean him any harm, either?"

The lamia laughed, the sound a low rumble reverberating through the woods.

"That's between the two of us. I suspect someone got the better of him this time, outmanoeuvring him once more, and he has gone into hiding to salvage his pride. That, or he craves some of that dark magic that trails after you. Is that so?"

Her last words left my throat dry. She too could sense the dark magic. It was likely what brought her here. I needed to tread with caution and buy some more time to gauge her intentions before revealing what I knew of Zhar's predicament. As with all creatures in Syanka, I decided on divulging as little of the truth as sensibility allowed.

"It is, but it's not what you think, and the fault does not lie with him. Not entirely…"

But before I could elaborate, our conversation came to an abrupt end. Something whistled past my ear and landed on the lamia with a sickening sound as it connected with her flesh. Almost the same instant as it did, two of her heads roared in anger, and the third one, the one where the arrow had struck, wailed in anguish, for the arrow had pierced right through one of her eyes. A moment later, a man bolted past me, sabre in hand, aiming straight for the creature.

CHAPTER 16

…Nor Are All Knights Noble

When the man emerged from behind the trees, the lamia wasted no time. The head closest to the intruder snapped into action and struck him like a viper. Her jaws closed around his arm, but caught only his shirt's sleeve. The man tore free from her jaws a heartbeat before the lamia's other head closed around his own. He lowered his gaze to his arm and saw that her teeth had only grazed flesh. Blood blossomed on the sleeve of his white shirt, his face twisting with pain.

The lamia's jaws snapped once more, and this time the second head struck, but before she could make up for her first miss and tear the man's arm off, he pulled free from the closing jaws, leaving a bloodied piece of shirt in the creature's mouth. His hand tightened around his sabre's hilt, and he swung with a precise motion, once, twice, thrice, his lean body straining under the pressure. The creature's five remaining eyes widened with surprise. She was dead before she'd realised what happened. The lamia's thick heads fell and rolled to the side, lifeless. Silence fell.

I thought of Nana's tale where the hero had defeated the lamia by severing all three heads, from the stumps of which milk, honey, and wine poured afterwards. Except that this man was no hero slaying a beast, and the liquid that surged from the body was just blood. With a dull thump, as if realising there were no heads to sustain its blood flow, the creature's body collapsed, crushing the heads under its weight. A scream of desperation tore my chest open. How could a mere man crush the lamia so quickly? Her eyes, still visible from under her severed body, glazed over, and the smell of her blood lingered on my tongue. All the while, the leafy creatures remained frozen. I had the sinking feeling they wouldn't be waking anytime soon. The man turned to me, a self-congratulatory smirk playing on his face.

"Fear not, fair lady," he said. "The monster is dead and you are free."

"Free from what, you fool?" I snapped, unable to contain the rising anger. His smug smile faded, but he quickly regained his composure.

"You are in shock. It's only natural that a fair lady requires time to get her bearings."

Unable to look at him, I turned away and stared at the grim scene that had unfolded in mere moments, my eyes stinging with unshed tears. In Syanka, Gorovoi had said, you could will things into existence. That was how Naiya and I found each other again. Could I will the lamia and the leafy creatures back to life? I tried to imagine them alive. My mind breathed life into the lifeless sapling remnants and the lamia's dead eyes, but even before I tried, I knew rules in Syanka obeyed no one, and above all no humans. Syanka did what

Syanka wished, and, perhaps with more experience, I could have stirred the bodies back to life. Yet, the little knowledge I had gained in this realm was not enough to do so, if it was at all possible. The bodies remained very much dead.

"Is there anything I could do to ease your anxious mind, my lady?" came the man's voice as if from afar. I resisted rounding on him, but could not keep the accusation from my eyes as I measured him up: a hero come to life, straight from Nana's tales and in all ways the embodiment of one. Strands of unruly gold hair cupped his face. He had a lean, yet firm body, full lips and round, innocent blue eyes so compelling that almost anyone would find them enough of an excuse for his transgressions. His armour, a linked chain of silver, only underlined his broad shoulders. I felt anything but awe. I could not hold back, even knowing he would never grasp the significance of his deed.

"You didn't have to kill her! She meant no harm."

He stared at me in bewilderment.

"My lady, I've been tracking the monster for days now, and I assure you, she is a predator worthy of the hunt! I see you are gracious enough to attribute human qualities to it, but it won't change the truth; the lamia was a monster."

His voice carried a defensive undertone, any lingering warmth evaporating after my outburst. There was something rough about it too, an unrefined note that suggested he was no knight. I threw my hands in the air in exasperation, knowing arguing wouldn't change his mind.

"At least call me Jasna. I'm no lady."

"Yes, lady. I mean Jasna. They call me Saval. Pray tell, where are you headed?"

"I don't see how this concerns you," I replied in an icy tone.

"Well, see, now that I saved your life…"

"You did not."

"…my honour demands that I see you to safety."

I couldn't keep the mockery from my voice when I asked, "Does it now? Did you, by any chance, hear one too many tales of knights from the free lands?"

Saval's face reddened at the suggestion, but I knew I had struck a nerve when he did not deny it.

"And what do you mean your honour demands to see me to safety? Do you think I can't defend myself? It seems to me I was doing well on my own before you intervened."

He bowed his head in acknowledgement, though his eyes remained doubtful when he said, "I would still like to accompany you to a safer place. Let me make it up to you by escorting you out of this forest."

I didn't have the heart to tell him that, thanks to Gorovoi's protection, the forest was safer for me than it was for him. Still, I remembered the loneliness I had felt earlier. Spending some time around a false knight would be preferable to the never-ending intrusive thoughts. Besides, there must be more to him than being a vain, self-righteous knight.

"As long as you promise not to harm any creatures that cross our path," I said reluctantly.

"I give you my word that, as long as we aren't provoked, I will spare any creatures we encounter from the wrath of my sabre. Why are you rolling your eyes?"

"Oh… uh, I was just checking if another lamia was about to descend on us."

Saval nodded with approval. And this was how I came to be companions with a would-be knight devoid of any sense of humour. My resentment towards him still simmered under the surface, but I could not deny that the comfort of not being alone in an unfamiliar realm was worth putting up with his hubris for a night. One last time, I wondered if the leafy creatures played dead because they mistrusted Saval or if they were truly frozen for good. With a final questioning look in their direction, I climbed on Naiya's back and set off to seek shelter for the night.

As dusk fell, the eastbound wind brought a chill to the air, forcing us to hasten our arrangements for the night. We found a relatively secluded clearing in a grove and settled for it. All around us, the forest was alive with birdsong and the hum of insects, carrying on well after dusk. Saval, whose every word and gesture had an air of grandeur, took care of both the fire and dinner like a true knight would. In the meantime, he regaled me with tales from his days in Syanka. From what I gathered, his life had been much like mine before the day he had discovered a portal to Syanka, hidden in plain sight behind his house.

"A good omen," he explained as he piled wood to build a fire. Nearby, Naiya snorted in disbelief. His voice instantly assumed a defensive undertone. "I speak the truth. That's what everyone from my village said, that the portal could not have opened sooner. Lean times had befallen us, for a hala destroyed our fields each summer's end, just before the harvest. It was decided that since the portal had opened near my house, I would venture in and hunt down the creature. Alas, I have not found her yet. But I have killed other foul beasts, a moroi and the lamia."

"She was no foul beast," I protested, but Saval waved my words aside and launched into an epic, no doubt embellished tale of how just the other night he had fought a moroi until the creature lay dead at his feet. Despite still harbouring resentment towards him, I listened with growing interest. From his dialect, it was easy to tell he was no noble knight, hard as he tried. Still, I found more sincerity in his stories than in his misguided attempts at chivalry.

Moroi were creatures of the night, also known as dead

people walking under the guise of darkness, searching for human energy to feed on. According to Nana, they were the reason night and evil walked hand in hand in people's superstitious minds. Despite the embellished story, killing a creature like that sounded like no small feat.

"I have always been unnaturally strong, even as a boy," Saval confessed. "Never knew my father, and my mother never talked about him either. Word spread that a roving spirit had visited her one summer night. Soon after, she began to show. Early the following spring, she gave birth to me. It took only a few years for my strength to emerge. A gift from my father, they said. When I discovered the portal, it quickly became apparent that my destiny was to venture into Syanka and find its secrets. Once here, I had no doubt that disposing of those monsters was my destiny. At first, everything seemed so unreal. All the colours were brighter than anything else I've seen. And some of my thoughts seemed to come to life before my very eyes. I still don't know how to make that happen – nothing here follows any rules."

He stole a glance at me as if to confirm his observations. When I nodded, the relief that flashed across his face that he hadn't gone insane was unmistakable.

"Your people held no grudge against you for being different? They didn't think you were cursed for being fathered by a spirit?" I asked.

"Why would they do that?"

Saval sounded genuinely confused. His brow furrowed, his round cheekbones betrayed an air of innocence only people coddled since childhood managed to retain. I grew increasingly frustrated at his lack of comprehension. His birth and strength had surrounded him with unnatural circumstances, just like mine had. Except that in one case, people considered it a gift and in the other – a curse. I reached with my sleeve to wipe the tears that welled in my eyes and threatened to spill. Anger and shame – yes, shame, that I was scorned for the very deeds that won Saval admiration – overwhelmed me. Saval cast a quizzical look in my direction, saw my glistening eyes, and averted his gaze, embarrassed he had witnessed my weakness.

"My mother died giving birth to me, and my father, stricken with grief, could not bear to lose my brother to the Sultan's blood-tax. So he took off to Tsargrad. Only, he never came back. No word of him arrived and as years went by, we presumed him dead."

Saval's eyes grew wider with each word.

"Everyone thought from then on I bore a curse. Except for Iliya."

"He sounds like a good man," Saval said simply.

"He is. But because the fates can be cruel, one day the Grand Vizier passed by Morava."

I relayed the events as concisely as possible. Saval exclaimed at the right places, offered sympathy, and cursed the bad luck that had led to my predicament. I began thinking that perhaps he wasn't that bad. And I would be lying if I said his attractiveness did not stir an odd feeling within me.

When I finished my story, I paused, hoping for some unexpected wisdom. He coughed, his discomfort evident, and changed the subject to his time in Syanka. I winced and forced a smile. Sympathies ran only for as long as the damsel in distress was well-accepted and liked. A witch did not have that privilege.

A wave of exhaustion washed over me. Even with the false knight by my side, I felt more alone than ever, in a realm beyond human reach and isolated from Nana, Iliya, and everything familiar. All the while, Saval droned on about a creature whose trail he'd been following.

"I've been on its trail for two days now. At first, I had reason to believe he hunted the lamia you saw me slay, but then it became obvious he was the prey."

Saval was mid-sentence when the noise came. Its direction – the woods. His shoulders stiffened and his hand flew to the hilt of his sabre. At the same time as the rustle of leaves came, a warning neigh from Naiya alerted me to someone's presence, and the bushes behind Saval parted to reveal the intruder.

CHAPTER 17

THE DAMSEL IN DISTRESS

Saval was up in a heartbeat, sabre in hand, as if he had manifested it from thin air. Shadows from the fire danced across his face, and at that angle, a savageness otherwise absent from his innocent expression glared back at the darkness.

"Please," sounded a familiar voice as the figure drew closer to the fire. "I mean no harm. I need help."

As she emerged from the thicket of bushes, Maruna's dark eyes stayed on Saval, compelling him to listen. The would-be knight lowered his blade by less than an inch, the tension behind his shoulders the only betrayal of lingering suspicion. A rattling noise sounded behind her, somewhat dampening the effect of Maruna's plea.

"I'm human, just like you," she said, then pointed at me. "She can bear witness to it."

"Do you know her?" Saval asked, voice low. I paused, not

wishing to risk her joining us. The presence of Maruna soured my mood so much that I wished her gone no matter what. Yet, I felt a pang of pity stir towards her. Being alone in a land she hated must have taken its toll on her, perhaps even teaching her a lesson on cruelty. Should I tell the truth and risk having her around for longer?

But before I could decide, Maruna, after weighing her chances, abandoned all dignity rather than relying on my goodwill, and threw herself at Saval's feet, begging, "I speak the truth, most noble knight. I need your help! I have been searching for someone like you to save me from a terrible fate."

I couldn't tell how much of our conversation she had overheard, but it hadn't taken her long to learn how to entice him. All she had to do was paint herself as the victim, and Saval, ever the gallant knight, needed no further prompting to jump in and rescue the damsel in distress. She almost had him fooled when the chest of hissing snakes emerged from behind. Saval crouched, poised for attack.

"Is this chest not a gift, Maruna?" I asked innocently. She glared at me but didn't drop her act. Her next words were so theatrical that I was certain even Saval would not be gullible enough to fall for them.

"Please, brave knight, save me from these wretched creatures. They have been following me for days."

"Now, now, that's not a way to treat the river's gifts," I said, but Saval, who couldn't say no to a damsel in distress, snakes or no snakes, drew near the chest. He paused and regarded me for a heartbeat.

"So you truly know her?" He lowered his voice as if the two of us were conspiring, and blushed. "She's beautiful."

"Who? Maruna?" I asked, almost choking. "She's vile." But my words got drowned in between the surreptitious glances he stole after her. My heart sank. Maruna saw it too. For whatever unfathomable reason, Saval had taken a liking to her.

"So what if we knew each other?" I said shrilly. "Believe me when I say this, I wish I didn't. As for the chest, it was a well-deserved gift from the river."

"Lies!" Maruna yelled. "A vile hala cursed me with the chest! And she was in league with Jasna. She must have already revealed that she is a witch! A cursed one at that. Everyone in our town knows it. Oh, my knight, you must not believe a word she says! Misfortune follows her, and it won't be long before it finds you, too, if you spend enough time around her, believe me!"

"Oh, eat your heart that the river had a lovely gift for me, but only snakes for you!" I cried out. But both she and I could see Maruna had already won him over. Resisting what he believed was his calling proved simply too much for Saval. And understanding that he was being played by someone shrewder than himself certainly did not fall within his range of skills. Having arrived at a decision, Saval closed in on the chest of snakes, which had gone still. A low hiss of warning sounded from within, but for a reason known only to itself, the chest remained rooted in place.

Saval circled the chest warily, then prodded it with his blade. Before I could warn him against getting too close, the chest sprang open, clamping down with a snap that tore the sabre from his hand. Saval yelped and reached into his shirt's pocket as if to draw another weapon. The hissing, which had quieted, resumed with new intensity.

One snake lunged, but Saval slashed it mid-air with a dagger he produced from his shirt. Another followed; he struck again. The third, wiser than the rest, paused, watching.

The hissing inside the chest quieted. And then, cold eyes

fixing Saval, three more bodies slithered out. Maruna retreated hastily to the first line of trees. After witnessing Saval sever the lamia's three heads with his precise slashes, I had little doubt he would take on the snakes just as capably. That was, until one of them spat a thick green liquid in his face.

Saval howled, a pain-infused scream of agony. The dagger fell from his hand as he lifted it to frantically wipe the liquid from his face. His weapon flew discarded into a bush while he tried to scrub the snake venom with his shirt. Maruna faded into the forest, leaving me with Naiya's distressed neighing and Saval's quickly blistering face. The venom ate into him with unnatural speed. He rubbed it off with a sleeve, and where cloth met venom, the liquid devoured it like a starved beast, patches of cloth burning with a hissing sound. The snakes wasted little time. One of them lunged again, intending to kill.

If I didn't interfere soon, Saval was doomed. The petrification that gripped me finally loosened. I plunged my hand into my bag for Nana's dagger, but feared it was too late. By the time I had the dagger in my hand, the snake had already clashed with Saval's chest and bounced back with a pained hiss. Expecting his tunic and flesh to begin dissolving from the dripping venom, I screamed with frustration. To our shared surprise, Saval stood unharmed. Hope flickered across his face. The other two snakes slithered closer, eager to have their turn. Thoughts swirled in my mind, desperate to figure out how his chest had been impervious to the otherwise deadly poison.

Then I saw it: the faint gleam beneath his torn tunic. "Silver!" I shouted, flinging the dagger towards him.

Impossibly, his hand closed around the dagger, despite my awkward throw. He lunged towards the snake just as the creature went for his face. It took a single slash to sever its head, and the snake fell lifeless to the ground. Another slash, and the second snake, with no time to slither away, got pierced through the head. I had to avert my eyes when its two severed halves kept twitching as if itching to be reunited. Once the body was immobile, a hush fell over the scene.

After witnessing the fates of her two friends, the last snake recoiled, going back to the chest. Saval never let his eyes wander off his opponent as he slid off the tattered shirt from his shoulders. The chain underneath had frayed in a line that ran from his neck to his navel, splitting the vest in two. Saval shrugged it off and caught it mid-air before it fell to the ground. With a single deft move, he threw the chainmail over the snake, trapping it before it could slither back into the chest. Saval covered the distance between him and the snake in one stride and grabbed the chainmail.

The snake spat droplets of venom that left the chainmail sizzling, but Saval twisted the mail around its head before it could burn through. The hissing and thrashing stopped shortly. The would-be knight let out a sigh of relief, and our eyes met briefly. He nodded, and for a moment, mutual understanding sparkled between us. Together, we gingerly stepped to the chest and peered inside. Its empty insides glared at us from its gaping maw, the foul stench rising from within the only clue something nasty had been dwelling inside.

"Good thinking on your part. With the dagger," Saval said with a ragged breath.

"Thank you, but it was all you in that fight. You dealt with the snakes rather capably."

"I take it, unlike the lamia, you don't consider them your friends?" He smirked, dispelling the tension. The foul smell intensified, and Saval wrinkled his nose in disgust.

"The venom animated the chest," I said. "It must lose potency once exposed to air."

"How do you know so much about such unnatural things?" asked Saval, the warmth in his voice all but gone as he drew the sign of the cross across his chest. I tasted something sour on my tongue at his words. People like Saval and Maruna, instead of being grateful that this knowledge had saved their lives, seemed intent on making the person pay for any bit of wisdom that went against their own beliefs. Most of what I knew came from Nana's stories. The hero that killed the hala had possessed a silver dagger, a detail that was sealed in my mind from the countless times I'd heard the story.

I shrugged, ready to dismiss his remark, but the sudden tension behind Saval's shoulders told me he had fallen back to regarding me with caution. I wanted to blame Maruna's influence. Brief as it had been, its mark on Saval stung much like the snake's bite. Just then, a rustle of leaves announced Maruna's return as she emerged from the line of trees. She didn't even bat an eye as she flung herself towards Saval.

"My hero, I knew you would save me from the vile creatures. You have my gratitude, my knight."

Saval's cheeks reddened, and he muttered that it had been nothing, really, for he was simply performing his duty.

"Not nothing, my knight. What you did was a true hero's feat. And to think that Jasna sided with the hala that cursed me with those horrid creatures!"

He raised an eyebrow at me and said diplomatically, "This must be a misunderstanding between the two of you. I should steer clear of it."

"It's not," I said, unwilling to play along with Maruna's pretence. "You have obviously taken a fancy to Maruna for whatever reason only known to you, so you might not believe this when I say it, but she isn't good. And what I've discovered in the past few days since going through a portal, partly thanks to this excuse of a person, is that hala – or lamia for that matter – can be good or bad. Just like people. And the hala we met did not side with anyone. She merely let the river give us a gift that reflected our souls. Hers was black as the night, and brought her a chest of venomous snakes. Let that speak for itself."

Maruna's face had also gone as red as Saval's, though for a different reason. She looked like she would love nothing more than to claw my face as she snapped, "Why can't you act normal for once, Jasna? Always different, always special, obsessed with ungodly stories and unnatural beasts. No wonder Iliya left, even he knew you never truly loved him."

Saval crossed himself again. Maruna's last words made my heart go cold. I didn't want to admit it, but I had been questioning whether Iliya truly needed my help. I tried to convince myself that it was nothing more than Maruna's ugly attempt to get at me. Yet, her words still hurt; the thought that Iliya never returned because he didn't want to see me, echoed my own fears. But I wasn't going to let Maruna know how deeply her words had cut me.

"Oh, and you are here because you hate everything that has to do with witches and the unnatural? How come you jumped into an ungodly portal so eagerly?"

"Why, that was merely to make sure you got your comeuppance, Jasna," Maruna said, a thin smile playing on her lips.

"Of course you did. You couldn't bear the idea of not ruining anything good that came my way. You had to go against everything you stand for – which, let's face it, isn't much – even if it meant going through a portal to make sure you prolonged my suffering. You are vile, petty, and small," I all but spat at her. "And this quarrel is ridiculous and stupid."

"I think it's time for you to go," Maruna said coldly. "We

want nothing to do with you. Have you not seen it yet? Wherever you go, misfortune follows. Take your evil ways and beasts with you, and use your witchcraft to get as far away from us as possible."

I looked at Saval, but he firmly avoided my eyes, busying himself with bandaging his blistering skin.

"Look, my mother always said not to have dealings with a witch," he said at last.

"The same mother who bedded a creature of Syanka?" I snarled. Saval's neck reddened, but Maruna had no intention of missing her chance.

"You're not welcome here, witch," she said, eyes greedy with excitement. "Go. Away."

"You are acting like a child," I replied, yet I couldn't help but feel like one myself when my eyes welled with tears.

Maruna gave me that look of hers, the one that combined both pity and disgust, which she had mastered just for me. A sadness like bile lodged in my throat and burned my stomach. Without giving my next action further consideration, I stepped by the dying fire, grabbed my bag, slung it across my shoulder, recovered the dagger from the snake's lifeless body, and walked away. Naiya, who had miraculously remained where I'd left her, neighed softly as she heard me approach. As I patted her, I noticed my hand tremble from all the emotions I was trying to contain. Embarrassment, above all, that I had not faced up to my childhood bully, but also resentment. Saval's easy belief in my wickedness stung, and though I hated to admit it, Maruna was right about one thing – perhaps I never loved Iliya beyond a friend.

"You will pay for it, Maruna, one way or another," I whispered before climbing on Naiya's back and riding off into the darkness.

CHAPTER 18

AN EERIE VOICE SPEAKS A WARNING

Naiya, who by now had grown used to following the red thread, did so even in the dark. As for me, I was able to locate it only when dawn paled the sky. My thoughts, a tangle of confusion, kept going back to Maruna's words.

"Now is a time as good as any for some truths," I told Naiya. She snorted in what I took for an agreement. I sighed. "Iliya deserves better than half-truths. I love him, and sharing my life with him would be the greatest joy, but I cannot give him what he truly wishes for."

My thoughts turned to my mother, who had died giving birth to me. Each year, at least two women in Morava met the same fate. It tripled in a bad harvest year. With people leaving for better prospects and men taken as blood-tax, the town was shrinking into a desolate village.

I refused to share the fate of those women and risk my life

giving birth to someone I might never meet. My mother's death had sealed that. Marrying Iliya and having a family was his desire, not mine, and if I ever saw him again, I knew I owed him the truth. But first, I had to find him. The thought lent me a brief burst of strength before exhaustion caught up; sensing it, Naiya halted and refused to continue.

"Always looking out for me," I said to her drowsily. An idea struck me as I absentmindedly stroked her mane. "Zhar will know what to do. He understands I have to get Iliya back, yet he's been hiding things from me. We need to press the zmei for answers on how to find him instead of blindly following a thread. What do you think?"

Naiya neighed softly. I took it to mean another agreement. That night, I slept on the hard forest floor with next to no protection, hoping that Gorovoi's domain stretched there to offer shelter. Sleep came surprisingly quickly. So fast did it descend upon me that one moment I was wishing I could speak to Nana and hear her advice, and the next one I found myself in Zhar's prison.

"If I am here now, move freely and see your prison the way it is, why can't I rescue you from the comfort of my dream? Will it work?" I asked Zhar with a hint of desperation the moment the dream solidified. Maruna's words still lingered at the back of my mind. Suddenly, an oppressive urgency told me I couldn't waste any more time. How long had I been in Syanka? Three days? Longer? What if a year had passed back in my world?

"Jasna, calm down. Breathe," came the familiar voice of the zmei as he emerged from the darkness. "I sense your heartbeat is abnormally fast, even for a human."

"I need to get Iliya. Enough with this meandering around. Tomorrow I find you, no matter how far you are."

"Would that it were so simple," said Zhar and a shadow fell

across his face. "The key to setting me free is finding out who my captor is."

"I don't have the time," I said more pointedly than I'd intended. I willed Zhar to understand. Last night had changed something, giving my journey an urgency that twisted my insides with icy fingers. Zhar's next words came out in a growl, a low rumble that reverberated through the cave and shook me to the bones.

"Are you saying what I think you are saying? Have you changed your mind?"

I paused, uncertain how to unravel the thread in my gut that demanded I find Iliya. I needed the zmei to help me get to him, yet there was no time to spare.

"And how long will it take to find you? Months? Weeks? What will the time spent here mean in my realm? Nana's tales always cautioned that time passes differently here than back home. I'll come for you, this I promise, but I need to find Iliya and my shadow. For all I know, every hour here steals a day in my realm."

"Need I remind you of our deal?" the zmei said, exhaling a threatening puff of smoke. "You don't want to make an enemy out of me, little worm."

"You are right. I don't. I just want to find Iliya. He might be hurt, if at all alive, and I have been keeping the truth from him for so long. But I had to be honest with myself first. Had I known, we would have never reached this point. He would still be in Morava, and I–"

"Would have no shadow or be dead altogether?"

I had expected the zmei to continue with his threats, but he suddenly seemed weary, and for the first time, I noticed the toll his imprisonment had taken on him. His scales had lost that shine with which they had reflected the torchlight, and instead appeared dull, much like the dimmed mischief in his eyes.

Specks of fire flickered from Zhar's breath and whirled around. He was right, I needed him. Moreover, I had committed to finding him first. The next time I spoke, my words came out evenly.

"Time is not on my side. And I have been wasting it. I can't bear to spend another day wondering whether I'm too late. Every moment I linger in Syanka, something puts me one step forward and two steps back. I've had enough setbacks, and I need to go to Tsargrad. I owe Iliya that much. Give me something to shorten the journey or a clue about who imprisoned you. You must have learned something by now."

My desperate plea did little to convince the zmei. A brief moment of hesitation that flashed across his face was the only indication he had considered my words. I grew increasingly convinced he hid something from me.

"You need to trust me, Zhar. All of this is for nothing if you don't. I forgive you for not telling me that using the potion would alter the red thread's course, but that means I won't tolerate any more secrets between us."

Just then, an invisible wind blew a sigh on my skin. I would have paid little attention to it, had the cave's air been less stifling. But so it happened that when air met skin, I was watching the zmei. It was why I saw him stiffen, his nostrils flaring as if to catch the scent of someone I could not see.

"This can't be true," he muttered to himself. "I sense her, yet she's been gone for so long. What kind of sorcery is this?"

"Zhar, are you speaking to me?" I asked, growing apprehensive. The zmei sniffed the air and closed his eyes, as if recalling a familiar scent. Just then, the dream shook. I tried to grab one of the cave's more jagged edges that lined the wall, but failed. The vision shook once more, and I knew I was about to wake. Just before I blinked my eyes open, the air carried a distant female voice to my ears.

"Ah, you're so close to finding him, beautiful girl, but he's not yours for the taking. I sense the one hunting you has caught your scent. Too bad, I need you both to free me..."

The voice waned, and the cave's heat leeched out, replaced by the forest's hard floor. With that, the dream ended as I jolted upright, tired and shivering. A fine layer of frost coated the ground. My breath steamed in the cold, and my body refused to move until I'd worked some blood back into my feet. I dug out the last slice of bread from my nearly empty bag. The bread was stale and stone cold, barely food at all. I gave it to Naiya, who bumped my shoulder and sniffed it with interest.

"Here you go," I patted her fondly and was rewarded with a moment of serene contentment where no zmei, Vizier, or Maruna existed.

With a sigh, I climbed on Naiya's back. Her body soon shared its heat. Last night's sleep had brought little relief, so I spent the day brooding as the sun trailed our journey. The red thread wound along the path, sometimes vanishing as if to toy with me. All the while, my stomach growled and my thoughts turned to the female voice from my dream, wondering if she was Zhar's captor. One thing was certain; Zhar knew her. An old-time nursery rhyme came to mind.

"Soaring high into the sky,
The zmei's looking like a tiny fly.
Something missing he is searching for
The glass eye of the wizard bound his soul in times afore."

"That's horse waste," I muttered, then added quickly, "Sorry, Naiya."

She halted, which I took as a sign that my apology was not enough.

"I said I was sorry!"

Then I saw the reason why she'd paused. We had left the forest, and the horse was standing on the last patch of grass just before her hooves were about to hit the sand. The red thread ended there. Ahead stood what at first I thought to be a large rock formation, but a glance upwards revealed an opening just below a jagged top that curved outward like a giant claw. I knew with certainty the cave could be only one thing. I had found Zhar's prison. Between me and the zmei's confinement, the beach sprawled its sandy toes, and on my left side the sea waves lapped at the place where Zhar was held captive.

It was the first sea I had ever seen, taking shape only once I fixed my eyes on it. Waves crashed into sand, the scent of salt sharp on the air beneath a purple sky and a fading crescent moon. I slid down from Naiya's back.

"This is where I needed to get to," I told her as I used my fingers to comb her mane. "Thank you for helping me and for always being so good. I don't know what your journey onward will look like, but I know it's going to be worthy of its own tale."

She neighed softly, lowered her head, and gently bumped her nose to my forehead. I put my arms around her neck and buried my face in her mane. In truth, I wondered whether Naiya would blink out of existence like the darting bird that had changed the thread's course.

"I hope you are happy, no matter where your path leads you," I said hoarsely and, with a last pat on the back, sent her trotting back to the forest. After she disappeared between the trees, I stepped on the beach, leaving Gorovoi's domain behind.

Sand shifted under my feet as I crossed the beach to the rocky formation. The sun hung high, stripping the beach of shade. It was the otherwise cloudless day that tipped me off that something was wrong. When I lifted my gaze and squinted against the sun, a winged shape eclipsed it. For a moment, I foolishly believed it to be an angel. Then I remembered that there were no angels in Syanka, and my hand shot to the dagger in my cardigan. My heart sank. There was only one thing the shade could be. A hala. She ploughed through the air with determination that said she was out for blood. The woman's voice from Zhar's prison echoed in my head.

The one hunting you has caught your scent.

My heart leapt from my chest and into my throat as I frantically considered my options. Returning to Gorovoi's domain meant I postponed the inevitable. The hala would be waiting for me the moment I left the forest's safety. My only choice was to make a run for the rocks in hopes I could find a hiding place.

I picked up my pace, my trot turning into a run soon after. The creature's silhouette drew closer. I ran until my lungs burned and my legs buckled – still, the hala's shadow grew larger. All the while, my thoughts raced ahead of me. If she'd found me so easily, my scent must be plain to every creature in Syanka, especially outside Gorovoi's domain.

Then a shriek tore the skies in two, warning me that she would be descending. Despite the fear fuelling my frantic run, I was soon out of breath, and not long after, my pace slowed and did not quicken, no matter how much I willed my legs to move. That was when the creature dove from the sky, and I knew she was the same hala that had hunted me back in Morava.

CHAPTER 19

CHERRY BLOSSOM, SILVER CHAINS

I was still too far from Zhar's confinement when she made for the ground. I could feel the parting of wind from her wings, so close was she now. With a cry of triumph, the hala circled above me like a vulture closing on its prey.

We both knew I had nowhere to hide and no means of defending myself, so she let me stagger towards the rocky formation for a while longer, like a cat chasing a mouse for the pure joy of the hunt. When I neared Zhar's prison enough to have a spark of futile hope ignite, she landed before me, her wings sending grains of sand flying around. A small smile tugged at her lips. I dared not move.

"You should have known better than to hide. I would find you eventually."

Her voice sounded sweeter than the muffled noise I'd heard when I'd hid in Nana's cupboard. Nothing sweet lurked

160

behind her hungry stare, nor in the long claw-like nails ready to sink into flesh. When I spoke, I did not hide my desperation.

"Was my shadow at the well not enough to sate your hunger?"

She sniffed the air in anticipation and took a step closer.

"Ah, I remember it well, the day of your grandmother's pitiful attempt at deceit. I knew she was keeping the true prize away, but there was no easy way for me to go around your house's wards. Still, the fates must be on my side to let me in on your scent. Neither your grandmother's charms, my sister's woeful attempts to wash out the dark magic's smell in the golden river, nor Gorovoi's protection, nothing could hide you from me for long. I shall enjoy devouring your essence very much."

"So there is no way I would come out of this alive?" I asked in hopes of buying some time. Her eyes reminded me of the sea at our side, except that a storm brewed behind them. Despite her next words, her pupils dilated with hunger.

"Alive? Of course you will be alive. I am not a monster, dear. Alive you shall remain. But soulless – for the dark magic clings to the remnants of your soul like a disease only I can cure. Would that not be preferable to you, to have no darkness haunting you?"

"Preferable to having no soul? Then I'm better off dead. I wonder then what it is that makes you less than a monster because I don't see it."

The hala paid little attention to my harsh words as she took another step towards me, her lips twitching in anticipation. Her wings, still spread, folded around me.

"Stay still, girl," she said almost gently. "This won't take long and it won't hurt. I promise."

Under her wings' embrace, a hush fell. The sea no longer

lapped at our feet and the screams of the seagulls died down like a distant memory. For a moment, I wondered if losing my soul would be easier than living with the tattered thing I had left. It wasn't like having a soul had turned out all that well for me. The hala, the captor whose name I didn't even know, lowered her head as if to give me a kiss and, for a moment, I stood still. There was no way for me to wriggle free of my confines. Even if I tried, the slightest movement would alert her. Yet, I couldn't let the opportunity slip. My hand found the dagger inside my cardigan. All I had to do was draw it and use it, but I made no move.

The hala, as if having sensed I would not resist, curled her lips, exposing a sharp set of teeth, then inhaled my scent, her nostrils flaring with pleasure.

"Such powerful magic," she whispered. "Yet it carries a sweet scent. I shall enjoy it very much."

Her breath brushed my cheek as she leaned in, our faces getting uncomfortably close. Though by human standards I was tall, she still towered above me. Her breath smelled of cherry blossom. Our eyes met and for an instant, a spark of understanding flew between us. She lowered her lips to mine, eager to drink my essence. Her wings squeezed me tighter, her breath warm on my lips. Her eyes grew unfocused, and she was about to close them when something in mine must have told her I did not intend to lose my soul that day. But before she could react, I twisted my wrist free and drove the dagger straight into her belly.

As her shriek pierced my ears, I sank the dagger deeper until the hilt met flesh. The hala's grip around me loosened and her wings hung limp around her as she slumped to the ground. She whimpered in pain and we both stared at the blossoming wound, neither of us quite believing what I had done.

I reached for the dagger, but her hand clamped around my wrist before I could pull it free and my eyes met hers. In them, beyond the pain, I saw disbelief give way to the realisation her life was about to end. As her life seeped out, the truth that I had killed her struck me like a wave.

I slumped next to her, unable to tear my eyes away from her wound. Blood soaked her white dress, the stain spreading further as life left her body. Her hand gripped mine when I freed the dagger, now coated in blood, from her limp body. Then her hand slid away from mine, her last strength flowing out of her. The hala's laboured breath turned metallic with blood. All the while, our eyes remained locked.

"I should not have underestimated you," she gasped in between wheezing breaths. "Don't make my mistake and underestimate yourself."

I remained frozen, staring at her in shock. Blood soaked the hand I had used to retrieve the dagger, and I hastily wiped it on my cardigan. I was not proud of what I did next. Too ashamed to look at the hala and knowing that she had little time left, I fled. I couldn't face her dying, a reminder of what I had done, so I ran. Still, the image of her final moments remained etched behind my eyes.

Only once I reached the rocks did my racing thoughts slow down, at last allowing me to assess my predicament. If I wanted to reach Zhar, I had no choice but to climb the impossibly high rock, wet and jagged from the sea's touch. The cave, chiselled into the upper side of a steep rising rock, appeared almost impossible to get to and the rock itself was too slippery to find safe purchase.

I attempted to scale it anyway. I dug my fingers into the rock, but the sea's spray had turned it slippery. Each grip lasted only seconds before my hands slid free. I had to pause, so I hauled myself up to a small landing. My face burned with the effort, yet I saw no other choice but to continue. My cardigan was torn, and Nana's bag that miraculously hung around my shoulder seemed to be one tear away from falling into the sea below. Aware of the pathetic image I struck, I was, for once, grateful for the lack of witnesses.

My arms shook. I couldn't hold my weight much longer. The sun rolled across the horizon and the scant remnants of light reflected the rock's wet surface. Iliya's face flashed in my mind, a reminder that he counted on me to bring him back. The Grand Vizier's ominous words echoed in my head.

You will come to me of your own free will.

The warning blazed behind my lids when I closed my eyes. I had survived Syanka, its creatures and foibles thus far. A petty Vizier that craved my body did not scare me any longer. It was, in fact, his promise that gave me a second wind. I wasn't going to be another severed shadow in Yerleg's collection, and I wouldn't let Iliya perish under the Grand Vizier's cruelty.

With an undignified huff, I hauled myself up again, grabbing a jagged edge that pierced my palms. And then I did it again. And again. My palms bled, and the rocks dug into my flesh with sharp edges, but still I hauled myself up. When the moon was high in the sky, I finally reached the opening, drenched in sweat and with barely any strength left to stand, let alone face whoever it was that had managed to imprison a zmei. Apart from the throbbing pain spreading through my body, my empty stomach growled, reminding me how long it had been since my last meal.

Forcing my feet to move took my last speck of willpower as I entered the cave's mouth. Unlike my dreams, no light greeted me. Unlit torches lined both sides of the cave's entrance. A rapid chill ran through my body as I ventured in, tracing the walls with bleeding fingertips. Darkness enveloped me not long after. Almost immediately, a pungent smell assaulted my nostrils, and I came to a halt just before I stepped on its source. The tip of my shoe met something spongy that made a wet smacking sound upon contact.

A loud snap followed, and all the torches lining the cave's walls lit at once, much-welcome warmth filling the cave within moments. Unsettled, I wondered what had triggered the torches, but came short of answers. To my immense relief, the immediate surface appeared to be flat, with no edges or crags ahead. That sense of relief did not last long as I noticed what had produced the wet, squashy noise. The dried guts strewn across the floor formed a crude trail, as if something had dragged a meal deeper inside. I followed.

For once, I was grateful for the scant breakfast I'd had. My empty stomach heaved with disgust, and the stench grew even more unbearable now that I knew its source. I wiped my foot on a dry surface and hurried along before the last of my resolve had wavered.

I passed from one dark chamber to the next. When my fingertips brushed the wall, just like at the entrance, torches flared to life.

I thought my skin must be interacting with an enchantment, but the torches didn't ignite until a few moments had passed. In the third chamber, I finally noticed the bloody traces left by my fingertips, still raw and bleeding from the climb. Blood got absorbed into the wall like salve on skin. The wall pulsed faintly, and the torches flared. The observation sent a wave of uneasiness across my body as I stepped into the fourth chamber.

"At last," rasped the voice from my dreams. Exhaustion had stripped away its mockery, leaving only relief. The torches, already lit, needed no blood this time. It was by far the largest chamber, and Zhar was at its end. Thin silver chains bound his body.

He was somewhat different from my dream. His scales were brighter green with a hint of yellow. In tales, zmei loomed larger than men, but only just enough for the hero to prevail. Zhar was either an exception, or fairy tales downplayed zmei's true size. He filled the entire wall which he leaned against, his body stretching up to the cave ceiling. I swallowed my fear and resolved to approach him with reverence. As I neared him, his eyes opened, and I gasped with surprise. They were old and tired, not at all how I had seen them in my dreams.

Zhar's next words carried a note of amusement. "Why are you so surprised, Jasna? Did you not expect old age to catch up with an ancient being?"

"It's just that you look different from my dreams," I said, and the words rang hollow, even to my ears. Perhaps it was the flickering torchlight, but I thought the zmei smiled.

"In your dreams, you saw the version of me I remember myself as. That youthful me is long gone. My eyesight has been deteriorating for a while now, and my bones feel the hard floor chill like never before."

Old age gave him a layer of dignity I had not seen in my dreams. Yet despite his size, he appeared emaciated.

"Have you been fed at all while here?"

"Look around you, and tell me what you think," he grumbled. I glanced towards the guts that had mapped the way to him, and swallowed. When I didn't answer, he said with a sigh, "Enough sustenance has been provided so I don't starve to death."

"And you never saw your captor?" I asked, though I knew the answer. Zhar huffed, and a stream of smoke exited his nostrils.

"I haven't had any unexpected revelations since we last spoke. Enough dawdling. Get on with setting me free before she catches a whiff of you."

He was, once more, not trusting me with what he knew. Instead of pressuring him, I ignored the edge in his voice and focused on the task at hand.

"How am I meant to set you free?"

"Have you learned nothing from your time in Syanka? You seem to possess the ability to fend off lamia, hala, and befriend leshy. Setting me free would be child's play in comparison."

Once more, I ignored the edge in his voice. His chains reflected the torchlight with a glow as if winking playfully at me.

"I just wish the chains away. That's it, isn't it? Will it work on an enchantment?"

"Why don't you give it a try and see?"

So I did. I focused solely on the silver chains, wishing them out of existence. Nothing happened. All the while, Zhar regarded me impatiently but remained silent, his gaze urging me to keep trying. This time, I studied the torchlight and how the glittering chains reflected the flame. Though my attention was solely on the chains, my eyes grew unfocused, and the chains merged together before my unsteady vision. I imagined them dissolving, melted away by the fire. So focused was I on holding that image in my head that I didn't realise Zhar was whimpering until the noise echoed between the chamber's walls. My vision snapped back to the present, and horror and guilt tore at me as I watched the silver melting into Zhar's body. The chains dripped like wax, searing into his scales. Zhar's howl shook the cave, but the silver kept sinking deeper, as if his body itself was swallowing it.

"Jasna," he said, and that was all he could manage. His scales sizzled, and not long after, the stench hit me – not just charred scales but something almost sweet, like roasting marrow. My stomach turned. The image of the chains melting shattered in my mind. Still, even after willing them to stop, they continued fading into his skin.

"I'm so sorry, Zhar. Gods, what have I done?" I threw my hands in the air. I willed the chains to stillness, but the silver had already melted into the zmei's skin. Zhar trembled and howled as large, round tears rolled down his cheeks.

At last, the sizzling mercifully ceased, though the stench of burnt skin remained. After one last whimper, Zhar went quiet, though whether that was good or bad, I could not tell. Over and over, I apologised, but the zmei remained silent.

"Please. Is there anything I can do to lessen your pain?"

For a little while, we stayed in silence, Zhar's mind withdrawn to a place far away. Then he cocked an ear, as if listening for something. His first words to break the silence were not what I had expected. His voice came out rasping and sounded as if it cost him a great deal to speak.

"Your debt to Syanka and me is repaid."

"That's it? Look, I'm truly sorry that I hurt you. I still don't understand how magic works in Syanka and I can hardly wield it. I promise, I will try to do better next time."

He sniffed the air and tensed. In his eyes, I found apprehension, the pain of his burned skin giving way to a more pressing fear. He lifted his head and sniffed the air again, as if the stale cave had grown rank with a scent only he was privy to.

"What is it?" I asked, his fear rubbing off on me.

"You should leave. It's not your problem anymore."

"Excuse me? I'm risking both Iliya's life and mine to come and save you from whoever did this to you. I daresay it is my problem! Not to mention you promised you would help me get Iliya back. Or did you forget about our bargain?"

But Zhar hardly paid attention to my words. Instead, he stepped gingerly to the wall he had been chained against, and for the first time, I noticed the cave ended here. The way back was the only exit.

"No one was outside when I came in," I said, more to myself than to him.

"Just leave! Listen to me, girl. Head for the exit now."

A faint laughter stole between the walls' cracks and brought with it the smell of a spring meadow. The hysteria behind it offset any pleasant feeling induced by the laughter's jingle. My suspicion that the zmei was hiding something was about to be confirmed.

"You know who's behind this, don't you? You know that female voice that spoke before."

"I have a feeling that I do. Though that's impossible," he said as his massive body shuddered.

"You should have listened to him, pretty girl, and run. Not that there would be a place to hide." A female voice spoke, and a small, ghastly shape filled the entrance. She stole a brief glance in my direction before heading towards the zmei, who still huddled against the wall. All pride had leeched from his face when he held her image.

"Impossible," Zhar repeated, his apprehension now mixed with reverie. "How?"

The woman studied him. Her edges blurred, as if she were a reflection in a pool. Where she stepped, the torchlight dimmed, repelled by the cold emanating from her. When she addressed Zhar, it was as if her cold voice absorbed all the heat his burning scales had released.

"Hello, my love. Did you miss me?" she said at last.

CHAPTER 20

THE SECOND HEART

"*R*umina." Zhar savoured the word like a long-forgotten taste. He said her name with wonder, like reciting a poem to a lost lover. Rumina returned his astonished gaze with a cold one.

"How?" he asked again, and I had the sudden feeling I was an intruder, an unwelcome privy to a conversation long overdue. Her mouth was set in a pout that reminded me of the zmei's petulance, yet her icy stare hardly softened as she held Zhar's eyes. The zmei drank the sigh of her faded image as someone long thirsting for water in an endless desert. Their silent communion made me uneasy, the two of them seemingly unaware of my presence. Then the apparition's eyes slid to me and hardened once more.

"Have you replaced me with someone new already? She is, after all, young and so very pretty." Her velvet voice trailed off.

"Never!" Zhar exclaimed with sudden vehemence. "Not a day has gone by in which you haven't been on my mind!"

The air had grown uncomfortably stuffy in the time they had taken to measure each other up. My skin began prickling with the heat, and suddenly I struggled to breathe. The draft had stopped, as if no air came in. My heart sank, knowing that Rumina must have sealed the exit. Zhar remained oblivious to the lack of fresh air, as though the sight of her meant he was at last free. If I wanted to get out of the cave alive, I had to take matters into my own hands.

"Rumina, or whoever you are, trust me, I have enough things to resolve on my own without getting tangled up with someone like Zhar."

The apparition regarded me cooly. Zhar seemed lost for words, his eyes never leaving the ghost's, so I attempted to salvage the situation once more.

"We didn't know it was you who had chained him. I promised Zhar my help in exchange for his assistance in getting my betrothed back."

"*We?*" was all she heard.

"Look, it's clear that you two know each other–"

"Know each other? I'm certain my beloved here must have glossed over how we met, if he bothered mentioning it at all," she said. "To an outlander like you, it must seem impossible for a human to fall in love with a zmei."

"Or zmei with a human," Zhar grumbled. Rumina, or the ghost of her, ignored him. Though her white dress was tattered, it spoke of a higher status. Her once lustrous hair was now tangled in knots, giving her an even more wild appearance. When she next spoke, the story spilled from her lips as if it had been waiting for a while to be told.

"As fate would have it, I was no ordinary woman. Born the princess of all zmei, I received the three wise men's gifts – as all royal children did. But in doing so, I unwittingly paid a price for my parents' mistakes. You see, my mother, the queen, refused to marry the third wise man's son. She chose my father instead, and when the scorned son learned of it, he took his own life. Many years later, the day of the three wise men's gifts arrived. The first wise man gifted me longevity – I would not cross to the other side until age had touched my face, until brown spots marked my hands. This is why I linger still, unable to move on after my untimely death."

"The second gave me sight – the ability to see what others could not. This is how I came to love a gluttonous zmei, one others deemed beyond redemption. The last gift came from the man who blamed my mother for his son's death. He gave me the power to feel pleasures only granted to humans. But there was a cost: every fortnight, I would transform into a human for one day and one night. It was this one day in a fortnight that I had to bear the burden of being stuck in a human's body when the false knight found me. And I learned what it is to be a woman in a world shaped by men. That proved to be fatal."

Silence followed Rumina's story. Zhar kept his eyes on the cave floor, but that did little to hide the heavy tears rolling down his cheeks like beads. The air in the sealed cave grew more stifling with each breath. The implications of the knight finding Rumina in her most vulnerable moment rang in my ears. Her face, ghastly as it was, carried such sadness that it shattered my heart. For the first time, I noticed a wound, as if the hilt of a sword had struck the back of her head. Blood crusted around the dented skull.

"I failed you," Zhar sniffled. The sound of his defeated voice brought tears to my eyes.

"It is done," she said, her voice harsh. "And you have moved on to someone better."

"Jasna? I'm helping her get her lover back from the Grand Vizier. Or was helping her before finding out that a part of you still lives. I would never do this to you, my sweetest. Two centuries might have passed, but my love for you still holds true."

"The Grand Vizier has her lover?"

I mumbled, "My betrothed. Not my lover."

"Tell me about it," she insisted.

So I did. When I finished, she scratched her nose with wraithlike fingers in a gesture that seemed more habit than itch.

"What a cursed thing being a woman can be!" Her voice grew bitter. "It was the lust of a man that killed me. And it seems it nearly killed you, too. Beware of what lurks in the Sultan's palace and use what skills you have to outsmart the Grand Vizier and his dark mage. You may go now and save your shadow and your betrothed," she said abruptly. She seemed sad, yet resigned to being left behind. I could not imagine a fate worse than being doomed to forever roam Syanka as a wraith. But Zhar was not ready to let go.

"My dear," he said. "I'm never leaving you again. How can I make this right? How can I help you move on to the afterlife?"

"Have you had enough of me already, to be so eager to be rid of me?" she asked playfully, but the sadness in her eyes remained.

"Never!" Zhar's vehemence brought a blush to my cheeks. Suddenly I missed Iliya, Nana, and the simple life we'd had. Rumina took pity on the zmei and elaborated with a gloomy smile that gave her face an even ghastlier air.

"To move on, I need my second heart to be destroyed. Yes, the tales are true. The firstborn royal zmei has two hearts to ensure their survival. The first one we are born with and the second one, forged by the first zmei that roamed Syanka, we receive at birth. Twenty hearts were forged, making sure they lasted eons. I received the last of those hearts."

"This is how zmei rule for so long," said Zhar, and his yellow eyes sparkled.

"Indeed. It's a secret known only to rulers, as the second heart keeps true-born monarchs invincible. Once one heart dies, be it of old age or in the unlikely event the zmei falls in battle, the second heart replaces it. Provided there's a body to do so," she added. That silenced my next question and extinguished the brief flicker of hope in Zhar's eyes. As it was, her body had been gone for centuries, depriving the heart of its host.

"So all I need to do for you to find peace is destroy your second heart?" Asked Zhar, somewhat despondent. "I'm not going to kill you... again."

"I'm already dead, my dear. You can't kill something that hasn't been alive for a long, long time." She gave him a ghost of a smile. "Though you will need help retrieving my heart."

Her eyes flickered back to me, and my chest tightened at the thought of yet another task keeping me from finding Iliya. My distress must have been clear on my face, for Rumina shook her head reassuringly.

"No, you don't have to go immediately. First, find your shadow and your beloved. Then help me. I have waited long enough as it is. A few more days won't hurt me."

"I'm not helping her," protested Zhar, much like a petulant child. "She nearly abandoned me here to rot."

"Oh, what a way to thank me for setting you free," I snapped at him. He stepped towards me menacingly, but I found my fear of him all but gone. After having dealt with the hala, I felt too tired to fear a half-starved zmei. My hand slid to the dagger tucked in my cardigan, and I waited for his next move. Rumina's ghost stepped between us.

"Don't be so pinheaded, dear. Would you not have done the same for me if my life was in danger? You would have forsaken everything to help me."

"This is different," he protested, but Rumina shushed him.

"How do we find your heart?" I asked, cutting in before the tension had worsened.

"Well, see… that's the tricky part. Its whereabouts are in a tiny chest–"

"Thankfully, I have acute eyesight," Zhar said.

"…in the deepest lake in Syanka…"

"Karasu," Zhar supplied.

"…in a glass ball…"

"A heart in a glass ball?" I blurted, uninvited.

"…in the belly of a monster to keep it safe," Rumina concluded.

"I can see how that could prove challenging," Zhar admitted. "I don't see why I need Jasna, though."

Luckily, Rumina's initial disdain and suspicion of me had evaporated. She now regarded me with sympathy stemming from our shared lot. When she addressed Zhar, her voice carried a honeyed undertone.

"Two centuries, and you haven't changed a bit. You need to understand that Jasna is her own person, and she still went after her beloved first while being held responsible for crimes she did not commit. You would have done the same for me." She paused and her eyes lingered on me fondly, as if the two of us were conspirators against a hostile world. "You need Jasna because only a woman can destroy the heart. A safety measure to keep usurpers – men and zmei alike – from claiming the throne."

"So it's the heart that tethers you here?" I asked. Rumina nodded.

"It pains me that we have to do this," said Zhar. Reluctantly, he emphasised the word 'we,' which hopefully meant he had set aside any hostile intentions.

"It's the only way, my dear," said Rumina, and as her gaze held Zhar's, her eyes softened, and I thought I glimpsed something of the old Rumina, unburdened by her tragedies. She was hauntingly beautiful with her serpentine green eyes and ghastly skin; I wondered what she would have looked like in her true zmei form. Just then, a breath of fresh air touched my skin. Not realising how much I had needed that, I inhaled a large gulp of it. It filled my lungs, scattering away the mist that had dulled my thoughts.

"I've opened the way. Go and find your companion. And Jasna," Rumina murmured, stepping closer until her cool presence brushed against me. "Never let other people have a say in what you do with your time on earth, let alone determine your self-worth."

Her words echoed those of Nana and Gorovoi, and I found that a part of me was finally starting to believe them. I wanted to tell her that I wished things had turned out better for her. But before I did, a thought that had gnawed at the back of my mind finally took form. Something about her holding Zhar captive made no sense, and I finally knew what.

"You made all this possible," I said. She raised an eyebrow, and I thought I detected an air of mischief about her. "You were never jealous of me. You only let us believe that. You needed someone – a woman – to destroy your heart. Someone you could trust."

"Did I now?" she asked softly. Zhar looked at her with quiet pride, as if he had expected nothing less.

"You held Zhar confined so he could form the connection with me after the dark mage's spell left a trace of me and linked us. And now that I'm here and you've heard my story, you know I will help you."

Rumina's eyes were lit by the lingering torchlight. She did not need to confirm my words for me to know they were true. In the end, she inclined her head in acknowledgement.

"I tried other ways," she said defensively. "I sent a dear friend, the lamia who kept me company for a century, to find Zhar before I was forced to imprison him, but she never returned."

I didn't have the heart to tell her the lamia's fate, so I steered the conversation away.

"Once we find Iliya and my shadow, we will find your heart, and you will rest in peace," I promised.

CHAPTER 21

PEARL AMIDST PEBBLES

I gave Zhar and Rumina a moment alone. On my way out, I thought of what love meant to them and what mine for Iliya was. For I did love him. I loved him as my dearest friend, someone I wanted to share my fondest memories with. But not in the way Rumina loved Zhar, and most certainly not romantically.

Outside, the moon and the infinite blanket of stars shone with a brightness that put my realm's night sky to shame. A chill ran through the air, though for once I did not mind after the cave's stale and stifling breath.

When Zhar emerged, his glistening eyes were the only hint of what had transpired between him and his long-lost love. Once outside, he drank the crisp air even more eagerly than I had. Then, after he'd savoured his newfound freedom, he spread his vast, sinewy wings, turned towards me, and said, "Well, hop on then. What are you waiting for?"

I regarded his scaly body suspiciously as I clambered on.

"A saddle would have been nice," I muttered, my teeth rattling in the cold air.

Zhar snorted. "What zmei would ever be saddled like a horse?"

As he said this, he spread his wings and took off, forcing me to grab one of the spikes that ran all the way from the centre of his neck down to his tail. Riding a zmei was, bluntly put, bruising. Scales lined his spine, making the ride worse. My thighs chafed where his scales rubbed against my skin, even through my clothes. Once airborne, I had to ask Zhar to slow down as the wind continually slapping my face brought tears to my eyes.

"You'll get used to it," the zmei said gruffly, but heeded my request. From up high, I saw Syanka's realm with new eyes. It stretched before us, lush with forests. Lakes dotted the surface, reflecting the moon with a silver glint.

"How do we get out of Syanka?" I asked, my voice barely rising above the noise of flapping wings. He either ignored me or did not hear me at all. The zmei seemed to be driven by some innate purpose as he ploughed into the sky, oblivious to my struggle to remain planted on his back.

"You aren't flying to the Vizier's palace, are you?" I shouted, the wind that slapped my face stealing my voice. Zhar grunted in confirmation. "You are destroying Rumina's heart first. Do you even intend to go to Tsargrad?"

"Don't be foolish, it will take but a day. What's that compared to the time that Rumina has lost?"

In my experience, it took more than a few hours to get through the hurdles Syanka threw at me, but if I wanted him to fly me to the Vizier's palace, I had to find a roundabout way to convince him to do so.

"How did Rumina fall for someone so testy?" I asked instead.

"You know, to this day, I cannot tell you why," Zhar replied, the fond memory giving a softness to his voice. "I once visited a feast in her honour, thinking only of indulging in costly foods and wines. And there she was, shining like a pearl amidst sea pebbles."

My teeth rattled once more, this time in agreement as the zmei went on.

"And she never treated me like someone lesser, nor did she despise me the way others did. We would talk about distant lands and realms, and she would admire my adventures, always eager to hear more. Funnily, I used to joke I was her curse. Though perhaps," he said, sobering up, "in a way I was. That knight would never have dared come close to her, had she not run away with me."

His voice trailed off. That was the most I'd heard him speak, and for once, I felt at a loss for words.

"It's not your fault," I croaked at last. "A curse is a curse, and trouble would have found her no matter what."

"Alas, you may be right," the zmei sighed. "I'm not certain if that should bring me any consolation."

Having decided he had shared enough, with a flap of his wings, he sped up, cutting through the sky with fierce delight. In the silence that followed, I considered what a blessing it would be to stay in Syanka, the place of wild magic and untamed creatures, and learn more about it and those who called it home. After all, what did I have to go back to? Risking being burnt alive for crossing the wrong people? But no, I could not leave Nana on her own and I had to find Iliya first. At the thought of Nana's fragile health, my heart longed to see her and make sure she was looked after. I worried she would be left with no water, and that the loss of this year's harvest would leave her starving.

Ahead, the sky paled as the sun heralded the new day's beginning. Cold air mixed with raindrops still beat down on my face when Zhar descended towards one of the mountains' peaks dotting the surface below.

"Is this it? Is this the place with Rumina's heart?" I asked, as he landed heavily. My stomach chose this moment to remind me how hungry it was with a long, mournful rumble.

"This is the place. But first, we both need sustenance," the zmei said.

Despite his size, Zhar proved to be an efficient hunter. A growing number of small animals – two rabbits, a squirrel, a finch, and a nutcracker – lay at my feet in no time. After taking my pick with a rabbit, Zhar gulped down the rest and used his fiery breath to char the rabbit's meat. He blew a narrow, focused jet of flame that would have worked fine had he skinned the rabbit before cooking it with his breath.

"I forgot. It's been so long since I made something edible for humans," he apologised as bones crunched between his teeth.

"How did you learn to crisp meat so flawlessly?" I wondered. "I can't imagine that you need to have it cooked."

"Rumina required human food for the one day in a fortnight she had to spend as one."

"But how do you control the fire?"

"I stop the stream as soon as I exhale," he said patiently, with a haughty air as if explaining to a child.

"I didn't even know zmei can breathe fire. None of Nana's tales mentioned that."

"We mostly can't. Most of us, at least. Why do you think every human court desired me as a guest even as they hated me for devouring their feast?"

"Oh," I said, never having given it any thought. "In Nana's tales, zmei are rare and visit people only in their greatest time of need. Though, not much else happens besides the hero defeating the zmei. How come you can breathe out fire and the other zmei can't? Are there many of you to begin with?"

"You ask too many questions," said Zhar with a deep growl. "And we have little time."

I must have had a look of utter disappointment on my face, for he glanced at me and sighed.

"Fine, then. Each of us has a unique talent. Mine is fire. Rumina's is… was," he corrected himself and a note of sadness crept into his voice, "ice. She could exhale a stream of ice, and that's why her scales were bluish-green."

"And yours are yellowish-green," I supplemented, and he grunted in agreement.

"But not all zmei have such obvious gifts. Some have the power of healing, for instance. Others have impenetrable scales. Only… a few of us remain. We used to have a kingdom, but ever since the new religion embedded itself in people's beliefs, we have been less and less needed or invited. A lot of us simply went to slumber. Others faded."

"Faded?" I frowned. Zhar rolled his eyes.

"Must I explain everything? We die only if we happen to do so in your realm. In Syanka, when we fulfil our purpose, we become one with the earth and sky. We fade like a sigh in the wind."

"That's beautiful," I said, once more in awe of Syanka's wonder. Zhar's gaze drifted to the horizon.

"Beautiful is one word to describe it. But it could also be sad to lose someone you have known for centuries. After Rumina's disappearance, the kingdom grew smaller and smaller. No heir came forward to claim the throne. Bickering among her cousins led to many deaths. So now zmei are rare even in Syanka."

"I'm sorry." I wanted to pat his back, but decided against it upon seeing the zmei's scowl.

"Well, we can't change the past, but we can make one thing right." Zhar sighed, and two tendrils of smoke escaped from his nostrils and faded away. "Let's get that heart destroyed."

I nodded, though my body reminded me of all the aches that had built up throughout the journey. Killing the hala and then scaling the cliff had taken its toll on me. Though the bleeding had stopped, the pain had settled with a constant throb that did not let me forget even for a heartbeat that it was there.

In the end, some elderberries growing in the bushes surrounding the lake had to do. It hardly helped. I felt faint, perhaps from the thin mountain air, and forced myself to focus on the task at hand.

"Is Rumina bound to the cave?" I asked.

"Her ghost roams only in the confines of where her physical body has been."

That somehow made sense in Syanka's rules.

"Then all we need is to swim to the lake's bottom, hunt the monster, and carve it up?" I asked uncertainly. "I doubt it's going to be that easy. And what about the monster? Do you know what it is?"

It seemed a lot of sighing went on from Zhar's side when he had to answer my questions, but sigh he did as he explained.

"If the creature is what I suspect it is, it may cause you some distress to know what we must do next."

"You mean it will be distressing to gut a monster and search its insides for a heart," I summed up. "I can't deny it's gruesome, but growing up with Nana has taught me a thing or two. You should see her skin a rabbit with a single move."

The lake Karasu, though deep, was so clear and pristine that no creature living in its depths could have escaped our notice. I peered over the edge, but if anything stirred its waters, I did not see it.

"He knows we're here," Zhar said softly, his low voice still loud enough for any creature in the vicinity to hear, even if the large zmei casting an equally massive shadow had somehow escaped their notice.

"Care to let me in on whose guts we're prying your beloved's heart from?" I asked, trying to dispel the uneasy feeling that lodged itself in the pit of my stomach.

"It's a vodyanoy," Zhar said. "I'm sure of it."

Of course – I should have figured it out myself. What other creature from Nana's tales would live in lakes or rivers, if not a vodyanoy? Thankfully, vodyanoy were not benevolent; they lured people to their deaths. That made it easier to regard this one's imminent end as unfortunate, yet inevitable.

"That should not be an issue, then?" I said, relieved. "Coaxing it out and trapping it will be tricky, but after seeing you hunt, I know it's not impossible. If I need to do the actual gutting, I will. I gave my word I would help Rumina, and I intend to honour that word."

Zhar sighed once more and assumed that haughty tone he seemed to have reserved for me.

"It won't be that easy. The vodyanoy you find in your realm are corrupt things that lure their prey to rivers and drown it. This one is just a recluse who suffers from severe anxiety."

"What do you mean?"

"Well, he lives in the highest, most secluded place he could find to be by himself. No fish lives here, so he must be barely sustaining himself on small prey it catches outside the lake."

"I get that the creature is troubled, but I'm sorry if I don't feel bad that he isn't out there luring people to their deaths. I'm struggling to see what the issue is. And when did you grow a conscience?"

"I didn't," Zhar grumbled. "But I thought your misguided sense of justice might be in the way of dealing with the vodyanoy."

"I'll try not to think too much about it," I promised. "In any case, we're doing this for Rumina."

But I would be lying if I said I felt as sure of myself as I sounded. Anxiety, a feeling all too familiar, made me sympathise with the creature despite my better judgement. Fixing me with serpentine eyes, it seemed Zhar knew my thoughts as he said, "I will lure him out and kill him. All you need to do is search for the heart after he is dead."

"How will you lure him? By starving him?" I asked, hoping the answer was a resounding no.

"I've considered it," said Zhar. "But that can take a long time. I have no other choice but to drink the lake. It's a shame, having to destroy the most pristine lake across all realms. Though being incredibly thirsty somewhat eases my conscience."

"Of all times to discover you've got a sense of humour, it had to be now," I said and patted the zmei's side.

"That wasn't a joke. Most zmei are lucky to have one gift that sets them apart. I have two. Fire and great appetite. Though sometimes it's more of a curse, really."

"You mean gluttony?"

Zhar's teeth grated as he smacked his lips. "Is that what they call it in your tales?"

"Don't blame me. I wasn't the one who came up with the

tales," I said nervously. He stared at me with his unsettling serpent eyes for a moment, then his gaze shifted towards the lake and the tightness in my chest subsided.

"It's lucky for you that I have this talent, so you won't have to wait for months to lure him out. Vodyanoy survive in the harshest of circumstances." He grunted as he lowered his head towards the water and began gulping it down, the motion of his jaws producing a loud slurping noise.

Though I had no way of determining if it was true, there was little doubt Zhar was a large zmei, even for his kind. What I remembered from Nana's stories confirmed my suspicions. Still, as much as Zhar's belly could hold, and I was sure of its large capacity, drinking up the lake should have taken ten zmei his size. After he had sated his thirst, and the lake had gone down by a quarter, he paused.

"The cave Rumina had me trapped in wasn't exactly rich in food or water. I was thirsty," he added. Then, with no warning, his maw opened and discharged a hot stream of fire that singed the tips of my hair. The lake's water sizzled as the fire touched it and clouds of vapour rose into the sky. This time, the lake diminished at a much faster rate against Zhar's fiery breath.

"Won't the vodyanoy boil in this heat?"

"If I persist long enough," Zhar said between breaths. It took a few exhales of fire for the lake to come down to a bubbly pond, revealing muddy layers of earth that used to be its container. When only a thin layer remained at the bottom and reeds peeked above the water level, he stopped and continued gulping down the remaining water, unbothered by the heat he had induced. His tongue lapped up the pristine waters casually, revealing more and more of the bottom. Still, there was no sign of the vodyanoy.

"It seems we were wrong, and the monster isn't here," I

said conversationally. In truth, a growing part of me hoped it was so. While sweating under the heat, it occurred to me that the vodyanoy was likely a living being with thoughts and desires much like Zhar and me. Perhaps he even had a family living in the pond the zmei had all but emptied.

"You are doing something odd with your face," the zmei said. My hand instinctively felt for my cheeks, surprised to find them moist. "I knew you would back down."

"No, it's not that," I murmured. "I only wish to know why he's living so reclusively. Is it because of a tragedy or because he is so mean that no one can stand being around him? And even if that's the case, is that a reason to kill him and gut him?"

"What if he has feelings?" Zhar repeated in a mocking tone. "Jasna, get a hold of yourself. He's a creature doomed from the start! Do you think he doesn't know what he carries inside?"

"But–"

"The zmei is right," sounded a deep, sad voice. It came from the newly uncovered muddy floor, which stirred and rose. Soon two eyes peered at me and the zmei, the only clue a living being had been hiding in the mud. The rest of him, his small, round body and long, webbed hands, were brown with a greenish tinge, much like the mud he had been a part of just a moment ago. To say that he looked pitiful would be an understatement. His green eyes brimmed with sorrow. Even Zhar, for once, regarded him with pity.

"I have agreed to store her ladyship's royal heart until such time as she requires it."

"The time has come for her ladyship to have it back," Zhar snapped, wasting no time.

CHAPTER 22

THE HEART THIEF

The vodyanoy did not protest, but his thin lips trembled and his eyes filled with tears. My heart went out to him.

"There must be another way," I said, an idea taking shape in my mind. "I'll use whatever magic Syanka has granted me to will the heart out of you. Syanka has odd rules, but it has worked thus far. I did it with the zmei's chains, and I don't see why it wouldn't work for you. After all, if you are no monster like the stories claim, you shouldn't have to suffer for it."

The vodyanoy regarded me with those sad, round eyes of his as if I had gone mad. At first, he reminded me of the rogue domovoy I had encountered at the caravanserai. Though wider in girth, he was of the same height, his slimy, wet skin glistening under the sun. Unlike the domovoy, his webbed fingers betrayed a tendency to prefer life underwater.

The vodyanoy caught me studying him and did not hide

the disdain from his voice when he said, "You don't understand. I have carried this burden for so long. I desire nothing more than to be rid of it. What are you waiting for? Get on with it and cut me open!"

"We'll find another way," I said, wringing my fingers in desperation, but my words sounded more like a plea than reassurance. During this brief interaction, Zhar had gone suspiciously quiet. When I turned towards him, he was regarding the vodyanoy with a newfound interest that did not sit well with me.

"I've heard of you," Zhar said. "You are the vodyanoy who is loath to talk to anyone, terrified of his own shadow for fear of offending it."

"What are you talking about?" The words came out sharper than I had intended. In truth, I did not like what Zhar was implying. The vodyanoy, though clearly shy, still had the courage to speak to us. To my mind, being terrified of his shadow was yet another tale that had started out as somewhat true, then swelled like a river in flood until the final story bore little resemblance to how it began.

"There's more to it," the vodyanoy said. "You ever heard of the Dolen Harman?"

I shook my head, but Zhar stared at the creature in disbelief, and something like awe showed in his eyes. It reminded me of Zhar from the stories, the cruel glutton who held no regard for others. I did not like that in the slightest.

"That's not possible," he said. "You?"

"I was the one who lured the entire village to its death in the nearby river. At the end, its waters flowed red with the blood of the village people. For that, I have to repent every day of my miserable existence."

"Would you look at that, Jasna? You have the monster you wanted to slay after all," Zhar said slyly, clearly enjoying my growing discomfort. I chewed over the words, my mind refusing to believe this creature that barely reached my waist could bring ruin to an entire village. I was not ready to write the tiny man off without knowing more.

"Why would you do such a thing?" I asked. The vodyanoy sighed and opened his mouth, but Zhar answered instead.

"It's his nature to do so. Domovoy protect the hearth and vodyanoy lure people into the depths of their domain."

"The only domovoy I ever met was anything but interested in protecting anyone's hearth. He was a rogue who wanted only to feast on fear and anger. Why should your nature determine all your actions?"

"Because life is simpler than you make it out to be," said Zhar and thin smoke curled up from his nostrils. "Sometimes things are just the way they are and there is no deeper meaning behind them."

I ignored him and turned to the vodyanoy. "Your anxiety. How did you develop it?"

The vodyanoy sighed, and his murky eyes filled with tears.

"One day, not long after my deplorable deed, a witch passed by the village remnants. Not expecting to find it desolate, she set off to discover the reason behind its people's demise. Once she learned the truth, a snap of her fingers and a potion from her bubbling cauldron cursed me with consciousness. Until then, all I had known was the way of the vodyanoy, or how to prey on people. Not that what I'd done was an excuse. It was my nature, you see. But the witch showed me it didn't have to be this way. It was too late, though. Having this awareness felt worse than being on dry land with no water in sight. I have tried to repent as best I could since, but the truth that I ended an entire village remains."

"You tried to repent by hiding from everyone?" Zhar asked.

The vodyanoy sighed and lowered his sad eyes as tears rolled down his frog-like cheeks.

"By helping rebuild the village and inviting people to repopulate it," he said in a rough voice. "Though considering what I had done, nothing was enough. I became a recluse and now spend my days being too ashamed to face others. Now go on, hate me. I deserve it."

"So you can continue stewing in your own self-resentment? Give you what you want just like that? I don't think so," Zhar said, drawing ever so close to the vodyanoy.

"Why did you agree to hold Rumina's heart?" I asked, ignoring the zmei. The vodyanoy heaved a deep sigh and cast a dirty look at me that implied I was at fault for prolonging his misery.

"Because she promised death at the end. See, I was too much of a coward to do it myself."

"That's my Rumina, alright," said Zhar and a puff of smoke escaped his nostrils.

"Go on," the vodyanoy hiccupped and pointed at his chest. "One blow from you would be enough to end my miserable life."

"Jasna, I assume you agree we should put an end to that?" Zhar asked without sparing a glance towards me. I got the impression that he cared little for my reply. I hesitated. On one hand, the vodyanoy was a murderer; on the other, he knew it, and it tormented him.

In the end, Zhar didn't wait for my reply. He gave me but a heartbeat to agonise over finding a way out before lashing out with startling speed. A single claw slashed through the vodyanoy's chest. Zhar's eagerness should not have surprised me, yet both the vodyanoy and I stood frozen in the face of his cold-blooded murder, the disbelief only registering in the creature's eyes when the cut blossomed red. His round eyes, previously brimming with tears, seemed to dry up as if his death deserved no mourning. As his blood streaked down his naked body, mixing with mud, the vodyanoy turned his eyes towards me and whispered, "It was the only way. It's the way I wanted it."

As he collapsed, I grabbed his shoulders and lowered him down, easing the fall. Staring blankly at his glossy, unseeing eyes, I could not believe how quickly he'd gone from a living creature to a shell of what he had been a heartbeat ago. Anger stirred at the zmei's callousness.

"Well, what are you waiting for?" Zhar grumbled, oblivious to the anguish that tore me on the inside. "Take the chest out. Don't tell me you've changed your mind. Ugh, humans and their fickle nature."

He leaned down and prodded me with his nozzle. Thinking about what I had to do next brought a surge of bile to my throat. In a day, I had murdered the hala and was now about to gut a vodyanoy and fish his insides for a chest that contained a heart. Unabashedly, I leaned away from the body and emptied my stomach's contents onto the grass. The zmei grunted in disgust.

"Like I said – humans. Unreliable. Here, let me help you."

With that, he extended a claw and deepened the slash, tearing the vodyanoy's chest wide with little effort. I gagged, fighting back another wave of bile, and plunged my hands into the open chest. Nothing stood out in the bleeding mess. The creature's guts spilled out and a rotten stench filled the air. Unimpressed, the zmei prodded me once more.

"I don't see it," he said. "It must be hidden from the eyes of males. You will have to get your hands dirty and search for it."

"Give me a moment," I rummaged inside the vodyanoy's open chest. The once-beating heart was easy enough to find. My hands came out covered in slime and blood, but I gripped it tight. I held the heart out and inspected it, blood dripping between my fingers. It was heavier than I had imagined, and something green jutted from it, as if someone had wedged it there as an afterthought. It took all my willpower not to faint as I peeled the tiny chest from the vodyanoy's heart.

"Why did I not think it would be an actual chest lodged in his heart? Even you can't deny how disturbing this is."

"What is it?" Zhar asked and stared at my hands as if they were empty. I opened the grimy chest, and a tiny heart enclosed in a glass sphere stared back at me. Zhar inhaled sharply, which suggested he had at last seen the heart. After wiping my hands on my already muddied cardigan, I emptied the chest.

The heart pulsed inside the glass ball as if full of life. Both Zhar and I regarded it with awe. For a moment, we lowered our guard. That was all it took for a birdlike creature to sweep down from the skies and snatch the heart with its talons.

It all happened so fast. One moment, the glass ball pulsed in my fingers. The next, it was gone, snatched away by the creature as Zhar roared and cursed.

"On my back! Now!" He bellowed, but despite how terrifyingly deranged he looked at that moment, I had my feet firmly planted on the ground. I'd had enough of being dragged into other people's battles when I had to fight one of my own.

"I'm going to find Iliya. I'm not wasting any more time. You had my word that I will help you retrieve the heart, and I did. I think Rumina can wait until I save Iliya."

"You dare defy me?" He growled as he stared up into the sky, both of us painfully aware of the time we wasted arguing.

"I need to do this and I mean it. I need to go. Please understand."

He hesitated briefly, then bumped me with his head, which resulted in me stumbling a few paces.

"Hop on."

"I said I wasn't coming."

"Hop on."

"I said…"

"I heard what you said, and I won't take long. Now. Hop. On."

He kept bumping my side with his head throughout our ridiculous exchange. Aware that it wasn't our most dignified moment, I sighed and, with a heavy heart, clambered onto his back. My palms sensed his eagerness to take off, his skin pulsing with anticipation, but that did little to ease the heaviness that tightened my chest. Without further ado, the zmei spread his wings and took off.

The vodyanoy's blood was quickly drying on my hands when I used them to steady myself mid-air. Zhar's body bore the scars of the chains that had melted into his flesh, and my hand instinctively traced the line of one. The zmei shuddered, but even the remnants of pain did not deter him from chasing after the thief.

If the first ride across the sky had been bumpy, this one demanded all my strength and willpower for me to remain on the zmei's back. My eyes started watering almost instantly as we surged against the wind and the inside of my thighs chafed against the zmei's scales.

"How will you find the creature?" I yelled, but my voice was drowned out by the flapping of wings and the beating of the wind. I paused, thinking, while Zhar plowed through the air as if his life depended on it. The creature must be female if it could hold Rumina's heart, though knowing that did little to help in hunting it down. We soared just below the clouds, and his searching eyes, lowered to the ground, appeared to be following something. Shared tension emanated like a current in the air.

A few moments passed before I noticed the small white spot that appeared ahead of us. Then the spot grew into wings that fluttered rapidly against the current. As we closed the distance, I was finally able to see the bird for what it was: an ordinary eagle. Under any other circumstances, it would have looked massive and quite majestic. Next to the zmei, it appeared small and unimpressive. Impossibly, Zhar caught up with the eagle, despite the zmei's much larger and at first glance clumsy body. The eagle, sensing the tide turn in our favour, let out a panicked squeak and dived for the ground, the zmei at its heels.

"Don't kill her," I yelled at the zmei, but my voice got lost, carried away by the wind. Zhar plunged downwards without slowing down. The eagle's panicked flapping grew frantic, but with a final powerful beat, the zmei overtook her. Zhar ducked below the eagle and craned his neck towards the bird of prey. His jaws closed around the eagle's foot that clutched the heart in its talons. The bird continued the torrent of squeaky noises, pleading for her life. A gust of wind slapped me in the face like a wake-up call as my suspicion that the eagle was just a bird got reaffirmed.

"She doesn't know what she's doing, she just went for the shiny object she saw," I screamed at Zhar as his jaws all but swallowed the eagle. I nearly lost balance and slid off the zmei's back. Once I regained my purchase, I tried to climb up the zmei's neck and yell my message in his ear. His scales dug at my already raw thighs, every wingbeat peeling a layer of my skin. Unperturbed, the zmei descended, oblivious to my struggle, the frenzy of the chase giving him a bout of strength.

"Slow down! Slow down, Zhar! She doesn't know what she's doing! Besides, you will swallow the heart if you devour the eagle! We need to get the heart!"

He finally heard me, and his wings beat against the wind,

ending the near free fall. Unfortunately, in the meantime, the eagle had weighed her chances and decided her odds of survival weren't great. She craned her neck towards the zmei and her beak pecked at his eye. The zmei roared, setting the bird free from his jaw's grip. For a moment, the eagle sagged, drawn towards the ground. Then she beat her wings frantically and dropped Rumina's heart.

"See what you've done?"

For the second time, Zhar roared in frustration. The eagle did not make it far before he closed down on her in a last act of vengeance. His jaws snapped around her body, with her head the only part sticking out of the zmei's mouth. Then a wet, crunching noise followed, and the eagle went limp. With one gulp, the zmei swallowed the bird.

"NO!" I yelled again, but he was too busy diving towards the ground, as if he had any chance of finding the heart in the sea of green below. We were still a fair bit above the ground when I lost my balance. It happened right when Zhar swallowed the eagle and let out a streak of fire, catching me off guard. A heartbeat was all it took for me to lose my grip, slide down from his back, and plunge towards the ground. The wind had me in its clutches in no time, though that did little to slow down my fall.

I gave up on reaching for Zhar almost instantly. It became clear he wouldn't match my speed before the fall ended. Despite that, falling to my death felt endless. My heart pounded against my chest, but inwardly I felt calm, shock numbing what was to come. I was about to die and that was all there was to it. My mind went out to Iliya, and a wave of sadness washed over me when I thought I'd never know what had become of him. I had failed the only people that cared about me. I'd put Nana in danger and I should have been honest with Iliya about not wanting to marry him. At least with me dying, Maruna would get what she had always wished for – getting rid of me for good. The ground was so close now that I could see the individual flowers peeking shyly at the sun.

My thoughts ran back to Nana. She would have loved to see Syanka. Or perhaps she had already. There were so many things I didn't know about her and would never find out. The ground below was beautiful, lush with fields of green, yellow, and brown, all seasons coexisting together, hugging the silver path that led to wherever you needed it to go. With a last sigh, I closed my eyes and braced for the impact.

CHAPTER 23

THE ROAD TO TSARGRAD

Dying turned out to be much like hanging above the ground in suspension, though I had expected it to involve much less pain. After all, everything was said and done. I thought death would be weightless. Instead, my neck bent at an unnatural angle, blood rushing into my head. A horse's nicker, the roll of carts, and a soft chatter of distant voices – too far away to understand – had no place in what I thought the afterlife should be. Something coarse dug at my wrists and ankles as if intent on keeping me hanging mid-air. Part of me wanted to pretend I was asleep, still in Syanka, dreaming of my next adventure.

What convinced me to blink my eyes open against the blinding sunlight was that death and the afterlife still hurt, and I needed to know why. The first thing I noticed was that my wrists and ankles were indeed bound by a tightrope. I hung from a thick pole that connected two large carts pulled by a horse and a bull. In between, my limp body dangled like a piece of meat ready for roasting. Apparently, dying also involved a throbbing headache. I was no longer convinced my demise had been final.

The chatter paused, and I shut my eyes in time for the half-ripped curtains that fell on the side to part. A shadow fell across my face. I held my breath.

"She's still out," said a male voice with a strong dialect. The shadow dissipated and I could breathe again. *She's still out.* Those few words had given me more information than I could have hoped for. Unfortunately, that also created an equal number of questions. From the brief glimpse I had managed to catch of my surroundings, I was positive I was not in Syanka any longer. The colours, dull compared to the vibrancy of the silver path, reminded me of a half-finished drawing in the sand, washed away and lifeless. It was like the story went; once you had seen the silver path, you'd never be happy settling for something less. Except it hadn't been just a road, but an entire realm that I had stumbled into, one I ached to return to.

The man's dialect told me I must be close to Tsargrad, his speech southern like that of the merchants who visited Morava's market. Over time, the empire's three languages had merged into a common speech, its mixed words intelligible in part even to those who did not speak it. Even through the bits and pieces I understood, the question of why they had taken me captive remained. Binding me and leaving me to dangle under the scorching sun was hardly a sign of good intentions. And if they were travellers, the only reason they would capture and bind me was if they thought I would fetch some gold. My looks would bring a good price, so they would be fools not to sell me into service. To whom, and for what purpose, I had no wish to know.

The warm air on my skin and the blooming poppies told me it must be late summer, and the Grand Vizier's words echoed in my mind.

You will come to me of your own free will.

The slow pace of the carts gave me time to think of ways to escape. A growing chafing from the ropes that bound me soon turned into numbness. If only I had something sharp to cut through the rope... though that would have been useless, given I had no free limbs to do so. At some point, I remembered the sling bag Nana had given me, and for the first time I noticed its absence. With a sinking heart, I realised my chances of escaping were slipping away.

The journey continued at the same steady pace for the rest of the day. I drifted in and out of consciousness, my head too heavy to think. My throat and lips soon felt hoarse and dry, and a dull throbbing wedged itself in my limp head. The occasional chatter from my captors reached my ears, but despite my best effort, I still couldn't make out any of the words. From the voices that filtered through, I could only tell that the cart contained at least four people, one of whom was a woman and another one a child. After the sun had rolled behind the horizon and the last light was fading into a bruised purple, the carts stopped and three men, a woman, and a boy emerged.

"Still out," the woman said, and I almost sighed with relief until the boy exclaimed, "I saw her open her eyes earlier when she thought no one was looking! She's pretending, mother, I swear!"

"Well done, my vigilant one," the woman said, and I cursed myself for not being more careful. Someone prodded my arm, and I gave up the pretence. Dusk still coloured the starless sky, and a silver moon greeted me when I opened my eyes. Enough light slipped between the cloth draping the carts to reveal my captors.

All three men had sun-kissed, weather-beaten skin, black hair, and brown eyes, though that was where resemblance ended. White streaks of hair ran across the first man's beard and hair, and he had a calm presence that eased my nerves by a notch. The woman, though quite young, had an air about her that told me all major decisions went through her first. A fine scarf protected her dark hair.

"What is your name?" she asked in a thick accent, her words slow and careful, as if translated from another language. I noticed the boy – who closely resembled her – staring at me, so I smiled. He regarded me with a vacant stare, and I winced, shifting my gaze. We had stopped at a grove made of tall, lanky trees. The surrounding area looked secure enough for setting up a night camp.

"Speak, girl," one of the men prodded me when I failed to answer. I narrowed my eyes at him but kept quiet.

"You have nothing to fear from us," the woman said gently, though the warmth in her voice did not touch her eyes. One motion with her bejewelled hand was all it took for the man to leave the two of us alone, followed by his other companions. The woman untied the ropes that bound my limbs, first the ankles, then the wrists. Having gone numb from hanging the entire day, my body collapsed on the ground with a dull thump, completing my undignified introduction to my captors. The boy, who still watched from afar, sniggered, and the men smiled, suppressing a laugh.

The pain of blood rushing back in my head took over any other immediate concern. I gasped for breath and rubbed my feet and wrists while life flowed back, drop by drop. By the time I was able to stand, the three men had set up camp for the night. A fire soon crackled and, though the grove offered little protection from the otherwise bare landscape, it afforded the men the chance to spot any intruders from a distance, giving them time to ready themselves for uninvited guests. All the while, the woman waited patiently, her polite smile saying my presence was but a minor nuisance. Finally, she sighed.

"My name is Didar, if that helps."

"Jasna," I croaked with a voice that had been out of use for too long. Didar raised an eyebrow at the distance, still refusing to meet my eyes lest I continue acting like a frightened doe. I took the opportunity to study her. She was of small stature, yet had a way of commanding attention about her that left no room for negotiating. Her kaftan had a belt with pouches and flasks tied around it, weighing it down. She reached for one flask and untied it. Didar then handed it to me and urged me to drink. With blood still rushing to fill the veins in my trembling hands, I removed the cork top and downed the contents, grateful for the much-needed water.

"And what would a young and exceptionally beautiful woman be doing all by herself, lying unconscious by the side of the road?" she asked, her otherwise rough voice turning soft once more. With a start, I realised her question was a veiled way of asking if a man had discarded me there.

"It's nothing like that," I said hurriedly. "I was... well, you may find it hard to believe, but it was not my intention to wake up... here."

Wherever here was.

The last bit, even if unspoken, hung heavy in the air. Didar continued with the same soft voice, as if soothing a wounded animal.

"I can help you with your pain if someone's hurt you. I have herbs and some healing sap that soothe such aches. You only need to ask."

"You tied me with a rope and left me under the sun for an entire day, from which my wrists and ankles are still bleeding, and now you are offering to heal me?" I asked incredulously.

Didar finally shifted her gaze towards me, her dark eyes regarding me thoughtfully. When she spoke next, she sounded guarded, the pretence of softness all but leeching out from her voice.

"Men like to think they are in charge, especially when it comes to women's bodies. My brother, for instance, was the one that found you and thought, there's a beautiful girl in need I would not mind helping. He wouldn't say it himself, but I've had a brother, two husbands, and a father for long enough to know their thoughts. They either see themselves as the heroes or the conquerors, when in reality they are neither."

She paused, as if waiting for me to confirm her words. I returned her gaze, but said nothing. For a moment, Didar seemed disappointed, as if her speech was something that had been supposed to get me talking. She quickly regained composure and pressed on.

"Wait here," she instructed me, as if I had anywhere to run. She then disappeared inside the nearest cart and came back a moment later with some bread and sweets, which she handed over to me. Famished, I swallowed down all my objections to accepting food from my captor and bit into the bread. It tasted divine. Soft, perhaps even made this morning. It melted on my tongue and sent warmth through my stiff limbs. My stomach growled in appreciation.

"Thank you for sharing your bread with me," I croaked. Though grateful, I still did not intend to open up to her. Didar waited for me to continue, so I chose my next words with care. "As to what happened, I hardly remember. I woke up and found myself tied to your cart."

Her raised eyebrow told me she did not quite believe me.

From the middle of the grove where the men had set camp, the smell of roasted rabbit curled through the air, setting my mouth watering.

"You woke up just like that? What were you doing on the road by yourself? Surely you remember some of what happened. Were you travelling with others?"

"I was travelling alone to Tsargrad where my betrothed is. He is in the Grand Vizier's palace," I said coyly. Didar's focus did not waver when she shot back.

"Where is your accent from? You sound like you are from the northern parts of the empire."

"Vidna," I lied casually. Vidna was a town east of Morava, far enough to confirm her guess. My exact whereabouts were no concern of hers, and though I thought the lie wouldn't take hold, it did. Didar nodded as though it made sense, though Vidna was a town no bigger than Morava and equally obscure. I knew of it because it bordered the sea. It was where some of our seafood and other exotic foods Nana and I could never afford came from.

"And why is your betrothed in Tsargrad?"

"Come, Didar, dinner." The older man's shaky voice interrupted Didar's interrogation. She cast an annoyed look at who I assumed was her father, but did not argue. She motioned for me to follow as she joined the three men and the boy, all seated around the fire. One of the younger men remained on watch throughout dinner, dagger at the ready, as he fixed the road with his chestnut eyes.

"This is Jasna, from Vidna," Didar introduced me. The boy regarded me curiously, but his eyes remained cold. "She is off to Tsargrad to be reunited with her betrothed."

That produced a surprised look from the man who shared some of Didar's features. Her brother, I thought, the one who had supposedly found me and tied me to their cart. One look from Didar quieted whatever he was about to say. The men soon fell into a comfortable chatter, and the boy dozed off. Despite the need to stay alert, my eyes couldn't remain open when the warmth of the fire spread through my body. For a short while, all the pains that had accumulated throughout my journey dissolved, or at least numbed down, and I thought that perhaps not everyone was out to get me. Then Didar sent her son to the wagon, leaving the adults to talk, and proved me wrong.

"Here, have more," her brother said with a thick accent as he offered me a roasted apple.

"A pretty girl like you should not wander alone. Even with a skin kissed by the winds, you would fetch a nice sum," said Didar as she drew closer. She reached a bejewelled arm and ran her hand through the length of my hair. Her bracelets made a hollow clunk when they met, suggesting the stones adorning them were fake.

For a moment, my vanity took the best of me. I reached toward my face and found the skin less smooth than it used to be back in Morava. The adventure had taken a toll on me, and like Nana had warned, any beauty faded with time. Perhaps mine had come to an end earlier than expected. Didar stayed uncomfortably close, her wind-beaten face mocking my vanity.

"So that's what you intend to do with me," I said, unable to hold the bitterness from my voice. Didar's husband snorted, but her brother shouted something in a language unfamiliar to me. Didar hushed him with a finger, and despite glowering at her, he obeyed, and I could not help myself but admire her for the obedience she so effortlessly commanded.

"See, my brother, Baha, thinks it would be a waste to trade you for mere coins. Men and their fickle nature always come in the way of profit, though to be quite honest, I see why you would appeal to any man. This would hardly come as a surprise, but Baha is quite infatuated with you."

Despite the fire's proximity, an icy chill ran throughout my body. I avoided Baha's eyes as Didar went on.

"He would like to take you as his wife. He says it would lessen the burden of the road to have a pretty thing like you by his side. My husband and I, we are of a different opinion. We prefer dealing in coin. Even humble travellers like us should not mix with the likes of you when someone else might have a better use for you. So, as you can imagine, I tried talking Baha out of it. I said to him, desires come and go, dear brother. Have the girl for a night and sell her, make a profit. But once he'd seen you, there was no changing his mind. Men! The heart wants what it wants, I suppose."

I glanced towards Baha, who smiled at me shyly, unaware of what was being said. Even though I was the object of his desire, it wasn't him I feared, but Didar, who spoke with the cold calculation of someone comfortable holding other people's lives in her hand. Yet, as someone used to getting what she desired, my silence unsettled her. Her jaw tightened and she shot me a dangerous look as my silence stretched.

"Well, girl, what do you think?" she pressed. "Do you accept my brother's offer? It would be unwise to say no, given that you have no other prospects after the way we found you. You'd spare yourself trouble by agreeing... unless you want to get off on the wrong foot with us, that is."

"It's not possible for me to accept your brother's offer," I managed at last, and she cocked an eyebrow. Her father chuckled softly.

"And why is that?" he asked, addressing me for the first time.

"Because I am already promised. And though that seems no issue to you, there is someone else who will be displeased –

if not offended – to learn you have taken what he has already claimed for himself."

"Your betrothed? I doubt he'll miss you all that much after seeing what Tsargrad has to offer to a young man," said Didar, more amused than threatened. Her words picked at the scabs of the old wound Maruna had opened. I mustered all the courage I had.

"Why, Didar, you of all people must realise that it's not a single man whose heart I hold in my hands. After singing praise to my looks, you won't be surprised to learn that it's no other than the Grand Vizier himself who took interest in me."

A moment of silence followed, and I thought I might yet convince her that my words were true. Then laughter erupted from all sides. Didar and her father both chortled, and once the latter had explained the supposed joke, the other two men followed suit. Didar said something in the men's language and her brother nodded.

"At least Baha won't get bored with a silly girl like you. Beauty fades, but a good sense of humour is what makes marriage last."

I waited for the laughter to die down while considering my options. As much as it pained me to act subservient to a man, I saw no other option. If I succeeded in convincing them of my unlikely tale, they might lead me to the Vizier. Slim as those chances were, I would still take them over being Baha's wife.

"Have you seen the Grand Vizier or ever been in his vicinity?" I said with as much authority as I could muster. "Have you ever even glimpsed any of the women that are part of the retinue? The Vizier takes what he wants, and I promised him I would be in Tsargrad before the summer's end. And, as you might have guessed already, a man like him is best not kept waiting."

"You would say that, wouldn't you?" Didar's eyes narrowed

with suspicion. The men fell silent, waiting for her to translate.

"You are visitors here, aren't you? Your husband and brother seem to be. How would you know what the Vizier desires? Do you think a man so well-travelled would not take what he desires the moment he lays eyes on it?"

"You are still betrothed, no?"

Though she wasn't convinced, the men's smiles turned sombre.

"Not for long. Ever since the Grand Vizier laid eyes on me near my home, my betrothed had not slept. He eventually set off to beg the Vizier to release me from joining him in Tsargrad before summer's end. He never came back."

I could sense I almost had her. She leaned closer, and something in her expression changed. The mockery dissipated, turning into greed instead.

"And imagine how grateful a man with unlimited wealth such as the Grand Vizier would be when someone safely delivers his prize."

In a low voice, Didar delivered the message to the other men. Her husband nodded and, after a disappointed look towards me, so did her brother.

"Lucky we found you on the road to Tsargrad then," said Didar. "Unfortunately for you, I'm not one so easily deceived. Lies come at a price in our troupe, girl. We are honest merchants," she added, as if the idea were novel to her.

"And because you are," I said calmly, "you will bring the Grand Vizier what is rightfully his, and get handsomely rewarded for it."

Didar's eyes travelled across my face and figure, assessing. I could tell the greedy merchant in her warred with the sensible woman. At the end, she sighed, and said, "I suppose you are pretty enough to even catch the eye of a man such as the Grand Vizier himself. My brother and I will discuss this. But for now, you need some sleep. We will speak of it tomorrow."

With that, she ushered me into the cart. For the first time in a while, I found myself alone. The three men positioned themselves close, loosely surrounding the cart. A low chatter rose, in words I could not decipher. Besides, I was too weary to make sense of their conversation. So I closed my eyes, embraced the aches throbbing through my body, and slept.

CHAPTER 24

The Thread Between Worlds

Sleep did not bring me peace of mind, and neither did it last long. Once I entered the stage between waking and dreams, I felt my mind slip away to a familiar place.

"Jasna, at last I found you. I've been searching the dream-world for days." A voice I knew all too well sounded behind me. When I spun around, Zhar's muzzle swam before my eyes. Behind him, Syanka's landscape solidified, bringing a wave of relief that my connection to the zmei remained.

"What happened? Did you find the heart?" I asked, my eyes searching for clues to his whereabouts. The landscape gave away little. Green patches of grass speckled the ground as far as the eye could see. Motley flowerbeds sprouted all around.

"How did you survive that fall?" he asked in turn. His concern came as a surprise. Zhar, a somewhat childish, yet ancient zmei, had grown fond of me. And I was equally stunned to discover I cared for him too. "I searched everywhere for you. After you… after you fell, I expected to find your body, but there was no sign of it. So I thought, there might be a chance you still live. And if you live, you will eventually sleep. Tell me. What happened?"

I hesitated, remembering that how I had ended up back in my realm was still a mystery.

"In truth, I don't know," I admitted. "I woke up back in my realm, only to find myself captured."

"Captured? By whom?" Zhar huffed. An angry angry fume of smoke escaped his nostrils.

"They claim to be merchants, but I'm not convinced. One of my captors wants me to marry him."

This time the zmei's outrage manifested itself as a full stream of fire, the heat of which I felt, impossibly, even in my dream. I waited for his outburst to subside before continuing.

"I think they are travelling thieves, though they call themselves merchants. If so, they must have a price. Merchants or thieves, gold speaks the same language to people like them."

"Well thought! What did you offer them?" His praise brought warmth to my cheeks. I missed him, his humour and even his fickle nature, and I missed Syanka.

"To take me to the Grand Vizier, who no doubt would be grateful for their services and express that in suitable terms."

It was touching to see Zhar approve of my plan. My fall must have shaken him more than expected. Perhaps seeing the ghost of his beloved had stirred feelings he thought long gone. It reminded me of all the questions I had for him.

"What happened to Rumina's heart?" I fired off the first and most pressing one.

Zhar's eyes were aglow, but he simply said, "I have located it."

"You have? But how did you find it? Can you touch it? I thought only a female could destroy it."

"Again with all the questions," he said grumpily, but I was sure the grimace he made was him smirking. "I have a mouse guarding it until you come back and destroy it. All I had to do was call in a few favours. A surprising number of creatures rushed to answer a zmei's call."

"But couldn't a female creature destroy the heart?"

Zhar hesitated. Something in his eyes told me that despite the goodbyes exchanged, he wasn't ready to let go of Rumina yet.

"I want you to do it. And so does Rumina. I will help you get Iliya back, and then we will destroy the heart for good. But first I need to find you. Do you have anything helpful I could use to locate you?"

"I don't know our exact location. I think we are close to Tsargrad, the travellers said as much. They wouldn't be considering taking me to the Vizier if we weren't. We have taken shelter for the night at a clearing surrounded by a grove. It doesn't offer much protection from forces of nature or from people for that matter, but it provides a good view of the road."

"Hmm," Zhar said with a sigh. "That's not offering much."

"I know. We are travelling in two covered carts. Maybe that will help you locate us from the skies. One has a faded red canvas drawn over it, and the other one is white. Or used to be. Now it's more of a dirty yellow-brown."

"Right, I get it, it's filthy." The zmei sounded amused.

"But how will you get out of Syanka? I thought you needed to be summoned to earth?"

"I do, unless there is a portal that's already open, but that's not very likely. We need an object like your Nana's axe to open one. Sadly, we are short on anything similar."

"It's never easy, is it?"

Zhar exhaled a curl of smoke that spiralled towards the sky, thinking.

"There's a way. It requires you to summon me. That will open a portal for me somewhere near your location at the time of summoning."

"How do I do that?"

"Well, first, a drop of your blood should do," Zhar said, prompting a groan on my side. "Don't worry, I'm jesting."

"Oh." I sighed with relief.

"It's a raskovnik that you need."

I rolled my eyes. Of course we would need a rare flower of legends.

"And where am I supposed to get a magical herb – or maybe a flower, depending on the account – that's near impossible to find?"

"Well, what do your Nana's stories say?"

I frowned. While the flower had been a recurring item in her tales, the way to find it had not been very clear. The hero that had fallen to Syanka through the well had used it to go back to his realm. That was all I remembered. Then I recalled an overlooked detail.

"I need to find a turtle's nest and look for the raskovnik around. Her tales always emphasised that turtles nested nearby."

"Very good, very good. Other chthonic creatures, like hedgehogs, can also lead you to it. Chthonic means they are of the underworld," Zhar explained with a haughty air.

"But what do creatures of the underworld have to do with it? And the raskovnik itself – how is it supposed to let you into this world? Isn't it meant for finding treasures?"

"Ah, all the questions," he said, though amusement coloured his voice. "Splitting my head in two, but we are getting there. Listen, I don't know when you are going to awake, so I'll be brief. Raskovnik is a plant that is notoriously hard for humans to find, yet it grows everywhere. Look for meadows, places where turtles nest, hedgehogs have their offspring, and the underworld opens its maw."

"Yes, that's incredibly helpful," I interjected, annoyed. Zhar ignored me as he continued.

"Most think raskovnik's uses are limited to locating treasures, but few are aware of its true purpose. It used to be widely used for travelling, for it opens a ley line between worlds. It can create a portal to Syanka and even allows its owner to descend to the underworld. Its only limit: often one has to cross more than one realm to reach their journey's end."

"Ugh," I groaned, dampening the zmei's enthusiasm. "Does it mean I have to stumble through all the realms before finding my way to you if you cannot come through? Provided I don't get lost–"

"Let's cross that bridge when we get to it. For now, we need the portal to navigate my way over and find you. The other thing you need to know is that the raskovnik is often mistaken for a herb because it looks like a clover. What only a few know is that when it blooms, a single red flower blazes in the centre. It's a rare sight and it unlocks all the plant's magical properties."

"That would help," I said, suddenly weary of all the travelling, the wrong paths taken, and everything that had happened in between. I missed Nana and Iliya, the quiet nights when he walked me home, followed by Nana's stories. Then I remembered all the vitriol the people from Moravia harboured, and that brought a sour taste in my mouth.

"You are angry," said Zhar, sensing my agitation. "Why?"

"Just remembering what awaits me back home," I answered in a small voice.

"You don't have to go back, you know."

"I know, but–" I began saying, but a sudden jerking of my arm took me by surprise. A voice was saying something with great urgency. It sounded like whomever it belonged to was terrified.

I had no time to alert Zhar as his image dissolved and I opened my eyes. Sweat broke on my brow and I sprang to my feet, losing my balance. Didar's hand shot to grab mine and steady me. The cart I had fallen asleep in moved, an agonisingly slow motion compared to the urgency that had forced me to my feet.

"What's wrong with you?" Didar cried out. The two of us were alone. Through the curtain, I noticed the other cart, tethered behind, moved just as slowly. "You sleep like the dead. Oh, never you mind," she hushed me as I began forming a half-coherent reply. "We are being chased."

"Chased?" I pulled the cart's fold apart only to be greeted by a dark sky, clouds obscuring any light from filtering through. Despite the disorienting noise of carts, hooves and people, I could make out three shapes outlined on the horizon. As soon as I noticed them, the galloping sound of their horses followed. They were closing the distance.

As if creatures straight from Syanka, all three stallions loomed larger than any other horses I had ever seen. Their riders, three men shouting for us to halt in the name of the Sultan, were all well-built and radiated authority.

"It won't be much of a chase," I couldn't help saying. Didar scowled at me, but had no time to contradict me, as it was at this moment that the chasers closed the already diminished gap.

"Was running even an option?" I muttered, finding the situation more amusing than it had the right to be. Didar, clearly displeased, lashed out.

"You think this is over for you, girl? That it's a mere coincidence that the Sultan's warriors have chanced upon us? How will they even know you are one of the Vizier's toys, anyway? As if they will believe a simple girl like you, no? Or perhaps they'll consider it only after they've had their way with you."

That dampened my already short-lived triumph. The horses surrounded the cart, and it lurched to a halt. Didar shoved me to the side and stuck her head out to hastily convene with her brothers. Their harsh language revealed little of what they were saying, though that became clear a moment later when Didar turned towards me.

"You will be our bargaining tool, girl. Tell them what you told us about the Grand Vizier and pray they believe your tale."

As she said that, she began dusting off my clothes and combing my hair with her fingers. I almost felt sorry for Didar and her brothers. Trying to outrun the Vizier's officials had been a stupid idea, and it wasn't like they didn't deserve what was coming. As to my fate, it swung from being at the mercy of one captor to another. I had promised myself not to let others dictate my fortune, yet at every step my resolve was thwarted. Now it appeared that fate had once more caught up with me.

"Out," a man yelled. We obeyed. The clouds above had parted just enough to reveal a faint moonlight that illuminated my new captors' faces.

The three men wore the rich kaftans and bejewelled bork hats of the Sultan's private army – the janissaries. Their sabres gleamed in the moonlight. But it was the musket resting on their leader's hip that took my breath. One shot from it, and I'd be dead before I hit the ground.

Having realised the grave error they had committed in trying to outrun the janissaries, Didar and her small troupe already knelt with hands outstretched and clasped before them in a gesture of complete surrender.

I had no clue if I had to kneel or not. You bent a knee for the Sultan and the Grand Vizier, perhaps lesser Viziers, but soldiers? Their status brought nearly as many privileges as a Vizier's. As former slaves recruited as young boys into the Sultan's army – I would know, for it cost me a brother – they were both feared for their unscrupulous behaviour and revered for their mastery with the sabre and loyalty to the Sultan.

I was awkwardly standing above the kneeling Didar and her troupe, unwilling to kneel myself, yet reluctant to draw attention, when the man on the right spoke.

"What a beautiful creature," he said, the ruby in his bork hat sparkling in the faintly in the moonlight, his dark eyes fixed on me.

"She seems a bit too old," the man in the middle said. His build was smaller than that of the other two men, though he seemed to compensate for it with an unmistakable ruthlessness that hardened his features.

"Nonsense. She's just been under the sun for too long. Skin like hers isn't made for travel. A good bath and a set of clean clothes, and you will be singing praise to her beauty. Looking at her, I can see why the Sultan has expressed such a strong preference for foreign women in the past," the third one said, a man with a wide jaw and broad shoulders. The smaller man snickered, but the first one said nothing and instead stared at me with an intensity that seemed to sear into my skin. I couldn't help but notice that his eyes did not ogle me with the hunger I had come to associate with men's eyes. Instead, he regarded me with curiosity.

"What brings you to these parts?" he asked curtly. Though

his question was aimed at the group, he addressed me as if I were their leader.

"If you would permit me to speak, honourable one," Didar said, and despite the ambivalence I felt towards her, I couldn't help but admire her audacity to draw attention to herself. Indeed, the man I had thought to be the leader of the three raised an eyebrow at her, prompting her to speak.

"This girl is promised to the Grand Vizier," Didar said, bowing lower. "But if the Sultan wished to claim her, who are we to refuse?"

A sly smile played on her lips when she said that. Hatred scorched my heart, but she wasn't done.

"The girl being promised is why we were making our way to Tsargrad. We were escorting her to safety when you... found us."

"Is that so?" asked their leader, his voice laden.

"Indeed, honourable one," Didar continued, emboldened. Somehow, she failed to notice the threat in the janissary's voice. "We are simple merchants, and we had to help a girl in need, especially when the Grand Vizier wishes her in his palace—"

"So you were delivering the Grand Vizier's prized possession out of the goodness of your heart? And it had nothing to do with the Vizier paying you good coin?" interrupted the cold-eyed man who had called me old. He had a glint of amusement in his eyes. "Oh, no, let me guess. You never even thought about a reward. You were merely doing your duty."

Didar mumbled under her breath that gold would be welcome, but not necessary. The man, though, wouldn't let it go.

"And where exactly in the empire are you from? Your companions don't seem to be versed in our language much, if at all. Unless they're mute, of course."

"Enough, Ilkay," barked their leader, and the man fell silent. I resisted flinching when his eyes lingered on my face. "What is your name, girl?"

"Jasna," I answered. His frown deepened, as if my name scratched at a memory, so I ventured. "Do I know you?"

He studied me, silent. No recognition sparkled in his eyes, only that same unsettling intensity. Too late, I thought I should have added Didar's 'honourable one.' Already out of my depth, I wondered if I would ever reach the Vizier's palace or perish still pondering the proper form of address.

"We shall take you to the Grand Vizier," said his companion.

"For a price," added the man called Ilkay with a sly smile.

"And risk the Vizier's ire? I don't think so. She could be spinning this wild tale to reach her own ends," their leader said.

"Since when do you care about what Temir has to say?" Ilkay cut him off. "I doubt he'll turn away someone with her looks. Besides, we don't answer to anyone but the Sultan. And from what I hear, he'd be more than pleased to have Temir vexed."

"I've heard the same," said the third man. "The Sultan won't tolerate Temir's ambition much longer."

"Where did you hear that, in the brothel you paid a visit to last night? She stays with us until the matter is resolved. As for you," Ilkay turned towards Didar's group. "You will cede all food in your possession and consider yourselves lucky that you are walking away with your lives."

"But what about my son, honourable one?" Didar asked, both humbled and desperate. "He is still growing."

"Appealing to a sense of honour won't get you far, woman," the third man said before the leader could reply. "You'll find we have none."

"Unless it comes to defending the Sultan's, of course," said Ilkay in a way that implied that he held no allegiance to anyone but himself. All the while, their leader remained silent, his dark eyes studying me. At last, when everyone turned towards him, he shifted his eyes and regarded Didar's troupe.

"It will take you only half a day to reach Tsargrad. You may keep what's left of your water after the horses are done. If you speak the truth and you were headed there, you wouldn't mind going half a day without food."

Didar nodded reluctantly and cast a venomous look in my direction, as if them being robbed of their food was my fault. I returned the look in kind.

CHAPTER 25

THE JAVINA

In the end, the soldiers ransacked the little possessions Didar's family had. Ilkay took great and obvious pleasure in turning their caravan upside down while the leader sat on the side, lost in thought. Despite the dislike I harboured towards Didar, I felt a pang of guilt when the horse pulling their carts got confiscated to be saddled as my ride. When the horse, a brown mare that accepted me with no objections, cantered away, I avoided Didar's eyes, which were full of tears and unspent rage.

The leader's name turned out to be Sirak. I learned this from Zareh, the man in the middle, who also rode by my side while the other two scouted ahead. He chattered on, more to keep himself occupied than entertain me. All the while, I kept my eyes on Sirak's back. He hadn't spoken to me since we'd ridden out, yet I could still feel the weight of his stare.

"It's because the Sultan and Viziers are busy keeping the

peace in other territories that are staging uprisings," Zareh was saying, oblivious to my agitation. "Bayas has tasked us with hunting down rogues. If you ask me, we need to show it's the Sultan who keeps the peace and not the Grand Vizier. There have been some tensions regarding the Grand Vizier's rising power."

You will come to me of your own free will.

I had not spoken until then, and when the words came to me, I flinched. Zareh shot me a questioning look, mistaking my flinch for weariness.

"You need to keep up, otherwise you'll have to share a horse with one of us. If you are worried about Sirak delivering you to the Grand Vizier, you have nothing to worry about. At least I hope not," he said, frowning. "He might come across as somewhat crass, but in the end, if taking you to the Grand Vizier is against your will, he won't do it. Although lately, he's been rather distant with all the unfortunate events weighing on his mind."

"Unfortunate events?" I asked in a low voice. Though his horse had pulled ahead, I was sure Sirak still overheard us.

"It's that damned sense of honour of his." Zareh shrugged and adjusted his bork hat. "His mind has been quite preoccupied lately. Like I said, he's dealing with the janissaries' latest rebellion in the north on the Sultan's behalf. Say, how come the Grand Vizier discovered you?"

His question was so sudden that it caught me off-guard, and I answered without thinking.

"His camp was near where I live. As soon as he'd laid eyes on me, he decided he had to marry me."

"That's Temir, alright. He takes what he wants, but he could offer a lot to a young woman like you if you provide what he desires."

"I would rather not," I said dryly. "I'm betrothed. Besides, what gave you the idea I was a rug to be wrung out and passed on to whoever wanted to use it next?"

My words lashed out like a whip, and Zareh recoiled and began mumbling apologies. Though his thick beard gave his face a harshness that made you think twice before disagreeing with him, there was also a hidden tenderness, an understanding of the predicaments of others, a surprisingly rare quality, especially in someone of his rank. I almost regretted my words, but there was no taking them back. When Sirak's stallion galloped further ahead, Zareh confessed in a low voice.

"Sirak is an odd one, I'll tell you that. He doesn't take part in the consolations we need to survive the road as soldiers. Pardon me saying this, but we need the comfort of women every now and again. He never engages in such frivolities, and some see this as distant, while others praise his dedication to the Sultan. One thing is for sure; he's a great warrior. It might be due to him being taken so young as blood-tax. The former Sultan scouted him himself and trained him well to serve as his most loyal soldier. Whatever he saw in him fifteen years ago paid off."

My mouth went dry. Fifteen years ago. When my brother was taken. Except that his name had been Sivo and not Sirak. Janissaries assumed new names when taken, but that was a thin thread to pursue, for the number of boys that departed for the capital every five years was in triple digits.

The first warning sounded in a worried neigh from the two horses ahead. A lone tree towered in the otherwise bare landscape. Its branches, dry and gnarled, reached toward the sky in a silent prayer. Something else waited there too, but I couldn't yet make out what.

"Don't you even think of slowing us down." Ilkay called from ahead, his voice sharp with excitement. My thighs burned in protest as the mare's canter turned into a gallop. The janissaries' patrolling had paid off. They had spotted something and, even from afar, I could tell it wasn't human. It slithered down the tree like a giant black snake, tendrils stitching together in a shape that solidified and moulded itself into a female form. As we neared, dawn coloured the horizon, though it was still too far to cast proper light on the creature.

"Stay behind," Sirak warned me. Reluctantly, I pulled my mare to a halt and waited for them to ride ahead, then followed, curiosity outweighing caution. Soon, I was close enough to see what writhed against the tree. My breath caught.

Even before the three men closed a circle around it, I knew it for what it was: a creature not of this realm. And not just any creature, but one woven from the very darkness as the shadow at Syanka's well.

"What on earth is that?" asked Zareh as the shadow stood tall, its limbs contorted and its neck cocked inquisitively. Its head lacked everything a head should have, not only mouth but also eyes, nose, and even cheeks and a forehead. The only way I knew it to be its face was because of the thick, luscious hair made of dark tendrils. Something in its outline gave me a moment of unsettled pause. Its distinctly female build was that of a tall woman, its shapes and proportions oddly familiar.

"Not of earth," Sirak replied. "But of the other creatures' realm. Syanka."

"You can see it too?" I asked, the growing certainty that this ugly thing was part of me twisting my insides with icy fingers. The three men took their eyes off the creature and fixed them on me.

"Are we not meant to see it?" The customary mockery in Ilkay's voice had given way to suspicion. I didn't know the answer to that. I had assumed the creature would be visible only to me and others from Syanka, if it was the same shadow that had torn free from the well. The creature's neck twisted and turned. If it had eyes, they would be staring at me with a clear, hungry gaze. I forced myself to meet its stare, and in that, its connection to me became apparent. It had the exact build as mine, the same legs, arms, hair, face, all down to the jawbone, yet it was anything but human. Its skin was that of shadows coiling together into darkness. In a state of constant shifting, they stitched themselves together as if from thin air. Behind me, someone cleared their throat.

"Since you seem to know more than we do, why don't you enlighten us?" The edge in Sirak's voice made it less a question than a command.

"I don't fully understand it myself–"

"Try us." This time he barked the command.

The four horses circled the creature, but kept their distance, wary of its every move. It seemed almost harmless now, the way it stood there, as if confused by what it was doing there. I didn't know how the thought came to my mind, but I was certain that stitching itself together in this realm had taken its toll on it. Much like me, it did not belong here.

"When the Grand Vizier built a statue above the well, he did it in my honour and so he made the statue in my image," I said with a hoarse voice. "It was only later when I fell ill that I found out his dark mage had entombed my shadow inside its structure."

My words produced varying reactions among the three janissaries. Ilkay tut-tutted while Zareh sucked in a breath. Sirak's face betrayed nothing, but his knuckles whitened on the horse's reins. One thing was sure. Trapping shadows in structures was a tale they were familiar with.

"Do you mean to tell us that this," Zareh said, catching on

to the implication first and pointing toward the creature, "is your shadow?"

I nodded. I knew with certainty the creature was not unlike the shadow from Syanka – another piece of me, ripped away. Was it even the same part? How many more were out there? Did other splinters roam the realms, waiting for me to pick up the pieces?

"How are you still alive, then?" asked Ilkay. "Surely severing your shadow to bind it to a statue would kill you."

"I don't know," I admitted. From the varying degrees of disbelief written across their faces, I could see my brief account had not won them over. And why should it? With a creature made of darkness as my only witness, who would believe someone left with a sliver of their shadow? And, more importantly, why was the creature just standing there, as if waiting for a cue? It unsettled me more than I cared to admit.

"Try a better explanation," Sirak urged. I pursed my lips and spoke reluctantly.

"My betrothed went to Tsargrad to beg the Vizier to cure me from the illness that struck me shortly after the statue's unveiling. The Vizier must have taken pity on me and listened to Iliya's plea, for soon after I made a full recovery. If the mage bound my shadow to the statue, this thing might be what's left – a shred of darkness that doesn't belong in this world. I don't know if it's here to reclaim the rest of me. What I know is that the Vizier holds the answers. He knew I would follow, even before the summer's end. That's all I know."

I laced my fingers together behind my back, hiding their shake. Let them believe the Vizier's mercy saved me. The truth of Nana's magic and Gorovoi's spell would mark me a witch.

In the silence that followed, the four of us regarded the creature. Its head tilted, as if listening to words only it could hear. Though I could tell it was malicious by the feeling of dread in the pit of my stomach, I couldn't say why. At last, Ilkay broke the silence.

"Unfortunate. But the Vizier's wants outweigh yours, girl. Now, what should we do with the shadow creature? I say, let's give it a taste of my sabre."

Despite his bold words, Ilkay paused and waited for Sirak's assent, his hand resting on the hilt of his sabre. Zareh had reassured me that Sirak wouldn't act against my will, yet Ilkay's words troubled me. I couldn't ignore that the shadow creature was a part of me. An ugly, crooked, unrecognisable part of me that I would rather not face, but a part of me nonetheless.

"I know what it is, though I doubt that would be of much help," Sirak said slowly. "The creature is of the undead, born from your shadow being welled. When enough essence gets severed, a shadow like that is born. It haunts whoever it belongs to until it drags them to the otherworld with itself."

I couldn't help but notice that no one commented on how odd it was for a janissary leader to have this knowledge, or the lack of reaction he got compared to when I showed a similar grasp of creatures. No one called him a witch.

"How do we deal with it?" Zareh asked.

"Deal with it? Why should we? It's her doing, not ours. There, I've said it all. The rest is up to my sabre," Ilkay said with disdain. Again, Sirak paid no heed. He seemed captivated by the creature, as though he longed to dissect it and uncover its secrets.

"I'm going to name it," Sirak cautioned. "I don't know what good that will do, if any."

He didn't wait for our assent when he slid down from his horse, eyes fixed on the dark mass that bore my liking. Its head cocked, and the shadows where its mouth should have been stretched into a smile. Not at Sirak, but at me. The air thickened, and the horses shied back. Even Ilkay's sabre hand trembled.

"This is not a good–" Zareh began, but Sirak spoke over him.

"You are a javina. A creature of the underworld, born of Jasna's trapped shadow."

For a long while, nothing happened. I didn't realise I had been holding my breath until I sharply exhaled. Ilkay laughed, but his face remained serious.

Then, just as the tension eased, the ground shuddered, as if something beneath us had awakened. The creature moved. Two dark slits where its eyes should have been opened and its head rotated at an unnatural angle to regard Sirak, the one that had named it. Then it lunged for him.

My scream was drowned out by the commotion that followed. The other two men dismounted at the same time with an efficacy that made the same movement on my side appear slow and clumsy. By the time I had sprung to my feet, Sirak had drawn his sabre in one hand and was reaching for the musket tucked opposite to where the sabre had been. The creature, javina, as Sirak had called it, lunged for him and as it did, another tremor from the ground split it open in two. A chasm ruptured, widening with an uncanny speed, at first as a mere crack and then as a tear large enough for a man to fall through. As it expanded, it left me, Zareh and Ilkay on one side, and the creature and Sirak on the other.

Sirak did not waver. He dealt a swift blow that cut through the creature's abdomen just as its outstretched arms went for his neck. The creature staggered and came to a halt, and I could have sworn its faceless expression was one of surprise. It glanced down to the sabre buried in its stomach, but made no motion to yank it free, nor did it show any signs of pain. No blood blossomed from the darkness of its body.

The janissary's leader twisted the sabre's hilt and sank it further, despite the creature paying no heed to the metal buried in its body. Its arms sprouted into action, fingers lengthened and grew like branches that wrapped around Sirak's neck. Again, he acted with speed, taking advantage of the little space left between him and the creature. Sirak pulled the sabre free, then buried it again in the javina's body. He struck again and again, but the sabre cut only smoke.

Then the creature opened its just-formed mouth and let out a long, screeching noise. It pierced my ears, and I had to clap my palms over them as the screech grew louder. Even Sirak was unsettled. His brief hesitation was all the javina needed. Its fingers, already cupping Sirak's throat, pulled him towards the chasm's gaping maw. In the last moment, just before the inevitable fall, the creature fixed me with black slits that stood for its eyes, their message clear. Its sudden attack had never been about Sirak. It knew that once it dragged the janissary down with itself, I wouldn't stand there watching a creature made of my shadow steer someone to their death. It knew as well as I did that I would see no other way but to follow.

CHAPTER 26

THE NAV

It all happened in what felt like an eternity, yet it took less than a heartbeat. Zareh read the look on my face and knew what I was about to do.

"No!" he yelled, his arm stretching toward me, but he was too late. By then, I had dived into the crevice that had swallowed Sirak. The last thing I saw before I plunged into darkness was the pale dawn that made its way toward us. Somehow, I knew that if we'd lingered just a while longer after sunrise, the creature would have had no power to pull Sirak down. That must have been its plan all along, and the shadow's gambit had paid off.

Once more, I fell into the unknown, the thought of everything I had left behind chasing after me. I thought of Syanka ⋯na and wondered if Zhar would find it in himself to ⋯o would he enlist in my stead to destroy her ⋯ngly, it saddened me that if I died, I would never get to explore Syanka with its ever-changing landscape, nor would I get to meet more of its peculiar creatures. I would never know what became of Iliya, and this journey would have been for nothing. Just like the fall in Syanka, I had little time to ready myself as the surrounding air grew colder, and I closed my eyes, bracing for the impact.

The fall ended with a wet thud. Something soft and moist broke my landing, clinging to my skin. I gagged and rolled over, a sickly green glow pulsing beneath me. Whatever enveloped me felt like a giant cotton cloud, big and soft enough to counter the speed with which I had fallen. Even with my eyes closed, I could tell darkness had given way to light. It prickled my eyelids with warmth, and when I opened them, a subtle gleam greeted me. The light came from the plant-like heap that had cushioned my fall. Though still dazed, I had no time to spare, so I forced myself to take in my surroundings, hoping to spot Sirak and my shadow.

Instead of Sirak, more of the eerie plants greeted me. They lay speckled here and there in what appeared to be a vast and endless cave. The plants, resembling a giant glowing moss, gave off a bluish-green light that cast strange, shifting shadows. Water dripped from high columns of stone that stretched upwards, as if coming from a ceiling invisible to the naked eye.

I climbed down from the plants and sighed in relief that I had lived through the fall. Despite being underground, the air did not feel stifling. The ground was rocky, with slippery patches forming here and there from the dripping water. Sirak and the shadow were nowhere to be seen. A closer look revealed the plants parted to make a clear path, which I followed.

As I walked, the silence was interrupted only by the constant drip of water on stone. I wondered where the shadow had dragged Sirak. They should have landed somewhere nearby, yet they had disappeared without a trace.

Something glinted under the greenish light and without thinking, I picked it up. A large silver coin similar to the gold grosh coins used throughout the empire rested on my palm. Almost immediately after I had foolishly touched it, something half-human shot up from a hole in the ground and went straight for my ankles. A rotten smell hit my nostrils just as the thing stirred. Icy fingers closed around my ankles and yanked me off balance. I toppled down, trying and failing to grasp for purchase.

The hand clutched my ankle, cold and blue, though whether the tinge came from the plants' light or was its natural colour, I could not tell. I sensed its hunger for my flesh in my throbbing leg, its grip so strong that it sent a wave of numbness across my limbs. Frantically, I grabbed the creature's ice-cold wrist with both hands and tried to pry it off my ankle. The creature did not waver, not in the slightest. I went for its fingers, prising them apart one by one. Once again, it didn't react. Instead, its grip tightened, and it began dragging me towards its lair. This forced me to stop struggling and brace against its pull.

My hand shot for the nearest plant, guided by its faint light. It felt odd upon touch. Soft, moss-like material covered the twigs branching from it. As soon as I tried to hold on to it, the moss treacherously slid free under the palm of my hand, even as I clutched harder. Inevitably, I slid down towards the creature's lair.

There was no mistaking that it was no longer fully alive, the stench emanating from the lair and the creature itself confirming my initial suspicion. Its eyes, devoid of life, contained only hunger. At the sight of fresh meat, its twisted mouth produced a long slimy line of drool. With one last pull,

I slid down into its lair and hit the ground with a painful thud.

A dark, but shallow hole greeted me. The undead creature seized my shoulder, dragging me towards its gaping maw. Its translucent skin clung to a body that reeked of rot and death, and bile surged up my throat. I retched onto the creature, and its moment's hesitation gave me the chance to wrench free and look up to see–

"Sirak!"

The shadow shifted, and the creature's gaze snapped to the intruder. Too late, I realised my cry had betrayed him. Abandoning stealth, he crouched and thrust out his hand.

"Grab it," he panted. At the same time, the creature let out an outraged wail. Sirak didn't have to prompt me twice. But before I could take his hand, the creature seized my waist and wrenched me back, a second scream of rage splitting the air.

"Sirak!" I yelled once more, this time more urgently.

Though I had expected it, the blow landed hard enough to send me reeling. With a kick of its leg, the creature cut under my knees and sent me to the ground, where it pinned me down, rendering me useless once more. I almost laughed at how quickly I'd broken my promise not to rely on anyone else. Yet, here I was, not long after, waiting for another knight in shining armour to sweep in. Tears stung my eyes at the realisation and my resolve crumbled. At that moment, heart raw with fear, exhaustion, and shame, I wished more than anything that I hadn't lost Nana's knife.

A dull thump followed and Sirak landed in the lair next to the creature. Before it had the time to react, a kick in its calf forced it to drop its grip on me and fold. In the blink of an eye, Sirak had his sabre out of its hilt and delivered a neat cut that severed the creature's head. It rolled down as the body collapsed, and the faint light behind its white eyes was extinguished.The body gave one last twitch, then stilled. Sirak pulled me to my feet, and I brushed at my cardigan, though the grime of my journey clung stubbornly.

"Thanks," I said begrudgingly, more annoyed at my helplessness than his timing. I'd followed Sirak down to the abyss to save him – not the other way around.

We scaled the uneven wall and were soon back to the surface of the underworld we had found ourselves in.

"Where's the shadow?" I asked, glancing around as if it might leap out and shout 'Surprise.'

Sirak shrugged and took stock of me, checking for wounds. When we had steadied ourselves, we followed the path woven by the blue plants. I studied him in turn. Annoyingly, he seemed unruffled despite the ghoulish creature we'd just faced. His dishevelled hair fell over one side of his face, hiding a scar on his left cheek. His light brown eyes held a steady calm that jarred with the chaos we had endured. I wished I could claim the same. Beneath the eerie glow of the plants, I was certain I resembled the undead creature more than the living.

"The shadow," he said finally, breaking the silence. "It's born from your soul. Do you know what it is?"

I hesitated. He had called it javina. The name sounded familiar, but I couldn't place it anywhere in Nana's tales. Even after having come so far, I still didn't know how it was possible for me to live while a part of my essence – my soul – was severed. Whatever magic was used to splinter it had been dark and vile enough to create the creature that had dragged Sirak here. Suddenly, I didn't want him to think less of me for having my soul's pieces scattered across the realms. When I next spoke, my voice came out tired and defeated.

"It's an ugly, twisted part of my soul, but part of it regardless."

I braced for his next words of judgement. Who would choose to remain near someone whose broken soul dragged others into the earth? Yet Sirak's composure never wavered.

"It isn't your soul, but something born from it. Your shadow, yes – but more than that. It's your death."

"What do you mean? How is it my death?" Fear twisted my insides.

"Let's say that I've seen what a creature like that can do. The Sultan has his own mage, though he hardly ever meddles in dark magic of the kind."

"The Sultan entombs people's souls?" I couldn't hide the apprehension in my voice. My feet trembled as I walked, though whether from exhaustion or anxiety, I could not tell. Sirak laughed, but the sound – unnatural in the underworld – was swallowed by the vast chamber.

"No, of course not. If anyone would commit such a vile act, it wouldn't be his mage, but Temir's. The Sultan would never cross that line. Only fools meddle with dark magic." He said it as if reciting something he had heard dozens of times. His words sounded familiar once again. Perhaps it was only the cave's bluish glow, but I thought his composure wavered before he recovered. "There is one exception I wish I could forget. The Sultan needed to build bridges to cross his conquered lands."

"Do you mean the four bridges?" I asked, aghast. Did the Sultan entomb four shadows to ensure the structure's integrity? Sirak heard the panic in my voice and hurried to reassure me.

"He didn't require a shadow for every bridge. Only one of the four chosen people got sacrificed before the Sultan called off the magic."

"That makes it so much better." I rolled my eyes, but the darkness hid the gesture.

"He is not a cruel man," Sirak insisted, and for the first time his curt tone softened. It felt like if I pressed him, I would be prying into something personal. I steered the conversation into a different direction.

"What happened to her? The woman whose shadow got entombed?"

"Her death walked with her until the end of her life, brief as it was. Then she greeted her and they became one once again."

"What does that mean for me?"

"Once severed, your shadow became your death, bound to find you again. We all carry our deaths, but yours was torn away and its only purpose is now to return to you. And that can happen only when you die. The woman I knew didn't last long. She was still but a child when her death rejoined her. It is the way of the magic, or the curse. It drained her swiftly." Sirak slowed his pace. "Wait. How did you know it was the shadow of a woman, not a man?"

"Because such fates hunt women more often than men – and it's usually at men's hands," I said wryly.

Sirak nodded. "The purer the woman, the easier it is for the magic to take root. The Sultan's mage himself told me so. This is why many who tamper with shadow magic are called dark or corrupt: they meddle with forces best left untouched." He paused, uncertain. I had expected his next words, yet they still took me by surprise when he blurted, "That you're not dead yet baffles me."

Back in Morava, I would have taken such a blunt remark as a slight. After all I had faced in this journey, it only reminded me of Nana's candour. Sirak hesitated, then added, "My apologies. I've been working on my diplomacy skills for a while now."

"And how is that going for you?" I teased, hoping to lighten the mood.

"I have taken into interpreting the Sultan's intentions based on… oh, you meant it humorously."

"See, you can definitely take a cue. And to answer your question, my betrothed may be the reason I'm alive. When I fell ill, it seemed certain I wouldn't survive, until he journeyed all the way to Tsargrad to plead with the Vizier for a cure. As you can see, I am alive and well, so that must have gone according to plan."

"Yet he never returned."

"Yet he never returned," I echoed as we drew closer to an arch that separated the vast cave-like structure from what lay ahead. I hesitated, wondering whether I should let Sirak in on the truth of who had truly cured me. But something else caught my attention. I now knew why Yerleg had cursed me: once for refusing the Vizier, and a second time because he'd seen my reason to do so as a testament to my purity. His spell, aided by Zhar's power, had taken a deep root, scattering pieces of me across the realms.

Aside from the ghastly light cast by the plants, a mellow golden glow spilled ahead. Sirak tensed, his hand falling to the hilt of his sabre. I tried to ignore the aches flaring through my body, but they had only worsened after the fall into the undead creature's lair. If we were to be ambushed, I would be of little use. Sirak's next words could not have come at a worse time.

"The creature that brought us here – your death. It dissipated into thin air. I believe its purpose was to bring us here."

"And you are telling me this now?" I snapped. "Where did it go?"

"That I don't know." He hesitated. "But before it dissolved, I asked her to let me go and she faltered. A recognition sparkled behind her otherwise dead eyes, which makes me think she isn't wholly evil, but rather bound to master's bidding. If you could convince her to delay merging with you–"

"If Yerleg controls her, then I have no chance to do so," I said darkly. As we stepped into the chamber ahead, I asked, "Do you know where we are?"

"I think *you* already do." Sirak halted beside me. "We're in the Nav. The land of the dead."

If Sirak had expected me to be surprised or afraid, he would have been disappointed. I had already guessed as much. The place we had entered bore no resemblance to the one we had emerged from. A black river, much like the darkness my shadow was made of, ran without an end. While the other room had been empty, this one teemed with a semblance of life. Tendrils of dark matter shot up from the river, twisted and coalesced until shaping themselves into creatures much like the javina.

Upon closer inspection, we saw the shapes were as varied as the creatures that roamed the realms. Apart from human-like forms, many other creatures coalesced from the dark matter and shifted into shadow-forms. Dogs, horses, cattle, even ants and creatures from Syanka abounded. The shadow of a nine-headed lamia briefly covered the visible horizon before landing in the distance. The chamber, despite the bustle of activity, did not feel like a place of rest, but like a temporary stop, a prelude to something else. At the far end, light sifted from a tear in the wall, a soft glow that reminded me of the vibrant dusk in Syanka.

Sirak swallowed, and for a moment, he seemed more like a lost boy than the Sultan's janissary.

"Pray we don't meet any gods," he said at last as he resumed walking towards the river.

"Like Veles? I doubt it."

"Why would you? We've already met the dead and this is his domain."

He had a point. Yet, something was missing in the unfolding scene. The shadows that formed from the river's depths drifted aimlessly through the air or walked about as if uncertain what purpose their limbs held. Veles, the god of the underworld, was someone to be feared, at least according to Nana's stories. Sirak's caution was warranted. Or would have been if Veles were anywhere to be seen.

"I suppose lingering among the dead to guide them to the afterlife is beneath a god. He must have other concerns. Still, they seem so lost," I said as we drew closer. Until then, the shadows had ignored us. Reluctantly, we approached, hoping their indifference would last. It did not. As soon as they noticed us, a winged, human-like creature, likely a hala, shrieked, "Mortals! You don't belong here!"

"We are aware," Sirak replied cautiously.

Something bothered me. If Iliya was dead, this would be the place to find him. And I had to know.

"We are looking for someone," I said, my mouth dry. "Someone very dear to me. I need to know if he's down here."

Instead of a reply, the hala's shadow let out a long, high-pitched cry.

"She wants to know if her dear one is here," she cooed toward the other shadows. Some had already paused their aimless wandering to listen to our exchange. Their previous state of apathy got replaced by muted interest, enough for them to draw uncomfortably close. "No one from the mortal world dares enter our domain," the hala's shadow screeched.

"You say that's your domain, yet no one is waiting to guide you to the afterlife."

If Sirak had been tense before, my last words made him

radiate anxiety, his hand tightening on the sabre's hilt. The hala's shadow hissed, spitting tendrils of darkness that coiled in the air like snakes poised for attack. The other creatures' interest sharpened as their otherwise lifeless faces lit with curiosity.

"I'm right, aren't I?" I demanded. "Veles isn't here to guide you into the afterlife. That's why you drift, aimless, with no end to your journey. We can help you."

Sirak cleared his throat. I tried to elbow him into silence, but the hala's eyeless face didn't miss a thing. She lowered her head, following the gesture, and said, each word deliberate, "I don't think so."

She hissed again and slithered closer. This time, the creatures followed her lead. They closed in, a tight ring of shadows, tendrils of darkness stretching towards us until all light vanished, swallowed by their creeping presence. With it, our last hope of escaping got snuffed. Next to me, Sirak had his sabre out, slashing at the shadows as his other hand closed around mine.

"I don't want to stab you in this darkness," he rasped.

I had thought the shadows' bodies to be of no substance, that when they touched us, we would feel nothing. As with many other things on this journey, I was wrong. A cold dread curdled my blood at their touch. Without thinking, I seized Sirak's free hand, and even in terror, a jolt of astonishment struck me when he returned the grip. As the shadows closed in, tears clouded my sight. He was here because of me, and I couldn't let him die.

Just then, something glinted in the darkness into which the shadows had plunged us. Even through blurred eyes, I saw it beckon me. At the same time, icy fingers closed around my neck and the he clammy, deathly touch of the shadows almost made me forget about the glinting red object.

It sparkled again, red as a ruby. The shadows pressed in until no space remained, and I was suffocating. I couldn't even lean down to grasp it as I fought for breath. Then Sirak fired his musket. The shot did nothing to harm the creatures, but it startled them long enough for me to crouch and seize the red plant, only to find it rooted in the ground. With the last of my strength, I wrenched the stem of the flower that bloomed without soil. The only flower to bloom in the underworld, a beacon of hope where none existed.

"I summon you, great Zhar," I croaked with my last breath, cupping the raskovnik in my palm. At last, darkness claimed me.

CHAPTER 27

THE KEEPER OF THE DEAD

Warmth prickled through my fingers, spreading across my body. It brought a rare but fleeting moment of peace until the pleasant tingle twisted into a blistering burn. Pain clawed through my body, forcing me back to consciousness. Next to me, Sirak groaned, covering his face to shield it from the sudden heat that ravaged the underworld. The chamber blazed so brightly I had to force my eyes open to see its source.

"Zhar!"

Even with eyes drying in the heat, the zmei that filled my vision was hard to miss. The slow beat of his wings fanned the flames as he exhaled a stream of fire, a blazing curtain that forced the shadows back. The fire threatened to leave us gasping for breath in the stifling air.

"Zhar," I cried out, but the waves of heated air blurring my vision made it impossible to know whether he had heard me. "Stop the fire! Stop exhaling fire!"

He glanced down towards us, and saw me waving at him. His wings slowed down and he closed his mouth, ending the fire stream that was feeding the fire. From the other side of the curtain, the shadows appeared to be retreating to the far side of the chamber. They visibly recoiled as the flames licked closer, their forms singed like burnt thread. My chest tightened. No matter how frightening they were, the zmei's fire was doubly so. The last tendrils of black matter curled towards the river, as if tugged back to their source by an invisible force.

The fire sputtered and died, starved of fuel as the last of the yellow plants withered to ash. Relief washed over me and I turned to Sirak to make sure he was unharmed. He knelt on the ground, his knuckles white against the stone, gasping for air. His wide eyes were fixed on Zhar, who loomed over us, embers still glowing in his throat.

The zmei's voice cut through the silence. "I told you it would work – though the Nav is hardly what I had in mind for our next encounter. No matter. You did it. You found the raskovnik."

Then he noticed Sirak, and his throat flared once more, smoke curling up from his nostrils. "And who might that be?"

His tone implied that had I outed Sirak as a threat, he wouldn't have hesitated to scorch him into oblivion. I stepped between the two.

"No, no, it's fine. He is…" I trailed off as I came short of an explanation. The truth sounded more wild than any made-up story. If Zhar had eyebrows, they would be flying high on his forehead at that moment. "He is a Sultan's janissary who got dragged into the underworld because of me. Speaking of which, how did you get here?"

"I was guarding Rumina's heart when you summoned me and the raskovnik opened up a portal to you. In my hurry, I did something I had not meant to happen."

Guilt twisted Zhar's face. Sirak drew closer, curiosity winning over any fear of the zmei as we followed him to the bank of the black river. Shadows parted, giving the zmei a wide berth as we trailed after. At the very edge of where the river's bed lay, something round caught my eye.

"I held on to the guardian as the portal opened. I did not relish the prospect of losing the heart," Zhar said, not meeting my eyes. "The little mouse did not survive."

The zmei nodded towards the river where, at an arm's length, a new creature's shadow began forming. Tendrils unspooled, coalescing into a tiny body, ears, a muzzle, and a tail that was unmistakably rodent-like. The shadow sniffed the air, its eyeless stare somehow still carrying a trace of accusation towards the zmei.

"It wasn't my intent to kill you!" he rumbled, smoke curling from his nostrils. The shadow-mouse tilted its head, and Zhar's wings twitched, heavy with guilt. The mouse nodded, and Zhar cocked his head as if to listen to whatever it had to say.

"Can they talk? The shadows?" Sirak asked, addressing the zmei for the first time.

"You can't hear them?" Zhar sounded surprised. We shook our heads. "Count it as a blessing; their chatter is quite insufferable. They say the gods abandoned them, that they have no way forward."

"Can we help them?"

"It's not our burden," he snapped. The mouse's shadow bristled at his words. "It's not my duty!"

But his words broke off as Rumina's heart flared with light. We had no time to react before bright white rays burst free from the container, which floated above the river as if lifted by an invisible hand. Its radiance stood stark against the shadows of the dead, and for a moment both they and the living paused to admire it. The light gathered into Rumina's form, her chest aglow with a living heart. Then dark tentacles rose from the black water, wispy hands seizing it.

"No!" bellowed Zhar, who, like me, had remained frozen in place until then, enthralled by the light. Too late, he bolted towards the river. Just before he reached its waters, the same shadows that had cowered in fear at the prospect of being incinerated by the zmei's breath just moments ago moved in front of it and formed a wall with their bodies.

"Out of my way," Zhar warned as a thin line of smoke rose from his nostrils. The wall of shadows hesitated, but did not waver.

"Zhar, look!"

The heart container, held delicately by the tendrils, opened, and the light inside flared into full brilliance, filling the chamber with brightness and warmth that tickled my skin. So strong was the light that bathed us in its glow that, next to me, Sirak shielded his eyes with an arm and I closed mine.

When the flare of light faded to a more comfortable glow, I opened my eyes in time to watch it solidify into a young woman, the ghost of whom I had spoken to only days ago. No colour survived in the black Nav, even with the warm white light that currently bathed it. No colour except for the crimson beating heart inside Rumina's chest. She turned towards Zhar, her eyes full of tenderness. But before the zmei could reach for her, the light dissolved into the river's darkness, taking the shadow of Rumina with itself. Only the beating heart remained, as if still held by invisible hands above the river.

Zhar let out another, even more desperate cry. We watched

helplessly as the darkness shifted again, this time shaping itself into Rumina's true form – a zmei made of darkness. The heart container dissolved in the air and the shadow stepped forward. The other shadows dispersed, making way for it. Zhar's eyes held the sight of his beloved, willing it to come to life, yet knowing she was long gone. A few moments of quiet passed, in which the two lovers seemed to communicate something in the shadows' language that only Zhar was privy to. Then the zmei got a strange look in his eyes. He turned towards us.

"She is saying there is a way for me to see her every day. And it's the same way that would help the shadows move forward to the afterlife. They need a guardian, someone to welcome them, and open the doors forward. Until Veles is back."

"In Nana's stories, a zmei guided the dead to the afterlife, not Veles."

I nodded before my mouth fell open because it had been Sirak who had spoken, not me. Zhar and I gaped at him. Nana's stories? Those words should have come from my lips, not his. Sirak's eyes, full of confusion, flickered from me to Zhar.

"What? It's just something I remember from before." His voice cracked. "Before I was taken to serve in the Sultan's army."

The chamber of the dead felt suddenly stifling as my mind tried to wrap itself around Sirak's words. There were too many things I wanted to ask, questions the answers to which I knew would haunt me until my shadow and I became one once again. Yet, not knowing felt even worse. Feeling apprehensive and not at all ready, I instead turned towards Zhar and said matter-of-factly, "The shadows need you to guide them to the otherworld. You should stay. And this will reunite Rumina and you for eternity."

"But you need me in the mortal realm to face the Vizier. If I stay here, I cannot go back and help you," Zhar insisted. "I'll be bound to the dead."

"So be it. If I get out of here alive, I would have survived both Syanka and the world of the dead. Why should some Vizier scare me after all I've been through?"

Zhar focused his serpentine eyes on me. Whatever he saw in my gaze must have been enough. He nodded, though worry still lurked in his eyes.

"Still, if you need me for a short while, there is a way to summon me."

"All I need is to find another raskovnik?" I asked with a smile.

"All you need is to find another raskovnik," he echoed. Then, unexpectedly, he herded me to the side using his massive head. I giggled like a little girl.

"That's not very dignified of you," I protested weakly, but let myself be pushed aside. "What is this about?"

"You have been keeping something from me," he said, rebuking me. "Something very important."

I followed his gaze to Sirak, who tried his best to appear as if he wasn't eavesdropping, which made it all the more obvious that he was.

"It's not that I have been keeping things." I sighed. "I just had no time to prove my suspicions. And now he's done that for me."

I quickly recounted the events since the last time we had spoken in my dream. As with every moment on this journey, it felt like two forevers ago when Didar was telling me I was to marry her brother.

"And he doesn't know yet?" The zmei shook his head and a

puff of smoke curled up from his nostrils. "You need to tell him."

"I know," I said, throwing my hands in the air. Then, seeing his concern when his gaze followed Rumina's shadow, I whispered. "I know. It's just that... it's not that easy. What if he thinks I'm trying to trick him or take advantage of his position as a ranking janissary?"

"Good, given that you are."

"Yes, but... excuse me?"

The zmei sighed and readied his favourite tone, explaining his thoughts as though I were a child.

"If I'm not there to protect you when you face the Grand Vizier and his dark mage, what do you think is going to happen?"

"He will let me and Iliya go?" I ventured feebly. In truth, as much as I appreciated and needed the aid, I was tired of someone else helping me get out of a situation. Facing Temir and his pet mage was something I needed to do on my own.

"Just tell him," Zhar insisted as if he had read my mind. "He will know it to be true, if he doesn't already."

I nodded. While Zhar and I were having the exchange, a sense of calm had fallen over the shadows of the dead. Their aimless wandering turned into anticipation not long after the zmei had agreed to stay behind. Zhar cleared his throat and a puff of smoke escaped. The shadows retreated a little, but remained close, waiting for the zmei.

"Alright," he said, and for the first time since I'd known him, I detected a sort of excitement in his voice. "I don't know what exactly you expect from me, but I will do my best to guide you forward." When the shadows made no movement, he added, "You are now welcome to move on to the next chamber."

"I think they expect you to go to the entrance," I muttered

in his ear. By then, the air had cleared enough to see what lay ahead. In the distance, the black waters ran into another underground opening. A soft otherworldly light spilled, beckoning the shadows.

"Wait," I said, before Zhar had the chance to head there. "Could you do me a favour? I was wondering… is there a way for you to check if Iliya is here? Just in case."

Zhar nodded and his stare grew distant. He cocked his head as if listening to something. Rumina's shadow drew closer and whispered in his ear. I heard no words come out of her mouth, but when she finished, Zhar had my answer.

"He is not here," the zmei said.

"How can you tell? Does Rumina know something about him?"

"Ah, more questions." Zhar sighed, but at Rumina's prompting, continued. "The shadows share a connection that allows them to communicate. Which makes sense, given they come from the same place."

He pointed towards the river, from the depths of which shadows had resumed forming.

"What about my shadow, then?" I asked Rumina. After a short-lived silence, Zhar conveyed her message.

"She says that's different. Since you are still among the living, your death should not have come to life, though that's not the right word." He paused, as if waiting for me to appreciate his joke. My face remained serious, so he sighed and went on. "She is here, bound to you until you return to the living."

"Must she be?" I frowned.

Rumina's shadow mouthed something, and Zhar's voice turned solemn. "The dead do not bargain. And now, as their guardian, I must send you back. They don't like being disturbed either."

"How will you do that?" asked Sirak, who had approached us once more. He still regarded Zhar with awe, which the zmei found to be the appropriate attitude towards him. Just then, as if to answer Sirak, the light spilling from the hall beyond reached for Zhar with warm tendrils. It wrapped around him like a hug, and for a moment he basked in it, serenity radiating from him. When the light receded and dissolved into the air, Zhar's serpentine eyes were calm.

"Now I can open a portal to wherever I want," he said. "Should you need help, you need only call me."

"With a raskovnik that's nearly impossible to find," Sirak pointed out.

"Help will be available to those who call for it," the zmei said vaguely. "And now it's time for you to go."

With that, Zhar lifted his foot, and a sharp claw slashed the air. Where the claw sliced, light, much like the one that had been surrounding him a moment ago, formed and quickly expanded into a portal.

"We will meet again," the zmei promised. "One way or another, in life or in death; I don't know if I'll be able to reach you in your dreams again, but know that you are in my thoughts."

Rays of sunlight spilled out through the door and into the underworld. I hesitated, reluctant to part with Zhar. In the end, I closed my arms around the zmei's thick neck, his chin resting with surprising gentleness on my shoulder. Rumina's shadow waved with a dark wing, and I stepped into the light with my brother by my side. From the portal, sunlight bled into the darkness – golden, real, and so familiar. Zhar bent his head, and for a heartbeat, his forehead pressed to mine. Neither was ready to say goodbye. "Until next time," he whispered. Then his wings swept forward to shepherd us through, and the light swallowed us whole.

CHAPTER 28

Roots Remember

Zhar did more than return us to the land of the living. He opened a portal straight into the Grand Vizier's palace. We stumbled into a walled garden, daylight blinding us after the darkness of the Nav. I could hardly believe it. At last, I had made it to the palace. And, by the heavy scent of late-blooming flowers, it was still the end of summer. Just as the Grand Vizier had foretold.

I shielded my eyes with one hand, blinking against the glare. Beside me, Sirak checked his weapons, then retrieved a knife and handed it to me.

"I have my sabre," he said. "And a musket that's no use now. It's empty."

He discarded the weapon into the nearest bush. I held the knife, feeling a little less defenceless, even if I would be of little help should the Vizier's soldiers attack. As my eyes adjusted, I took in the garden. A few of the flowers I saw sometimes appeared at Morava's market, though always in small numbers and at a dear price. Nana would marvel briefly before dismissing them, saying the showy tulip bouquets were no match for our violet flowerbed. Here, tulips blazed yellow across the floor, broken only by a walkway and the odd cypress.

Sirak saw me marvel at the colours and said, "The palace has double walls with the gardens in between. The walls circle the area and have many smaller garden rooms full of flowers and trees. Each has a different theme, but it's usually the same bed of flowers across a chamber. We were lucky that your friend sent us to one of the more secluded parts of the gardens."

He had been about to add something when a shout from behind the outer wall made him pause.

"Form the ranks!"

Steel clashed against shields, a sound multiplied as more soldiers joined. Sirak stiffened. His eyes, wide with fear, searched the wall for a crack. The call faded into a sickening clatter of steel and boots, and the already warm air thickened with dread. The garden walls were the only thing between us and whatever army waited outside.

"I believe I know why there's an army outside," Sirak said with a frown, still desperate to catch a sight of what transpired outside the palace walls. "But it can't be. The siege wasn't being planned until autumn."

"The siege?" I repeated, a note of hysteria in my voice. Sirak nodded and pointed to the doors that led to another part of the garden towards which he set off. Mercifully, we encountered no guards as we made for the exit. We followed the wall that opened up to a larger garden of cypresses, purple hyacinths, and red roses. Bees buzzed about, unbothered by the imminent threat of an army in waiting.

"Zareh, one of the men who had accompanied me before the javina dragged me to the Nav, hinted that the Grand Vizier was overstepping his station," I insisted as we rounded a corner. The heat and overpowering flower scent brought a sick feeling that made my stomach churn. Sirak grunted in agreement.

"This makes getting your betrothed back more difficult. The Vizier bears no love for the janissaries, and if they are outside besieging the palace, it means we are in greater danger than I anticipated. My word won't hold any sway for long, especially in your predicament."

"Why are they doing this? Isn't the palace the Sultan's property?" I asked, the sense of dread only blooming further. The gardens hinted at an opulence the likes of which I had never imagined, but also frightened me with how little I knew of where I was. I felt like a pawn moved across the board while complex politics transpired inside the palace's walls.

"It's more complicated than that," said Sirak. "In the past few years, the Sultan has been travelling on various campaigns throughout the conquered lands. He's made a habit of retreating to one of his residences to spend time alone with his concubines."

His last words carried a bitter note. I regarded him with poorly concealed curiosity, but did not press him further. Sirak continued.

"In the meantime, the Grand Vizier has been amassing power as quietly as possible, thinking the Sultan is naïve enough not to notice. Naturally, his brilliant mind has had Temir outmanoeuvred from the beginning. Bayas has been rallying janissaries for a while now, strengthening our ranks and recruiting over the quota."

"Recruiting." I couldn't help but laugh. "You mean taking little boys as blood-tax against their will?"

"The Sultan is not like his predecessor," Sirak said harshly, much to my surprise. "The one that took me as a boy was a cruel man and did not value his soldiers. Bayas does. He offered us a new life, expanded our power, and never spared resources for us."

"All out of the goodness of his heart, no doubt."

Sirak whirled around, his cheeks reddening. For a man who had likely killed for the Sultan more times than he could count, any slight against his master clearly touched a nerve. His voice cracked like a whip. "The Sultan is kind. You don't know what you're talking about."

"What would I know?" I said bitterly. "I'm just a provincial girl. But even I can tell you – a kind man doesn't face revolts from the people he claims to rule with mercy."

Sirak's jaw tightened. "Those revolts come from fools like the Grand Vizier. From fools mistaking kindness for weakness."

He flung a hand toward the distant roar of soldiers as evidence for his words. I wasn't ready to let it go.

"I've heard stories," I whispered. "Of boys taken against their will from their homes, who grew up forgetting who they were, raised only to kill. Many forget their roots. But not you, Sirak. So why?"

His eyes darkened, but when he spoke, his voice was quieter.

"He was kind to me when no one else was."

I hesitated. My resentment wasn't just about the Sultan's cruelty. It was about what he'd stolen from me – my brother, my father, my whole life before I even had the chance to live it. When I lifted my gaze to meet Sirak's, his eyes, the colour of autumn leaves, were warm.

"The Sultan is not the reason you are so upset, Jasna," he said, his voice gentle. "So what is it?"

Despite the commotion beyond the wall, I was sure he could hear my heart hammering against my ribcage.

"I wasn't trying to challenge your beliefs. But by now, you must have noticed some resemblance between us."

What I meant as a simple remark sounded more like a plea. The garden had gone still, the stench of sweat and violence from outside the walls hanging in the air. No trace of birds remained and even the bees' constant hum had gone silent. We halted by a bench and I slumped on it. Sirak followed. Black and white mosaic tiles in concentric patterns covered the parts of the floor and walls. For a moment, the armies beyond the walls and the dangers within seemed to vanish. All I could hear was the pounding of my own heart as I waited for Sirak's next words.

"Your javina, born from entombing your shadow – the death that follows you everywhere, is a creature visible only to its intended. Yet I could see it. Why?"

"I think you already know why," I said. A shadow fell across Sirak's face, and my heart sank, not ready to be rejected. The words poured out, unguarded and confused.

"Then explain why my two companions saw it too. Only kin can see each other's death, or so the stories say. Some claim those born on a Saturday can see it, but I doubt all of us were born that day. What troubles me most is how familiar you are with my past. You flinched when I mentioned Nana's stories." He hesitated, his eyes no longer meeting mine. "There's something I didn't tell you. I had a sister. And a father, too. He took care of us, though he grew less and less present after my mother's death."

My eyes had welled with tears during his outburst. I wanted to tell him that I didn't know why everyone saw the death that was meant for my eyes only, but that it mattered little since we at last had found each other. But once he had unleashed the stream of words, Sirak had to say all that troubled him, so I let him speak. All the while, he regarded me like a man who'd been searching for something he could not name.

"In my heart, I knew it was true," he said, his eyes wide with hope. "You are about the same age she would be now. And though I was too young to remember much else, I know you are her. A janissary's training is meant to erase the names and places of our past lives, but I remember her eyes. Dark green, the quiet of a forest before the storm. The rarest kind. Much like yours."

Though both my vision and his were blurry now, our hands still found each other's. For one brief moment, everything made sense. I felt at peace. Then Sirak asked, "What happened to our father?"

"You haven't seen him?"

A rustle that sounded like feet crunching on leaves broke the stillness. Startled, Sirak dropped my hand and sprang to his feet, sabre drawn. My palm closed around the knife he had given me, feeling anything but threatening in my cardigan – once blue with yellow flowers, now so tattered and thin that it felt like wearing a shirt under the summer heat beating down on us. Both exits appeared clear of soldiers or servants. Sirak's tension, visible in his shoulders, did not ease.

"What is it?" I whispered. The air was still. Then came a rustle of leaves.

"Hidden doors," he mouthed just as a flash of silver caught my eye.

"Down!" I yelled as I shoved him hard. He stumbled back a step – just enough for the dagger to miss him and sink into the trunk of a cypress. A man stepped from the slender trees, his green robes and matching turban blending into the foliage.

I barely had time to steady myself before the assassin

produced a second knife, this time aimed at me. I dropped flat to the ground just as the blade hissed past my ear. Unfazed, the man advanced, his eyes burning with bloodlust. A third knife glistened in his hand, and I rolled, bracing for the strike.

Caught up in his knife-throwing game, he missed a root sticking from the ground and tripped at the same time as Sirak dealt a blow with his sabre. The sabre whistled through empty air when the assassin stumbled. The man, however, was not quick enough to regain his balance. Sirak grabbed his shoulder and hauled him upright. He then placed the sabre's tip at the assassin's throat.

"Who are you?" he said in a voice laced with murder.

The man spat in his face. Sirak pressed the sabre's tip enough to draw a streak of dark blood that ran down the man's throat and coloured the hem of his green robe. A bead of sweat formed on the assassin's forehead. Still, he remained silent.

"Why would you try to murder a janissary? You know the penalty is death."

The blossoming blood turned into a gushing wound with a flick of Sirak's wrist.

"Please," I heard myself plead for the assassin's life. Sirak ignored me, his face twisted with bloodlust. The man gagged and gasped for breath, blood trickling down from his wound. I pushed myself up on bruised palms and brushed the dust from my hands.

"I won't ask again," said Sirak in a low voice that nonetheless carried the promise of violence. "The next one will kill you."

With great effort, the man produced a barely audible sentence, punctuated by gasps for air.

"The Sultan... he's desperate to find you. He thinks... the

Grand Vizier... has you. And the Vizier... decided to use this... and let him think so."

"So Temir thought he could get a head start by using me as a bargaining chip?"

A gurgle was the only noise confirming his question.

"Sirak, please!" I begged again. "He was just following orders."

Sirak hesitated, then lowered his sabre. Sweat ran down the assassin's face and mixed with his blood.

"A word of advice. Be a good little soldier and obey the Sultan, your sovereign, not the Vizier, even if he is the one that employs you," Sirak said and produced a thin rope from his kaftan's pocket. "Here, help me tie him up."

Once the assassin's wrists were bound and his mouth gagged, we left him behind a bush and exited to the next section of the garden. A sea of jasmines greeted us, their floral fragrance so heavy it pushed the threat of battle into the distance.

"I wish Nana were here. She always has something up her sleeve," I said.

"She always did," Sirak agreed. All the violence had leeched from his face, and I found it hard to believe he was the same man from a moment ago. Still, I couldn't shake the image of the raw blood-hunger he had about him when holding the assassin at a sabre's point. One did not become the Sultan's deadliest soldier by showing mercy, I thought, and the notion left a bitter taste in my mouth. Not wishing to dwell on it, I said, "I wish you had seen her when she opened a portal to Syanka and helped me escape Morava. It was as if she were young again, so determined and fierce."

"Morava," he said, the word foreign on his tongue. "I had forgotten about it."

It warmed my heart how easily and unconditionally Sirak

accepted me. I told him about Nana and how our father had set off after him only never to return. I even recounted the events that had forced me into Syanka and what I had seen there.

"It does bother me," I confessed eventually, "that everyone could see my death. I think my shadow was severed into more than one part and Nana helped me get back the bits that belonged to me. The ones only I could see. But my death was left roaming the realms in search of me, free for everyone to see. I have so many questions, but somehow always fall short of answers. Nana would know exactly what to say, but it's not like I can ask her…"

I paused to catch my breath, and in the short-lived silence, Sirak's hand found mine once more.

"It's been lonely without her. Despite meeting all these creatures, my first thought is always of her. I want to tell her of all my adventures and see her eyes sparkle with mischief once again. I'm glad I found you, though. And I hope to see our father soon."

My words had given Sirak time to reach for the chain hidden beneath his shirt.

"Father never found me. I fear the worst since he never returned. But the silver lining is that Nana didn't leave me with nothing, even when the Sultan took me in," Sirak said as he pulled out a small pendant. It was round with a polished dark green stone in the middle. When Sirak opened it, there was nothing inside.

"It's empty," I breathed out an air of disappointment.

"She said that in a moment of need, it will be there to guide me."

"Perhaps the pendant itself will provide guidance. In Syanka, I had a red thread leading me here, and then I drank a potion that turned into a bird and moved the thread to show me the way to Zhar. Nana knew much more than what she was letting on. I'm sure we'll figure out how to trigger whatever the pendant is meant to do."

"We'll see. I trust Nana's words."

"She really made extraordinary things possible, didn't she?"

We sat in silence for a moment. Then the green stone began to glow faintly. At first, I thought it reflected the sunlight, but the glow soon intensified, casting flecks of light across Sirak's face. I couldn't quite place it, but the deep forest colour reminded me of something I had seen only recently.

"What…" Sirak began, but changed his mind mid-sentence and instead said, "The pendant is warm to the touch. Try it."

He took it off his neck and handed it to me. Indeed, it tingled pleasantly against my hand, warm enough to be felt at the touch of skin. The ground quivered. A crack sounded beneath us, startling me enough to drop the pendant. Sirak caught it just as roots sprouted from the floor. We had no time to react when, with unexpected agility, they turned towards us and lashed out. While still holding the pendant with one hand, Sirak unsheathed his sabre the moment I held out the knife, ready to cut my way through the writhing tendrils.

Branches whipped upward, reaching for Sirak. He slashed, but more rose. Where his sabre severed parts, new saplings grew and reached out as if animated by an invisible force. Like tendrils, they wrapped themselves around my wrist, rendering my knife useless as it fell on the ground. Sirak wasn't faring any better. A root relieved him of his sabre and bound his wrists in the same manner as mine.

"They're not going for us, but for the pendant!" I gasped. Sirak cast a dubious look at me but held out the still-glowing pendant for the roots to grasp. The moment he did, the tendrils reached hungrily for it and wound around it, holding the pendant in suspension in the space where Sirak had let it go. Inside the circle of tendrils, something shifted.

Sirak saw it before I did. With a hand now free of the roots, he lifted the sabre from where it lay on the ground. His eyes grew wide with surprise upon noticing the thing that stared at us from inside the opening the roots had woven.

"The javina, the Nav, the zmei, and now this," he muttered. "I hope Nana knew what she was doing when she gave me the pendant."

"She knew," I said. Calmness settled over me. For the first time, I wasn't walking into the unknown alone. "And so do we. We need to find the Vizier. Bring Iliya back. And stop the siege."

CHAPTER 29

THE LADY OF PESTILENCE

*C*uriosity got the best of me as I approached the thing enshrouded by the saplings, ready to hurl myself to the ground one more time, dignity all but forgotten. The tired, mud-coloured eyes staring back at me were not what I'd expected to find. A vaguely familiar creature stood there, looking close to collapse. Swollen lumps of pus bulged across its body, and each wheeze rattled its chest. It looked half-dead, yet when its murky eyes fixed mine, calm lucidity stared back. Then one boil burst, yellow liquid trickling down its arm. My brother and I recoiled in unison.

"That's what Nana sent us?" Sirak asked morosely.

"Hey, I didn't ask to be here either," the creature grumbled. I had thought it was male, but the voice had a note to it that said it was actually female. At that moment, two things occurred to me. The dark green stone at the pendant's centre reminded me of Gorovoi's eyes. The leshy had promised help when needed, provided it was within his domain. Perhaps the cypress trees and the Sultan's luscious gardens fell within that domain as well.

"Gorovoi sent you, didn't he?" I asked the creature. She stared at me for a while, as if measuring me up before nodding. I turned to Sirak to share my second insight.

"I know what she is," I said carefully. "But you have to promise not to get upset when I tell you. I've seen her before, in the caravanserai on the silver path. It's the chuma."

Sirak hastily stepped away from the creature, colour draining from his cheeks. "Are you sure it's really the… the chuma? Why would Nana give it to me?"

"By now you know that much of what Nana told us as stories is true," I said, at first uncertainly, then with growing conviction. "She must have known Syanka was real all along. I have no clue how far her knowledge stretches, but she knows things no other human does, like how to open a portal there or how to negotiate with a hala. So why not have an actual plague as an acquaintance if all these other things exist? It's just like Nana to have the unlikeliest of friends."

"What are we supposed to do with a disease? Help us die quicker?" Sirak asked dubiously.

"Calling someone a disease isn't very nice, you know," the chuma said, and both Sirak and I stilled. She had been silent for a while, so we had somewhat rudely excluded her. "You could have simply asked me what I was. I, too, have feelings."

Sirak hurriedly reassured the chuma that we meant no offence. Nana had given the pendant to Sirak, but it had been Gorovoi that had sent her to us, which meant the two of them must be better acquainted than I thought. Once again I wondered if I would ever get the chance to ask Nana all the questions I had gathered in this journey and tucked in the sleeve of my cardigan for later. One thing I knew: Nana wouldn't have given Sirak the pendant if she didn't think it was useful.

"The pendant only opens as a last resort," I said. "Which means we are closer to the Grand Vizier than we thought."

Sirak scratched his chin. "It's true that this exit leads to the palace, but I don't see how the chuma is helpful unless we want to die before facing him."

My next words sounded as if they came out of someone else's mouth.

"We won't be dying – hopefully. But people who cross our path might have to. Is it true you can taint whoever you wish with your plague?" I asked the creature while pretending I did not see Sirak pointedly staring at me. Had I truly just suggested an enemy deserved to die? I had killed the hala, was I considering killing again?

"So what if I can?" she said defensively, as if I was accusing her of having had too much fun with her powers. "Doesn't mean I go around touching people. Not very often anyway, but accidents do happen. I've retired."

Sirak was about to ask how it was possible for a plague to retire, but his words died on his lips when I elbowed him in the ribs and mouthed 'some other time' over the creature's head.

"But will you help us if needed? We have to confront the Grand Vizier Temir and plead with him to release my betrothed."

"Ah, a love story." The chuma sighed longingly. "Nothing compares to a good love story during a plague outbreak. Lovers living their last days in agony, yet their love lives on in stories even after their slow and painful demise."

"No one's dying," I said hurriedly. "No one on our side, anyway."

The creature let out a disgruntled 'hm,' but did not protest further. The roots and saplings around her writhed apart, and the pendant clattered to the floor. Sirak hastily retrieved it, eager to keep Nana's last gift safe.

"We just need you to intimidate a few people. Persuade them to… contemplate their mortal lives and how unfortunate it would be if they were cut short," Sirak said. For someone who claimed to be retired, the chuma looked awfully disappointed she wouldn't get to do what she did best. Still, she shooed the last bits of roots away and nodded, her hungry eyes drinking in the sight of the palace walls with all the potential victims inside. I suppressed a shiver.

"We will also need you to look less conspicuous, if that's possible," I added in a rush before the chuma strode inside.

"You want me to assume my other form? That can be done. However, there is another matter we need to settle. You have to promise me that you'll abide by the terms of our agreement. My condition is that I will repay the debt I owe to the pendant's owner by helping you. And then you will release me from its confinement. Are these conditions agreeable to you?"

Sirak and I nodded.

"Out of curiosity, what did Nana do to have the chuma indebted to her?" asked Sirak. The chuma frowned, and a pustule burst. I gagged, and Sirak struggled to breathe, yet the chuma remained oblivious to our distress.

"Who is Nana? Is she my current owner? I have been bound to this pendant for centuries. Every owner says they will set me free after our bargain is fulfilled, but when they need my help no more, they always forget to do so. It's only in Syanka that I get some respite from the tedious life of being stuck in a pendant."

"That's awful," I said as I considered the consequences of setting the plague free. After all, humans did not need her help to spread disease and misery. Yet, the chuma had promised she was retired, but who knew what she would do once set free? Sirak's thoughts must have been similar to mine, for he muttered in my ear, "We'll face that problem when the time comes."

"I would rather set her free than be responsible for the enslavement of another creature," I said under my breath. It was impossible to tell if the plague heard me, because at that moment she began transforming. Her limbs elongated, ulcers vanishing beneath fresh pink flesh. Golden-brown hair spilled down her shoulders, and a white dress clothed flawless skin, her crimson lips stark as blood in snow. Both Sirak and I must have gaped at her with our mouths open. A glance at us made her exhale sharply as she said, "This is exactly why I prefer my other form."

"We didn't mean any disrespect," I assured her, praying Sirak would have the decency to stop ogling her. He tore his glance away with a frown.

"Forgive us for being insolent, but your new form is hardly unnoticeable," he said.

"Oh, my most sincere apologies," the chuma snapped. "Should I change back so that I would please the great Sultan's emissary?"

Sirak's face turned a shade redder, and he muttered that no change was needed.

"Worry not, my powers remain as they are. A single touch is all it takes for someone's beating heart to still."

We couldn't help ourselves but take another step back. I had the feeling that this imperious woman, plague personified, had seized command.

"Don't worry," she reassured us once more before heading towards the palace, leaving the gardens behind. "I have no desire to come near either of you."

"That was uncalled for," I muttered under my breath, and

Sirak chuckled. As we entered the palace through what I had imagined would be a much grander entrance that instead appeared to be a back door, another cry from outside shook the walls.

"Arrows notched and at the ready!"

I inhaled sharply and shared a glance with Sirak. We both knew we were running low on time, and being under siege on the wrong side of the wall was not what I had come here for. The feeling of impending doom clung to me, bringing back the sense that someone else was forcing my fate upon me.

"The Sultan uses the arrows command as an intimidation tactic," Sirak said, as if his words were meant to be reassuring. "He likes to draw out the moment as much as possible to force the other side to reconsider their actions."

"Does it work?"

"Somewhat. But Temir is way too clever to fall for that."

"Naturally."

"With her on our side," Sirak said, pointing at the chuma, "we have little to fear."

His words rang hollow in the long hallway we found ourselves in. Cool air swept over my skin, but relief faded when a cold prickle ran up my neck. I couldn't say when the sudden feeling that we were being led into a trap formed, but it only intensified with each step that plunged us deeper into the palace. Sirak must have sensed it too. His next words betrayed a sense of unease.

"Forget what I said. It's way too quiet."

Deserted chambers trailed behind us, the quiet only growing as we pressed deeper into the palace. The chuma led our small party with a confidence that said she knew what she was doing. When I asked her if this was her first time in the palace, she looked at me oddly and said, "What gives you the idea it isn't?"

"Not reassuring at all," Sirak muttered as we shared a glance.

"But surely you know your way around?"

It was Sirak, who was too busy keeping his eyes peeled open for potential threats to notice that the question was aimed at the chuma, that answered.

"I know the palace like the back of my hand, though it's been years since I last visited. As janissary initiates, we were required to live here before the Sultan sent us on campaigns." He paused, as if recalling something unpleasant. "That was also before Bayas started holding court at his seaside residence. The palace is divided into courts, and despite all the changes, the janissary court remains the largest."

As he spoke, a breeze carrying the smell of salt filled my lungs. When we narrowed down a hallway, a breathtaking view opened beyond the large bay windows: the sea stretched endlessly, waves rippling under a summer breeze that stirred the gossamer curtains. I paused on the balcony, reminded of Syanka and Zhar. I missed both dearly.

"This is the view that greeted you every morning?" I asked Sirak, pointing towards the sea. He nodded.

"There is so much more to see if we survive this. I'll show you all the wonders the Sultan's empire has in store. That's a promise."

Despite the enticing offer, I found myself longing for something else.

"I owe it to Nana to visit her first."

"Of course," Sirak nodded. "We'll go together. No one will dare accuse you of witchcraft after that."

"Let them. They don't scare me anymore. And then..." I took a breath and at last voiced my truest desire. "After that, I would like to go back to Syanka. And I would love for you to join me."

But before Sirak had the chance to reply, a commotion ahead drew our attention. We dashed forward to see the chuma grab a guardsman's wrist and squeeze it almost lovingly before letting it go. The man did not even stagger, instead quickly regaining composure. His dark eyes carried a promise of blood. The chuma's bizarre inaction seemed to doom us – until the man cried out and collapsed, his hands clawing at his face. His screams shattered the silence of the hallway as he began scratching his face, hands, legs, and every part of his body.

"It hurts," he whimpered in between screams. "Make it stop, please. Make it stop."

"I might have overdone it a little," the chuma mused, frowning as if trying to recall the proper dose of plague she should have delivered. The man writhed, skin torn and bloodied. He clawed at his skin until crimson welts covered his body. When I noticed the yellow pus mixed with blood, I was grateful for not having had a proper meal in a while. Otherwise, I would have emptied my stomach on the floor.

"Put an end to this. Don't you see he's suffering?" I hollered at the chuma, not caring who would hear us. It was too late for that, anyway. The man's screams had long alerted anyone in the neighbouring corridors of our presence. Sirak was ready to end the man's suffering with his blade when the chuma stepped past him and lightly touched the man's forehead. His screams, which had turned into a hoarse screech, ceased almost instantly, his twitching legs the only hint he still lived. His eyes took on a glassy look, and his kicking turned into convulsions that died down shortly after.

"Apologies for that," the chuma said calmly. "I haven't used my ability in a while."

"You just tortured a man. You didn't just kill him – you put him through the worst kind of agony," I spat.

Sirak muttered, "Not to mention we could have questioned him first."

"I said I was rusty, didn't I?" The chuma bristled, oblivious to the suffering she'd caused. "It's why you wanted me to take the lead, right? To dispense with anyone who stood in the way."

With that, she went ahead as if nothing had happened.

CHAPTER 30

At Musket-Point

Though we had no argument against the chuma's last words, Sirak and I grew increasingly uneasy in her presence. As we crossed the countless hallways and emerged in and out of courtyards, the suspicion that a clever trap was closing in on us would not leave me. It took either deliberate planning or a catastrophic event for the empire's heart to lie so empty.

Abandoned janissary quarters greeted us, our steps echoing across marble in the unsettling quiet. Even with the siege, it seemed unlikely all guards had fled. Sirak's rigid jaw betrayed his own unease. Only the chuma ventured deeper without a flicker of doubt.

We kept to the outside walls as much as possible and went inside only when having to cross different quarters. Sirak insisted it would lengthen our journey, but to lessen the chance of being ambushed. The prospect of being out in the open for everyone to see us unsettled me, but I trusted him and his knowledge of the palace enough to keep quiet.

"We are about to enter the second court," Sirak warned. A narrow passageway between the janissary courtyard and the kitchens announced the court before it swam into view, the summer heat making its rooftops shimmer like a mirage. I stole an uneasy glance at our surroundings before venturing into the building, but there was no sign of anyone following us. The feeling that we walked deeper into the trap made my shoulders ache with tension.

"It's not the harem." I sighed with relief after noticing the more rugged design of the red brick buildings. Sirak suppressed a smirk at my obvious reluctance to be walking in on the Sultan's many wives. Somewhere close by, a fire burned despite the warm day, grey smoke curling from a chimney into the clear sky.

"How do you know it's not the harem?" Sirak asked, still bemused.

"Because I have a nose?"

The unmistakable smell of coffee, one of the many wonders I had seen at Morava's market, as well as melted sugar mixed with other aromas, such as that of rising dough, wafted from the long passageway. It could only mean one thing. We were about to enter the palace's kitchens. Suddenly, the reminder that I hadn't had a proper meal since sharing Didar's dinner made my knees buckle and my stomach let out a long and desperate growl. The chuma halted, shaking her head so that a cascade of smooth curls bounced around her face.

"It isn't the time to sate your human needs. The air carries the iron tang of blood and it won't be long until the battle commences."

Sirak ignored her and steered me towards the kitchen.

"Let's get some food. I doubt the Vizier will mind. Or notice, for that matter."

"Isn't it too dangerous? Lingering and risking being seen?"

"As our companion pointed out earlier, her touch can kill, so we have no cause for worry."

"I wouldn't want to murder innocent maids and cooks in case we get ambushed," I said, but still followed him, my stomach demanding to be fed no matter the cost. To my relief, the kitchens, much like the rest of the palace, save the unfortunate guard we had run into, were deserted.

"Help yourself," Sirak said, though he didn't have to tell me twice. A table waited, still heavy with baklava and loaves torn but untouched. The sweet, yeasty smell was stronger than fear, so I wasted no time. The chuma stood guard at the door, her lips pursed in a thin line of disapproval while I helped myself with the feast in front of me. If the fear of what lay ahead had let me succumb to despair moments ago, it now faded into the back of my mind, chased away by the food that filled my belly. For a moment I let myself believe we were safe, just me and my brother, eating in peace.

"Let's get Iliya back," I said as we made our way out of the kitchens. Upon exiting, a different type of unease settled over. It turned out that clear thinking went hand in hand with a full stomach. The insanity of us confronting the Grand Vizier and the dark mage while an army waited outside the walls seemed to at last seep through my tired mind, the seed of doubt quickly blossoming.

The chuma needed but one glance towards me to sense something of what transpired inside my mind. She pouted her impossibly red lips.

"You humans and your constant need for reassurance.

Don't you see what a bad time this is to harbour doubts? Hold them hidden until our bargain gets fulfilled."

But Sirak had paused and was regarding me with both understanding and sadness, as if all the invisible scabs I carried were peeled to bleed raw for anyone to see.

"It must have been a very long and lonely journey for you," he said gently, and I did my best to avoid his stare, blinking away the tears that blurred my vision. "Not everyone is brave enough to set off on such a path and still end up where you are, even against all odds."

"I was forced into it when my people decided they were better off if I were dead," I said with a shrug, once more trying, and failing, to put up a brave front.

"You didn't have to come all this way, yet you did. That's not nothing."

"I had no choice unless I wanted to be burned alive. Another time," I added in a rush when I glanced at the chuma's exasperated face. She did not mince her next words.

"Poor pretty girl, being mocked for being so special. Must have been excruciating."

"Leave her be," Sirak cautioned. The chuma's words reminded me of Maruna, another bully I had once thought on my side. The comparison made me rethink my alliance with the creature. After all, I hardly trusted her to deliver on her side of the bargain. The chuma's retort was already on her lips.

"Or what? You are going to risk an incredibly painful death? I think not."

"You are right," I said. "I'll stop whining. But the pain of being mocked your whole life for not being enough or fitting in a frame drawn for you by others is something you should understand better than most."

Her eyes narrowed, but she only said, "The Grand Vizier

will use your lack of confidence against you. Beware when you face him and his dark wizard. Both prey on any weakness they sense."

I gritted my teeth, but said nothing. She was right, I could not let any sentiment cloud my judgement regarding what lay ahead. We crossed over to the next court and were once more greeted by deserted hallways that led to another stone and brick chamber with tall windows. Eight domes, all painted with geometric patterns of red and blue, stood high on the ceiling. The walls, lined with enclosed cases, contained riches such as I had never imagined.

"The treasury," Sirak explained, "where the other janissaries and I used to get paid. If you wanted to make a rich woman of yourself, now would be the time to take some of what's in those cases and forget about dark mages and Viziers."

Though his light tone said he was joking, his tense expression had a pleading edge to it, as if saying 'take the ruby necklaces and gold plates and never return to this wretched place.'

"You will never find the royal treasury stripped of guards. I hope your betrothed is worth forgoing that opportunity," he said instead.

"Would you steal it and just go? Abandon your duties?"

I knew the answer even without his affirmation. Something about the loyalty he had exhibited to the Sultan earlier had told me as much.

"No. I have nowhere to go."

"You have me and Nana," I began saying, but just then, a case laden with gold and jewellery shifted ever so slightly. The faint scrape of metal followed before the cold muzzle of a musket pressed against Sirak's back. The sound of my pulse hammering against my ribcage drowned out every thought.

"How nice of you to pay us a visit, Sirak," said a familiar

voice that, even though I had heard it only once before, was seared in my mind. The memory tasted sour on my tongue as I recalled the day at the well that had heralded all events that had followed.

"Yerleg," Sirak said, not hiding the contempt in his voice.

"And I see you brought company. A most pleasing outcome for the Grand Vizier. He was once again right that you would come crawling to him by the end of summer," the Vizier's dark mage said as he stepped out of the shadows that had concealed him until that moment. It would be more accurate to say the shadows parted for him, like smoke dissolving into thin air. They were made of the same darkness that we had seen just hours ago in the Nav.

"You have hold over them. Over the shadows of the dead." I gasped at the same time as the realisation drained the colour from Sirak's face.

"Ah, yes. The Grand Vizier himself thought you cleverer than most. Smart for a woman, anyway, not that this is a requirement for him," Yerleg said as he licked his lips. "You weren't clever enough to obey him at his first command, though. Imagine all the pain it would have saved you and your beloved. Iliya, was it? Now, where is your companion?"

I cast a confused look around the treasury. Did he mean the chuma? She should have intervened by now, yet she was nowhere to be seen. Sirak cursed under his breath.

"The thing about creatures of Syanka," the dark mage drawled, "is that they can't be trusted to be there when you need them, especially when they know they're cornered. I prefer to deprive them of that possibility and instead bind them to serve me. A much more reliable method."

"Like you bound Zhar to use him for his power?" I asked with venom. The dark mage only laughed.

"You seem to find friends in the most useless of creatures… and people," he sneered, his glance full of disdain as it slid back to Sirak. Yerleg had called him my friend, so at least he knew nothing of us sharing blood. For all he cared, we were just strangers whose lot had been thrown together.

"At least her friends don't have a penchant for theatrics," Sirak retorted. The dark mage merely extended another one of his wry smiles.

"That's not the sharp reply you think it is, my dear boy. You have been lucky enough to firsthand witness the grandest of Viziers conquer lands and people, yet you still underestimate his power." Yerleg went on while his smile sharpened with every word. "Again and again, your ignorance wins over wisdom. And you, girl—" his gaze flicked to me, "just as mediocre as your brother."

Yerleg paused as if to savour our reaction. "But what's the matter? You two are looking awfully pale. Did you think that I, the Grand Vizier's greatest mage, hadn't figured out your little secret? That two mortals, bound by blood, are crossing the land of the dead, caused quite the stir among my shadows. Did you think they wouldn't whisper in my ear of what transpires in the Nav and the realms beyond? No? Then the more fool you are. But enough of that. I would advise you to obey my orders if you want to find out your beloved's fate. And mind you, I have no need of weapons to force you to obey me."

When the dark mage steered us towards the far exit, we had no choice but to comply; the musket pointed at my brother's back was enough to force us to do so. The royal treasury seemed much less imposing now. Fear left no room to marvel at the precious stones and ornaments in its cabinets. We remained in the same court, arriving after crossing just one more hallway. It chilled me to think we had come so close to the Grand Vizier, only to be delivered into his hands at musket-point. Another entrance greeted us, this time the two heavy doors creaking open seemingly on their own. No doubt the dark mage thought himself impressive. Yerleg could not help but gloat before he pushed us inside.

"In times of war, it's the servants who flee first – that's why the palace is so quiet. The Grand Vizier remembers those who have remained loyal to him and rewards them richly. As for deserters." He let the words hang. "You'll see soon enough. But for now, be ready to meet those who remain."

"How kind of you to warn us," I said.

At the same time, Sirak sneered, "There is no way you'll withstand a siege with a handful of people."

"You underestimate the Vizier's forces, as usual," Yerleg said absentmindedly and pushed the doors open to reveal what lay ahead. The domed chamber was brimming with people. Soldiers, servants, and other nobles – askeri – among whom I recognised some familiar faces I had seen at the well. The woman with the flawless complexion who had once envied my skin regarded me appraisingly. I didn't hide my contempt when Yerleg steered us towards a dais at the far end.

The chatter fell into a hush the moment we entered, and statesmen and servants alike parted to make way for the Grand Vizier's mage. Under different circumstances, I might have gaped in awe at the opulence that surrounded us. Even under siege, the riches that adorned both walls and people alike were anything but mundane, yet I had eyes only for the man that sat on the throne, the same man responsible for severing my shadow and almost killing me in the process. Sirak's grimace revealed his own displeasure at seeing the Grand Vizier seated on the Sultan's throne.

There I was, just as he had foretold. If he had foreseen that I would arrive at the exact time of his prediction, perhaps the Grand Vizier was the most powerful man in the empire after all. I glanced towards his dark mage and the musket he had propped against Sirak's back dissolved into thin air. Illusion, that's what it had been. And we had followed it without question. A thin smile played on Yerleg's lips as he delivered us to the Grand Vizier.

CHAPTER 31

A KIND WORD

The time it took to cross the hall and reach the foot of the Vizier's throne felt like an eternity. Once there, I wished I could be anywhere but at his feet, waiting for his mercy. I dared not look into his eyes for fear of what I would see. Triumph that he had, with one swift blow, conquered both the woman who refused him her hand and the Sultan's most fierce janissary. Now that I had at last reached the palace, I dreaded finding out Iliya's fate.

But I had come all this way to make sure he lived and to free him from whatever bargain he had struck, so seeing through what I had started was the only way forward. The Grand Vizier didn't immediately say anything, yet an air of triumph radiated from him. Finally, not wanting him to think I cowered before him, I lifted my eyes to find his already on mine.

He hadn't changed at all in the months that had passed

since last seeing him. His beard, just as well-kept as before, was flawlessly trimmed and his figure maintained the lean appearance of someone used to every meal's finest cuts. In contrast, I felt nothing like the Jasna he had encountered at the well. Yet, in the ways that counted, I was still me. Still riddled with fears, but resolved to fend for myself. When his gaze drank me up, I grew uncomfortably aware of how marred with dust and dirt my clothes were. My face and hair were in no better condition. The journey here had left its mark on me.

I chased the thoughts and straightened up. I wouldn't let a man dictate my self-worth. A sparkle of amusement flickered in the Grand Vizier's eyes, there and gone before I was sure it had happened at all.

"What do you bring me, my most devout mage?" He turned to Yerleg. The dark mage swooned at the Vizier's regard of him and pushed at the front of the dais to stand in front of his liege.

"You flatter me with your attention, most esteemed Vizier. As you predicted, so it has happened. I bring you the woman whose statue you commissioned as well as her brother, Sirak, the Sultan's army first-in-command," Yerleg said as he bowed deeply.

I couldn't help but wonder why such a powerful mage would kneel in front of a man whose entire power-grabbing ploy rested on his mage's unconditional obedience. Still, the Vizier possessed a certain charm, and unmistakable power emanated from him. Yet, I found it hard to imagine what possible prowess he could possess that would come close to the mage's skill in binding the shadows of the dead to his service. The Grand Vizier's attention shifted from his beloved mage to Sirak and narrowed.

"The Sultan's favourite pet," he said, savouring the words.

"How gracious of you to pay us a visit. Did Bayas let you off your leash?"

Yerleg let out an undignified snort that could have passed for laughter, but Sirak remained silent, unfazed by the Vizier's provocation. The Grand Vizier seemed to care little for a reply as he turned to address me.

"And your lovely sister, I see. Here at my mercy, just as I predicted."

This time Sirak did not keep silent.

"She is not yours to do with as you wish," he said through gritted teeth, and the Vizier laughed, a merry sound that rang high across the domed ceiling.

"Then why is she here?" he asked with that thin smile playing on his lips again. A flush crept across my neck when he referred to me as if I weren't even there. For all that mattered to him, I was a conquest that had willingly delivered herself to the slaughter. I had the sudden urge to shatter his perception of me, to break the illusion I was weak into tiny pieces.

"I am here for Iliya, Grand Vizier," I said, interrupting whatever Sirak had been saying. The Vizier's gaze slid away from my brother and fixed on me once more, some of the predatory look returning to his features.

"And who might Iliya be?"

"My betrothed, Grand Vizier. He came all the way from Morava on the cusp of summer. He wished to implore you to grant him your help and cure my illness."

"Ah, yes, I seem to recall something," the Grand Vizier drawled, and for a heartbeat I let hope take root in my heart. Then I saw the smile tugging at the corners of his mouth, and my blood chilled. "In that case, I have news for you, Jasna. Oh, do cheer up a little. I'm not some sort of monster, no matter how much you wished I were. The boy you seek is here, though he is a boy no more. He's become a man who goes by a different name these days."

I shivered, the instinct to bolt away from the Vizier and his pet mage coursing through my body. Still, I stood my ground.

"Toran, my boy, step out and let your beloved see what has become of you."

Though barely older than Iliya or I, the Grand Vizier referred to people as if years of experience stood between him and his peers, an attitude that allowed him to easily dismiss anyone who dared stand up to him. Yet at that moment, I cared little for his disdain, my entire focus shifting on finding Iliya in the motley crowd.

Not a day had gone by in which I hadn't imagined this moment, yet the man that peeled away from the crowd was not who I had expected. In my mind, I had imagined Iliya changed from the unimaginable cruelties the Vizier had inflicted upon him. Though I knew it was Gorovoi's spell that had returned some of my soul back to me, I still wanted to believe that another splinter had found its way to me thanks to Iliya. What I had not expected to see was the man that now stood in front of me, pointedly avoiding my eyes – a richly dressed man who vaguely resembled my betrothed. His cheeks were rounder and his clothes were in a fashion not dissimilar to the Grand Vizier's own rich kaftan. I sensed Sirak's hostility grow by a notch.

"Iliya?" I asked stupidly. I had also imagined the rush of relief I would get in seeing him, but all I felt was emptiness. His eyes reluctantly found mine and a flash of guilt clouded them.

"I'm glad you live and have regained your health, Jasna," he said awkwardly, and a glimpse of the old Iliya showed through a crack in his demeanour, one moment there and the next gone. A tall woman with sun-kissed skin stepped by his side, her gossamer veil covering luscious hair. My breath caught in my throat as she slid an arm around Iliya's, the gesture bringing guilt back to his eyes.

"Not that I wish to be imposing on your lovely reunion, but I think congratulations for Toran and his lovely bride are in order," the Grand Vizier said. "Which, I'm afraid, would make your prior agreement void. See, in coming here to plead for your life, he made an impression on me. Loyalty, courage, these are qualities I deem essential for my court and therefore reward richly. And if you were as affluent as I am, you would find people always have a price. His love for you certainly did."

Temir paused, and regarded me with a smile that only grew larger when he delivered his final blow. His gloating stirred a hot feeling that sat like a lump in my throat and left a bitter taste in my mouth. I knew what he was saying was true. People did not forsake their names or forget who they were unless they needed a new beginning. And Iliya adopting the name of Toran was a sign he had fully embraced the new role the Grand Vizier had thrust upon him. The Grand Vizier wasn't done gloating.

"It turns out he would rather follow his dreams of living a rich man's life than stay true to your love. Did you even know your former betrothed had dreams? A place in the palace, a lovely bride, that was an offer too good for him to pass on. Now, now, don't mar your beautiful face with tears. Your former betrothed tells me you never held much love for him. Or are you that embarrassed to admit it? Fear not, you can still please me. Once the Sultan is taken care of, I intend to be a merciful ruler and grant you a place in my court, though not in such a prominent position as you might have hoped to hold."

Yerleg bared his teeth at me, a grotesque mimicry of a smile playing on his lips. My hand flew to my face to cover the tears I hadn't realised were there. I wasn't crying because the Vizier had called me out on not being in love with Iliya. My former betrothed's betrayal, though not entirely unexpected, still stung. There, in the middle of the Grand Vizier's court full of people, I couldn't help but feel more lonely than I had felt on my entire journey throughout Syanka. Iliya's betrayal wasn't just a wound – it was the death of every memory I'd clung to. The boy who had braved mountains for me now hid behind a stranger's name and the Vizier's gold. My journey had been for nothing. My final words sounded as if someone else spoke them.

"I don't expect you to understand," I said in a hoarse voice. "If I held no love for him, I wouldn't have come all the way here to make sure he lived and was well. As for your most gracious offer, celebi, I will have to refuse."

"Do not mock me, girl," the Grand Vizier snapped. "Your dedication and beauty once moved me, but devotion gets you only so far and beauty fades sooner than you think."

He gave me an appraising look as if to say, 'Look at you, what makes you valuable to me is already fading,' but I found his judgement had no hold over me. It was at this moment that I noticed a shadow take form on the side, close to the dais where the Vizier sat. With all eyes fixed on our interaction, even the dark mage missed the chuma appear as if out of thin air. Someone shifted awkwardly at the back, but to my surprise, didn't alert the two men. I used the opportunity to pay back the Vizier's words in kind.

"Believe me, grandest of Viziers. I know beauty doesn't last forever. But fear not, I have other tricks up my sleeve."

At that, the chuma stood tall in her human form, a beguiling image of a woman, her red lips the colour of blood, her pristine skin suggesting nothing of her deadly touch. If anyone harboured any doubts about her nature, her next actions shattered them. With an inhumane shriek, she lunged for the Vizier, who, upon at last noticing her, immediately abandoned all dignity and pretence of regality and hurled himself to the ground. That sent him scrambling down the dais, on the opposite side of the chuma who had almost touched him with her proffered hand. Her vital mistake was going for the Grand Vizier instead of Yerleg.

In a split second, the shadows behind the throne shifted and solidified, as if they had always been there, only now stepping into sight. But it was only one shadow that caught my eye, a distinct female form made of darkness, moulded exactly to my proportions. My javina and my death.

"Stop! It's Jasna's shadow! You'll kill her if you touch her!" Sirak cried out, just as the chuma reached for the shadows. It all happened so fast that I had no time to wonder whether her abilities worked on shadows. The chuma hesitated, her outstretched hand freezing just before it found flesh. That gave enough time for people around us to bolt for the door, cries of fear bouncing off the walls. The Vizier, who had gone pale, had a look about him that said we would pay for the insolence. He got up and dusted his kaftan, a streak of purple returning colour to his otherwise shocked face.

"You dare bring this... this thing? In my own court?" The corners of his mouth frothed, his ragged breath puncturing each word, and suddenly I found it hard to breathe myself. At Yerleg's twitch of a finger, the javina listlessly moved by his side.

"I could end your court with a touch of my hand," the chuma snarled.

"But you won't unless you want her to die," Yerleg said and pointed at me. "Unfortunately for you, I know well how these bargains work. You won't get freed if your master dies."

"I serve no master," spat the chuma, oblivious to the dread

her appearance had spread in Temir's court. Yet, she made no move – we both knew when someone had outmanoeuvred us.

"You and your brother have proven most bothersome," the Grand Vizier said. "You are lucky I intend to be a merciful ruler and that promise begins from today. In that spirit, I have one more gift for you and your brother. Think of it as a bridal present. Guards, bring out the prisoner."

"A pitiful attempt to regain authority," Sirak grunted, but his voice wavered. He too knew we were cornered.

The chuma remained frozen, as did my death. Something in her listlessness bothered me, and an invisible thread tugged at the corners of my mind, waiting for me to catch it.

The guards did not take long to return. They brought in a scrawny man with matted black hair that stuck in clumps to his face and neck. A patchy beard obscured most of his profile, streaks of grey running through. His downcast eyes hid the rest of his features, rendering him unrecognisable. Though the man evoked pity, I failed to see his relevance to the unfolding scene. When I turned towards Sirak, his face had gone white. The man was close enough for my brother to reach over and steady him, but when he tried, the guards shoved him away.

"Unfortunately, my guards have strict instructions – no one but them is to touch your father," the Vizier croaked, still ruffled by the chuma's sudden appearance. "What's the matter? I thought you'd be pleased to see your long-lost father?"

My breath had gone out of my chest at the Vizier's words. One glance at Sirak's face told me the Temir was telling the truth. This man, the man who I had thought was dead for so long, was my father. Which meant that all these years, my father had been alive, hidden away, and held captive by the Grand Vizier.

"You monster," I cried out. "You… vile… monster. Why?"

"Why? Why have I kept a man as a bargaining chip against the most promising boy in the Sultan's janissary school? The boy that the new Sultan had taken a special interest in? I don't know, Jasna, you tell me."

The man lifted his head, and my throat went dry.

"You monster," I repeated, but the desire to fight had all but fled. The socket where the man's left eye should have been was a sunken pit of scarred flesh. He lifted his hands towards me and Sirak, and both of us replicated the gesture, but the Vizier's guards pushed us back, once more refusing to grant us even this small mercy.

"My guardsmen had a bit too much fun torturing your father, I'm afraid. But fear not. The transgression hasn't been repeated," the Vizier said, as if that concluded the matter of my father's carved eye. An ugly look twisted Sirak's face when he turned towards Temir, the promise of revenge clear in his eyes.

"It doesn't matter. The Sultan's armies will breach the walls any time. You stand no chance."

"Don't I?" Temir said, unfazed. "That remains to be seen. Rendering you useless to your master has certainly been my pleasure. What choice do you have, but to do my bidding from now on? That is, if you value the lives of your long-lost father and sister."

And as if on cue, a horn blared, followed by a wave of shouts and the sound of steel meeting steel. Chaos had erupted outside. A collective holler of surprise followed, then of rallying the troops, and soon enough – too soon for any battle to be won – I couldn't help but notice a note of desperation in the soldiers' voices.

"You'll find that while the Sultan was busy moving his harem to his new palace, I have been recruiting soldiers to aid my cause," the Vizier said, that annoying smirk of his playing on his lips. "With some persuasion from my most esteemed mage, there is little your beloved Sultan could do to stop what's coming, let alone to reclaim his palace. Of course, I wasn't stupid enough to keep my new soldiers cooped up in here. Servants!" He barked. "Make sure the soldiers on our side are ready and give the signal."

He waved at two of his servants and they immediately exited the chamber. I frowned at Sirak. How had we not seen any of the soldiers Temir spoke of? My brother seemed equally confused.

"Don't make yourself too comfortable. The siege will break soon enough. I'm afraid the Sultan's soldiers won't last long after facing my special force."

My father lifted his eye and fixed the Grand Vizier with a stony stare. Even his guards flinched and shared a look as if privy to a knowledge we did not possess. In my father's stare, I found a broken man who had at last seen a glimmer of hope and who would do anything to cling to that last promise. As much as I felt the need to, I had no time to go through the conflicting emotions that his presence stirred within me. One thing was true – Sirak and he shared the same eyes, the firm set of their jaw, and were even of similar height and build. I might have forgotten his appearance, but there was no mistaking he was our father.

Outside, the cries of soldiers rallying turned into screams of horror, too fast for the reason to be anything else but a massive army squashing the Sultan's finest janissaries like bugs. A brief moment of silence followed. Sirak and I shared another terrified look just as applause erupted around us, every noble ready to flee only moments ago now scrambling to congratulate the Vizier and his mage. My death, the same one that had dragged Sirak with uncanny strength down to the depths of the Nav, stood still. The thread tugging in my mind finally unraveled.

"It's the shadows. The dark mage is controlling them," I gasped, my voice barely audible in the loud chamber. Sirak inched closer, straining to hear my words. "It's the shadows. Yerleg is making them slaughter the soldiers. That's why their screams sounded so helpless. They know they stand no chance. They know it would be over soon."

Sirak's eyes grew wide when he realised that what I was saying was true. I turned towards my father, and found him staring with his one eye at my brother and me, drinking in the sight of us like a man whose life had at last regained some of its meaning. No matter my conflicting feelings about him leaving me, my heart shattered at the sight.

"I have one more surprise for you," the Grand Vizier said. "Bring in our most esteemed guest."

Two more soldiers peeled themselves from the wall and hurried to obey the command.

"What do we do?" I whispered, but Sirak gave no acknowledgment that he had heard me. I followed his stare to find it fixed on the chamber's large doors. He had gone terribly still. Only his hand betrayed a slight tremble. I noticed Iliya and his new wife retreat further into the crowd, my former betrothed's gaze avoiding mine. Contrary to him, his wife's eyes immediately found mine, and she did little to disguise the hostility in them when she slid her hand around Iliya's as if to claim him for herself.

Then the doors swung open again, admitting the two soldiers that escorted a man needing no introduction. A hush fell amidst the crowd of sycophants as the Sultan himself entered the throne room in chains.

CHAPTER 32

THE LAST CONTRACT

When the current Sultan, Bayas, came to power, his portrait circulated the empire for everyone to see their new supreme ruler. At the time, I had thought how well he fitted into the role, with his portrait exuding an air of majesty, as if to declare, 'This is what I was born for. To subjugate you is my divine right.'

Now, in his battle armour, a chainmail shirt and four gold plates protecting his chest, even in defeat he struck a pose more splendid than his portrait. Yet the helmet obscuring his forehead could not hide the tired lines that ran along his face.

Though a man of small stature with most towering above him, Bayas still naturally commanded everyone's attention. As soon as he entered the throne room, Sirak's fists clenched, as if refusing to accept that the man he had so devoutly served had fallen from grace. But there was something else there too. When his eyes followed the Sultan, they took on a tenderness

I had not expected to find there. Our earlier interaction in the gardens came rushing into my mind. At last, I pieced it together. My brother's feelings were more than loyalty. They were love. And judging by the Sultan's gaze – softness touching the corners of his eyes when it rested on my brother – the same held true for him.

The invisible string connecting the two men snapped when the guards dragged the same Sultan they had sworn allegiance to and callously hurled him to the ground in front of the dais. A triumphant smirk played on the Grand Vizier's lips.

"My friend," he greeted the Sultan, the words rolling off like honeyed mockery. The Sultan lifted a gaze to his second-in-command, all warmth leeching from his dark eyes.

"You are no friend of mine."

The Grand Vizier's smile only widened.

"Now, now, no need for bitterness. The better man has won, surely even you will acknowledge it? Or have you been too busy building your new harem to notice what was under your nose this entire time, my former liege?"

The chamber erupted with laughter as though cued by an invisible signal. Sadness crossed the Sultan's face, and I averted my gaze to find the chuma staring at me as if trying to tell me something. The woman's eyes slid to my shadow, who stood listlessly by the dark mage's side, and this time I understood.

The javina, forced to be here against her will, held hostage by the man that had created her, was part of the solution. Yerleg controlled her, but her purpose was to reunite with me. Could I probe how far our connection went? Perhaps the thread that bound us ran deeper than the dark mage's thrall over her. She had, after all, dragged me to the Nav of her own accord. Something else resurfaced too. Sirak's words in the

Nav – her hesitation when he'd asked her to let him go finally made sense. Would I risk diminishing the little chance we had of living through today? I saw no choice but to find out.

I cleared my throat, hoping to get her attention, but the noise got drowned in the cacophony of jeering. The Sultan regarded his former nobles with an impenetrable stare, and their merry mood was dampened by a notch.

"You laugh now and mock, but what of tomorrow, when someone else disposes of your new leader? Will you mock your Vizier the same way as you laugh at me now?"

His words had the desired effect. The smile on many smug faces wilted, though a few retained their haughty demeanour. One of the latter was the Grand Vizier, who waved with a hand as if to dismiss the disgraced Sultan's words. I spotted Iliya among the crowd, a look of confusion on his face. The implications of serving the Grand Vizier above all others seemed to be at last catching up with him.

Temir rose from his new throne and leisurely walked up to the former Sultan.

"You will find it's not as easy to dispose of me as it was of you," he said in a low voice that still carried above the crowd. "And you know why that is? Because, unlike you, I always anticipate everyone's next moves. I, unlike you, see who is scheming against me from one corner of the empire – shall we now call it my empire – to another. Besides, I have the best mage money can buy."

Yerleg, who, like everyone else, was too distracted by the Vizier's speech, missed my gesture to the javina. I felt Iliya's eyes burn a hole in me, yet I counted on him keeping silent for old time's sake. 'Please,' I mouthed to her, again and again. 'Help us.' At last, the javina cocked an eyeless head towards me in acknowledgment.

You are more than the pawn Yerleg has compelled you to be.

I willed her to understand, to somehow hear my thoughts. I begged her with my thoughts and with my eyes, praying that some of Syanka's magic had followed me in this realm.

If I hadn't been looking closely, I would have missed her barely perceptible nod before darkness exploded in the throne room. The last thing I saw as it engulfed us was the javina bending her back as tendrils of darkness split her chest open. Screams followed, but the darkness spread too fast for anyone to stop it. I had time only to grab Sirak's hand before a nightmarish blackness coated the air. More screams erupted, the stillness lasting for a heartbeat before everyone blindly scrambled for the exit. Unless we wanted to be trampled to death, we had little time to take control of the situation.

"Get our father," I yelled at Sirak at the same time as the Grand Vizier's voice rose above the screams.

"Yerleg, the Sultan! Don't let him run away!"

"The chuma is on the loose! Yerleg, the chuma," another voice shouted.

"The doors, get to the doors! Guards!"

"They won't budge," a desperate voice cried. "They're sealed from the outside! We're trapped!"

A high-pitched scream heralded the panic that spread like a wave of Zhar's fire. Maybe it was hysteria, maybe it was hope, but when I saw them scatter as though the plague chased their heels, I burst out laughing.

"It's the chuma! She's mocking us!" someone yelled, mistakenly attributing my manic laughter to the chuma.

"Don't provoke her!"

But the crowd's frenzy had reached a point beyond reasoning. A tide of bodies surged, pressing us against the doors. The air grew uncomfortably warm so fast it made breathing hard and my clothes suddenly felt too tight and itchy, suffocating me in the midst of the body wave that had us trapped in a deadly embrace. Sirak's hand grew sweaty and slipped from mine. The only way I knew he was still close was because he kept shouting the Sultan's name above the crowd.

"Don't you dare move, janissary!" Yerleg's voice sounded from another corner, the direction hard to pinpoint amidst the frantic commotion. "I have what you are after. You and your cursed sister better stay where you are or your father and Bayas die."

"What do we do?" Sirak breathed a wave of hot air in my ear. We were moments away from suffocating in the middle of the crowd. Then, a different type of scream chilled my blood. It was inhumane and more like a howl, as if a wounded animal was dying in an unimaginable agony, the scream its last attempt to expel death. The worst part was that I'd heard it before. The guardsman had shrieked the same when the chuma's touch left him writhing.

"Thank you for helping me find you, mage. You've made ending this so much easier." The chuma's calm voice rippled through the crowd, confirming my suspicions. What followed trumped the nightmare that had been unfolding until then. A cacophony of screams rose from where the dark mage had last spoken. The chuma was paving her own way to us. Left and right people started collapsing, their screams filling the room with dread. If we wanted to live, we had to act fast.

"Temir has our father and the Sultan," Sirak said in a panicked voice. It was too late; by then, the chuma's touch had doomed more people to an agonising death.

"Stand still! Don't move or that thing will get you!" Shouts rose from all sides, only driving the crowd into greater panic. Another wave slammed against the door, but it didn't budge. If I wanted anyone to survive her deadly touch, I had to do something. The chuma couldn't tell foe from friend – and I couldn't watch her kill more.

So I shouted, "Chuma! You are murdering innocents! This has to stop now! Our agreement is fulfilled! You are free to go!"

I didn't think my words would carry above the cacophony. For a moment, my heart sank, thinking all was lost. But then, just as suddenly as they had started, the screams of agony died. My ears still rang with their echoes when the chuma's voice sounded seemingly from all corners of the chamber.

"Consider our bargain fulfilled. At last, I am free…"

A strange feeling swept the room. The chuma's human form lit the darkness: a hauntingly beautiful woman, bright as day, her white dress spattered with red speckles of blood. Then her light was snuffed out, and she was gone. The darkness my javina had cast dissolved into the air, and daylight poured back in.

The doors swung wide, and a collective sigh broke from the crowd. Fresh air rushed in. Sirak wasted no time. He seized my hand and pulled me towards Yerleg, who lay sprawled among the other casualties of the Vizier's court.

In the end, the chuma's touch spared no one, high or low status. That the mage who once bound death could be so easily unmade felt almost disappointing. All it had taken was one of his own shadows turning on him.

We pushed through the dissolving crowd. A few lingered behind, unwilling to miss the spectacle's end. The Vizier and the Sultan had tumbled to the ground beside Yerleg's immobile body. I tried not to dwell on the red blotches blooming across the dark mage's skin, but the image had already seared itself into my mind.

The Sultan was the first to regain his bearings; the defeat that had weighed his movements earlier was all but gone. He dusted his kaftan with studied ease, his eyes already sweeping the room, storm clouds brewing in them. They held a promise that all who had betrayed and deserted him would pay. Next to me, Sirak exhaled in relief at the sight of his liege. I let them have a moment as my eyes searched the hall for signs of our father.

It was his missing eye that identified him in the pile of corpses. I hadn't expected to react so strongly at the sight of his lifeless body. Something inside me broke at once. My knees gave way as the realisation struck: I would never see him again. The next moments blurred, and when my vision cleared, I was on my knees, clinging to Sirak, both of us weeping before the man who had been our father.

It felt like a cruel joke to find him now, only to have him taken away from us in the blink of an eye. So I mourned him – the father I had not known, the father I always believed had chosen my brother over me. Yet, he was the only father I had, and losing him unleashed grief that had been long due. I was suddenly glad the chuma was gone. Had I known her touch would bring my father's end, I would not have set her free so willingly.

I could barely recall what happened next as I sat there, my eyes stinging from tears. I remained close to my father's corpse until it was removed by the returning servants. The Sultan said something about dealing with traitors, starting with the Vizier. Sirak, in a state just as dazed as mine, apprehended Temir. Though the former Grand Vizier looked nothing like the magnificent figure that had occupied the throne – his scuffed kaftan and ashen face a testament to his fall from grace – he had gone quiet, calculating, as if still plotting his next move. All the while, bits and pieces of conversation floated in the air, but I was too tired to catch their meaning.

"And the shadows?" The Sultan was asking one of the few soldiers who had survived their assault.

"Gone, celebi," the man replied, relief written across his face. He pointed towards Yerleg's immobile body. "Dissipated after his death. They seemed eager to go, celebi. Can't imagine the glaring sun was a pleasant experience for the dead."

"All the better," Bayas said, concluding the issue.

The rest of the day passed in a haze. When we ventured outside, I noticed the javina was still there. She lingered under the thickest shade near the first court's wall, but even that seemed to make her uncomfortable. Worse still, though most wisely avoided her, a few cowardly noblemen had taken it upon themselves to taunt her, albeit from a safe distance. The jeering stopped once they saw Sirak, and the men scattered, casting one last look at the place of my death. I resisted the urge to call after them for the cowards they were.

"Thank you," I said to her. "For standing up to Yerleg and saving us despite his hold over you. I don't know how you broke his thrall, but I am grateful that you did."

My shadow regarded me silently. Then, just barely visibly, she nodded.

"Why did you do it?" I asked without expecting an answer.

"Because you showed her kindness, and asked for her help even when everyone else feared her," Sirak said as he drew closer. The javina cocked her head as if in agreement.

"I'm sorry that I was afraid of you," I said, lifting my palms as a peace offering. "It must be hard, having to roam the earth, waiting for your other half to join you. I will gladly become one with you when my life draws to an end. I used to fear you, but I no longer do. Still, you'll have to wait for my time to come."

My death lingered there for a heartbeat before dissolving into the air like a sigh – there one moment, gone the next.

"Where do you think she went?" Sirak asked.

"Somewhere she can find peace, I hope."

A thought occurred to me, and warmth spread through my body.

"Father's shadow. It must be reunited with our mother in the Nav."

Sirak's face lit, hope sparkling in his eyes as he extended his arms towards me. We stayed like that, arms wrapped around each other, until someone cleared their throat behind us.

"Who is this, my most esteemed janissary?"

Sirak carefully stepped aside, letting me go. I spun around to find the Sultan regarding us with an inquisitive expression laced with what I thought was jealousy.

"Great one," Sirak bowed formally, and the Sultan glared at him as if the sign of respect from my brother were more a gesture of mockery than reverence. "Allow me to introduce my sister, Jasna."

"Did I hear correctly?" Bayas cocked an eyebrow. "Your sister?"

"It transpired that the former Vizier here held our father hostage for–"

"For twelve years," I cut in. Out of the corner of my eye, I saw the last of the nobility slipping into the palace depths before being forced to face the Sultan's fury. Iliya and his new bride were among them. It stung for a heartbeat, seeing him slip away from me so casually. Then I remembered I had found my father just to lose him again, and the sting of his betrayal subsided in the face of a much greater loss.

"Is that so?" the Sultan asked, turning towards Temir, who was now held in custody by his own men. "In that case, your punishment, which was going to be severe to begin with, will now involve some further, shall we call them... creative methods? My guards can do with you as they please. But worry not, they won't kill you. Did you think I've gone soft and would let you and the nobles' betrayal go unpunished?"

Temir's dark blue eyes filled with hatred when they found the Sultan. He said nothing; there was nothing he could do – he was, after all, defeated. Former Viziers had tried, and met the gallows for their insubordination. Temir knew what awaited him. The guards, on the other hand, shifted with obvious discomfort, their shoulders sagging under the weight of guilt. One of them, a large man, blanched, but quickly regained his composure and nodded.

"We await your orders for what will happen to us, celebi. We have shamed you and deserve the punishment."

"Your punishment will be decided in due time, for I am aware you acted on orders. The rest of the court, however..."

He let the rest of his words trail.

Suddenly, I felt exhausted and could not help but question my involvement in a coup I had not intended to participate in. Though I had learned of Iliya's fate and dealt with the Grand Vizier, I had lost a father in the process.

As if having read my mind, Sirak's hand slid into mine and squeezed it reassuringly.

"I miss Nana," I whispered, so that only he could hear me.

"As do I," he said at last. "Let's go pay her a proper visit, what do you say?"

CHAPTER 33

ONE CHAPTER ENDS

The palace bustled with wounded soldiers, healers, and workers restoring the walls. Everyone seemed to serve a purpose – everyone but me. The Sultan demanded Sirak at his side at all times, and in those days we barely spoke. I considered assisting with the bandaging of the wounded, but every time I did, my father's lifeless body surfaced before my eyes and I found myself recoiling in dread at the sight of even the smallest wound.

In the end, the only thing I could do was to make certain my father's passage to the Nav went as smoothly as possible. He was buried in the main garden, a rare honour, and they even named him a hero for enduring the Vizier's torture. Yet my only solace was the thought of him joining my mother in the Nav.

I had crossed realms to save Iliya, only to find he wasn't in need of saving. The anger that had carried me here ebbed, leaving only the thought that I could at last live life on my own terms.

The Sultan let me roam freely around the palace after reinstating it as his primary residence. Any protection I received from him and his first janissary meant people treated me with reverence that made me uncomfortable, not only because I was not used to it, but also because it gave me a status gained through a man's favour. Much like the begrudging acceptance granted to me by being Iliya's betrothed back home, I felt this was a facade that would shatter the moment it faced resistance. I did not intend to linger and be proven right.

The Sultan made it clear he would punish all nobles who had supported the Grand Vizier's failed coup attempt. Since Iliya was one of them, I had to wonder what his fate would be. Despite what had transpired between us, I still did not wish him ill.

On the day of the Grand Vizier's execution, a week after my father's death, I was walking down the hallway, flanked by the two guards assigned to me by Bayas himself. Late summer sun spilled through the windows overlooking the sea, the air thick with salty humidity that lingered on my lips when I came upon Iliya.

Just like in one of Nana's romance-infused stories, we ran into each other at the intersection, where one hallway met the other. The difference: no spark jumped between us, no wave of relief at the sight of him washed over me. Instead, I froze, a seething resentment I had not realised I harboured bubbling to the surface of my mind.

"Jasna," he said. My name rolled off his tongue reluctantly and I couldn't help but think of all the years of camaraderie spent together, only for it to end so poorly.

"Congratulations on your marriage," I said icily. Then, as an afterthought, I couldn't help but add, "I wish you and your conveniently rich wife eternal happiness. Though now that the Vizier is no more, I wonder what your title means to the Sultan."

The words left me before I could stop them. I regretted them instantly, but it was too late. Yet instead of striking back, Iliya's face softened.

"This is not you, Jasna." My shoulders slumped with the journey's heaviness weighing on me. I longed to lose myself in one of Nana's stories. "You never truly loved me, did you?" he asked, his knuckles white on the hilt of the silver dagger tucked in his kaftan.

"Isn't finding my way to you through all the realms enough to convince you? I loved you. But I wasn't…"

"In love," he finished.

"And what about your new bride?" I asked, unable to meet his eyes.

"We manage." He rubbed the new wedding band on his finger. A smirk tugged at the corners of his mouth, bringing out the boyish face I was so used to seeing back home. Despite his curt words, his smile suggested he was already fond of his wife. I tried not to dwell on the fact that just months ago the same smile that lit his face had been reserved for me.

"At least you won't have to put up with Maruna any longer," I said, smirking. "Did you know she followed me to Syanka only to spite me?"

Iliya's smile broadened. "Tell me everything."

He laughed, and to my surprise I found myself laughing too. Something barely perceptible shifted between us. We were friends again, and it was enough. We walked to the execution in the reopened first court, our footsteps in harmony much like they used to. On the way there, we chatted about everything and nothing. Iliya told me about Viziers who had committed various transgressions over the past few decades and described their executions in more detail than I cared to know. For this execution, the Sultan had chosen a traditional rite in which Temir was to race the gardener. If the Vizier won, he was to be spared. If he lost, the gardener was free to use whatever tools he had at his disposal to execute the Vizier. History favoured the gardeners, for they had won nearly every race. Even with the threat of death hanging above one's head, few Viziers had kept as fit as a man well-used to honest labour.

The largest crowd I had ever seen had gathered to witness the event at the first court, their enthusiasm not in the slightest dampened by the late summer heat. The smell of roasted nuts and sweat filled the air as the crowd's cheers rose above it.

"Something about their blood thirst doesn't sit well with me," I muttered to Iliya. He wiped his damp palms on his kaftan, nodding.

"Agreed. They must be well-acquainted with violence by now. The old Sultan used to have the heads of his slain enemies impaled at the first court's doors. The stench, I was told, became unbearable," Iliya said as he leaned forward, his eyes bright with mischief.

"That couldn't have been a pleasant trip to the market. Imagine living in the palace and having to pass by severed heads each time. I never asked you," I said, the laughter dying in my throat. "Did the Sultan punish you for siding with Temir?"

Saying his name felt good, as if it dispelled an air of mystery and authority that had up until then lent the Grand Vizier power over my life. Iliya seemed uncomfortable for a moment, then shook his head. His fingers twitched on the hilt of his knife.

"The Sultan was merciful, far more than Temir had

suggested. He forgave us, seeing I'd had little choice in whom I served. Even so, he let me keep my title." His cheeks flushed, and I wondered if he felt pride or shame.

"You needn't feel embarrassed that you have made a name for yourself. Not in front of me or for my benefit."

He nodded and a companionable silence fell while we waited for folk to gather around. Just before noon, the sun beat down on us with waves of scorching heat. Combined with the cacophony of the square full of people, it made the scene feel almost like a dream.

The guards hauled out the disgraced Vizier who wore nothing but a modest cotton shirt and torn trousers that revealed bruises stretching all the way from his face to his bare arms and calves. His lean figure already displayed signs of food deprivation, his sunken stomach visible through the thin shirt. Still, he maintained an air of superiority, and the determination to win this race was clearly written across his face.

"He might actually win this," Iliya said, echoing my thoughts.

The Sultan's gardener was already waiting at the starting point. A short and stocky man with broad shoulders, he had a look of calmness about him that betrayed nothing but confidence in his imminent victory. The guards hauled the Grand Vizier next to the gardener, and the former staggered, but quickly regained composure. He was not spared jeers from the crowd.

Seeing the two men facing each other as equals, I realised why the Sultan had insisted on having the race. It would be one last humiliation for the already disgraced Grand Vizier to break a sweat trying to outrun a commoner. There was little chance a man beaten by his guards for a week would outrun the fate that awaited him. Word of the Grand Vizier's failure would spread across the empire like wildfire, and soon no one would remember the rebellion against the Sultan. What they would recall would be how the Sultan's gardener outran and then killed the second most powerful man in the empire.

As the two men readied themselves, the crowd broke into a chorus of cheering and heckling flung at Temir. The latter ignored them, his eyes on the path that lay ahead.

"The Sultan isn't even here," Iliya muttered. I searched the crowd as we joined the nobility that occupied their own tents, leaving the crowds unprotected from the sun. There was no sign of him.

"His absence is saying that he is confident in the outcome," I said, for the first time realising I had ruptured a layer of skin from biting my lip with anticipation. "Or that it matters little what happens – the Grand Vizier is already disgraced."

There were no speeches or ceremonies to mark the occasion. A servant waved a flag, and the two men bolted towards the market's gates. The crowd erupted, their shouts trailing the two men. Under the high noon sun, both competitors' faces reddened fast, and in no time sweat soaked their backs and faces.

It was a short-lived race. Just before the finish line, the Vizier pulled ahead. My heart lurched. But then, like a bird of prey toying with its victim, the gardener swept past, barely finishing first, but winning without a doubt. The hush that fell among the crowd lasted for a mere heartbeat before it once more erupted in cheers.

I found myself unable to tear my eyes away from the disgraced Grand Vizier as the realisation that his life was about to end flickered across his features. His red sweat-coated face drained of colour until it was white as a sheet. In the end, when the gardener executed him with his weapon of choice – a scythe –

it turned out distinguished men bled and died just the same as commoners. Whether that was a consolation for the rest of the onlookers, I could not tell. That chapter, which I had been unwillingly drawn into, concluded with the Grand Vizier's death.

Iliya and I parted as friends. His wife's glare bore into me when he joined her in her tent and the two exited together for the feast. I tried and failed to suppress my grin when she placed her hand on his shoulder and squeezed it to remind me he was hers.

Sirak joined me on the way to the feast. These days, the Sultan spared no means to wash away the memory of the events that had unfolded barely a week ago. Still, with all the soldiers that had perished in the aftermath of Yerleg unleashing the shadows, the halls remained half-empty.

"Is the Sultan going to recruit more janissaries to fill the gaps?" I asked as we walked into the palace. Thick new carpets muffled our steps on the way to the feasting halls.

"Yes." The fabric of Sirak's kaftan rustled as he turned to me. "But I won't be going on any of the new recruitment campaigns."

"Yet you would not object to boys being taken," I said, a tinge of bitterness touching my words.

"I am but a man, Jasna," Sirak sighed. "What do you think can be done against centuries of practice, even in the position I currently hold? Besides, not everyone objects to it. Some, as you know, welcome the possibility of their sons holding elite positions."

I had no answer for that, so instead, I asked, "Do you know what you'll do next?"

Though daylight spilled from outside, the hall was dark enough to warrant torches. Their light cast a shadow across Sirak's face when he leaned to whisper in my ear.

"The Sultan wouldn't admit this, but he believes I could turn into a liability if I were to remain in his proximity."

"Because of what you feel for each other?" I whispered back, hoping my bluntness did not offend him. But Sirak simply nodded.

"There's some civil unrest at the southeast border that needs to be taken care of. The Sultan thinks it's a good consignment for me to take. But first, we are visiting Nana."

CHAPTER 34

The Girl Who Cheated the Wind

The first signs of autumn hinted at the change of seasons when we arrived in Morava. A hue of rust tinged the leaves, and the crops along the way bore that golden shade that heralded the end of summer. A small crowd had gathered at Morava's square, with everyone eager to make way for the janissaries and their entourage. It mattered little to me. An odd sense of peace, once an impossibility, had fallen over me during our journey home. As I watched people bob their heads with respect and mutter among themselves, I knew the feeling for what it was – acceptance. Though I had not forgotten all the hardship Moravians had put me through, I had forgiven them for never recognising me as one of their own. Only scars remained, born from a childhood of desperately longing to please everyone enough so that maybe they wouldn't treat me like I was the chuma.

"Is that Jasna?" someone from the crowd asked incredu-

309

lously, loud enough for the voice to carry over the cheering. I rode a white mare, a generous gift from the Sultan himself. Though she would never replace Naiya, I couldn't deny the bond that was forming between us.

"Jasna? Jasna, is that you?" The breadmaker's familiar voice reached my ears.

"Is that janissary mad? Travelling with her?" Maruna's mother called out. "She's a witch!"

"Oh, shut up, Ana."

"She's not even that pretty anymore." Another voice cut in.

The chatter rose and swallowed the rest. I was aware of the redness creeping up my neck and cheeks, yet the exchange did not come as a surprise. Nana had prepared me for this moment a long time ago. Her warning that beauty didn't last forever and that one day mine too would fade rang in my ears as if it was yesterday when she had delivered the warning. Yet, I had not expected the freedom my weather-beaten face now gave me.

A prickling at the back of my neck warned me of something malicious. I scanned the crowd again to find a familiar pair of eyes trained on me. Maruna and her knight had made it back. She stretched a hand over her belly, as if to protect an unborn child from the danger she imagined I posed. Next to her, Saval gaped at me as if having seen a ghost. I waved at them and smiled. Saval reddened and Maruna's lips curled as if in a sneer. It only broadened my smile.

"The witch lives, and you can't make her leave this time, you vile creature," I said, savouring the words.

"What's that?" asked Sirak from the gelding next to me.

"A ghost from the past. Nothing more," I said, this time loud enough for people to hear as I locked eyes with Maruna. She tore hers away first.

And as I uttered this, I knew it to be true. Moving past her, my eyes searched for Nana, but she was nowhere to be seen. Probably nothing to worry about, I thought, but despite that, a feeling of foreboding lodged itself inside my chest. Nana never attended such gatherings, not only because of her growing fragility in the past few years, but also owing to her dislike of 'All that foolish gawking.' It was at this moment that someone else had the gall to yell, "That's the witch who unleashed the hala on us! Our lands got scorched because of her! Get her!"

"Don't be a fool, Pavol. No one tells a hala what to do." Someone else protested.

"She's bad news, no matter what you say. Her family is cursed," Pavol said. "Look at that statue at the well. It gives me the chills knowing what came out of it. Ungodly."

I didn't have to turn around to know people were crossing themselves against evil.

"Isn't that her brother, little Sirak?" someone else said, shifting the crowd's gaze.

"Aye, it is him!"

"Not so little anymore, it seems."

"Sirak? Didn't he get taken as a janissary?"

"Do you not have eyes, you fool? What do you think he is now?"

Someone laughed and another onlooker cheered, dissipating the tension that had been brewing under the clear autumn afternoon. I led the small procession to Nana's house, Sirak following close behind. We had entered from the opposite end of her house and the well, so we had to go all the way past the square, the narrow streets, and the houses that dotted Morava. And there it was, just as I remembered it. But the wrongness only deepened: the porch where Nana usually knit gaped bare.

"She must be at the well, fetching water," I said, as the

parted curtains revealed an empty room. Sirak and I dismounted first, followed by the rest of the group, who maintained a respectful distance to give us privacy. Knocking on the door of my childhood house felt wrong, but I did it, ignoring Sirak's raised brow.

"Nana?" I said as I opened the door and ventured inside. An eerie silence, alongside the familiar smell of dried thyme and nettle, greeted us. I hastily crossed the room to find the door to the bedroom Nana and I shared was open. Inside, Nana lay in her bed.

"Nana!" I repeated, slumping to her side with relief, though it was short-lived. Sirak stood at the doorframe as if unsure whether to come in or stay there. Reaching for Nana's hand, at last I noticed the unnatural stillness with which she slept. I grabbed her hand then, certain that I was too late, that I had left her to live out her last days alone, with no one by her side to offer her support.

Just then, her fingers twitched in mine, and her eyes opened. Behind me, Sirak let out a loud sigh of relief.

"Nana! Nana, are you alright? What happened?" I veered on the verge of hysteria as my fingers massaged the inside of her calloused hand, as much to reassure myself as her. Her hand had gone gnarled, with age spots peppering it, spreading to her neck and face. Age had crept on her like an unwelcome guest. But what made me gasp were her eyes, her beautiful green eyes and the specks that dotted them, were half closed, unseeing. I traced prayer circles around her palm as I tried, and failed, to hide my apprehension at her frailty. I had been gone for the summer only, why had she aged so? Though my illness had already slowed her considerably even before I'd left–

"Jasna, child," Nana said, and her deep throaty voice sounded more ancient than ever. "Did you find Iliya?"

"I did," I said, choking back tears.

She feebly squeezed my hand, and then, as if knowing exactly what had transpired, asked, "Did the big city get into his head?"

"It did," I said, and the tears I had tried holding back started freely rolling down my cheeks.

"I never thought that boy had much to him… apart from always yearning for more than he had," Nana said, not unkindly.

I sniffled as Sirak stepped into the room. "There is someone here to see you, someone that has been missing you very much."

Nana's eyes shifted to Sirak, and despite the blurry curtain impairing her vision, her face beamed with recognition. In that instance, she transformed, as if in a matter of moments years shed from her shoulders. She propped herself up on her elbows.

"My boy," was all she said before her eyes welled with tears. The next thing I knew, I was sobbing, and Nana was crying, and Sirak found himself in her arms, not bothering to hide his own tears. We cried for the little boy he was when taken by the Sultan, for the years he had spent apart from us, for our father, who had wasted in the hands of the Vizier, and for all that was lost and gained in between.

After some time, when the tears had dried, and the words that needed saying had been said, Nana got up, though the effort cost her considerably. Just like before, she moved to her chair in front of the empty hearth. To hide our apprehension at finding this new Nana, both Sirak and I fussed around her, trying to ease her discomfort. For in every move of her body, pain disguised itself as age-induced fragility, her muscles and tendons protesting each time they had to be put to use.

Sirak and I both rushed to tell her of the events since we

last saw her, our stories taking up the better part of the evening. Nana had her eyes closed as if asleep, but every now and again she would open them and stare at us, her gaze piercing through our souls despite the blurriness that had settled there. It felt as if Sirak had only left for a while, almost as if he never went away. Almost.

When I mentioned Gorovoi, her eyes turned glossy, distant. The memory of one of her old tales rose unbidden. In it, the king of the leshy had fallen for a mortal, and they'd had a daughter together. A daughter with forest green eyes. Nana's smirk widened as if she had read my mind, and she got a wistful look, which neither confirmed nor denied my suspicions. Instead, she said, "Syanka seems like a fine place to visit. And maybe even stay for a little while."

Something else bothered me more, and I could not help but voice it.

"Nana, do you think I'm incomplete without my shadow? If my death is roaming the earth, doing whatever it is that lost shadows do?"

Nana reached for the yarn and needles on the side of her chair and absentmindedly continued working on the socks she was knitting, not needing to use her eyes to know how to work the needles. For a moment, it felt like the past few months had never happened and Nana was about to tell me a story. Then, her hands trembled, and the stitch came loose. Her composure faltered for a moment, and she set the yarn and needles aside, her hands still trembling.

"Your soul is yours," she said, her voice steady but firm. "And your death is part of you, but no more than that. It's not you, and it does not define you. Besides, even with a missing piece, you still have more soul than the people that would claim otherwise. If your journey has taught you anything, let it be that. Listen to no one's judgement but your own, and live as only you can."

I squeezed her hand, hoping the gesture conveyed how much I had missed her. Then I continued my story. When I reached the point where I had met Sirak, she grew pensive, as if reminiscing about all the years lost. As I finished recounting our journey to the Nav, she said, "I'm glad Zhar stayed behind to help those poor lost souls cross over."

"Why?" Sirak and I blurted at the same time. Something in her tone unsettled us.

"He'll soon be greeting me," she said plainly.

"Nana!" I cried. "Don't say such things!"

"Alright then. Let me tell you a story. I haven't used my voice in a while, so lean closer and listen carefully."

Silence settled as we sat at Nana's feet, the floor still warm from the early autumn day. A hush fell over the birds in the trees as they paused to listen to Nana's story.

"Have I ever told you the story of how a girl cheated the wind and made it carry her to the magical realm of Syanka? No? I'd wager my last grosh I have, but you want to hear it once more. Very well, then, listen. Once upon a time, a poor woman lived in a village far, far away. Her only consolation was her daughter, for whom she would do anything. One day, the mother decided to bake bread for her girl…"

We listened to her tale until sleep muddled the borders between truth and story, and I found myself turning into the girl who cheated the wind and made it carry her away. When Nana's story ended, Sirak woke long enough to see us to bed, then settled on the floor as sleep gathered us all into its embrace.

THE DOOR BETWEEN REALMS

Nana drew her last breath in the early morning hours, just as dawn coloured the sky crimson. We cremated her by the birch tree near the front porch. A part of me had known this would be our last evening together and that she wouldn't live to see another day. Yet I had hoped against hope the world wouldn't be so cruel, tearing us apart so soon. Sirak's face mirrored my grief. A small voice inside my head couldn't help but whisper, again and again, 'What if you'd been here? What if you had never left? Would she still be alive?'

The two other janissaries who accompanied us helped set up the pyre. Though Morava had churches dedicated to a sole god, I wanted to give Nana the burial she believed in, and none imposed on her by others' beliefs. No priest attended the ceremony and none was needed. My eyes, swollen with grief, blurred each time they fell on her small, lifeless body, wrapped in white cloth, her calm face the only part of her that was visible. In the end, I closed her eyes and mouth as we set the pyre aflame. Even with Sirak's hand in mine, I had never felt lonelier as when we said our farewells.

It was a fine day, not a single cloud disturbing the sky's endless blue. Moravians from all across had gathered, and begrudgingly, I let them pay their respects. Nana's reputation, if not always impeccable, had preceded her. Even those who had whispered against her came to pay respects, for everyone remembered the healer who never turned them away.

Maruna and her mother, at least, had the decency to steer clear. Grandmother Ona was there, her wide eyes fixed on Sirak's every move as she drank in the sight of her long-lost grandson.

None of it mattered, though. Nana wasn't coming back.

"I wonder if anyone apart from you would come to my funeral," I told Sirak, perhaps selfishly, as we watched the smoke of Nana's remains ascend to the sky. Before he could answer, something caught my eye and made my heart swell with an unexpected burst of hope. The unlikely flower winked at me, its red petals standing out in a sea of fading autumn green. I let go of Sirak's hand and squatted to cup the raskovnik in my palm before plucking it carefully. Once the fire had engulfed Nana's body and her soul had flown to the Nav, I opened my palm where the raskovnik lay. Sirak's eyes grew wide, and it felt as if the rest of the world paused when my breath grazed the flower.

"Zhar, I call you to my aid."

For a few moments, we stood in silence, the line of mourners thinning as one by one they took their leave, unaware of what was about to happen. Then, a warm wind coming seemingly from nowhere blew over Nana's ashes, scattering them over the land, from our house to the caravanserai, sending them dancing as if stirred by an invisible hand. Where they touched the ground, flowers broke through the earth, growing wild and in full bloom, from daffodils and hyacinths, to marigolds, and even white roses. When the last speck of ash had settled, and Nana's body had returned to the earth, the warm gust of wind ceased and instead, a beat of great wings took its place and ruffled Sirak's hair.

A collective gasp rippled through the remaining onlookers when Zhar landed beside me. A woman screamed and bolted. Others followed; those who stayed stared with a mix of fear and awe. But it mattered no longer. Zhar's eyes found mine, and a question formed behind them, as if asking, 'Should I make them pay for all they did to make you feel unwelcome?' I shook my head and his massive body relaxed a little.

"It is good to see you again, Jasna," the zmei said. "Rumina sends her best."

"Is she alright?" I asked, and the zmei nodded.

"She is not ready to move on to her next journey yet, and that's fine. She is welcome to stay with me for as long as she wishes to."

"I imagine that means she is staying for a while." I almost smiled before a fresh wave of grief engulfed me. The zmei regarded the remaining onlookers absentmindedly and a cloud of hot smoke escaped his nostrils, sending the last of the crowd scattering hurriedly towards Morava.

"I know why you called me today." His voice softened. "I'm sorry about your Nana."

He spoke to both Sirak and me, and for a moment his reptilian eyes contained more humanity than many Moravians had shown.

"What you did with her ashes was beautiful. Thank you," Sirak said, and the two of us were crying again, but the grief had softened into a bittersweet ache, as if the darkest clouds had been driven away by Zhar's warm gust of wind, letting a ray of hope peer in.

"You should know that she is in the Nav, and she is grateful for the moments the three of you shared. She says she was ready to follow me there." He cocked his head as if Nana's voice carried through the Nav and whispered straight to his ears. "You shouldn't blame yourself – it was her time to go. So you need to stop asking yourself if there was anything you could have done. There was no other way. There rarely is when the time is here, no matter how much we fool ourselves into thinking that we could have done more."

I nodded, and some of the invisible lump that had lodged itself in my throat melted a little. I believed Zhar and knew that Nana wouldn't be around forever. But letting her go was harder than I had imagined.

"There is one more thing I can do for you." Zhar's eyes sparkled with mischief as he said that.

Sirak figured it out before I had.

"Not so soon." His words sounded like a plea. My mind at last caught up with what the zmei was offering. Something stirred in me and a glimmer of hope broke through the curtain of grief.

"You can do this for me?"

"I am the lord of the Nav," he said with more smugness than I had thought possible. "Mine are the crossroads of the realms."

I nodded, my path finally clear. A pleasant scent of fresh flowers reached me as I regarded the house I had grown up in one last time.

"I wish we had more time together," Sirak said and lifted my hands in his. "I never thought I'd see you, father, or Nana again. And now that it's you and me that's left…"

He let his words trail off, their meaning hanging heavy in the air.

"You could come with me, you know. I could use someone at my side and you may not hate it as much as you think. I promise."

"I'm sure I'll love it," he said, and sadness crept into his voice. "But I can't join you yet."

"Is the Sultan so much more important than me?" I let bitterness seep into my words. My brother gently squeezed my hand.

"No one is more important than you. But I have to see this chapter through."

I thought of Iliya and my own chapter that I had needed to see closed, then nodded, understanding.

"This is not to say I won't find a way to you."

"I know." I sighed and wrapped my arms around him in a final hug.

"Ready?" Zhar grumbled with his characteristic lack of regard for anything remotely sentimental. "The portal won't wait forever."

I rolled my eyes at him and stepped away from Sirak. With a slash of his claw, Zhar cut the air open. A shimmering light appeared and then magnified, pulsing once, twice, growing faster and faster until a fully formed door made of light stood in front of me.

"Thank you," I told Zhar and nodded to Sirak.

Then I stepped through the portal, to the realm I belonged to more than anywhere else. Syanka greeted me like an old friend, and I knew that even as one chapter drew to an end, another one was about to begin. Behind me, the portal winked out, closed by Zhar's fiery breath. Ahead, Syanka's winds whispered, beckoning me to follow – and, for the first time, I answered.

AFTERWORD

Thank you for reading *The Girl Who Cheated the Wind*. As an independent author, I don't have a publisher's marketing team behind me – it's your voice that makes all the difference. If you enjoyed the book, please consider leaving a short review or star rating on the store where you bought it or on Goodreads. It helps new readers discover Jasna's story and keeps the Woven Realms alive.

Your support means more than you know.

— M.E. Moirin

9 781919 232331